I0706093

Ankou's Unsharpened Scythe

Jack Passey

Paperback ISBN: 978-1-964664-01-9
Hardcover ISBN: 978-1-964664-02-6
eBook ISBN: 978-1-964664-00-2

GLOSSARY

Anti-nautilus – the twenty-nine and a half-day spiraling track of a vent from approximately eighty degrees south latitude to the North Pole. The anti-nautilus is a mirror image of the nautilus but shares points of origin and termination with the nautilus.

Apical Frame – the frame representing our physical, corporeal existence. Also a frame deeper in the frameset that has been repopulated by a pikirovatel/ trouplongeur (called a reconstituted apical frame) and has, therefore, become the physical, corporeal reality to all associated with that segment of the frameset and its reactivated standard progression of time.

Archived Frame – a one ten-thousandth of a second, topographical, three-dimensional, semi-holographic, retrievable facsimile of an apical frame. Archived frames can be repopulated by pikirovateli/trouplongeurs, causing them to become reconstituted apical frames.

Archived Vent – a vent that has completed its twenty-nine and a half-day nautilus and whose aperture becomes affixed to the first archived frame (the first ten-thousandth of a second) of the following new moon. Archived vents circulate and descend within the frameset, intersecting other archived vents, providing an ascension of pressure from petram to principal apical frame.

Blanc-Becs – individuals that exist as umbrae in the Gontlets. The Blanc-Becs lived on the Earth at a time that corresponds to the current frameset, less than one hundred and twenty years in the past, and died a Gontlet death. Some of the Blanc-Becs know that they are deceased, some do not. Most of the Blanc-Becs choose to reside at the supra-principal apical frame Gontlet.

Disengaged Umbra – an umbra that is no longer secured to the moorings of its hull. This includes the Blanc-Becs, the Lifers, the Dovolniya, and any pikirovateli/trouplongeurs in the process of Pik-ing, from abandonment of the hull at an apical frame to recoupling with the hull.

Dovolniya – individuals that exist in a realm outside of the frameset, but that visit the Gontlets in pairs. The Dovolniya lived on the Earth, experienced a Gontlet death, and were removed from the Gontlets to an unknown location by the Inscrutables.

Exiles – entities banished to the frameset and its Gontlets from a region beyond the frameset for sedition. The Exiles do not have, nor have ever had, a hull. The Exiles never lived on the Earth in its standard sense.

Frame – a one ten-thousandth of a second, topographical, three-dimensional representation of the entire Earth. There are active apical frames and inactive archived frames. Once a frame is created, it falls for one hundred and twenty years until it is fused with the Petram as an irretrievable, immutable record.

Frameset – the totality of all falling frames in their one hundred and twenty-year descent. There are 37,765,440,000,000 frames in the frameset at any given moment.

Gontlet – the space between two frames. A variety of entities can inhabit these spaces, including the Exiles, Lifers, Blanc-Becs, Dovolniya, Inscrutables, and, temporarily, any pikirovateli/trouplongeurs in the process of Pik-ing. When frames fuse with the petram, these spaces are compressed out of existence. Pressure from this compression works its way to the principal apical frame through the vents.

Gontlet Death – a physical death, not associated with the vents, where the umbra is released to inhabit the Gontlets.

Gravure – intelligence, understanding, memory, and experience permanently imprinted on the umbra.

Hull – the material organism that interfaces physically with a corporeal reality; the physical body.

Inscrutables – a race of beings that exists in a realm outside of the frameset, but that visits the Gontlets in pairs to remove individual umbrae from the Gontlets and escort them to an unknown location outside of the frameset.

Kwazants – the expansion or amelioration of aspects of the mreg.

Lendemain – a native umbra that has severed its connection with its hull and has recoupled with its hull at a reconstituted apical frame deeper in the frameset.

Lifers – individuals that exist as umbrae in the Gontlets. The Lifers lived on the Earth at a time that corresponds to the petram, greater than one hundred and twenty years in the past. The Lifers know that they are deceased, and that they are, more or less, stuck in the Gontlets.

Merovingian – a society of French natives who originally discovered the vents and who want access to those vents strictly controlled.

Moorings – points within the hull to which an umbra anchors. Any umbra can secure itself to any moorings, but only the native umbra is a permanent resident. Lendemains, derivations of the native umbra, are also reliable residents of their native hull if their mreg consistently subordinates the native umbra and any other coexistent lendemains. All other Umbrae occupying a non-native hull at the moorings (xenoumbrae) are only temporary residents.

Mreg – the aggregate of the umbra's attributes, to include size, density, luster, power, color, etc. Developed aspects of the mreg determine how securely a lendemain will latch to its native hull and how much control it exerts over other umbrae occupying its hull (i.e., the native umbra, other lendemains, xenoumbrae).

Nascent Vent – a newly created vent whose aperture is affixed to the principal apical frame for its twenty-nine and a half-day nautilus. Pressure accumulating in the frameset due to aged-out Gontlets is released through the aperture of a nascent vent at the principal apical frame.

Native Hull – the hull in which a native umbra is born. A weld is created between the native hull and the frame associated with the moment of birth through which the update runs.

Native Umbra – the umbra with which an individual is born. The native umbra is anchored to the hull via its moorings. The native umbra is permanently integrated with the hull until death. Any prolonged separation of the native umbra from its hull constitutes death. A lendemain recoupling with its native hull does not displace the native umbra.

Nautilus – the twenty-nine and a half-day spiraling track of a vent from the North Pole to approximately eighty degrees south latitude, extending from the beginning of one new moon to the beginning of the next. All nascent vents begin their course with a nautilus. Archived vents rotate between nautilus (north to south spiral) and anti-nautilus (south to north mirrored-imaged spiral), back and forth, descending as they go, until the entirety of their twenty-year depth is pressed out of existence at the petram after its one hundred and twenty-year lifespan.

Petram – the accumulation of all frames that have completed their one hundred and twenty-year descent. Once frames have fused with the petram, they cannot be accessed by pikirovateli/trouplongeurs and, therefore, represent an immutable, truly historical record.

Pik (Pik-ing) – the act of severing one's umbra from the moorings of its hull to propel the umbra through an apical frame, into a vent, through a Gontlet, ultimately recoupling with the hull at an archived frame deeper in the frameset, resulting in a reconstituted apical frame.

Pikirovateli/Trouplongeurs – individuals that use the vents to access archived frames deeper in the frameset in order to recouple with their hull at an earlier age.

Principal Apical Frame – the topmost apical frame representing the objective reality, opposed to reconstituted apical frames deeper in the frameset that represent only a reality subjective to an individual pikirovatel/trouplongeur and all associated with that reconstituted apical frame. Though termed a frame, the principal apical frame is the original from which all other frames are created and is thus not a true frame.

Reconstituted Apical Frame – an archived frame deeper in the frameset that has been repopulated by one of the pikirovateli/trouplongeurs and is now an apical frame to all entities that were associated with that past frame. A particular reconstituted apical frame is only such for one ten-thousandth of a second as the reconstitution travels up the frameset, frame by frame, at time's standard progression. All individuals associated with the progression of reconstituted apical frames are *living* in that term's accepted sense.

Subvert – a member of a Russian society that regularly accesses the vents and opposes the Merovingian's philosophy of limiting access to the vents.

Umbra – the immaterial organism that occupies, animates, and vivifies the hull. Any member, temporary or permanent, of the Gontlets other than probably the Inscrutables.

Update – a daily reconciliation accounting for all changes made within the frameset from the deepest iteration of change to the principal apical frame. This reconciliation occurs at midnight along the longitudinal line that cuts through Carcassonne, France. Only pikirovateli/trouplongeurs effect changes to the frameset beneath the principal apical frame. The update is summative, incorporating all changes made by all pikirovateli/trouplongeurs in all regions, at all points in time, to include all effects of effects of effects. Individuals without lendemains are not conscious of the update or what has changed. Though powerless to prevent any prior changes or the effects the system has calculated, lendemains are conscious of these changes.

Vent – an approximately twenty-year deep columnar void circulating in the frameset that releases the pressure accumulated by the system when Gontlets are pressed out of existence. This pressure is released into the open system of the supra-principal apical frame Gontlet through a nascent vent. The superior aperture of vents is affixed to the principal apical frame for their initial twenty-nine and a half-day nautilus, then to an archived frame throughout the remainder of its lifespan, descending toward the petram with that archived frame.

Xenoumbra – any umbra occupying a non-native hull.

Day -1

Chapter 1

"This is just a courtesy call. This is just a matter of policy.
This is just an act of kindness to let you know that your time is up."
– "Courtesy Call," Sixx:A.M.

The house is silent <<as the grave, appropriately>>. It's a rare, conspiring kind of silent; the kind of silent that gives audience to the languid thrashings of an entitled mind. It's an underwater kind of silent, where counterpoint screams are muted and indiscernible. It's a kill yourself kind of silent.

I say silent, but looping in the darkly curtained halls of my unrealized expectations is the icy euphony and disconsolate cheerleading of some grunge ballad. <<Did grunge have ballads?>> The distillation of this euphony is shuffling the coils and threads of my coronary arteries around in a clutch of vague paradoxes. I can't tell if it's affirming what I've done or condemning what I'm about to do. Or some third option. It's hard to be objective when you take everything so personally. Though, I'm not sure how the interpretations of a disconsolate grunge ballad will have any effect on the outcome. Maybe it's just supposed to be the song that plays as the credits roll.

I'll keep takin' punches until their will grows tired . . .

Sounds more like condemnation.

I've been rolling this ziggurat-capped, deranged mistranslation of prescription bottle orange around in my keyboard-cramped fingers for some minutes now, self-discussing the prospect of my own late-term abortion. Twenty-eight years late.

I'll swallow poison until I grow immune . . .

Definitely not affirmation.

Ambivalence may have slowed my approach to this sinister crossroads, but I am undeniably here, and it's pointless to continue negotiating with a piper that's already half way out of town with my children. This is what happens when you don't pay your pest control bills—they pile up and become unmanageable. So I either pay the debt or be okay with a bad credit score <<repossession might be a better metaphor here>>. In other words, I come to terms with my life as an irreversible plan B, or kill myself. Just after a forking break in the road, signs for Resignation and Death, with their respective distances <<Resignation – ∞, Death – ☺ >>, are posted in opposing directions. Plan C was to develop an indifference to ambivalence, but my procrastination is walking through the outskirts with that option tucked in the breast pocket of a pied tailcoat.

It's a good thing I don't have any afternoon plans.

Now that grunge ballad is playing at seventy-five percent playback speed. I think it's trying to mirror my state of mind—tired and drowning. If those dark curtains could get any darker, they're darker.

With each quarter revolution of the prescription bottle's polluted dusk, the next rank of the phalanx rends the stale, barrel-vaulted sky with its crunchy tumbling of a battle cry. There is blood in its mandate <<or at least a thick plasma>>. The next quarter revolution, the next rank's battle cry. The next quarter revolution, a single hoplite breaks ranks and tumbles out a delicately tapping knell. The more I roll, the more formidable a beast inevitability becomes. It's approaching Chinese dragon ferocity. <<Not sure how ferocious Chinese dragons can get, but they always look angry.>> The next quarter revolution, the rank shrieks its muffled toppling. My floppy consciousness is turgid with their drug-crazed war preparations, spear tips dipped in cardio-lullabying balms, barrel-rolling in their nuclear winter-obscured garrison. The conscripts await the decree. <<I don't mean to marginalize my own death, but the suspense is still a little light.>>

The moment probably doesn't warrant such derailment, but I'm backflashed to my tenth year, accompanying my adrenaline junkie <<I can't think of an antonym for *adrenaline junkie* that wouldn't also sound sarcastic>> mother to Fort Gordon's Bingo Palace when my dad was deployed to Arkansas <<Dad's rarefaction because Mom thought Afghanistan, where he was actually stationed, sounded like a murderous profanity>>. Ms. Rose would delicately pinch the handle and crank the cage with fingers as gnarled as the branches of a corkscrew willow and a radiation of veins more prominent than the fingers themselves. I was always expecting her to hand me a poisoned apple. Her entire stooped body would gyrate with the motion of the handle as the cage completed its times and seasons. Bingo balls rumbled, roaring like heavy rain on a steel roof in what seemed superfluous crank after crank after crank. Ms. Rose, her voice as gnarled as her fingers and modulated like the wooden staircase of a 1910 Victorian, creaks, "W(ATSON)-820!"

I study the pills. WATSON 820. Bingo!

I had to pay my dealer four impacted wisdom teeth for these pills. I'm standing at this fork in the road, watching that musician leave town with my children, wondering how I'm going to die quietly, die privately, die definitively, die without the ignominy of a lot of vomit, die undiscovered for at least a month. Remember that scene in *Die Hard* where John McClane hands his unsuspecting enemy, Hans Gruber, a gun? It was like that, but the gun is loaded and I'm going to turn it on myself <<it's a loose comparison>>. Only a ninny would need anything more than a carton of ice cream to work through the aftermath of construction tools pulling bone out of bone, but when you use phrases like, "Black out at the wheel," and, "Pain-induced serial murder," when asked how you handle pain, dentists err on caution's side <<an ironic kind of caution since I'm using his mercy for my mercy killing>>. Whether it's a solution to your problem or a *solution* to your problem, a 30-count bottle of narcotics is a panacea.

Unless the problem is texting drivers, I guess. Or human trafficking.

Rolling . . . rolling . . . rolling . . .

It takes me three child-proofed attempts to spin the cap off <<clearly I'm committed>>. I tilt my nostrils over the mouth of the thinly titian pill bottle.

That chemical bite resonates; I know exactly how it feels. The bitter cup it must have drunk to sweat such caustic blood; I feel like we were drinking buddies. And here we are, sharing our Gethsemane with . . . well, naturally, with no one.

I know comparing my memory foam plan B life to flesh-tearing, bone-snapping agony is a greasy blasphemy, but meiotic metaphors aren't going to steel my nerves. And I should probably avoid references to people that kept themselves alive through life-ending horrors—now I'm back to that coil-shuffling clutch of vague paradoxes that feels like condemnation.

I will hold the candle 'til it burns up my arm . . .

I don't really want to kill myself; I just want to be dead. And I can't figure out how to be dead without somehow killing myself. If I could will myself dead, I'd will myself dead. And I don't want to step in front of a bus or in any other way entrust this enterprise to any force that isn't as dedicated to my demise as I am. <<If you call this dedication.>> That crazy accomplice <<he has no idea how I'm abusing his mercy>> dentist of mine was the bonanza of all windfalls. Now I can die on my terms—quietly, privately, definitively, vomit-free, undiscovered. Though this unbalancing silence isn't helping at all. Or maybe it's my greatest ally. For the overthinkers, for the misinterpreters, for the betrayed, for the discarded—silence is a warzone. Accusations are so loud in this uncontested silence.

It's a stupid death wish. Indefensible, really. I was working on a manifesto that would make it sound philosophical or existentially matter-of-course, but it sounded more like satire. I tried to dress it up in a tuxedo and style its hair, but it remains a guttersnipe of selfishness feeding on the bread of hyperbole and capitulation. I had to settle on the thesis, You just wouldn't understand, to at least obviate the wiles of the problem solvers; Recondite fatalistic inevitability, if there are a lot of follow-up questions; also, It's genetic. I drove off the cliff years ago and trying to fix me in freefall will only make the eventual impact all the more startling for everyone.

In the final analysis <<not a pun>>, it's just a creeping tastelessness. Not in a literal, gustatory sense, of course, but everything was becoming a hum of palpitating grays while the redolent filet mignon that was supposed to be my life grew cold and inedible at the other end of the table. It's tasting glory and then having all your taste buds removed. It's death of the soul by a thousand cuts. Well, one big gash and then a thousand self-inflicted nicks to keep the wound open and gurgling.

By all accounts, by all appearances, I have everything. But when you only want one thing, when you've devoted your entirety to that one thing, having everything *but* that one thing is almost worse than having nothing at all. *Languid thrashings of an entitled mind . . .* Maybe *entitled* is a little hypercritical. It's as much entitled as expecting a diploma when you'd completed all the university's graduation requirements is entitled. It's the logical expectation of a harvest to reap after the seed is sown. I had sown the seed. If such a thing is possible when considering life's enormity, I was a big deal in high school—courted and wooed <<maybe a little petting //over the clothes//>> by high-powered college football programs from Florida to Washington, Southern California to Michigan, because I had this unique ability of rendering a man horizontal who was running away from me vertically. It's apparently a rare and coveted skill, and consequently pays better than being able to see the future, heal people, or time travel. I was supposed to be the next Jack Lambert, the next Troy Polamalu, the next T.J. Watt. And here I am, none of those things. If it was a fanciful expectation I developed from collecting football cards or meeting Jack Ham in person, surely the devastation would be commensurate. I'm not a crazy person <<unless you consider paranoia, freaky cleanliness, and pathologic people pleasing crazy>>. At seventeen, I was this armored berserker that dined on offenses and chewed up the hopes of other hopefuls' proud parents. Then, at the end of my senior year, I had a career-ending injury and that was that. Taste buds removed.

Some would say that not being a once in a generation this or that is an arrogant, irrational, and presumptuous reason to kill oneself. And, generally speaking, if I wasn't that one in a generation, I would agree. But the effect of juxtaposing the glory of the was <<and should-have-been>> with a decade of the inglorious wasn't <<and never-will-be>> wraps every second that hammers by in a prickly and electrified slow-squeezing anaconda. If you've never played sports, if you've never been truly good at anything, if you've never been passionately one-dimensional, never mind. There's no reasoning with you.

I devoted so much of my time to football. It's all I had. It's all I was. If I ever had time to think, it was about football. After graduation, everyone went their own way and I was left holding my shell-shocked shadow like a mine-dismembered battle buddy. Life began trimming away the remaining post-high school fat, and instead of a lean emotional fighting weight, I was linear emotional dead weight. No width, no depth. No future. If I had something else, anything, I would at least have some two-dimensionality to lean on. In a slightly painful instant, I emerged from my Garden of Eden into the lone and dreary world. I had turned mortal and everything started to ache.

Life started getting stuffy, like the already open windows needed to be opened. Silence became itchy. Being alone was like being in a room with your parents while they're yelling at each other. I thought maybe I had a slow-bleeding hematoma that was squashing what little identity I had left into my brainstem.

Inevitability has become a ten-headed hydra.

I'm avoiding the use of the phrase *identity crisis*. It's not that I wasn't sure who I was anymore, it's that I was sure I was now nothing. It was like blinding a sculptor or cutting a surgeon's hands off. It was complete identity dissolution. Life became a series of stock pursuits to shamelessly outflank humanity and play hide-and-seek with my own mind—loud music, binge-streaming everything, immersing myself in work, relocation, sequestration, around the clock sensory saturation. It worked for a while, then it didn't. My teens turned into my early twenties, my early twenties turned into mid-twenties, mid-twenties turned into late twenties, and all the while I squander my *now* pining after the days before that damnable injury.

The defeat was so enervating I didn't have the energy to multi-dimension-alize myself. I just was. For a decade. As a result, every aspect of my person, personality, affect, appearance, habits, and mannerisms is a translucent and tran-quilizing amnesic. I'm a faceless extra in my own life. I have become my own evidence of the existence of ghosts. I'm completely untethered to self or society. And if I had always been like this, I suppose life would be pretty good and I would find pleasure in the inane, for there would be nothing to compare it to. But there is this shredded beast of a Tyler Durden that emerges in those unsaturat-ed, crepuscular moments of shifting phases of consciousness that delivers orbit cracking, zygomatic splintering, maxillary shattering, ethmoid crushing blow after blow after blow.

Life rises and falls on expectations and comparisons, I guess.

This stalling is either solidifying my resolve or helping me come to terms with my reality. Either of which, I feel, will have the same outcome. Like Patch would say, *Sometimes indecision is the best decision.*

Inevitability has become Behemoth.

It's time, I guess. I'm sure inevitability can't get any bigger than Behemoth.

I pour myself a glass of Mountain Dew. I don't want my last stroll down these darkly-curtained halls to be a vinegary -ide, -ate, -ic, -acid chalk. If I'm going out on a low note, I want to at least go out on a high note <<Mountain Dew>>.

The spear tips of the hoplites are perched with twitchy anticipation along the top edge of a rank of locked shields. I fill my mouth with the glass-smooth elixir of the gods and let it pool at the precipice of my throat, my head tilted to facilitate the phalanx's advance.

And . . . the phone rings. Of course. I've gone so deep underground I forgot what a ringing phone sounded like. <<I'm actually proud of that.>> I guess I could talk to Mom one last time. Maybe I can bury a goodbye in some small talk.

Turns out, it's not Mom. Life <<and death, incidentally>> rises and falls on expectations, comparisons, and assumptions. This caller has the sassy impu-dence to register its identity: Sanborne & Esche. Interesting. For spammers bold enough to identify themselves, I can spare a few pre-death moments to inflict some drawn-out, sugary malice. Might as well take someone down with me . . .

"Yes, this is he . . . Whose attorney? . . . I have an attorney? . . . I mean, that's my name, but I'm not—I don't think I have a grandfather by that name . . . Oh, yeah, then that is my grandfather. His first name is Elliot?

"Ah. I don't think I've ever heard his real first name before. He was always having me call him by all these different names. I think Patch is just the one that I remember using more than any other . . . Yeah, I guess eccentric is the word . . . Why do I need to be sitting down? . . . He's a pilot? . . . He has his own plane? . . . Where is Omsk? . . . Wait, you're saying he's dead?

"No, yeah, I'm still here. I'm just . . . I mean, it's just really weird to hear . . . Yeah, I'm okay. You're a lawyer, right? Why am I hearing from a lawyer, not the police or a doctor or something? . . . Executor of his will, really? . . . I don't know why he would have done that. I haven't seen him in years. I thought he had a lot of family around.

"Well, like I said, he was a strange guy . . . This afternoon? You mean today? Yeah, I guess. Yeah . . . Sure. Four o'clock . . . I can just map it. Sanborne and Esche, Downtown Salt Lake, right? . . . Okay. I'll see you at four."

The house is silent <<as the grave, appropriately>>. It's a rare kind of silent, a head-clearing kind of silent. It's the kind of silent that gives audience to . . . I don't know, clarity, maybe. A new reality is pushing a heaviness onto my diaphragm. It's an unalloyed and confusing kind of sadness. I was sure that old man was immortal. His exhausting joie de vivre was a self-circulating fountain of youth. If swashbuckling was still a thing, Patch <<my now-late grandad>> was a swashbuckler. Were there swashbuckling philosopher gunslinger alchemists that could fly?

I know death is supposed to be sad, but this feels more like a heaviness borne of gratitude, maybe even happiness. Albatrosses are littering both paths diverging from the fork and my ears start ringing. I feel like I'm being held under uncomfortably hot water. I can't care about this—today's death is supposed to be mine!

But, and I am loathe to admit it, it is a mathematical certainty that the debt I owe to that swashbuckler is insurmountable. And I'm not even that great at math. I'll execute your will, old man; that will be my swan song. Then back to my death business.

The mass of the past hour reaches critical and I start crying. Just regular crying. No convulsions, no heavens cursing, no catalepsy, just a pure expression of sadness doing what it naturally does. Have I ever cried like this before? I never really had a cause to cry as a kid <<other than my dad dying, but I could never find a break in Mom's crying to sneak in a turn>>, and everything since has been your garden-variety weeping, wailing, teeth-gnashing. I've been tucked into the warm covers of this egoistic implosion for so long it didn't occur to me that there may be other entities with minds and identities and lives and torments and deaths of their own. And this particular mind and life was extraordinary, salt that gave the world its savor kind of extraordinary. Patch was a lightning rod and a prism and a mirror for everything manic and happy and light.

I didn't think the curtains could get any darker, but the world feels like it just blacked out.

Chapter 2

"The only way you can beat the lawyers is to die with nothing."
– Will Rogers

I am not agoraphobic. I may exhibit all the symptoms of agoraphobia, but *phobia* implies irrational, and my cautions are based on empirical data, astute observations, and an overactive sense of smell. The fact that it's really anthropophobia dressed up as agora<<not>>phobia may be a little irrational, but whose pride isn't a potent pig lipstick? <<It's why I don't trust journals.>> People assume trauma with agoraphobia and are more sympathetic. With anthropophobia, people just think you're somewhere on the spectrum. I tell myself it's more about time management than fear of leaving my house, so temporophilia rather than agoraphobia <<anthropophobia>>, but even when it would save me time to leave the house, I generally won't leave the house. Besides, security consciousness and self-preservation shouldn't be implications of irrationality. It sends the wrong message.

If it wasn't for my Mountain Dew addiction <<Fountain Dew, that is; I know Dew comes in cans and bottles that can be delivered to my door>>, I'd be a shut-in. <<And people say addictions are bad . . .>> Inertia and all that. If there's no promise of Dew, leaving the house is a violation of physics. Besides, leaving the house is such a mobilization. By the time I'm presentable, essentials gathered, house secured, and at the garage door, the power of Grayskull I called down is already pooling as mental lactic acid. Then it's miles of lung-flushing deep breaths so I'm not David Banner–activated by drifts of Utah drivers that spurn the hospitality of green lights. But I'd leave the house for Blood Bath & Beyond <<one of Patch's hundreds of alternate identities I had to cycle through over his years of here and there>>. And that's it—I'd put on my big boy pants for Mountain Dew and Patch errands. And possibly wildfire evacuation if turning on my yard's sprinklers didn't stave off total destruction.

It's about the scarecrows, my anthropophobia. Humans are basically plague rats—personal space-violating plague rats with loose vocal cords, bad hygiene, and no respect for time or privacy. No matter how aggressive the social cue, no matter how blending the camouflage, I'm flushed out with their small talk and friendly inquiries on a spot-lit stage with a microphone and captive audience. I'll never understand it—in our magnificent world of self-checkout lines and home delivery and automated ordering, people still want to *talk*. And they're not satisfied with comments in a vacuum; they want you to respond! They want a dialogue I'm never prepared for but always tensely expecting. And they speak so loudly!

Every time I'm accosted with response-eliciting words, my mind flips through all possible replies without ever choosing one, and I'm just *there,* scrolling, mumbling, inaudible, incoherent, until one of us just walks away. Okay, well, maybe it's not that bad, but that's the impression I come away with. If I say something trite, I come away from the interchange looking stupid; if I say something brilliant, *you* come away from the interchange looking stupid. Lose-lose. The only winner here is agoraphobia <<anthropophobia>>. At six-foot-four, two hundred and seventy pounds, I'm not really afraid of people, I'm just afraid of how stupid they can make me look.

I've been told I need to stop overthinking things.

As I roll my effeminate, globular Ford whatever into the teeth of the afternoon, my vampiric skin recoils from the barbs of fresh, handpicked sunlight. I'm even squinting through sunglasses <<the sun is a big blazing ball of headache>>. Bluetooth sinks its incisor into my phone's playlist and fills said demoralizing, may-as-well-be-a-high-school-cheerleader's-cabriolet with a classic rock song I've heard eighteen thousand times but have no idea who sings it or what the title might be.

The riffs close their eyes, lean against a tree, and start a countdown of hide-and-seek with unsolicited thoughts tasked to breach the gap between regret and shame. Sensory saturation is an impregnable fortress.

Twenty-seven point four miles, round trip. I can do this <<I'm making a bumbling attempt at shadow boxing and I make sure my dashcam is facing *away* from the cab>>. The lawyer, the Holiday clerk <<Hello, it's a refill; I do have a rewards card; here's $1.06; have a good day>>, home.

This is it, Sanborne & Esche. Black block letters on a glass façade. Office hours placard. This guy has a real eye for style. I don't know what I was expecting, but lawyers being boring would only be a stereotype if less than one hundred percent of lawyers were boring.

I'm standing in an office furnished with boredom, framed certificates and degrees of boredom on the walls, stains of boredom on the carpet. I can't even smell anything. I'm guessing that's what boredom smells like. I regret not bringing that bottle of pain killers with me. If he tries to winkle secrets out of me with the spell of his boredom, it could have served as a last ditch cyanide capsule. And what's with all the books? Aren't these all online now? Shelf upon shelf of perfectly sequenced boredom.

He greets me, Garrett Sanborne, Esq. <<Is esquire still a thing?>> Everything about this guy is a brilliant radiation of neutral and inanimate. He thanks me for coming in on short notice. <<The venom is circulating . . .>> He says something about Patch. <<Losing consciousness . . .>> He asks if I've ever been the beneficiary of a will before. <<I'm chewing on my tongue to stay upright . . .>> I should get out more often—I'm already feeling way better about myself. I pull my phone out and start recording his voice so I can save money on melatonin.

He sits me down in a gray chair that has a distinct boring feel to it and starts in on the executor business. Hopefully this doesn't show on my face, but I'm flexing my calves under the chair as hard as I can without cramping so I don't lose consciousness. We're fencing with our épées of awkwardness—I'm struggling to ask clarification-eliciting questions <<fléche>> and he has no idea how to clarify <<corps-a-corps>>. I'm using six small words to refer to one simple legal concept <<flunge>> and he's frozen in confusion, making no effort to meet me half way <<parry>>. I keep having him repeat himself because I'm processing each six-syllable word as its own complete thought. I don't get the impression that he's trying to impress me, he just doesn't know any layperson synonyms for the words he's using. Can you dumb down *probate*? Do I really need to know how sound his mind was at the drafting of the will?

En garde. Pret. Allez!

"So, what does a will executor do?"

"We don't use the term *will executor* in legal vernacular. You are the *executor of his will*. The legal term *personal representative* is also acceptable."

Right.

"You will be responsible for managing the disbursement of Mr. Dillinger's assets to the respective parties according to Mr. Dillinger's desires as directed by the will."

In other words, your grandfather wants you to hand his stuff out to certain people.

"Sounds like a lot of work." I don't really have any reference for how much work is involved; still just scrolling.

"It's not. You and your mother are the only beneficiaries listed in Mr. Dillinger's will."

<<A real fencer, this one.>>

"Really? Just the two of us?"

"Yes."

I watch his boring face, sure he's going to add something. He doesn't.

"So . . . as the *executor*" <<I purse my lips and give it a half British accent to make it sound more official but it ends up sounding French and riposte>> "I just take what he left me?"

Humorlessly, he muddles, "In theory, yes."

"In theory? Meaning, that's not how it's going to work this time?"

"Correct. The majority of the physical material that has been committed to your disposition is immediately available. The remainder will become available relative to the heed you pay the instructions outlined in the manuscript."

Now imagine an automaton saying all that. And then layer it with a cadence where each syllable gets its own metronomic click at 260 bpm.

"Manuscript?"

"To further elucidate the nature of your grandfather's arrangement, it will be necessary for us to convene at his apartment in town." <<He had an apartment here?>> "Contextual documentation will provide further clarification." I have him repeat that. "Would you prefer to drive with me or drive yourself and meet me there?"

"I can drive myself." Your gray, kryptonic cube of catatonia has drained all my powers and all that mental lactic acid is back. I seriously feel like I haven't eaten in three days after that exchange. Are lawyers cheaper than anesthesiologists?

That Mountain Dew can't come soon enough.

CHAPTER 3

"Smells are the fallen angels of the senses."
– Helen Keller

I follow the gray kryptonite cube down East Broadway for thirty seconds <<Mr. Esquire must be a fellow agora-averse //not phobic!//; we could have gotten here quicker on foot>> and park across the street from a four-story apartment building. It looks both old and new. Climbing the west-side staircase to Patch's fourth-floor residence, it becomes apparent that each floor is its own apartment. We pass through a locked turnstile at the top of the staircase <<now I know where I get my paranoia>> and enter a clean and featureless landing in need of carpet stretching that spans the entirety of the apartment's face. A plaque affixed to the front door reads: Who would cross the Bridge of Death must answer me these questions three, 'ere the other side he see. This is definitely Patch's place; he loved that movie. We make it across the bridge of death due to no bridge keeper. And a key.

Through the front door is a small vestibule presided over by an iron-wrought chandelier <<one would expect to see gargoyles perched on this medieval monstrosity>> and matching sconces mounted to four scrolling, fluted corbels that support the base of a domed ceiling twelve feet above. The only other furniture occupying the vestibule is an old, three-legged stool and a free-standing coat rack. Archways open in three directions to a large, continuous space divided only by what looks like the polished trunks of ancient trees, each crafted with its own cornice, frieze, architrave, and capital. Through the eyes of the vestibule's archways, it looks vast. Everything is wooden and robust and gorges itself on the room's light. Why did he never say he had a place in town? It looks like he's had this apartment for a while.

Antique drafting tables and free-standing chalkboards <<chalkboards, for the love!>> are spaced throughout the contiguity of space, tilted at every angle like a satellite dish farm soaking up alien intelligence. A single Louis XV-style leather armchair sits in the center of the room, placidly reading a newspaper among and despite the anticipatory clamor of the chamber. The drafting tables are covered with the trappings of investigational insanity—specimens pinned to boards, microscopes, jars of marked and unmarked substances, functional parts of musical instruments, old cameras, varieties of optics, dry scales, fabrics hanging in stiff dryness, bottled tinctures, equations etched on table tops, wax seals, engineering instruments, open maps, notebooks abused by the manic markings of the magi <<not one of his nicknames>>; everything is in a state of assembly or disassembly, dissection or resurrection. Intelligence saturates every element in the room, fidgeting and restless, awaiting the return of their Arthur to pull Excaliburs from stones of serendipity and revelation scattered about on their islands of inquiry. It's everything you'd expect from a modern-day Renaissance man. If he was, indeed, modern. It was hard to tell sometimes if Patch was the anachronism or modernity itself, with all its Dark Ages sureties.

I become aware of some winsome beckoning that draws me farther into the apartment's entrails. I'm pulled to the threshold of the studio where lies a blood red welcome mat inscribed with the white-lettered phrase ASSUMPTIONS DIE HERE. I know I'm here to be digested, so I slip my shoes off and take a single step into the temple's pharynx . . .

That indelible smell . . . the subtlest inhalation and I can recreate every version of every dimension of his person with perfect accuracy. My mind is a 3D printer and there he is, rubbing his eyes and stretching his well-preserved back. I can feel his forehead pressed against mine, a handful of my shirt waded up in his fist while he bellowed one of his <<what I called>> Listen Up, Laddies: *There is no such thing as accidents, my boy, only negligence, stupidity, and bad planning!* It's a smell as distinctive as his erratic, colorless eyes; the wool three-piece suits he wore every day; his always-healing knuckles; the sharp pitch changes in his voice when an excited syllabic stress would attack; the High Life wax-curled ends of his mustache; and a laugh that sounded much like insanity itself. It's old leather and antique mahogany and the age-absorbed pages of a first edition and India ink and Kiwi Shoe Polish and the Brylcreem he used to keep the hair out of his face. It's a turn of the century smell. It's the smell of home.

Obey the law, ya wee parsnip; it has teeth!

Memories that were out of reach before that trigger start multiplying on impact like the bouncing proliferation of cluster bombs. The tree-lined brick paths to and from happy memories are daisy-chained with detonating souvenirs. Casualties are piling up at the door of the temple to be used as burnt offerings made by fire, a sweet savor unto the gods of my preservation. I don't think humans are meant to experience this kind of deluging recall. All the richness of my life is spasming in my chest and my sweatshirt becomes a map of tears. I can't remember the last time I experienced a pure distillate of either happiness or sadness, let alone both on the same day. The past decade has been a mishmash of whatever is to the left of sadness, to the right of happiness, and pureed red herrings somewhere in the middle. The highs were dug down and the lows were filled up in a perdition of pity. My great contrast of uncluttered affect had become nothing more than a flat, torpid hum of paralysis. And here I am, stretched to both poles in some improbable temporal conflation. I can hear Patch with his smug, singsong assurance, *Coincidences were invented by the statistically idiotic to avoid accountability!*

I move as reverently as a man my size can manage and sit in the armchair in the center of this holy of holies. Squeezing my eyes shut, I draw long inhalations through my nose, trapping with snapping metal teeth all the nostalgia my cannonading lungs will allow, breath after paroxysmal breath. He's lurking in the shadows of the vestibule, that automaton. I can feel his hot breath fogging up all of my mind's mirrors. Normally, this kind of display would stoicize me with an acute performance anxiety, but there is an otherworldliness to that smell that melts the elements of my delusion-calcified self-consciousness with fervent heat. It might be the first time in my life that all sense of self-awareness has simply fallen away. I don't care what I look like. I don't care what I sound like. I just need this regression. That smell, that sweet respite, that is inheritance enough.

There is no such thing as giving offense, only taking offense! echoes off the columns.

I can feel the freshly-laundered, threadbare comforter pulled up to my chin and dramatically tucked into the entire outline of my body; fingers threaded into the plaited undergrowth of my incorrigible hair; the silhouette of the curled end of a moustache framed in the residual hall light crowding the cracked door, eagerly awaiting the day's closing remarks. A steady and masculine Eddie-Van-Halen-brown-sound-distortion-grain voice surfaces to a depth just above whisper, "I wonder if you will ever know how much you are loved." And then it would all go black, and I would lay there in a perfect, hermetic warmth, wondering if I'll ever know how much I am loved.

Though I had a good sense.

Bernie McBattlewater <<I can't believe I remember these names>> had an authenticity about him that made him almost as much an abstraction as an individual entity. He was a sort of lost angel, carrying on with these advanced faculties until he could find the portal he'd erroneously locked himself out of, and this seemed to allow the abstraction to permeate everything in his blood circle. It <<he?>> was the blazing interface between the arteriole of truth and the venule of its terrestrial representation, and if you were within that blood circle, you were passing through what felt like a rarefied plasma. Patch was from Scotland, so there was nothing *tender* about him, but he so deeply loved that it seemed he could weaponize the abstraction. I should probably stop using the term *abstraction*. I don't know if I'm characterizing an entity or a force or a manifestation or what, but the only term I've ever dared use to sheathe this double-edged concept is *intelligence*. And I don't mean intelligence as a capacity or an ability or a function, but as an autonomous will that enlightened <<in all of that word's literal and figurative angles>>. It was an electric, magnetic density that whispered brightness and illuminated better directions. When Patch was around, seemingly wielding this intelligence, things were easily understood, capacity was tumid, possibilities multiplied, memorization was easy, and thoughts, useful thoughts, spilled over as self-sorting, explicit, and intelligible torrents. And I was always happy. Early on, I just thought this feature was another one of the quirks of his immediate presence, but there were moments when he would be in another room or something and this abstraction would shatter into a plasmatic flurry of excited creation and collaboration. Patch may have invited them <<them?>>, but they were definitely guests, not the host.

I wonder if you will ever know how much you are loved. There are a thousand definitions of love. There are a thousand nuances to each definition. But this intelligence was the primevality that spawned them all. It was the spark and the ember and the heat of every intermediary. It was a love that supported until you were self-supporting. It was a love that accepted until you came to terms with what was unacceptable. It was both paternally conditional and maternally unconditional. It was a manifestation so foreign to my routine experience and I would just idle in this lattice of interwoven evening sunlight and rabbit pelts. My heart would be consumed by a fire that didn't consume. This warmth of effulgence was squeezed into every channel of my body and it lit up the entire surface with a caressing, electrical storm that no other human experience has been able to replicate since.

Patch and his abstractions . . .

My breathing recovers and I'm lying in that perfect, hermetic warmth under the threadbare comforter. Patch's merry band of schisming plasma people make good and sure I know how much I am loved. With such a reminder, I wonder how I was ever able to forget. As my eyes open, I can see through a lacrimal haze the grainy apparition of the automaton standing over me. Light is flexing in and out of me and his presence there makes rot of its sanctity. No offense, Garrett Sanborne, Esq., but you are the abomination that maketh desolate.

His arm is extended and a brown letterhead box is growing out of the sleeve of his suit coat. I stand and dry my eyes on my sweatshirt like a disgusting slob.

"What's this?"

"This is the aforementioned manuscript."

"Oh." I handle it like it was pulled from the Ark of the Covenant <<which might actually be here somewhere>>. "I thought . . . there might have been more to it than that. You couldn't have handed this to me at your office?"

"I think your reaction to this room is sufficient testament to the fact that such a course of action would have been inadvisable and potentially reckless."

Touché, Mr. Estate Attorney, sir. Wait, *reckless*?

"What do I do with it?"

"What would you do with any manuscript?" I'm amazed that he's able to say that without sounding sarcastic or condescending. "The twenty-four file boxes on the eastern wall accompany the manuscript and will be delivered to your home tomorrow morning. As with anything in life, you are free to dispose of said material in whatever manner befits you. However, Mr. Dillinger has drafted explicit instructions in the first several pages of the manuscript regarding their handling. He prefers that you read the instructions before making any definitive determination regarding its disposition. I have also been instructed to inform you that a great deal of money attends these items, and the manner of its disbursement is outlined in the manuscript's introduction."

Jumpin' Juggernaut had money?

The grainy apparition of rot starts for the front door, my indication to follow. The moment the door to the temple's outer court is closed and locked, I feel the gutting banishment of being back in the lone and dreary world.

'Ere the other side he see. I scan the words' blessing with my fingers.

"The funeral is tomorrow, Friday, at 5:30 p.m. at the Temple Hill Cemetery Chapel."

"Funeral? He hasn't been buried yet? I thought this . . . estate stuff was taken care of after the funeral."

In very lawyery fashion, he waits for the intonation of a verbal question mark to distinguish between my ponderings and an actual question. "He respectfully requests your attendance."

Respectfully requests? Who *respectfully requests* the presence of people at his funeral?

"Would I be able to come back to this apartment at all in the future?"

"Just heed the directives of the manuscript and we'll go from there. We want to take care of you in a way that makes sense according to what we know."

My mind is tumbling in breaking waves over that statement. According to what we know? What the helter skelter is that supposed to mean? In a way that makes sense?

He circulates through the turnstile before I can ask follow-up questions.

I lean my forehead against the front door and inhale through my nose with purpose. More tears channel through the alluvium of my nose and hop to the bunched carpet below. I can hear him in there: *There are a million excuses to NOT do something!*

Though I hope this isn't the new me, it sure feels good to cry like this.

Chapter 4

"I will make my way through one more day in hell."
– "Indifference," Pearl Jam

We want to take care of you in a way that makes sense according to what we know.

Seriously . . .

That phrase was square and compass engineered to be mathematically amoebic. It's Patch-style ambiguity used to masquerade apocalyptic horsemen as routine Pony Express mail carriers. It's not reassurance, it's a warning.

I heft the letterhead box like a curious Christmas present. There must be an entire ream of doom presaging paper in here. This thing is Pandora's fruit of the Tree of Frankenstein's Monster so I hold it as far away from my face as my long arms allow. I'm using such loitering absurdities to postpone my fate. Now I have to see how long I can do this before my shoulders give out. This suspense-stretching delay reminds me of Patch's nasal spray runs. We would be in the middle of an ignore-Mom's-pleas-to-let-me-do-my-homework conversation, when he would abruptly stop talking, and his nose would crinkle. That cue, the subtlety of the wings spreading and the bridge wrinkling, that meant On your mark, and, Get set. I'd instinctively clutch the armrests of the chair and await the crack of the pistol. He'd pull a 1925 South Bend Co. Studebaker pocket watch from his vest pocket, hold it aloft with his thumb on the detonator for the explosives rigged to all my fast twitch muscles, and stretch the suspense out to near false starts . . . then, GO! I would tear through the house, no regard for my own safety or that of the bric-a-bracs stupidly teetering on top heavy furniture. Mom would shout, "Stop breaking my house with your games, you two!" Patch announced each second with increasing volume and drama. I'd be back in twelve point three eight seconds with his off-brand nasal spray in a victorious pant. Unless I didn't break the record, then it was head-shaking shame and back to our conversation. Either way, he got his nasal spray and my speed was challenged.

There's no way to describe his . . . I don't know what to call it. Ubiquity? He wasn't the canvas, he was the imagination. He wasn't Leviathan, he was the ocean currents. He was a gas filling all available space. He was loud energy. *If you don't listen to your mother, there will be hell to pay; and you can't afford it!*

It's a cursed treasure, this is. If I open it, it can only mean war, pestilence, or unparalleled fortune. More like unparalleled fortune after surviving the war and acquiring a natural immunity to the pestilence. Bro Manjigglies was a man of extremes. It was always work, work, work with the old man. *Life is work!* And a shoulder-to-the-wheel, plow through to-do lists would be manageable and predictable, but Patch is all about explorations and unfoldings and tortuous, solvable, irresistible riddles. *The manner of its disbursement is articulated in the manuscript's introduction.* When he says introduction, he means the introduction of a nursery of raccoons into my comfort zone to poop in all its corners. My trustworthy, intrusion-buffeting intuition tells me to chuck this temptress into the fire. I know I said this would be my debt-cancelling swan song, but this is way more than executor of a will.

I squarely center the Manuscript on a circular, rattan placemat on my dining table and walk to the bottle of suicide on the counter. The hoplites have settled into their afternoon nap, purring battle cries, spear-tipped lullabies turned on their handlers. I shake the bottle a little. These post-*Cat in the Hat* Brittanys and Connors don't seem so menacing now. Was that really just this morning? It already seems like an episode carefully wrapped in doilies, concealed in a breakable heirloom, stored in a forgettable attic corner, and cryptically referenced in journals discovered generations later. Time flies when you're fencing estate attorneys, I guess.

I'm still a little tipsy from Crackbaby Fitz's golden electricity nymphs so I run the water in the sink and dump the phalanx into the drain. So . . . that's that.

Life is weird.

I motion to busy myself with perfunctory chores—the banking, loading the dishwasher—but I can hear how amused the Manuscript is by this. It knows it has burrowed its head up to the shoulders in my attention. It's like sitting in front of heaven's acceptance/rejection letter. Fine, whatever, I'm not afraid of Revelstoke's ramblings <<my abdominal muscles have been flexed for an hour>>. Besides, I know there's no use in trying to outmaneuver the eventualities of this Manuscript, whatever it is. Even if I chucked it in the fire, Granny Two Step <<these names are my teen years>> would have anticipated that and there'd be another copy on my doorstep in the morning. All twenty-four of those file boxes may be filled with extra copies, for all I know. He was a scare-the-shittyknickers-off-you kind of thorough.

Should I wait for the other boxes to get here tomorrow morning before opening this thing? <<Just open it.>> You can't trust that guy with lids! <<The only way out is through.>> Is there no other way? <<There is no other way . . .>> This isn't an inheritance, this is torment! And I just know he's somehow spying on me right now as part of his *jolly rompery*, or whatever he used to call it. I should check all my outdoor cameras but I don't want to indulge the insanity of thinking a dead swashbuckler is peeping through my windows. I don't *always* have to pander to my paranoia. If I'm being honest with myself <<which is rare these days>>, I don't know what I have to lose; I'm dead as of this morning. I'm on borrowed time—the loan yoked with an onerous interest rate and the most demanding of creditors <<read: loan shark>>. Besides, life transitioning from unbearable to unaffordable is a step up, right?

I am not statistically idiotic, so I can't dismiss the timing of my deliverance. And this is the second time Old Man Scurlock has snatched me from the jaws of a salivating abyss. Apparently, his real name is Elliot Dillinger. I just found that out today. Coincidentally, that's my name as well. I didn't know I was named after somebody. Thanks, Mom.

Though this Manuscript will end up being a worm that never dieth and will eat me like wool, I acknowledge with much disinclination that it will have the best of intentions. Patch has always been benevolent that way. All traces of spare time and comfort and predictability and relaxation will be smitten with the east wind and devoured by insects, but only a fool would argue that a terminal *nothing* beats a purposeful *something*. And if a purposeful something doesn't break my life's water main fairly soon, I'll be back to inventing reasons to see a dentist. What am I not considering? Oh, yeah, he's an eccentric swashbuckling lunatic that thinks lessons can only be learned through immersion therapy! Also, the promise of money . . .

I hear the brown sound feedback from my fridge magnets: *You know if something's good for you if it's easy to quit. Vices take it personally and try to destroy you if you break up with them.* Maybe I'm overreacting. <<I'm absolutely not!>> I could at least read it. If it's hard to quit, I'll know it was pestilence. Easy to quit, unparalleled fortune. I can't believe this is my new unavoidable reality: fretting over unfolding a treasure map. In my defense, there are sure to be more booby traps than booty.

I'm stalling again. I never seem to be in a hurry to do things these days. Maybe it's this table; it does have an ambivalence-breeding kind of grain to it.

Chapter 5

"[Kids] don't remember what you try to teach them. They remember what you
are."
– Jim Henson

My dad was in the army. Like any kid folded up in his sharp-cornered, geometrical world, I didn't care what he did as long as there was no qualitative change to the quality of my life. Which was a good life, despite being an only child. My dad did a good job of doubling as father and sibling, both making sure I brushed my teeth and ganging up against Mom in protest of unreasonable bed times so we could watch *Raiders of the Lost Ark* for the fiftieth time. I remember hearing terms like *signals* and *SATCOM* and *datalink* thrown around in his conversations with Mom, but even now I'm not sure what he did in the army. I should probably ask Mom; it's a little embarrassing not knowing. Dad was killed in Afghanistan when I was thirteen. RPG, they say. He was over there so much, Mom was resigned to the fact that Afghanistan would murder him. So sure, that when he *was* home, Mom was in tacit mourning, and it began to feel more like a funeral home than your standard *home* home. Sometimes, in his presence, she would drop what she was doing and just start crying. It was a strange time. I don't know if her death sentence made it easier to deal with his death or harder to deal with him while he was alive. I could tell by his helpless glances at me that he didn't like being a ghost. He was gone so much during those years I don't remember much about him, but I do remember that he was a good dad. He was the Thorazined version of The Great Cataract <<another of Patch's names>>, but just as attentive. He was intrusive when it was fatherly to be intrusive and unobtrusive when it seemed a matter of motherly inroads. I was so busy consoling my inconsolable mother <<sitting her down and watching her cry, mostly>> that his death didn't really have the opportunity to affect me that much.

Within a week of his passing, my dad had, in essence, been replaced by an older, juiced version that seemed totally unaffected by everything going on, like he was hired by a service to maintain the household's uninterrupted operation. Patch swooped in like a hungry falcon and snatched up the prey of paternity. "Did you make your bed? Did you brush your teeth? Did you make out with any cute girls today?" His reaction to his son's death was the counterweight to Mom's, and he seemed very savvy about this, shifting deftly to keep all the plates spinning as Mom carelessly stumbled into them. He artfully reserved his own mourning, knowing that shuffling toward the fulcrum would create an imbalance and provoke some consolation that would short circuit Mom's healing. "He's much more your husband than he is my son," he would patiently remind her. She was quite stingy with the sackcloth and ashes.

One time I asked him how he came up with the name Patch <<which was used more frequently than any other name>>. His face went squishy along all horizontal planes and he looked at me for the longest time with genuine concern.

He finally said with a huff, "It's a common nickname for someone that wears an eye patch." Then he shook his head with great condescension and disdain and turned his attention to something outside.

He never wore an eye patch.

Salvador's Lama wasn't so much a fixture as he was a flare-up. His presence either was or wasn't—he'd either be over for three weeks straight or gone for a week. When he was around, he was like a smothering humidity—no privacy, no downtime, no peace. He had such a violent animus toward public schooling that he commandeered all my evenings to uneducate me and re-educate me, Patch-style. Nothing in the school curriculum overlapped with what he thought a wee barra my age should know, so I was schooled, unschooled, and reschooled all throughout high school. He sort of snuck all his indoctrination into the fun we had. And I was a naturally curious kid anyway. I would be in a Georgian-fauna, jury-rigged ghillie suit in the woods behind our house, Patch as my spotter, doing advanced trigonometry, atmospherics, physics, ballistics, and ethics to get a clean shot on distant enemy paratroopers dropping from an Il-76 at such-and-such speed at such-and-such altitude, and on and on and on. It was always like this—dizzying kaleidoscope wormholes of firehose-fed information and scenarios and perspectives and considerations and rapid-fire quizzes. It was education by onslaught. I found it sort of exhilarating, actually, even if sleep did devour me the moment my head hit night's pillow.

The academic blitzkrieg was all well and good, the death-distracting raucous recreation was hilariously unforgettable, but it was the linebacker drills that sold me on Commodore Battle Chicken's <<I have a notebook somewhere with all these names>> unsteering devotion. Hours and hours shifting, shuffling, reading, tracking, tackling, stepping, swatting, shadowing in the wretched atmospheric pools of Georgian skies. He was a machine. I couldn't evade, outwit, or outrun the old man until I was nearly sixteen. What Scot knows that much about American football? And who has that much mobility and energy at sixty-something? I'm twenty-eight and I get winded putting my socks on.

Come to think of it, I have a lot of questions that should have surfaced when he was around. <<What teenagers miss when they're a world of one . . .>> Why was he so easy about spending weeks on end at the bidding of my caprice, or doing what he thought would be best for *me*? Didn't he have anything better to do with his retirement <<I'm assuming he was retired>> than babysit some kid? Did I ever see him do a single thing for his own recreation or entertainment <<other than watch *The Princess Bride* and *Monty Python and the Holy Grail* with me>>? Did I ever see him sleep? I can't remember.

Questions are always welcome, my boy, but refusing to abide the answer because it isn't what you want to hear, that's never welcome. Never impose your demands on the truth!

His absences never really bothered me, even the slightly extended ones. I needed recovery days. His presence was so tumescent, I felt like I was in his swarm for days. Maybe he realized this, and that too much Mad Murphy would condense the bloating atmosphere to a downpour. When he wasn't around, I assumed he was sleeping off a speed-fueled high. After seeing that apartment, he'd probably discovered some compound that replaced sleep. Maybe that's how he made his fortune: herbal amphetamines.

I take a long draught of Mountain Dew as the universe that is Patch sits on my mind.

This frenetic, hyper-dramatic, loudly simulated life went on for several years, until I was seventeen. Then he was gone without a word. *Gone* gone. Mom said it was his turn to mourn Dad, but I never did find out the real reason. I'm not even sure Mom knew. She did say that, time or not, he gave us more than we could ever repay. I was still a little pissy and felt that I was owed something. Not sure what, but something. Maybe an explanation. Maybe a dad that didn't disappear. But, then, teenagers are self-focused brats, so what did I know? I never saw him again after that. Soon after he left, I got injured. If I was fork-tongued, I'd say my death wish is a symptom of all kinds of abandonment, and I'm mourning the loss of two fathers. But I must not be fork-tongued, because if I'm mourning anything, I'm mourning the fact that I was more devastated by that injury than a good dad's death. Than good *dads'* deaths.

Life rises and falls on the shame of rotten priorities and false attributions, I suppose.

Why are Mom and I the only ones in his will? Did he not have any other family? That seems unlikely; his was a generation of fertility. Where did all those sabbaticals take him to? I have no idea what he did for a living. How did he have money? He didn't act like he had money. In fact, I don't think I ever saw him *spend* money. And how were we living so comfortably all those years without a breadwinner? Were we being . . . subsidized? Was Jumpin' Juggernaut sponsoring Mom's bingo hall addiction? Our whole livelihood? Is Mom's reference to a debt we could never repay a monetary debt as well? I'm not entirely sure why any of this should matter, but knowing what I know about that sidewinding stress fracture, there are no *likelihoods* or *probabilities*. Everything is calculated, weighed, scheduled, coordinated, connected, sequential, completed, interrelated, stage-setting, and relevant <<did I forget any adjectives that connote *grand design*?>>, regardless of delay or digression. Everything has an echo. Everything is a type and a foreshadow. Nothing is singular or anomalous or coincidental. He's shifty that way. He's shifty in every measurable way. So whatever was or wasn't, whatever is or isn't, everything will be as he intended for it to be. The fact that I'm sitting in front of this Manuscript at this very moment may be the final act of his play, for all I know.

Again, he's scare-the-shittyknickers-off-you kind of thorough.

Even without the money hypothesis, Mom's right; it's a debt that can't be repaid. Everything I am is three parts Plugs Bigsby and one part puree of everything else. Maybe nine parts, one part. He was the dad I remember. Mom says that most of what I say sounds like it's coming straight from Patch <<she boringly calls him *Dad*, because, she explains, that's just what you call your

father-in-law>>. I assume it's complimentary; she's smiling when she says it <<and frequently shaking her head>>.

Evening light is stuttering through windows in the clouds, indecisively opening and closing. The sky bleeds out its colder pinks and venous purples. The last gossamer of spun sunlight infiltrates a glass pyramid I was gifted by a client <<for basically doing my job>> sitting on the sill of my kitchen window, and it casts its diffracted conversion in a perfect spectrum of soft transitions onto the center of the letterhead box. This is my cue, apparently.

Poop or get off the pot, Mom would say.

Do I have any nitroglycerin laying around? <<Why would you have nitroglycerin in the house?>> Should I take an aspirin first? <<Just open the box. >>

I press my thumbs and middle fingers into the sides of the lid and lift. I can see the lid quaking. Probably lingering caffeine <<I know better>>. My face didn't melt off. I didn't turn into a skeleton. So far, so good. I flip the lid over and place it reverently on the table to my left. Patch's fracturing plasma ghosts pendulate a censer, circulating an incense of mustache wax and almond lotion and pencil shavings across the title page. I press the tip of my nose onto the page and inhale. In, out. In <<hold it>>, out <<forcefully, to flush away any residual competitors>>. In, out. I consider resealing the box to contain the smell. Maybe this is enough. Maybe this is as far as I need to go. It can serve as a soothing music box for my nose. But I don't; because, how stupid would that be?

The title page is a sterile, optical white noise with *Ankou's Hourglass* printed in an old-timey typewriter font across the center. It's clean and innocent. This should pacify me, but it doesn't. <<Remember, Elliot, he's shifty in every measurable way!>> I pull the Manuscript out and push the box and placemat aside. I lay it on the table and adjust the pages that shifted to restore its cubical integrity.

Ankou's Hourglass. No idea what that means.

My future is stacked in a footprint of aseptic geometry, like a newly dedicated maternity hospital of seraph-hand hewn marble with all its layers of promise and renaissance. Maybe *naissance* is more apt, since I never got around to living life the first time.

Now I'm stuck between worlds. I feel like I've been locked out of my own pitiable paradigm and I'm back in the loading Construct.

I lick my fingertip, dislodge the title page from its penthouse, and place it face down on the table to my right with a little self-indulging ceremony . . .

CHAPTER 6

"Remember, all I'm offering is the truth—nothing more."
– Morpheus, *The Matrix*

The second page is blank. No Intentionally Left Blank caution. Third page is blank. My heart slips stiffly on an evaporative hope that the printer somehow failed and I could emerge from the Fire Swamp with a small shoulder wound. And . . .

Bummer.

The title page was typewritten, but this part is handwritten, with all the edits intact. Dicken's Specter always had such masculine and flawless penmanship. Maybe gentleman-adventurer is more apt than swashbuckler. There's no heading, no preface, no forward, he just dives right in:

Bone of my bones, flesh of my flesh, son of my son, greetings from an untenable grave.

Initial thoughts: use of the word *untenable* in reference to his death is a little disconcerting.

Tomorrow night, following the funeral, plot #408, northeast corner of Temple Hill Cemetery, my body must be exhumed with shovel and haste under the cover of night and, encased in liquid nitrogen marbles in the trunk of your car, driven across secondary roads to Duluth, Minnesota, where you will arrange with the Seaway Port Authority for maritime transport of my body to Casablanca, Morocco, where Abu Ahmad Al-Barimi will intercept the shipment at Mina'Wahed and transport by unmarked ambulance to Bait An-Naum where you will be waiting with $3,000 USD in cash to hand deliver to Fou'ad Alaoui, who will administer a life restoring dose of Baasi. Within ninety-six hours of burial my life becomes unrecoverable. Surely, there is but a step between me and death. Snatch me from a categorical death, my son! Your passport awaits at the receiving office of the Duluth Seaport (ask for Gail). You have been trained for this (Scenario 11)! Don't fail me, wee barra!

Pretty sure my bowels started backing up at the word *shovel*. I know it's senseless for someone like me to have brown paper lunch bags in the house, but for a moment I curse myself for not having any brown paper lunch bags in the house.

Oh, how I have missed this jolly rogery! <<Jolly rogery, jolly rompery—I was close.>> Bet yer gammie ticker's pure done after that quality mince! I miss our time, my friend.

You're kidding me . . .

Next order of business:

How in hell's halfway house was that an order of business? Yeah, my gammie ticker's pure done, you lunatic! Where would somebody even get liquid nitrogen marbles?

Whatever dread percolated in those prodigious and sportless guts of yours, good instincts on ya, laddie. All your suspicions about this manuscript are hardening to bone. I'm here to evict you from your life, if that's what you call this sodden broth you've made of yourself—meat and potatoes to stock strained of all its pepper 'n pluck. Thought I'd made a stout lad of ya! If Jack Splat had a look at you now. Enough to make ya cowk, ya wee bawbag! You shat your chance, laddie, now it's my round for a square go. Okay, I've had it out, ya numpty. Read and heed!

I remember him slipping into this swampy brogue when escalating passions would pit mouth against mind. Like this sample—I always knew it was English, but could only pick out enough to get that far. You could tell he wasn't always well-spoken. If I'm going on tone alone, it's a ranting insult. *Sodden broth* doesn't sound flattering. Remember to look up *cowk*, *bawbag*, and *numpty*. And that reference to Jack Lambert was just mean.

Consider your linebacker days, my boy. How much of heaven and earth would you move to reclaim that glory and take a hop over the fly-covered demise of that fateful injury?

He knew about the injury? Mom must have told him somewhere along the way. To answer your question, old man, all of it. With hell in tow. With all seven of its levels—if there are seven levels. <<I can feel all the muscles of my hip sockets tensing, like they're about to sprint, because I know he's somehow serious.>> I take a moment to soak in the whirlpool hot tub of that possibility.

Let that vision lay siege to the supply lines of your mind and ambush the scout of your every thought. What follows requires twenty thousand measures of confidence and objectivity. Take a deep breath. Go throw up if you need to.

I take a long drag of cold Mountain Dew through the fattest red straw the Holiday stocks. Bring it on, old man.

When you dream, your mind accepts the most absurd assumptions as incontrovertible reality and does not take inventory in the moment to reconcile the obvious discrepancies. Only when you awaken do you wonder how such improbabilities were so casually embraced. Your world is that dream state, and its parameters and partitions have been cleverly constructed to ensure you do not awaken. The real world is hiding, is hidden, in plain sight, just beyond the horizon of your wakefulness. Every now and again you will catch a glimpse of this real world, but the demands for the acceptance of this dream state are non-negotiable, and unwitting institutions condition you to doubt and discount from the cradle to the grave. You are in Oz and the wizard's curtain is tightly drawn.

Twenty thousand measures of confidence and objectivity, Elliot. You can do this.

With gratuitous well-poisoning, you are told how and why you see something before you see it; you are told how and why you believe something before you believe it. To question is to accuse, and another dose of anesthetic is administered. Blockbuster films dramatize its indisputable provenance. Day and night media demonize dissenters on a seasickening loop. Dissidence is ostracism. Your conditioned senses and intuition tell you: this is banking, elections, terrorism, discovery, scandal, and embracing the tenets of these constructs is essential to your status and well-being, even your survival. All you see, all you are allowed to see, is that which excites and enrages—politics, sports, identity sculpting, social causes, stock portfolios, streaming, wars, video games, social media affirmation. They are levers for increasingly saccharin-rich pellets formulated to prevent you from exploring the perimeter of the Skinner box, where the rifts exit to horrifying freedoms.

That's a horrible way to start. Maybe a less destabilizing anecdote or something. And what's wrong with sports and stock portfolios?

Consider a mouse running a maze. The mouse is clever, but the maze is malevolently convoluted. The mouse begins to explore. The professor and lab assistant argue about the layout of the maze as the mouse makes no extraordinary progress. The professor contends that running the maze should be its own reward—their eyes brightened by the exercise. The lab assistant offers a counterpoint: dozens of hand-selected mice should learn the maze so more advanced mazes can be designed and navigated to facilitate the advancement of the mice. The professor posits that history deposits all alleged advancement in landfills of arrogance, overreaching, and self-destruction. Lab assistant: history is replete with blinding phoenixes of flourishing recovery from such hubris. The professor plucks the mouse from its course, administers an electric shock, and places the mouse in a yet undiscovered corner of the maze. The mouse resumes its exploration for the first time, or so its bolted mind accepts. The lab assistant begins removing sections of the maze's walls. The professor adds wall sections depicting naked female mice in compromising positions, then shocks the mouse. The lab assistant inserts wall sections made of cheese. The professor spreads Nutella over the center of the maze floor and shocks the mouse. The lab assis-

tant inadvertently cuts the mouse in half while placing a section of wall in an arrangement less prohibitive. The professor shocks the front half. The lab assistant stitches the mouse up and returns it to the point of forward progress. The professor barricades the bacon reward and stands a shrewd guard. Then shocks the mouse. The lab assistant recruits members of the cleaning staff to slash the professor's tires in the parking lot. The professor kills the lab assistant's mother before the lab assistant is born.

This is the abstract of your reality. You are the mouse. The professor and lab assistant rearrange and redefine the maze. Your mind is erased every day to run it again.

Well, that clears everything up. I said a *less* destabilizing, not *more* destabilizing anecdote.

These two parties reformat and refine this maze, this dream state, by reformatting time. They also live in the maze, but they know the location of all the trap doors and secret hallways that lead to the real world, a world the dreamers cannot fathom. It is a world of ironic invisibility as our senses are, at all times, inundated by its inscriptions. The professor and lab assistant are expert with glitter and glitz. Every day we become more proficient at navigating the center of the maze, every day we applaud our proficiency. The corners and edges of the maze are unguarded but unexplored as we have condemned ourselves to the validations of the center. Mice are predictable creatures, and it takes little inducement to get them back on the hamster wheel—a little punishment, a little reward, a little entertainment.

Though the professor and lab assistant are at odds regarding the parameters of the maze, they do agree that there must be a maze. Mice become cannibalistic when they realize that their monarchy and majesty is mythical. With whispering walls and counseling corridors, the professor and lab assistant induce a self-circulating sleepiness and the dream state perpetuates. Presidents, magnates, prime ministers, tycoons, monarchs, dictators, cardinals, central bankers, consortia, mafioso, technocrats, oligarchs—our generic classes of powerbrokers—the inmates running the asylum. Parliaments, universities, agencies, corporations, churches—the asylum. The administrators and therapists (~~Merovingian~~ professor and lab assistant) make observations and take notes to determine how many floor tiles to the left the ping pong table should be moved in the rec room to keep the relative peace.

Though the dispute between the professor and lab assistant is far more chivalrous than my characterization, all the elements remain, and you are, as the mouse in the maze, the daily collateral damage of this duel. Think of these two more as pre-pubescent brothers playing a game of ~~four-dimensional~~ Risk. When one sees that the other is going to win, in a fit of sour competitiveness he overturns the board, blaming his loss on some unfalsifiable, nuanced contravention and demands a rematch. ~~You are one of the blue 1 army pieces, temper-tossed to~~

~~the four winds, retrieved from the kitchen floor near the vent with the rest of the collateral damage and placed with great etiquette before the lab assistant or the professor.~~ They always play again. It is always a new board. It is always war. You are always in the crossfire.

It is a genteel war of infinite fronts and flanks burrowing into the fertile soil of an impressionable and mutable history that daily overwrites itself as each frame shift, deep or shallow, lumbers in its muddy shoes to the surface of the final frame. Muted battles waged in railway stations, courtrooms, orphanages, board rooms, stock exchange floors, laboratories, theater dressing rooms; in Post-Soviet Russia, in Imperial Japan, in neo-Conservative America; fought in payments and promises, suggestions and winks; all are knit into the now that is click, click, clicking. ~~Recent past and present are so wholly inseparable, that an exchange in a 1930s Parisian café is, may I contend, categorically more relevant to the fate of the world than a declaration of world war this morning.~~

What in black whiteness am I reading? I think I might have been given the wrong document. This was meant for . . . for one of his lieutenants? His therapist?

With individual agendas, the professor and ~~Subverts~~ lab assistant sink into the past to outflank, dictate the battlefield, and turn generals. This reformatting of time is the expression of the petulance of the overturned Risk board. It is, in a general sense, change. It is not necessary to qualify the magnitude of any particular change, as some seem devastating when Monday morning quarterbacking but end up a hiccup, and some begin as a random mark on a tablecloth and spark thread-bending wildfires that char the present. Following a change of any magnitude, there is no restoring the original thread, and every day at 0000 hours, you lie in an ~~umbral~~ infirmary as the bandaged wounds to your reality heal into scars of a new reality. This reality, so-called, is ~~the constant adjustment to imperceptible and distant ripples that undulate through your imprinting,~~ what your mind accepts as historical memory because every subsequent moment of your life has been respectively altered ~~to overwrite~~ to support the acceptance of the new reality. Because you only have one mind in your body at present, and this overwrite defaults to that single mind, there is no consciousness of amendments. Tomorrow will be no different: ~~something will change, the stack will update, you will have, and have accepted, a new past.~~

One mind in my body *at present?* I want to say he's losing it, but I've heard myself say those very words many times before and I've always ended up the fool. I shake the cup and discover that my towering sentry of Dew has abandoned its post.

As a result of this overwrite, sometimes your circumstances change, but in the main, you are left entirely unaffected. The hitch is, as long as you remain inside this single-mind loop, wrinkles will pulse modifications through the stack, something will change, and you will never know what that something was. You have lived this moment a thousand times. It is impossible to say with what degree of variation you lived it; it is immaterial, really, because you will live it again another thousand times with a manicure. For this reason, we will need to duplicate you and dump a twenty-eight year-old spy in your sixteen-year-old body.

Come on, Elliot, you're smart enough to figure this out! I just have to ferret out the figurative from the literal. Okay, I'm a rat in a maze, I have accepted a false reality, I'm a POW in some crazy gentlemen's war, I'm locked in some *Groundhog Day* scenario, time doesn't really exist as I understand it, I get a new past every day. Got it. Classic Patch. What does this have to do with me being a linebacker again? Is he implying that a copy of the current me is going to be stuffed in the sixteen-year-old me? That has to be figurative, right? Am I, in effect, going to *be* sixteen again? Is that how I get out of that single-mind loop, by shoving a second mind into one body?

As it stands, you are not the subject of your life's sentence; you are an unwitting direct object. You are a slave to sequence, and your lockstep with time's march is the justice from which you must be a fugitive. Simply put, you need to be freed from this loop. Less simply put, you need to free yourself from this loop. I can promote you from maze mouse to lab assistant, but you must first become the subject of your life's sentence. Your proactivity must get ahead of your reactivity. Everything about your dream state world is a deafening machine that will swallow up your purpose and significance with the immensity and complexity of its noise, every façade of its Potemkin village will dazzle and bewitch, so you must focus and trust the process. Plucking you from the briars of the overwrite will not prevent the changes, but it will a allow you a fly-on-the-wall cognizance of them. It will allow you to sidestep their effects and become a greater contributor to discussions about parameters and partitions. Your life, this world, the aggregation that engineers your reality, it is just one version, a version that is dictated by people that are not you. I am not offering just another version or a second chance, I am offering insurance. I am offering life outside of time, life outside of determinism. I am offering counterpunches to fate's blows. It is impossible. It is unbelievable. You will think me auf me nut, but, as they say, faith precedes the miracle. You could use a miracle in your life.
I can move you through bedchambers and dark courtyards without having to fight the war proper, but you need to make fighting weight if we are to fit you into pre-injury Elliot, sixteen.

Now we're talking! I don't like where all this *fitting me into* and *duplication* gibberish is going, but the pre-injury Elliot, sixteen notion is promising.

There is a society of no renown and infinite import, a society that keeps the machinations of this world's substratum oiled and whirring by ventilating the compressive containment of time. Yes, yes, they overturn Risk boards and shock mice and speak cryptically of cold fronts in 1951 Bostonian parlors, but they alone hold keys. This society is governed more by a charter than an immutable canon, but there is one principle, a covenant, by which every ~~pikirovatel/trouplongeur, Subvert, Mero, and mapper~~ member of this society abides. It is its constitution and its currency. It is the precept that must manage the rudder through these channels. It is this: regularly dying is regularly living and you must always die on your own terms. Never let the Gontlets have you—they are for the dead! I see now that you have the courage to die. It is a good start, but no more pruning the dying branches of my dogged fatherhood with those shears again! It is the grossest manifestation of ingratitude! <<Uh . . . what? Did he know what I was planning to do this morning? It sure sounds like he knew. Is that possible?>> *Since this is your maiden voyage, I'll keep the gloves on, but so help me, by the brass feet and hoary head of the Almighty, if I so much as discern hangdog in the rumor of a west wind, the gloves will come off! I am arrayed for battle! I have trained my hands to war and my fingers to fight!*

You do not know enough to know what you do not know, so keep your questions to yourself for now. Nothing intelligent will come from musings and all needful answers will be provided in time. If I told you what was on the other side of those façades, you'd write the whole business off before we could get you fixed up. Nobody can stomach the sausage factory's fifteen-minute tour. If you want greatness, you have to prove you can be great. You need brick by brick, thinking and doing, endless drills in the soupy heat of the Georgian sun greatness. There is no back door. There are no shortcuts. You have to feel with acuteness the muscle cells tearing. I know your mind—you like structure and order and predictability and have ~~a mollycoddled~~ an aversion to even the salliest of setbacks ~~that should shame any respectable Steelers linebacker~~. <<Striking through a word doesn't make it invisible, you know. Of course I hate setbacks! Everybody hates setbacks! Who likes doing things twice?>> *This process is fraught with chaos and upending and bottlenecks and will provide the thunderous glesga kiss needed to knock those neuroses clean oot yer napper. That's the easy part. The hard part is not reading ahead. If you read ahead, the jig is up. The gills of this scheme are in the strict adherence to its progression. This beast needs to sniff you for a year to make sure you're not a sidewinder. One year! I got you past the rough patch; time to entrust your life to the Great Glass Canard!*

Oh yeah, I forgot about that one.

Remember when we would play Scotland Yard—you were all five detectives and I was Mr. X? There came a point in my endgame evasion where you would have to direct all of your resources to one last-ditch besieging and trust the soundness of it. You have reached that point. This is the course. If you are patient and thorough and disciplined, and work out each phase with diligence, you will be skinned unto blood, hardened unto bone, and you will behold the raw flesh. You, Elliot Dillinger, are a bloodthirsty linebacker and this day will I begin to put the dread of thee and the fear of thee upon the nations that are under the whole heaven who shall hear report of thee, and shall tremble, and be in anguish because of thee, and I will make thee a name of greatness and terribleness! They shall come out against thee one way, and flee before thee seven ways; their plague will be the sword without and terror within! Be strong, and quit yourself like a man.

Now away with you, and think nothing of this until Saturday. The twenty-four file boxes you saw at my apartment should be delivered to you tomorrow. The items in the boxes correspond to the instructions contained in the manuscript. Investigating the contents of the boxes before the instructions dictate will be as destructive to this process as reading ahead. Without context and explanation, the boxes' contents won't make sense anyway. Two blank pages separate each day's instructions. On the following Saturday, remove the intermediate blank pages, read that day's instructions only, and execute.

The tide is coming in. We have but a moment to resurrect that walloper of a linebacker before some splitjacked French masonry overwrites the lot of it. This is the crack in the Skinner box. Great and terrible freedoms await. Reclaim your rightful royalty!

Holy crack pipe, that was all over the place. And I was right, raccoon poop in comfort zone corners. At least I don't have to go to Morocco; that was a horrifying notion. Even the backroads trip to Minnesota with a dead body in the trunk sounded horrifying. Today is Thursday. I'm supposed to think nothing of what sounds like spring training for time travel till Saturday? But he can get me back. He can get me back to pre-injury Elliot, sixteen.

This rapture has severed all consciousness of my limbs.

Chapter 7

"Each morning when I awake, I experience again a supreme pleasure—that of
being Salvador Dali."
– Salvador Dali

Everything about today has been a month of Sundays <<the stay in your church
clothes and read quietly on the couch kind of Sundays>>, and it's still only 9:30
p.m. And I feel pretty good. I can feel the contrast of that uncluttered affect
re-broadening in weird ways. The death of a father and the excitement of a redo
can have that affect.

The Manuscript stands in its post-visiting hours stillness. At this hour, I
normally have the popest of rock music drowning out the whimpers of existential agony through headphones while I work, air guitaring arpeggios that don't
exist through the solos, cold Mountain Dew keeping me company. It's an intoxi-
cating kind of implosion, those hours are, a total detachment from anything real.
It makes tonight's workless quiet a peculiar phenomenon.

My thoughts are so obstreperous that the cricket-cracking, blacked-out
backdrop of suburban bedtime stories is enough extra noise. The humming and
growling of systems and appliances are all paused. The house is at rest. I listen—
there's an actual peacefulness to the silence in this cobwebbed kind of suspension. Apparitions of anguish aren't rending the peace with their barking and
barking. I feel settled. When was the last time I felt . . . settled?

I took the last hour or so to reread and study the mad blatherings of Sheikh
Jinn Jab. I wanted to take a second look after the initial anticipation had worn
down to swollen nubs. I'm kicking myself for never asking him a single question about his life. Was I that self-devoured? <<Emphatic yes.>> It is truly
embarrassing. My inability to sneak a question in is testament to his genuine
preoccupation with my interests. Or genuine preoccupation with concealing his
own. Possibly the world's most interesting man, my own grandad, my replacement father, and I'm learning about him through this text, half crossed-out. He
was such an enormous presence that every word I read reincarnates a dimensionality as active and loud as the reality it's derived from. He was silverback,
chest-pounding multimedia.

After breathing my warm breath on the glass, this is what I could make out:

The world around me, the world I perceive, does not exist the way I think
it does. It is somehow a fabrication so convincing that I am unable to see past
the illusion. I like the Potemkin village metaphor that Patch used. Everything I
fill my life with is an encouraged distraction so I don't stumble onto the truth or
actively seek it. All the institutions I have come to rely on for truth and surety
<<governments, the scientific community, news media, educational institutions,
international bodies, financial institutions, large corporations, militaries, everything with a face in general society, I'm guessing>> are agents of forgers, and
are, themselves, extensions of the forgery. I don't know if these institutions

know they are agents of forgers, but I don't get the impression they know. It would make sense that at least a few in each organization know. There are two organizations that vie for the real seat of power in this world—the Merovingian <<the entity represented by the professor>> and Subverts <<the entity represented by the lab assistant>>. These two entities are engaged in some kind of war that extends back into layers of the past. <<Is specifically fought in the past?>> The campaigns and incursions of this war result in changes to the past, and, though these changes are constant, they are all somehow permanent. At least permanent until midnight. Apparently, they affect every point in time from their origin to the present, and this is *updated* <<Patch's word>> at 0000 hours each day. But I am not able to perceive any of these changes because the reality of everyone affected is restructured accordingly.

It's like . . . it's like <<the concentration required to figure this out exceeds the remaining caffeine in my system>> this daily update is a tsunami and we're all swept up in it; everybody relives the altered reality from change to present, so it's the only version of life their time-bound mind has ever known. My connection to the linear progression of time prevents me from seeing or discovering the truth, prevents me from seeing or discovering any changes made, and I can somehow become freed from this recycling imprisonment. But I'm not able to accept the way this happens because of the way I've been propagandized my whole life. It needs to be incrementally unveiled for me to accept it. This requires me to abandon everything in my life that's a tangential distraction, focus my mind, and comply with Patch's process.

These changes are somehow the casualties of this war, and the means of gaining the upper hand by one combatant or the other. Each contender seems to have its agenda, but I don't think I was given enough information to know what those are. He said it was a *genteel* war, so I don't get the impression it's for the pursuit of power itself. The Merovingian seems to be spinning the illusion <<*splitjacked French masonry?*>>, but I don't know if the Subverts are involved in that as well or if they're just contrarians. They seem to be at least supporting the illusion if they agree that there must be a maze. Or one of many other possibilities. From the professor-lab assistant analogy, I get the impression that the Subverts want to liberate more people from this single-mind loop, as he called it. I can't prevent any of these changes from occurring, but once I've been pulled out of the sequential progress of time, however that is supposed to work, I can adjust course when I see their effects piercing my present with the daily update <<overwrite>>.

Patch never explicitly incorporated himself into this society, but I get the impression he's one of its officers. He claims to know where the trap doors and secret hallways are and he said he could promote me from a maze mouse to a lab assistant. That must require some authority, right? Knowing Patch, he's the king of the whole scheme, but if I had to place him in one of the two camps, he's definitely a Subvert. I don't understand the bits about regularly dying and regularly living or letting the Gontlets have me. Hopefully that will be explained because it seems to be consequential.

I spent some time trying to figure out how he might have surmised suicide from his untenable grave. It's fruitless. Any attempt to second-guess or outwit this clown is folly. I'm sure Saturday's read will include more twisted mockery.

I should really be working right now. I'm losing money. But who can think about work when there are such thoughts to be had? This morning I was in the belly of a great fish. Twelve hours later, it feels like Christmas Eve. Like I say, life is weird.

Life <<and rebirth, apparently>> rises and falls on expectations, comparisons, assumptions, and deliverance.

Chapter 8

"Life is like riding a bicycle. To keep your balance, you must keep moving."
– Albert Einstein

I can't just sit here in a haze with a stupid grin on my face till Saturday. Maybe work will be a reasonable diversion. Not a quality mince, per se, <<Morocco . . . that hoodlum>> but enough to kill some time.

I nudge my stitched-up mouse, and two oversized monitors open their bright eyes. A dozen PowerPoint files are scattered across their corneas in orderly disarray. I have a system. I start arranging images of the atlas, the axis, and C3 through C7 aesthetically around the canvas of one of the slides. I connect structures with labels using fine threads: the dens, transverse foramina, vertebral artery, bifid spinous process. Layer after layer of style and minimalist text until it's a conservative work of art. Today it's anatomy, tomorrow it could be computer coding. Then first century Rome. Then textiles. The Tactician prepared me well for this occupational army soup.

My mom never pushed me that much, she just kind of let me be who <<or what>> I wanted to be, good or bad. She didn't see any inherent badness in me, so that might have been as involved as she thought my development required. Besides, life with Patch around was like being a rabbit circled by a hawk, so drifting into forbidden paths was as remote a possibility as time travel <<which, I guess, is a bad example since time travel might not be that remote a possibility>>. I'm sure I was being surveilled most of the time anyway. Not that she would have had any idea how to make a man out of me, but since Patch took such an interest in that very ambition, it was probably a convenient out for her. I think, as well, that she never really knew how Dad's death affected me since she was a mourning-hoarder, and Patch was like one of those cheery, middle-aged women that gets babies to smile for pictures. Maybe she didn't want to poke the bear, just in case. However, after my injury she could see that my devastation littered the house like the spirits of a dead unkindness of ravens. She knew what mourning looked like. It might have been the first time in my life that she had occasion to sit me down and watch *me* cry <<figuratively>>. Patch was gone by then and I had nobody else, nobody that could have properly consoled in that sense, anyway. I must have sat motionless, unshowered, unresponsive, twice dead and plucked up by the roots, in a cause-less hunger strike for a week before it occurred to her that she might need to lower a bucket down. <<This certainly wasn't as grave as my father's death, so I was on my guard not to be perceived as yanking the rug out from under Mom's fifth year of mourning.>> It was probably one of her life's most awkward moments, but I interpreted it as brave and gentle. <<She was always gentle, but only brave in settings where the primary function was gambling.>> She walked up to me with this brand-new book <<you could smell the warm infancy of its press>>, placed it in a numb right hand that turned out to be mine, and said, "God just wanted you to know that the world needed your brain more than it needed your brawn." She quietly brushed some hair out of my face, ran her index finger knuckle down the lateral edge of my jaw, and walked away. She was not normally engaging or motherly that way. I felt that it was so courageous and meaningful of her to do that, I snapped out of the murkiest of the funk almost immediately. The disembodied unkindness was always there, but I was able to move around without stepping all over its squawk-less corpses.

I never wondered how much I was loved by Patch, but at that point I knew that my mom loved me, too.

I sat there for another hour before I actually looked at the book. I don't know why, but I was expecting it to be a self-help book written by a retired football player, some sort of *pick up the pieces and rebuild!* Which would have made me furious. It was the funniest thing—it was a PowerPoint instructional manual. A PowerPoint instructional manual!

Over years of her lamenting, we kind of disconnected. My mom had her sullen life and Patch and I had our frenzied fantasy worlds and football life, and rarely the twain would meet. She was always around, we would always talk over dinner, but I never got the impression she was that interested in me. Scripted questions were asked with moist eyes, a plastic smile, and a quiet, tired curiosity, like it was exhausting to just get the words out: "What did you learn today? Did you make any new friends? What was the best part of your day? How was practice in this heat?" That seemed the extent of her interest. Or the extent of her energy. She was just there to love me in her subdued, in-the-other-room way, and make sure I was fed. And that was plenty for me. Maybe since Patch's interest in me was like being in a swarm of bees, she didn't think two or three more bees would matter.

When I finally looked at the book, I heaved out an unconscious and breathy expression of wonder. It was confirmation that she knew absolutely nothing about me. Of all the Jaws of Life she could have used to pull me out of this fiery twist of mangled steel . . . not that I could have <<or would have bothered to in my prison, fed with bread of affliction, and with water of affliction>> thought of something more appropriate in the moment. She was always gambling, so I thought maybe she'd won it in a raffle and didn't want it to go to waste. Regardless, the book became a paradox—a seemingly random offering I felt had absolutely no connection to my life or situation would come to represent the other god I went whoring after. Other than amputated memories, a head full of Patch's ranting dicta, and unusable muscles programmed to eat the flesh of kings, and the flesh of captains, and the flesh of mighty men, and the flesh of horses, and of them that sit on them, and the flesh of all men, both free and bond, both small and great, it was all I had.

I was already fairly decent with PowerPoint and had a good eye for design, but that book, that lock pick, parted the pins and tumblers to my future. Within a year, I was working for a pay-by-the-hour service designing lecture slides for the biology department of a university in Omaha, Nebraska. In my typical golly-gee-goody-gumdrops-go-getter style <<I've always been a bit of a gutless people pleaser>>, aside from the slides themselves, I started devising elements for a full curriculum—peripheral study aids, essay topics, test questions, even test reliability and validity analyses—all for what a nineteen-year-old thought was beaten gold, and what the university thought was exploiting cheap child labor. This is the happy result of being taught wrong, taught how I'd been taught wrong, then taught right. In the end <<which quickly followed the beginning>>, they handed over all of the many reins of curriculum development to a teenager. <<It's possible they didn't know I was a teenager.>> I was the one-stop shop for the department's entire curriculum. Word of mouth and examples of my work spread between departments, between colleges, between institutions, across states, across disciplines, across educational levels, and, before I knew it, I was having to turn work down and increase my fee.

In a blink, Patch's axiom *Life is work!* was realized. Though, by that, he may not have meant life is all work and no play. Because I became a dull boy.

It wasn't football, but it paid the bills. Who am I kidding, I didn't have any bills. It padded my bank account. I kept Mom company for about a year, then we moved to Salt Lake City because she had some family there and didn't think being alone out East would be good for her mental health. Once we got to Salt Lake, I found my own place. It sounds like a good gig, I know, but when you spend twelve hours a day doing something other than what you're passionate about, your soul starts bleeding out. The money is only consolation at first. Those that have no passion for something are the lucky ones. There's no burr in their surfactant-oiled alveoli reminding them with every breath that they will never truly enjoy their second-choice life.

Though lucrative, the job was a tragically enlightening revelation. It spoiled my world a little. I became painfully aware of how little so-called experts knew about their own fields, and how little was actually known compared to their claims. Patch used to call science *epoxied argumentum ad verecundiam*, and I know exactly what he means. Loose theory is passed off as inviolability, peer reviewed literally means *reviewed by a peer*, researchers cite their own research, conclusions are stretched from faulty methodology to a distant pole of certainty, confounding variables are swept under lab mats, incongruent data is discarded, the publish-or-perish mandate breathes life into the most unrecognizable monsters, scientific laws are based on correlation rather than causation, funding guides conclusions—all under the auspices of the mighty and irrefutable omniscience of PhD. Then these *studies* are passed to media outlets to put a bow in its hair, paint its nails, and give it a good twirl. *In a recent study, scientists have discovered that* . . . Nobody goes back and checks the literature. They wouldn't even know where to look. And you can never question the science, because . . . argumentum ad verecundiam—you think you know more than a PhD?

In some cases, yes, I do.

It might explain why ten times a day I would hear Red Richthofen challenging the world's certainties with, "If you believe in that kind of thing."

Patch, if I'm as smart as he thinks I am, claims I can time travel. Sidestep time? Be plucked from time's advance? I've never heard him make a claim that wasn't rooted in plausible and convincing soil. I met even his most hysterical madness with shrugs because I couldn't come up with anything to refute it. And he had some of the wildest ideas—most of which I would quickly agree with before he'd get his nibs in me and start interrogating, parlaying, and sermonizing. Time travel is preposterous and impossible, and had it been the declaration of any other human, I would doubt and discount. But Patch is the best of noble men and the Tesla of his age. I have no reason to doubt this claim either.

So, tonight's project is cervical vertebrae. I can get into this. And the funeral—that should take my mind off things tomorrow afternoon. Temple Hill Cemetery Chapel, 5:30 p.m. My presence is respectfully requested, whatever that jackcrackery means. He's posthumously creating a guest list to his funeral? I know he's a planner, but come on . . .

Though this time travel angle might explain that.

DAY 0

Chapter 9

"Sometimes I arrive just when God's ready to have someone click the shutter."
– Ansel Adams

T-minus . . . eternity, it seems. Twenty-four short protracted hours and I begin to die and I begin to live. Like Patch always said, *The only way out is through.* I shouldn't be this eager; I know this gets much worse before it gets better. I just need to keep my eye on the Jack Lambert-with-ram's-horns-and-scorpion-tail prize. It really shouldn't be, but it's a prize worth thirty chargers of gold, one hundred priests' garments, an hundred baths of wine, and salt without prescribing how much. It's just a microscope slide of high school football in Georgia, yes, but with the breath of my lips, I slew the breachers; I was a slaughterer of kings, visiting my enemies with the flame of devouring fire, my fame hissing forth unto the ends of the earth. I taunted spectators like a blood-badged gladiator, his arsenal bathed in the liquid life of the lessers. It was the last time I felt like a man. Ever since, I have kept company with the lessers. I know that sounds petty and hopeless, to pine away one's days for the small kingdom majesty of high school football, but there it is—I am petty and hopeless. But before you judge, imagine launching your body five feet above a battlefront of clashing sweat and blood, crashing your body into a catapulted running back on fourth and goal with time expiring to singlehandedly secure a state championship victory. If the glory of that moment does nothing for you, I will concede to petty and hopeless.

I usually work late and get up late. It's easy. Well, more convenient than easy since I have clients in multiple time zones, but it does make life easy. My excited mind pulled a dastardly fast one on me this morning in its day-skipping impostures to convince me that it is Saturday. So, in this instance, I was up late, up early. I figured out the deception quickly enough, but couldn't get back to sleep, so I took the time to make myself a breakfast that wasn't pre-packaged. I'd forgotten how much flavor real food has.

Did somebody just knock on my door? What a foreign and alarming sound. I guess when you turn the white noise all the way down and your world's auditory canvas is a soft yellow pastel of distant rolling waves, life's sounds are startlingly loud.

Thus it begins . . .

Being the security-conscious <<read: paranoid shut-in>> homeowner I am, I tiptoe to the front door's peephole and look through at maximal distance so they can't tell someone's there. <<I don't want them shooting me in the eye through the peephole when it darkens, obviously.>> Behind the fisheye distortion of a man in a delivery uniform, I see a bulbous box truck with a back opened to several file boxes. It has been so long since there was someone at my door, I forgot I could have just spoken through the video doorbell.

I begin the process of dismantling the portcullis' many fasteners.

"Dillinger?"

"Yes, sir."

"I have twenty-four items from Sanborne & Esche Legal Office. Where would you like me to put them?"

"Right here in the foyer is fine, just not against the wall, if that's okay."

"Okay. I'll be out of your hair in five minutes."

"No problem. Do you need any help?"

"Nope. I got this."

Good, because this is all very irregular, and I'll need to keep an eye on you. I refuse to be the victim of any funny business. Besides, heating a home is expensive and insects have no respect for private property. I can't rest if things are scurrying or twitching or bouncing in my periphery.

After twelve roundtrips, he concludes our business with, "That's it, have a nice day."

"Do I need to sign anything, or . . . ?"

"Nope, it's all taken care of."

"Okay, thanks."

"Have a nice day."

"You too."

It was a cadaverous exchange and I notice that everything I say is blank and forgettable. What was his name? Where was he from? Could I not have asked at least that? No, Elliot, no! People are interest ambushers and goodwill exploiters and time bludgeoners! You ask where he's from and the next thing you know, you've been standing there for an hour looking at pictures of his newborn and his last trip to Florida! <<I should really start talking to people.>>

I confirm his official exit from my property through the peephole. Double-sided key bolt lock, security bar tucked under the doorknob and kicked across the floor to rubber stopper immobility, security wedge siren clicked on and kissing the threshold. I sweep out the entry and the foyer, spray some air deodorizer, and soak the doorknob with a disinfectant wipe.

I know that sounds clinical, but you can't hide from humans in a cupboard for a decade and not turn out a little weird. Cautious. Survivalist. I can appreciate that the reckless and disgusting majority technically dictates what *normal* is, but I swear I'm the normal one. If I'm the only one that survives the next super bug, give me whatever label you want. Oh, yeah, you'll be dead. Who's normal now?

I notice that one of the boxes is unmarked and sealed with an entire roll of packing tape. That goes on the bottom. One of the boxes is not sealed at all and says Open Upon Arrival on the top. That's definitely Patch's masculoimmaculate handwriting. I place that one next to the dining table. The rest are numbered and I move them to my office and stack for easy chronological access.

Security, order, and cleanliness restored. My encumbered mind is defragmented.

Now for this box. I set it on the table and crouch way down, so my head is below the table's surface. I nudge the lid up from below with a butter knife, so its bottom edge is resting on the top lip of the box. Then I jab the side of the lid with the knife so it slides completely off the top of the box and onto the table.

Even from underneath the box, the smell is overwhelming, like he's a genie coming out of a bottle of 1928. It's such a showered, groomed, and stately smell—what you'd imagine Zeus smelled like. Inventorying the box, it appears that the cosmetics themselves have conjured him: the red, griffin-stamped tub of Brylcreem, the "Look Your Best!" High Life mustache wax tin, and a small jar of J.B. Lynas & Son Cream of Almond lotion. I remember these being staples. Those, and the nasal spray. Speaking of nasal spray, his Studebaker is in here, his pocket watch. Why would his pocket watch be in here? I'd sooner find him without pants than without this watch. Did he die naked? I hold it aloft with my thumb on the plunger of the . . . wait a minute, this doesn't have a stopwatch function on it. Why was he always simulating a stopwatch? Are you telling me he was making those times up? That scallywag! And to think, I was moving heaven and furniture and tchotchkes to break those nasal spray run records! I can't believe anything anymore.

What else do we have in here? There's an old deck of Apollo brand playing cards. I remember these. He was always practicing card tricks on me with these. I pull the cards from the disintegrating box to see if this is the same deck he used. I remember he marked the back of the jack of clubs by adding an extra string to the lyre in the center of the card. Well, what do you know. What a hoot. I'm sure every one of these cards is somehow marked. He claimed he could detect the subtle temperature differences from the light reflecting off the different colors on the face of the card and would tell me what the card was simply by sliding his finger across the face. Thinking back, I should have just had him close his eyes. But knowing him, he would have anticipated that. He always had a stack of contingency plans.

Franka Rolfix camera. I've never seen this before. It looks like there are a few exposures left. Interesting. Where on earth would I get this kind of film developed? There's a leather-bound notebook with . . . oh, not this again. I have no idea what I did with that key! Why would he think I'd still have that key? The notebook is full of the written code Patch invented that we would use for all our communications he didn't want Mom privy to. I don't know if I can decode this without that key. Hopefully it's not crucial. <<The only reason this notebook would be in this box is because it *is* crucial. Patch doesn't do random.>>

The last item: a chartreuse photo box that has the texture of being recycled from hairballs. I open it with the same caution as the file box. <<You can't trust that imp with lids!>> Though consistent with the nostalgia of the box, I'm surprised to see actual photos drifting like flotsam in its little bay. On the top is a picture of me collapsed at the waist, hands on knees, recovering after a nasal spray run, Patch in his recliner clutching the prize above his head in an attitude of record-breaking victory. I've never seen this picture before. It is unmixed extemporaneity that seems the summary of an entire era. Clearly Mom is the photographer. How did she have time to take a picture when she was banshee-screeching from nose wrinkle to knee-clutching hyperventilation? Nicely done, Mom. I set it on the table and turn my attention to the next . . .

Time just stopped. Or maybe my heart stopped. Of all the things in this world that cannot be, I have stumbled on the cannot-est. Of all the levels of impossibility, this is impossible on all of them. Imagine a single moment that you would consider the pictorial quintessence of your life, the most defining image, something that epitomizes your entire identity, a four by six photographic prospectus, if you will. It is what you want to hand someone when they ask, "Tell me about yourself." You have to settle on a single still frame image. There's an excellent chance that this singular moment was never captured on film. And until this moment, it hadn't been for me either. In fact, I don't think a thousand attempts to stage this moment could have approached the exquisiteness that the spontaneity managed. I'm almost afraid to handle it. But there it is . . . I finally have documented proof that I was terrible as an army with banners; that though Saul has slain his thousands, I have slain my tens of thousands. It is my epithet and my epitaph. I can feel my cells recreating that moment: tensing, twitching, focused, unflinching, grunting with superhumanity. Vapors of uprooted grass and stale, sweat-trapped helmet inserts rise from its altar of incense. It's surprisingly clear for such a frenetic moment. The entire stretch of my six-foot-threeness <<I grew another inch after high school>> is splayed in starfish stretch, suspended three quarters of my height in the air, nearly horizontal in ephemeral flight, the fingertips of my right hand cradling the nose of a football. Opponents and teammates are all turned toward me in unfocused deflated and elated anticipation. I came down with that interception. It ended the game. I was a hero that day.

I'm just staring into the jetsam of the little bay, admiring this swelling rebirth and its shadows of a once happy and fearless Elliot. I finally pull the photograph, walk to my frosted glass design board, and hang it up with a magnet.

I know this may seem like a thickly exaggerated reaction to such a discovery, but I assure you, it is not. That was a life-fulfilling moment <<a fulfillment that didn't last very long, apparently>>.

Life rises and falls on the glory of moments.

I fish through the rest of the pictures. I haven't seen any of these before. It's obvious that Mom was the photographer for most, and for most I was an unsuspecting subject—my face sleeping on a dining table pillow of a diagrammatic depiction of how the French could have won the Battle of Agincourt <<one of Patch's many homeschool assignments>>; Patch and I playing Scotland Yard; backyard linebacker drills with Patch <<still in his suit>>; Patch and I in mid-celebratory launch following a Red Sox World Series victory. It appears that she cared much more about what was going on in my life than I noticed.

I hang them all up.

Speaking of suits, it just occurred to me that I don't own one. Is that still standard funeral fashion?

Chapter 10

"If you are out to describe the truth, leave elegance to the tailor."
– Albert Einstein

This disruption has carved out sinkholes of reflection-plunging silence, and melancholy is filling the gaps like an edematous infection. I can feel it spreading like a burning venom into my facial muscles, into the arthritis of my fragility, into my aching diaphragm. When I first heard the news of Patch's death, it was a welcome reminder of happier times. The Manuscript is feeling more like a familiar conversation and the true grimness of that news is starting to seize me. I can feel the sun burning out again.

But I still need a suit, so I should probably summon the power of Grayskull and wallow in the car.

Where would one get a respectable, monster-sized suit in Salt Lake City? I don't really have time to have anything tailored, so maybe some big and tall joints? My search for big and tall men's suits in Salt Lake City gives me . . . one result. One? That's it? Boglioli's on 100 South. Sounds fancy. And expensive.

The two-story façade reflects the bustle of 100 South <<by *bustle*, I mean homeless foot traffic>>. I can see towering and portly mannequins draped in garments that are clearly three times the fabric required for that of normal-sized people <<I hope that doesn't mean triple the price>>. Business appears to be slow, which is good. I'm not assertive enough to make quick work of these kinds of purchi <<a plural for *purchases*; Patch used it so often that *purchases* now sounds incorrect>>. As I approach the mirrored façade, I can see that a nice suit will not be enough bondo for this car wreck .

A bell announces my entry. I catch a scintillation of horror sweeping the associate's whole manner. It's the lightning preceding a quick snap of thunder into plastic politeness and effusive dismissals. Am I even too big for a big and tall store? "Mi scuso, signore. Very sorry, sir. Non abbiamo . . . um . . . we don't have your size qui . . . er . . . *here*. We don't have your size here." He's shuffling me out the door as he's translating for himself. "Ottimo negozio down strada . . . eccellente . . . *store* down . . . down *street*." He smashes a business card in my palm, points vigorously toward the south and shuts the door, bowing with his hand on his heart over and over, superimposed on the reflection of my disbelief.

That was weird.

The business card refers me to the Proper Gentleman, two blocks south on East Broadway. Sounds like a pimp store.

As I open the door to the Proper Gentleman, I immediately understand the significance of being rerouted here from Boglioli's. The analogy of the professor and the lab assistant and the maze and the moving walls is becoming less an analogy and more a sickeningly claustrophobic reality. Patch's groomed ghost is pouring out in waves of Brylcreem and mustache wax and stale wool.

Nothing will ever be as it seems again, for the rest of my days. I consider just walking away, but I know I'm in check and will eventually end up in this store despite a visceral rejection to being marionetted like this. He did say it was his turn for a square go, and he is a planner. Frickity frickwater frick . . .

The suicide reference, that episode at Boglioli's, this outdated time traveler outfitter . . . Patch is anything but dead. I better see a pretty convincing corpse in that casket tonight or I'm going to file a missing person's report.

"Sorry, I think I might have the wrong address."

"Wutterya in de market fer, b'y?"

"I was referred by Boglioli's. I need a suit."

"Yap, yap, yap, we gots just wutyer lookin fer. Let me haves a lookacha, b'y . . . forty-eight long, fer sure, just wutyer lookin fer, yap." Looking around the store, the closest thing to a clothing item I see is a couple of leather belts. "I'm tinkin solid black with dems dusted black paisley lapels, Australian Merino Wool straight from oover der Nundle Mill, no machine, b'y, teelored by 'and in de back der. Mmmm, oivory paisley oover de powder lily waistcoat, yap, power suit, fer sure, b'y, commands respect."

It's a toothless patois despite his full set of dental implants that are probably worth more than his store's inventory. I almost tell him I only speak English, but I'm counting on the fact that he's just thinking out loud in whatever language that is. I rhetorically ask myself if the day could get any weirder, but I already know it will.

Despite the dismantling accent, the proprietor's sharply sunburnt features and recessed scrutinizing leaven the deep, salt-etched lines of his cheeks and chin with a native intelligence. He looks like land hasn't been his life's primary residence, but that the deprivation has given him time to think. Or tink, as he'd haves it.

"Fer de tucker, we go wit de Poplin weave, 'gyptian 'undret percint, Giza-ferty five, two 'undret ferty tread count, stand collar whoyte. Best in de biz. Right classy, breatable, good fer de 'eat, and yer a big feller." I look around to see if he's actually talking to someone. "Wingtip boots, Varvatos, right classy, fer sure. Size twelve, wha? Yap, twelve, fer sure. Weddered ledder, Lord tunder-in' Moses, classiest on the island, yap."

I catch a lot of exotic <<expensive>> sounding international threads and leath-ers and clarify, "Oh, no, no, I'm not, like, taking over Columbia or anything. It's just for a funeral. I'll probably never wear it again after that." I try to push a short burst of quick-dying laughter out so he knows I'm kidding and serious.

The sea-plowed furrows of the proprietor's forehead dip into a fighting stance. "Funeral, wha'. Funeral fer who?"

I smirk and wait for him to break character. I know this whole conversation is just being read from a script and Patch is in the back somewhere enjoying this jolly rogery <<I like my *jolly rompery* better>> from his director's chair. The Mariner doesn't budge. "My grandad."

"Good feller?"

"The best."

"Aye. Well, don't get yer blood up, buddy. New customer discount. Don't fret aboat n'arn a dis and dat. Lord tunderin' Moses, we got yuz in de pocket. Viv!" A young woman, a gorgeous young woman, a woman so beautiful my scalp starts to sizzle, emerges from wherever Patch is hiding, straightens a few items as she slithers an uncoiling route to the front of the store, and stops at the proprietor with a patient, heartbreaking grin. I start feeling underdressed. Undressed. My tongue is swelling up and I have to consciously inhale. I'm out of practice with wowing attractive women because I've never had to do it. Girls were always trying to wow *me*. Where are some stinky football pads when you need them . . .

"Ya can'ts be crashin da funeral of a good man lookin like dat, b'y. Dis here's Vivian. Viv'll fix yuz right up. Grandfadder's funeral, Viv. Gots to look right sharp, dis buddy. I'll gets buddy's suit whipped up."

Vivian pats the proprietor on the back and summons me with a few back-handed index finger trigger pulls and an elegantly confident tone. "Come on back, big man." As Patch's shadow is cast in long angles from virtually every product in this establishment, I follow her back, fully expecting to encounter him in the crackfueled flesh. Have I mentioned how shifty that little guy is <<not saying *was* until I have some confirmation>>?

Walking behind Vivian into the store's penetralia is the best part of my day. Year.

She leads me through a congested stock room and into what looks like a gangster bath house with its white and blue shower tile floor. Vivian sits me in a turn of the century throne that looks more like an instrument of torture or execution than a barber chair, capes me, and leans my head back into what she tells me is a shampoo bowl. I'm relieved when, rather than an administration of electricity, a stream of warm water flattens my impossible hair. Proper grooming, it turns out, is way more involved than my ten-minute presentability standard. Just preparing to shave my face, Vivian has already exceeded the time it normally takes me to shave, shower, and dress.

I can tell my reflection in the mirror is weirded out by the novelty of this scene—a beautiful woman is making love to my face with oily hands and creams, running a straight razor down my voraciously vulnerable neck with warmly cool caresses, running her fingers through my hair, massaging my scalp, orbiting my eyes uncomfortably close to assess symmetry. It's the kind of thing that happens to other people, in movies, in big cities.

She is distractedly humming something pop-ish, which is a bullet dodged. Anything coming out of my mouth would have been cringey conversational lemons. Besides, it seems like she doesn't want to be disturbed in her strokes and daubs. For her signature, she four-finger scoops a marshmallow guts pomade from a regal, red container I would recognize anywhere. Brylcreem. It was the clean scent of my youth. The shadows around the room are gathering dimension and I can hear echoes of ceaseless wisdom <<don't tell him I air quoted *wisdom* with my tone>> :

It's not that people only use ten percent of their brains, it's that people are only using their brains ten percent of the time!

Just because a smart person says something, doesn't mean a smart thing was said!

Vivian steps back like she's unveiling her masterpiece. I'm disappointed that it's over, but in every way feel restored. As I look at myself in a mirror trimmed with photographs of Vivian's family, I have a revelation, like I can see a superior identity embedded somewhere between the bone and the skin that is waiting to be unearthed. I see a linebacker with the body of a leopard, the feet of a bear, and the mouth of a lion.

Then thoughts of how much this is going to cost push their way into the coat room of my consciousness. Do I tip her? Is that insulting? Do I include the tip at the register?

As this alien image stares back at me, something mindlessly slips through the door of the coat room I forgot to close behind me, something I didn't intend to be audible: "Who on earth are you?"

"You're welcome."

"I even *feel* like a different person."

"You're the same old Elliot you've always been. With a temporary upgrade, maybe."

I'm so stunned that I could be made to look like this I don't stop to analyze Vivian's disfigured reply. It's like my vision is coming back in expanding, concentric circles after a concussion. It's jarring.

"You're a magician, Ms. Vivian." I think my mind was simultaneously processing, "You're magic," and, "You're an artisan," and the summation of two wrong turns fortuitously ended up at the right location.

She doesn't respond to this comment, just squeezes my hand and holds my eyes with a quiet sort of desperation, like she's trying to communicate her kidnapping with a look. Normally in these circumstances I just mirror <<being the craven social survivalist I am>>, but my unconscious fixes my face in an arrangement of corrugator-dipping confusion. There's something strangely familiar about this moment.

The rest of my encounter with the Proper Gentleman is bizarrely consistent with the day—hurriedly maneuvered through the serpent's bowels to the exit, handed a garment bag and a box, new customer discount, "N'arn a yer loonies today, b'y," shoved out onto East Broadway because, "It be closin' toime," the jingling door closed and locked behind me, lights off. Sign flipped to Closed.

Not very inconspicuous, Patch.

But there was something, something the Mariner said right before the door closed that my social instincts had been accustomed to dismissing as platitudes.

It stung my pharyngeal taste buds like a metallic aftertaste. What did he say? "Make 'em proud, laddie." He said, "Make 'em proud, laddie." He was calling me *buddy* and *b'y* the whole time, not a single instance of *laddie*. And *laddie* is distinctly Patch. I'm standing on the sidewalk with, I'm sure, a vacant, open-mouthed stupidity even the homeless notice.

Through the façade's coffin lid, I can still see the vestige of Vivian's quiet desperation reaching out like an apparition. That expression is already haunting me like a tip-of-the-tongue recollection.

And there's no way he tailored this suit in an hour and a half. Life rises and falls on ridiculous improbabilities.

CHAPTER 11

"When a person dies he only appears to die. He is still very much alive in the past, so it is very silly for people to cry at his funeral. All moments, past, present and future, always have existed, always will exist."
— *Slaughterhouse 5*, Kurt Vonnegut

The footpath leading to the chapel is a quilt of molted black mamba skin stitched with pools of cooled lava sewn into bright black tar pits hemmed with never-healing scars of freeze-thaw. It's an ankle-turning hazard. And these brand-new Barbados Vivitar whatever boots aren't helping. It's hard to look cool strutting with the uncertainty of a newborn foal. At least they got the grass right—a wetly saturated Granny Smith frosting on a dirt cake of gummy worms and rotting Oreo crumbles.

Hewn from the shadows of trees, headstones of denuded sunlight stretch across a field of stone receipts exchanged for the deposited dead and on into Federal Heights. Some people are sixteen-foot obelisk important, casting robed, lording shadows over dozens of their prostrate and obscure subjects, administered by two-foot keystone vassals. Caste is immortal, apparently.

It's so quiet. It seems that even sound comes here to be buried.

I speak too soon . . .

Patch has recruited loitering ghosts to take potshots at me from behind the evergreens and cypresses that stud the horizon with spires and arches. I can hear the random exhortations whistling past: *Inserting yourself, uninvited, into another's conversation is the height of rudeness! There's no quicker way to slavery than owing someone money! Nothing epitomizes selfishness like complaining! No self-respecting girl is interested in a guy she can push around!*

This place, this oppressively quiet, call-before-you-dig landscape of death <<aside from that whistling crossfire>> is the antithesis of Patch. Could somebody that lived so loudly be in a place so . . . lifeless? Could he really be dead? When he left, never to return, leaving no word, I assumed he didn't want to be found and that was that. One- to two-week absences were fairly common, but then there was a third and a fourth and a fifth. Then it was a disappearance that felt like an abandonment. Between that and the injury, I wasn't in the mood to care about anything. But in the doldrums of that pall of emotional tar, why had I not thought to find him, to reach out, to thank him for snatching me from a darkening descent, thank him properly, as an adult? If he had an apartment in Salt Lake City this whole time, why didn't he visit? Why did you leave us, Patch? Where did you go?

I'm brought back to a similar scene of rattling nonplus fifteen years ago at my own dad's funeral, walking ten paces behind a mother who had been leeched of any sense of existence or identity or context. An angry kind of sadness made lead of my diaphragm and my exhalations burned with icy fire. It wasn't just sadness, it was a diorama of despair—helplessness, hopelessness, confusion, a childish peevishness that I wasn't allowed to exhibit a mourning that could be perceived as out-mourning Mom's, profound loneliness, a strike-slip dislocation of my understanding of the world. It was that buttoned top button, existential strangulation that pressed no matter how much I craned my neck.

Good times.

It wasn't just my father, or just my mother's husband that died—it was Patch's son, his *only* son. I don't think I ever considered that. He just bounced in like a wisecracking magician, waved his hands to misdirect for a while, then bounced out. But he was still out there somewhere. And it never occurred to me that he might be the one needing some misdirection. And now he's dead. When you live the up-all-night-sleep-all-day, decade-long pity party lifestyle, it's hard to get out of your own head. If I didn't feel schmucky before, I certainly do now. The last forty-eight hours have been one big Elliot schmuckfest. But since I'm now confident this is a con and that Patch isn't really dead, the weight of it all isn't sinking me any deeper than wondering if he might be hiding behind one of these headstones.

The sun's sluggish chariots are kicking up cool luminance as their advance to the Wasatch Front wanes. This is why I love November—a more pronounced wintry duality. My clothing has its own calm respiration and assures me I'll have no problem overthrowing the Columbian government. My face is smooth as water. I'm not scooping my iron-willed hair out of my face. I don't have a headache.

This feels really good.

The chapel is about fifty yards ahead. The face is a blaze of refraction, diffraction, reflection, collecting all the cemetery's crippled sails of light and harnessing them as a wall of transitioning glory. It looks like a waiting room for one of the kingdoms of heaven. <<Now I have a headache.>> Within five feet of the door, the entrants are consumed, unconsumed, and assimilated into a wall of pulsing fire that admits them to the third heaven; although, the fashion looks a little mafioso, so maybe second heaven.

People, crap . . . I forgot that people <<coffee-breathed, non-hand-washing, small-talk-making time thieves>> attend funerals. This is why you trust your gut, Elliot, and never leave the house. Maybe I'll text Mom and see if she'll be here. Though deplorably sad that I can't be in society without my mother, I don't have the wherewithal to experiment with my courage right now. And though texting Mom is always a gamble <<you get either indecipherably sequenced emojis or a novella in response>> I haven't seen her in a couple months and I'm sure she'd want to catch up. But if she didn't already know about Patch, would she be hurt that I knew and she didn't? Or would she be grateful to know either way? Normally this would just be me overthinking things, but Mom is fragile.

"El?"

Oh, no. Please tell me somebody doesn't know me here.

The backdrop of heaven's living room window allows me only a headless, limbless torso. The gait is languid and funerial, a paradox of slow strides and shuffling. I put my hand up to defy the refulgence of God's soul and peek under my thumb. Modest layers of comfortable blacks fill out the limbs.

"Hurry, hurry. This isn't something you want to be late for."

"Mom?"

"Hello there, my son, let's get in there."

"How did *you* find out about the funeral?"

"No time for that right now. It won't start for a few minutes yet, but I need your face in there."

Comments like that just add to the weirdness that has become my life. "Mom, why would anyone care if I was here? Is this really a funeral? Is he really dead?"

This stops Mom fast. She stands still for a moment and then turns to look up at me <<which is a face a foot and a half north of hers>> without lifting her head. She looks like an angry eagle under eyebrows that have flattened into an even line, expressing some irritated disappointment in stupid questions. Then she's right back to covering a remarkable amount of ground with that paradoxical gait.

I quietly express my bewilderment behind her back.

"Mom, how have you been?"

"Yes, yes, we'll get to that later."

Our approach shifts the angle of the conflagrant portal and the glass becomes transparent. It opens to a high-ceilinged temple of progressive sacramental modernity—sharp corners, silver steels and beige woods, clean lines, minimalist crucifixes, and a statement-making, un-elevated rostrum. Oh, and people. Lots of people.

This is seriously terrifying.

Just breathe, Elliot. Remember the counsel of Sir Peckish Hamburger: *Stress should be reserved for moments of clear and present danger! Never anticipate! Anticipation exaggerates reactions and wastes resources!* Okay, right, fine. Though the moment gives me no idea how to put that into practice, I should not stress until I know what I'm stressing about. I show up, pay respects, disappear. Piece of cake. Now I'm craving gummy worms. I need to get out more.

Mom can hear the groans of my overly dilated arteries and the valves of my heart slamming shut in jackhammer staccato. She looks back and winks at me as we cross the threshold. That helps, actually. If little old Mom's not nervous, I'm not nervous <<I'm about to soil these Nundle Mill Merino Wool pants>>.

As the hydraulic arm eases the glaring, celestial portal back into its casing, I get my first glimpse of the milling, droning congregation. My carotid arteries are like vacuums, sucking all the blood out of my head, and I'm instantly dizzy and squinting. I push the heel of my hand into my eyeball so the sensation of it keeps me from passing out. I'm distantly aware that my breathing has shallowed and I push it down into my belly so it isn't apparent in my chest. I can feel an unnatural pressure boring into the bones of my left forearm. I turn my head slowly <<slowly enough to avoid triggering some syncopic shutdown>> to investigate the constellation's searing outlier and find Mom's thumb knuckle-deep in my muscle. Her jaw is clenched in a panic smile that is one part concern, three parts confusion, and six parts fire-breathing castigation. I stretch my eyes wide open and force all the drama out in one quick puff.

"All better?" she more insists than asks.

In my defense, I am, in a single frame, struck with the realization that I have walked into the war room of seven nations greater and mightier than me. Every word struck through in the Manuscript that I assumed to be figurative, super-fluous, or irrelevant instead cements into a hard and stuffy reality ringed with folding tables of Danishes. <<Patch doesn't even like Danishes!>> The professor, the lab assistant, the mouse—these aren't analogs! Why couldn't you be figurative for once, Patch?

Whatever happened to that beast of a linebacker? I could really use blood-thirst right now.

My ears are still ringing from extreme blood pressure fluctuations, but can perceive the congregation's mutterings muted by the collective, laser-eyed inquisition burning holes in my dusty black paisley lapels. Which are pure class dope.

My self-consciousness feels sticky, unsure why my entrance would be any kind of spectacle. Everyone is standing still but there's a sense of pacing and taking notes. For some reason, because it's so uncharacteristic of me, I scan the room, and my eyes snag on a few individuals. The brief catches are expressions of reverence and interest and curiosity. A couple look like disdain. One, I'm sure, is contempt. Strange, coming from strangers who, I'm sure, have no idea who I am. It is evident that the Mariner is responsible for every article of clothing in this chapel, and there he is right there. And there's Vivian. Of course.

And nobody's speaking English. Great. What a fest.

At least it's an upgrade from my forejudged non-hand-washing, coffee-breathed type.

The fashion is a fusion of contemporary cuts, vintage patterns, elegantly clashing colors, and breathable functionality. The Mariner is obviously very good. I'm glad I chose to get a suit for the occasion; how awkward would khakis and a polo have been, right? Although, now that I say that, it dawns on me that I probably had very little to do with the fact that I'm wearing this suit right now. I can feel the wires anchored in my joints tugging . . .

Everyone is still staring at me.

I look back at Mom and she seems to be admiring my unspoken calculations. I should probably visit her more often; she ages in chunks when months lapse between visits. "So, how did you find out about Patch?"

Mom shakes her head and, with her version of amusement, says, "Your grandfather and his names. I forgot all about that."

"Forgot? That's the most prominent memory I have of him."

"Well, he had me call him Dad, so that was your thing. I've known a little longer than you, and before you get sensitive about it, your grandfather gave me strict instructions to let him tell you in his own way."

I hiss, "Mom! What in hell's haberdashery is that supposed to mean? Can't you hear how bizarre that sounds? *Instructions to let him tell me in his own way?*"

Her head drops to one side and I can tell that I've disappointed her again. "Language, El. And in a chapel . . ."

"Oh. What did I say?"

"H, E . . . ," and then she nods the rest with a little sanctimony.

"Oh, yeah, sorry. Sorry for the language. You just make it sound like he knew he was going to die, but I was told he died in a plane crash."

"Plane crash? Well, flying incident."

"Did he somehow know he was going to die?"

"He left nothing to chance, you know that. I'm sure he had this all planned out when he was in grade school."

Her refusal to make eye contact is troubling.

"So, are you saying that Patch informed you of his death himself?"

"Listen to what you're saying, Elliot. Inform me himself. The notion! I found out the same way you did—Mr. Sanborne."

"How did you know I was in contact with Mr. Sanborne?"

This time she looks squarely at me with an unblinking harpoon and says, with a little disappointment in my ignorance, "To what do these questions tend, my good son? I have known Mr. Sanborne for many years. We talk."

I guess there's no sense in trying to wrap my arms around any of this. "Did he happen to give you anything?" I don't want to mention anything about the Manuscript in case Patch wanted it to be a controlled item. <<Though, now that I let that thought effervesce, I realize that saying or not saying, doing or not doing, preaching to the Ninevites or fleeing to Tarshish, there is nothing I can do that won't land me exactly where he wants me, exactly when he wants me there.>>

"Give me anything? You tell me—you're the executor of the will. Mr. Sanborne said he'd read the will to you."

"Heavens, Mom, I was trying to chew my own tongue off just to stay conscious! He's like one of those soul-sucking Dementors."

"He's certainly not your grandfather. But to answer your question, he didn't give us *anything*, he gave us *everything*."

"What do you mean, everything?"

"Your grandfather's estate."

"Everything he owned?"

"That's typically what comes with an estate."

Rare cheek from Mom. "Why would he give it all to *us*?"

"Why would he not? Who else would he give it to?"

"His family?"

Mom looks a little confused. "We *are* his family."

"No, I mean, like, his immediate family: brothers, sisters, nieces, nephews? No?"

"I would say you don't know everything about your grandfather, but it seems that you don't know *anything* about your grandfather. Nan died when you were little, you know that. He has one living sister in Scotland, that's it. Your dad was an only child like you. There's no one else. Why would you think he had family?"

And I thought I didn't know anything about Patch before. This is humiliating. But if the last ten years have taught me anything, it's how to deal with humiliation <<let it fester and necrotize my will to live>>. I'll forego mention of the Manuscript until I have a better idea what she does and doesn't know.

"I guess I just assumed."

"I'm sure we're all the family he has here today."

"How did I not know any of this?"

"You had other things to worry about, El. Besides, your grandfather was a very private person and expert at keeping your mind otherwise engaged."

Mom watched the 1995 A&E version of *Pride and Prejudice* every Sunday for most of my childhood. Much of her dialogue is stolen lines. I reflexively grin every time she uses one because I don't think she's aware she's doing it anymore.

"Speaking of that, since we're the only family here—and I know this is a little short notice—I need you to say something about your grandfather after we get this thing started. I don't want any of these . . . funeral crashers taking any licenses with an open mic. I know they're dressed all fancy, but they aren't here just to pay respects or console."

I'm sure I just lost consciousness, though I'm still standing and looking at Mom through the remaining pinholes of light and color. I can feel my head unconsciously bobbing. She punches me in the sternum with her fat-free knuckles to restore my peripheral vision. Which works. And hurts a little. Then she flattens out the fabric she'd bunched up with her necessary violence.

Now it's time to stress. Voiceless screams through clenched teeth leak out as a frenzied-sounding sibilance. "Surely you're kidding." <<Mom is not the kidding type.>>

"At your grandfather's request. You'll be fine." I can feel the distal half of her thumb boring into my forearm muscles again. "You'll be fine," she reasserts with no hint of a mother's love.

I nod as the carotid arterial vacuums resume their work. My left forearm is going numb, I think. I survey my audience again. "If we're his only family, who are all these people?"

This time she looks up to fix our eyes, and after a suspiciously long delay says, "They are not family and they don't know your grandfather like we do."

Wow, isn't *that* the most unsettling non-answer I've ever heard? This intensity is starting to scare the living crap out of me. But I know better than to needle information out of that bingo-hardened broad. When Mom dodges questions, it means the answers are in a vault. Christmases, Easters, and birthdays taught me that.

I'm scrambling for something to say about Patch. There's no way I can come up with something impressive, or even passable, when I'm trying to stave off a digestive catastrophe and shrinking lungs. I don't know why I do this, <<I've never had a handkerchief anywhere on my person ever for any reason>> but on an impulse, I reach into the lining of my suit coat, locate the pocket, and, magically, pull out a handkerchief. The Mariner put a handkerchief in my coat pocket. That is presciently fantastic. I use it to daub sweat bubbling out of my forehead. Okay, Patch, what can I say about you? I'll just have to chalk this day up to another demoralizing loss. I can't seem to de-blankify my paralyzed mind. How would Patch settle me right now? How would he reassure me in his quit-your-self-like-a-man sort of way? What did he say at my Dad's funeral? *For what is your life? It is even a vapour, that appeareth for a little time, and then vanisheth away.* Ooh, that's good. Maybe I could use that. My mind tumbles over the edge of a waterfall; *The Lord killeth, and maketh alive: he bringeth down to the grave, and bringeth up. For all flesh is as grass, and all the glory of man as the flower of grass. The grass withereth, and the flower thereof falleth away.* I thought I was on to something, but now it's just getting grim. But I'm close . . .

A bramble of brilliance perforates my struggling composition and concepts in the Manuscript start congregating. I scan the attendees again. If I understand what I read <<if what I read could be understood>>, there is a high likelihood that, come tomorrow, none of this will have happened. My apocalypse of a eulogy will have been overwritten by a yoga class or a sermon on the immortality of the soul. These people are the rearrangers of reality. None of this will stick and I will be none the wiser. Hideous prospect, but it does help dull my nerves a bit.

"Mom?"

"Yes, dear?"

"Why is everyone staring at me?"

Again, without flinching, and this time squeezing my hand, she says, "Don't worry about that right now."

This cryptic old battleship is just dumping spiders on my nightmare. And she wonders why I never visit.

Mom slides her hand into the crease of my elbow and herds me toward the front of the chapel. I watch the Mariner approach at an intercepting angle with a collapsing limp that looks painfully Trendelenburg. I guess I hadn't seen him stand or walk in his shop. I can feel the earthward tug of half my body with every buckling step as he unbalances everything in the room. The rods of my eyes gather uncolored arcs of attendees bristling at the approach.

"Right sharp ya bees, b'y. Credit to da tailor, yap." He's running his hands over lapels, opening and closing pockets, tugging at the shoulders, smoothing things out. "Yap, right smart ya looks." Then he turns and lists to the right, like the scurvy mar'ner he bees, all the way back to a seat at the rear.

I look at Mom for some assurance that things like that are normal in society. I'm unpracticed. She's taken to winking at me a lot. I can't tell if it means Surprise! You have anthrax! or Being felt up by Popeye is standard funeral fare. This is what it's like with Campy Koosman in your life, even when he is purportedly dead. He's a light that burns away the recesses of superfluity with his supercharged enormity. Everything becomes significant and relevant and a concentrated precipitate of a thousand purposeful processes. The world becomes the pure extract of something squeezed with the pressure of colliding worlds and physical laws warring against physical laws. And sometimes it's just too overwhelming a realization for regular folk to do anything with. Everything is strangely massive and you know in your abstract, full of eyes before and behind, by contrast, that you were designed for something that exceeds on all sides the parameters of what would constitute a universe. <<That Rollie Fingers mustache and the smell of Brylcreem being the reduction of that effect in my firmament-bound teenage world.>> That contact with the Mariner just now meant something, I know it, but I'm too self-conscious to start checking my pockets. And I'm sure Patch is one of these characters milling about.

I don't know why I didn't notice it before, but there's a coffin here. My knee-jerk denial is trying to make sense of what it's doing here, though I know I'm at a funeral. I slip away from Mom and zombie my way toward a heavily vermilion and layered dazzle of jasper and sardine stone, smeared like finger paint in focused and unfocused depths. The lid is a bloom of clotted blood, swaying and settling just beneath the surface of the clearest tropical water. It was a polished mesmerism of a tomb. But what disrespectful cad would besmirch this somber occasion with a coffin, of all things! I'm quite incensed.

I run my hand over the blood-blooming water. It has heat and a heartbeat. It *is* more likely that he would vivify this box than that it should lay siege to an inevitable reanimation. What could possibly kill the Boatman's Boatswain <<this is one of his appellations, not an aquatic metaphor>>? It's just not sinking in; I have to lay this doubt to rest <<not a pun>>. I'm not sure I'm ready for this level of finality, but I try to open the lid. And wouldn't you know, it's bolted shut.

The noticeable increase in mumble volume suggests I might be making a scene. But, again, none of this will have happened as of midnight, so whatever. I'm in a position with my back to the attendees at the moment, so I put both of my hands on the lid in a display of mourning, bow my head, and just listen. If I'm already making a scene, maybe I can get something out of the moment. I can definitely hear French. It sounds snotty and dismissive, like someone's talking down, and out of, their nose. I took French in high school, but they're talking too fast and hushed to get anything. I think I heard, "Essaie d'ouvrir . . . ," which I think means, "Try to open . . . ," but I couldn't get the rest. There's also something that sounds full-mouthed and thickly consonanted. I can hear *da* and *nyet* here and there so it must be Slavic. That's it. Those are the only two I hear. And no English. They sound worried, maybe agitated, like there's something locked in this coffin they all want. I don't hear anything I would interpret as mourning, at least in tone. It's more sharp susurruses and gravelly malcontent. Both the French and the Slavs seem more consternated than concerned. I would have expected more grief at a funeral.

What have you gotten me into, Patch? And how am I supposed to get closure when you've bolted your coffin shut? I was counting on a body, something waxy and verisimilar that would sedate my jabbing paranoia <<or at least stun it>>.

I think my head is starting to clear. The audible, fermenting shifts and sways of the attendees are working the slivers out of my adrenal glands. Even envisioning my impending address before this rabble has little effect on my nerves. Maybe I'm channeling Patch's self-contractile, self-replicating, fluorescent energy through the placenta of this lacerated jasper womb.

"Let's take a seat, everyone. We're going to get started."

Weird, that voice sounds strikingly similar to Mom's. I mean, I know she's *here,* but what would she be doing calling things to order in this setting? I wander back to my seat, visibly confused as to why Mom is standing on the un-elevated rostrum, seemingly emceeing the event. And, she winks again. The more you wink, Mom, the more unsettling it gets.

"Thank you all for the sacrifices you have made to be here to honor one of the world's greatest men. Because that's why we're all here, to pay our *respects* to Elliot Dillinger." <<What is going on?>> "My name is Sandy Dillinger, Elliot's daughter-in-law, the widow of Elliot's only son, Eric. Being a meticulous planner, Elliot has arranged the program for this event and asked that I preside."

Preside? This brittle, mousy house of cards is going to preside over something? I really do need to visit more often; she's growing up so fast.

"We will not deviate from this program. Nous ne nous ecarterons pas de ce programme. C'est compris? Mui ni otklonimcya ot etoy programmi. Yasna? That includes tomorrow and yesterday, understand? Eyes don't die, so don't take any imprisoning liberties."

What? What just happened? Did I just have a stroke? I understood the first part and then it all started to wobble. My eyes make it sixty degrees to the right and left <<because my head is paralyzed, I think>> to see if I'm the only stroke victim. All my periphery allows is either bowed heads or nodding. Some mulish capitulation. Why would she dare lecture Patch's reality-unsteadying bugbears? <<I don't really want answers to these questions, I just want to be magically transported to my family room, but I'm sensing the futility of escape as rat maze walls are crashing down, shifting position, exploding all around me.>> I'm folding my arms and pressing them hard against my chest, but I can still feel my whole body jittering. The water is up to my chin and the remaining air is smoky. I'm back to mortified.

"Elliot has requested that Clovis Merovech offer the invocation. This will be followed by a scriptural reading by Misha Namyestnikov. Then my son, Elliot's grandson, will say a few words. Elliot's coffin will not be interred at this site, so there will be no graveside service, no need for pallbearers, and no need to loiter.

The Kronometrur will ensure that Elliot is laid to rest properly and *permanently*. Clovis . . ." Then she sits with perfect posture, shoulders back, chin up.

Oh, Mother. Oh, dear, dear Mother. What on earth are you into? She must have the Manuscript; she is clearly fluent in its language and concepts, especially the impermanence of events. This all feels wrong, like a more elaborate Morocco-type joke is brewing.

"Mom!" I'm back to hissing through my teeth. "What on earth was that all about? What are you involved in here?"

"Oh, I was just reading that from the script your grandfather gave me for this event."

Lies.

This Clovis character gets up to offer the invocation. The Mariner truly does exquisite work—every layer agreeing and disagreeing so perfectly in color, cut, and pattern. <<Though everyone here, including Mom apparently, is part of some secret society, at least this suit allows me to be a perfectly disagreeing layer.>> He interlaces his fingers at his chin and rests his forehead on his balled-up hands. What follows is a beautifully unpretentious French soliloquy. I don't understand a word, but I know an anthem served on silver solemnity when I hear it. I wish I had the foresight to record this.

Now Misha, I guess. I assumed Misha would have been a girl, but there are things I just don't understand about the world apparently. And I just noticed that, besides Vivian, Mom is the only female in the room. Other than helpless *kh*'s where *h*'s are to be, his English is quite good:

"And the angel spake unto me saying, behold the depth of the rivers that press time unfolded and heave its breath as from a vent, behold the fountains that issue forth the currents obeyed by the helmsmen; whoso hath ears to hear, let him hear and understand, where there is space, revolutions have been appointed, and where there is time, windows have been opened. The days and hours and minutes, the years and months and days, the times and the seasons are fixed from the days of its determination and no man knoweth them but what is revealed to those who have wet the earth with their blood and passed through the windows of the breath and sighs of the winepress of time."

Mom nudges me and whispers, "Forget these people. They don't know anything about your grandfather. Just be honest and then stop talking when you're done. You'll be fine." Then she winks.

Those infernal winks!

My jejunum starts wrapping itself around my great vessels. I'd forgotten about this part. I take a few steps to the rostrum and podium that aren't there to provide psychological distance and turn around. Everything is distant and blurred and muffled. *The joints of his loins were loosed, and his knees smote one against another.* I'm playing with the seams at the bottom of my suit coat and, even with significant concentration, can't consciously stop doing it. I run my hand across my jawline and am distracted by how close that shave actually was.

Somebody on the right side of the room mumbles, "C'est l'héritier?" Mom turns full around in her chair and shoots an unblinking scowl that translates as, "You have to the count of three." The left side of the room turns without turning and glares without glaring <<don't ask me how that works>>. The distending and muggy seconds become so unbearable <<to everyone but me, it seems>> that the gentleman to the reprobate's left elbows him until he gets up and exits the chapel in an embarrassed huff. And the whole right side of the room seems to sink into a collective ignominy as the celestial portal's hydraulic arm seals its banishment.

I'm done thinking things couldn't get any stranger. It's approaching the point of entertaining. No way any of this can be real. I need some antacids.

As I stand in my dizzying vacancy, I realize that the center aisle demarcates a clear division in the room. On the left are silks, high collars, cashmere beanies, long coats with fur-lined lapels, darks and darkers, scarves, turtlenecks, sash-type belts, vests that look like they're made from small bears, elegant embroi-deries, golden-lensed sunglasses, and no attempt to correct what looks like a lot of bedhead. On the right is style, layers of progressing complexity, experimental simplicity, surprisingly discordant coordination, and full heads of mythological hair. Nothing excessive, time-refined taste. I'm leaping here—the ones on the right are the Merovingian, the French, and the ones on the left are the others. I can't remember what he called them. Saboteurs? My mind is running on fumes. It's easier to remember professor and lab assistant. Subverts! He called them Subverts.

After Mom's unveiled threats to those that might be tempted to disturb permanence, maybe all of this *will* have happened tomorrow.

"My grandfather would have me call him by a different name every time he came over. Did he do that with you guys as well?"

Accented sobriquets start circling like bats: "The Cartographer, Miner," <<the less fluent English-speakers catch on to the game>> "Excavateur," <<he's corrected by a colleague, Digger>> "Leviathan, 121, Swabbie Jack-Tar," <<I laugh at that one>> "Kapatel, the Immortal . . ." It's almost whis-pered, and without any noticeable movement the entire room slumps into an ecliptic despair. It's the first indication that any of these kings and princes may have known Patch, let alone intimately. Tears appear. Faces are buried in hands. Fellow shoulders are massaged in gestures of consolation. So he *does* have this effect on everyone. Evidently, they don't share in my death doubt. But I should move this thing along. "I have a notebook somewhere in a box that is full of these names. He wouldn't respond to me, or even look at me, unless I used the day's properly pronounced and ordered name, so I just started writing them down for convenience. There are hundreds. One time he had me call him Blood Brother from Another Mother's Blood Brother's Mother-Brother. Even written down, it took me an hour to get it in the right order. And then it was disturbing when he told me what a *mother-brother* was. I wasn't sure how he was able to keep track of them. He had a lot energy, for sure, but I could always tell when he was a little more worn out because he would circle back to the name Patch. It was the only name he ever repeated. So, absent any nominal requirements, that's what I called him. I just found out yesterday that his given name is Elliot. I'd never known that." Mom is smiling a rare, authentic smile. I can feel my throat thickening and lower eyelids becoming reservoirs. "That's my name, Elliot Dillinger."

I pause to consider the significance of that realization.

"Patch . . . Digger, Miner, whatever, was so massively consuming, I felt like I was tumbling in a giant eddy in the middle of an ocean. I could never tell where he ended and I began. Even standing here at what I'm told is his funeral, I feel like we're all just some of his muscle fibers or bone marrow or something. When he would have to leave, I always had to take a day or two to recover. Even while I was recovering, this enormity would haunt me: *Don't impose your discomfort on everybody else; it's rarely their fault! Alcohol is for the emotionally weak!* <<Some of the Slavs shift uncomfortably in their seats.>> *The only thing better than articulating your opinion clearly is not articulating it at all!* This would eat up all my quiet moments, a Patch-absent Patch barking these quips. More than anything, Patch loved the language of the Bible. Every night he was around we would read from it, and as he'd leave, he always said the same thing, which he made me memorize: This day will I begin to put the dread of thee and the fear of thee upon the nations that are under the whole heaven, who shall hear report of thee, and shall tremble, and be in anguish because of thee. I will make thine arrows drunk with blood, and thy sword shall devour flesh. Descend into hell, break the gates of brass and bruise in pieces the kingdoms of iron! Though ye be troubled on every side, ye are not distressed; though ye be perplexed, ye are not in despair; though persecuted, ye are not forsaken; though cast down, ye are not destroyed. Now, my son, sanctify yourself: for to morrow the Lord will do wonders among you. Then he would look at me with a grave look and say, 'I wonder if you will ever know how much you are loved.'"

This is where I break apart. I clench my jaw so tightly shut to stave off full convulsions that it gives me a headache. My lungs have lost their capacity. The levees break. "Elliot Dillinger, wherever you are, whatever you're doing, I hope you're getting back everything you gave."

Everyone's nodding.

Mom said to be honest and stop talking when I'm done, so I sit.

"That was perfect and beautiful. I'm sure he loved it."

At least she didn't wink at me that time.

I can hear the benediction in some wilderness bordering my thoughts, but I'm gummed up in the stupefaction of how well that went. That should have been disastrous. That should have been my undoing. That went better than if I had prepared something. Have I always been able to do that? Have I just not had the opportunity? Taken the opportunity? Do eight-word conversational vignettes about the air quality in the city while paying for soda not count? Maybe I'm not as gelatinous as I think I am. Maybe there's some Jack Lambert left in me after all.

The service has concluded I guess, because Mom is shuffling me past people that clearly want to say something to me. Being the people pleaser I am, my body language is apologetic as its two hundred and seventy pounds are swept away by Mom's overpowering one hundred. Like my entrance, everybody is tracking my exit, everybody except one oddly dressed individual that sat in the back, across the aisle from the Mariner and Vivian, an individual that is cupping his hands over his mouth as if trying to light a cigarette.

A dark and hellish hue has taken the sky. Ripples of the darkest purple are faint in the highest heavens and I assign them the afterimages of the chapel's fluorescents. "Should we discuss what that was all about, Mom?"

"It's called a funeral, El. I know you've been to a funeral before, sweetie."

Pathetic evasion. And why is this woman dabbling in snark all of a sudden? "I take it that's a no."

"Your grandfather had some strange associates. You don't belong in that world. I'm just sparing you some heartache, like any good mother would do."

"The foreign languages, Mom, talking tough to people that look like organized crime royalty, what is *that* all about? Who are you?"

"Oh, that. Your grandfather warned me about these characters and told me what to say and how to say it. They just needed a stern tone. I'm still the same little Miss Mom."

No you're not, but whatever. I am and will always be the quockerwodger here. I should just embrace it and polish the wires. Life rises and falls on expectations, comparisons, assumptions, deliverances, ridiculous improbabilities, and, unfortunately, resignations.

Chapter 12

"A few words here about following people. People know they're being followed when they turn around and see someone following them. They can't tell
they're being followed if you get there first."
– Daryl Zero, *Zero Effect*

I'm back in my living room, swaddled in the depression of a well-developed couch cushion. I've been using noise as a painkiller for so long, I'd forgotten how unearthly the quiet sounds. It sounds windy. The vacuum of this room has a swell like the gluttonous undulation of a night-glazed ocean. I'm trying to cram that quiet into my mind, but the more I try, the more it becomes a particle accelerator. Loud within, quiet without. My associative reflexes nudge me to turn some reflection-burying music on, but, oddly, the loathsome silence feels like a cool palliative. Maybe because I know it will soon be loud within, loud without.

I should take this suit off so it doesn't get wrinkled, or whatever happens to thousand-dollar <<spitballing>> suits when you sit in them on a couch for too long. But being in this turbulently mindless gel feels so good right now. It's a displaced absenteeism that has a floating sensation to it. Patch is suggesting his finger-pointing animadversion from the kitchen: *Always take care of business first! Only the feckless and beef-witted recreate among disarray!*

Okay, Patch, I'm up.

I'm standing in front of my reflection in a kitchen window silvernitrated by rural blackness, drawing in one last breath of this impossible transformation. Impressive work, Vivian. I really do look good. It never occurred to me that I could be made to look like this. Maybe I never cared enough to take the time to find out. If you don't have any useful clay, why would you think to become a sculptor? However, I have money. And if that means Vivian's fingers playing "The Sound of Silence" along my jaw line every Friday, it might not hurt to experiment with some mild vanity.

Now let's see why that broken little Mariner was being so tactile. I unfold the handkerchief and hold it up to the light. Other than being monogrammed with the initials PGM <<you done slipped up, Patch>> and some wicked embroidery, it seems like your garden variety handkerchief. Inside the left breast pocket is a . . . I'm not sure what this is. It's a poker chip with the silhouette of a dead person lying in the middle of a lotus flower on one side and DbY on the other. It doesn't look familiar. Is this supposed to mean something to me? I should probably be better about inspecting high-end clothing handed to me for free by strangers. Today a cryptic poker chip and mismonogrammed handkerchief, tomorrow coveted time travel secrets.

My phone vibrates and notifies me that I have an email from The Left Lapel of Your Suit. The subject line reads, "This funeral isn't over." Great. There's no rest for the grandson of a thousand-layer Matryoshka-style fragmentation grenade. Maybe I should ignore it until the morning and just get some sleep while I can. <<Hilarious futility, Elliot.>> Tomorrow is Saturday and I need to be well-rested for Manuscript, day one! <<You're not sleeping with an email from The Left Lapel of Your Suit in your inbox.>> It's just going to have to wait. <<And it has an audio file.>> If you press play, Elliot, you can say goodnight to a good night's sleep. <<But an audio file . . .>>

I pinch the left lapel of the suit and run my fingers along its length. Yep, I can make out the topography of thin wires converging at a bulbous point in the fold. Hells bells, my suit is bugged. I'm glad I didn't get too crazy singing along to the music on the way home. And now I have to see if this ear-cupping hugger-muggery of a suit is spying on me at present. I should have known I'd be doing this tonight whether I liked it or not. Polished wires, Elliot, remember.

I pull a can of liquid lust, laughter, and love out of the fridge and prepare for a long night. The body of the email reads, "Get thee up, eat and drink; for there is a sound of abundance of rain . . ."

Way ahead of you, old man.

My thumb hovers over the audio file's icon with head-clogging hesitancy. It seems that every fifteen minutes I'm confronted with points of no return. I'm looking back. I turn to salt. I'm repurposed. I'm looking back. Fire from heaven consumes me. I'm repurposed. There has to be a way out of this loop. Which reminds me of Patch's stated purpose for this whole exercise—stepping out of hamster wheels.

Okay, I'm done being mystified and mortified by all this. Time to just work it out.

I press my thumb into an abundance of rain.

I can hear the subdued scratching of fabric washing over fabric. Funneled and amplified voices emerge from the surf and organize themselves into a dozen conversations. French. I hear a phrase I recognize from the funeral. Hey, wait, this *is* the funeral. It's an audio recording of the funeral. And there I was kicking myself for not recording it. Patch, you think of everything. I remember this part; I'm already standing at the coffin. This is right after . . . of course, right after the Mariner felt me up. *That's* what he was doing, he was turning me on. Maybe not the best choice of words after *felt me up*. Activating me?

A modulated whisper etches itself like crystal into the microphone: "Aurait-il pu se suicider? Cela aurait-il pu etre intentionnel?"

The response pours, as smooth as virgin olive oil, "Il n'a jamais pris parti; Pourquoi aurait-il fait ca? A quoi cela aurait-il servi? Non, chaque mot, chaque geste, cela avait un but avec L'Excavateur."

And then in a crystal whisper, "Dans ce jeu, le suicide a aussi son but, que nous puissions ou non voir comment."

I pull up a translation app, fix the settings to French to English, and restart the audio. The text populates, deliberates in spastic addition and subtraction as context accumulates, and settles on, "Could he have killed himself? Could this have been intentional?"

The oily reply spills over a wax tongue, "He never took sides; why would he have done that? What purpose would it serve? No, every word, every gesture, it had a purpose with the Excavator." <<Excavator—that must be the nickname *Digger* they mentioned at the funeral.>>

The modulated whisper scratches, "In this game, suicide has its purpose as well, whether or not we can see how."

The skittering translation bumps along. Olive oil continues, "Why did we trust him with everything? How do we function without a cartographer? Without *the* Cartographer?"

The response sounds distant and sentimental: "And he was the Immortal. He outlived us all. He held our collective memory."

Oily asks, "Has anyone tried to see what's in the coffin?"

Distant nostalgia man: "I tried. It's locked." Reverence is dusted like powdered sugar on their concern, but you can tell there's more to their loss than Patch himself.

"Alors, qu'est-ce qu'on fait de l'heritier? Sera-t-il un wild card ingerable, penses-tu?"

Olive oil pours with authority, "Continuez a nourrir les dead drops et briefez les trouplongeurs pour que sa derniere decennie soit un flipper. Et esperer que L'Excavateur ne lui en a pas trop dit."

My translator seems to be struggling with this one. It's running two steps forward, one step back, up an agility ladder. I think it's trying to find a French translation for clearly English words like *wild card* and *dead drop*. And people are afraid machines are going to take over the world . . .

Here we go: "So, what do we do about the heir? Will he be an unmanageable wild card, do you think?" <<Unmanageable? Am I something that needs to be managed? And why do they keep calling me *the heir*? Do they already know about the Manuscript?>>

The authoritative reply: "Continue to feed the dead drops and brief the hole divers" <<hole divers?>> "so that his last decade is a pinball machine. And hope the Excavator hasn't told him too much." So they don't know about the Manuscript then. And hang on, is that pinball machine they're talking about my life? Uncertainty is bad enough without adding flipper bats and slingshots and bumpers to it. Now I'm just anxiety for nothing.

<<Note to self: trouplongeur = hole diver.>>

I guess that's Patch telling me the Manuscript shouldn't be exposed to the elements <<i.e. hole divers or whatever>> on my dining table. But why would he have had me encounter these people if their paranoia was going to jeopardize his plan for me? How would I be a threat to any of their plans with my igno-rance? And if they can change stuff, how could I secure something that could be erased from my memory without ever knowing I had it in the first place? Was there a way to keep me anonymous until . . . stop, Elliot! Just stop! There are no loose ends or unintended consequences here, you must see that! Why are you trying to out-scheme a beast wide as imagination and deep as time?

The audio continues.

Mom: "Let's take a seat, everyone. We're going to get started."

A distant conversation slips into the folds of the lapelcrophone and I realize that was when I was heading back to my seat. The translator app categorizes it as Russian.

The translator seems to bounce along more quickly through this than the French.

A younger man whispers in convinced disbelief: "We understand that he was able to use stacked vents to dive with the hull, that stacking vents creates actual, physical openings."

The response sounds like a tuba amplified through a cantaloupe, an exquisitely low rumble finding its way around a tongue too fat and lazy to move out of enunciation's way. "That's impossible. If that was possible, we would have known about it."

The younger, more impartial seeming Russian counters: "If he didn't tell the Mero everything, it's likely that he didn't tell us everything either. Not taking a side is not taking a side. And nobody questioned the Cartographer."

Then Mom initiates the proceedings and I pause the audio. I forward the email to a secure email account for future reference. There may be more, but I get the idea, and I just want to be suspended in this deep end with my thoughts for a while.

Though drowsily peaceful, the house is filled with the noises in my head and the sound of my index finger tapping on my teeth. Clearly, Patch wanted me to have all this information, but what am I supposed to do with it? I can see it's fleshing out what was already mentioned in the Manuscript, but I don't have enough context to exploit it. It sounds like he had, or may have had, information that neither side was aware of. Would a supernova with nuclear joie de vivre kill himself? Was he taking that information to the grave <<wherever that ends up being>>? He was referred to as the Cartographer by both sides. What was he mapping? These vents? It sounds like I might pose some threat, one that needs to be managed by messing with the last ten years of my life <<which, eh, they weren't that great anyway>>. That takes me back to about the time of the injury. Is that relevant? It seems that they don't know about the Manuscript if they don't know how much Patch has told me. Not sure about things like hull, vents, hole divers, etc. I think I remember references to those terms from the Manuscript, but I read that like fifty years ago and can't recall specifically.

Patch's afterthoughtish canting echoes off the appliances' stainless steel: *Don't spend hours anticipating or embracing failed seconds! Sufficient unto that second is the evil thereof!* Maybe this will all become clear in the days ahead.

Curse you, Patch! You know I can't resist a good puzzle! All this and I haven't even started this Manuscript business yet.

I let a draught of gods and angels list over all available taste buds before letting it descend. My brain and pericardium are cooled and numbed. I'm soaking in a submersive pressure equalization and I can feel gravity dissipating. I remember this feeling last time Patch was in my life: invincibility, purpose, omniscience, enrapturing optimism. It is a baptism in the River Styx.

My calves and forearms are flexing in succession like a Newton's cradle.

Day 1

CHAPTER 13

"The best pace is a suicide pace, and today is a good day to die."
– Steve Prefontaine

A really weird dream yanked me into the morning just before dawn. It had that discomfiting, oracular vagueness that you're sure means something, but it's too otherworldly to superimpose any of its elements on a conscious reality. And usually with dreams like this, at the event horizon of consciousness, the details slip down a greased limbic drain before I can catalog them for any level of recall. But not this time. This time it was eerily stark and intact, and I had little trouble recreating its full scale. This was a new brand of dream. It felt more like a vision or a premonition, like it could be decrypted if I just paid close attention to normally elusive subtleties over the next few days.

The first thing I'm unconsciously conscious of is that I'm in my high school football gear, pads and all, except my helmet and cleats. I have a parachute on my back, and in the dream it makes sense because I know I might need it for what I'm doing. Though the sky is darkened with the disgruntlement of lead-weighted storm clouds, I know I'm in a landscape much like the Bonneville Salt Flats. I'm barefoot and sprinting at superhuman speed. I remember thinking, though I couldn't see them clearly, that the ridges of wind-swept salt would hurt the bottom of my feet if I didn't avoid them. There's the silhouette of low, black mountains in the distance and an icy white lightning occasionally snaps a crawling, branching revelation of the salty expanse. It was absolutely beautiful in its orderly flatness and I remember thinking that being there was like being in hell, but escorted by Michael, Gabriel, Raphael, and Uriel.

I look down, left, right, and know from all visual clues that I'm running hundreds of miles per hour. Of course, I have only localized and confined glimpses of what it feels like to be a god, but this has that sense of well-regulated, boundless, purposeful power. It's that supreme confidence of having full control of every physical faculty, like what you'd think an ibex is experiencing as it's scaling a cliff. As I run, I'm jumping over these giant pits. With the timing and assurance of a species whose life was spent, and livelihood depended on, clearing such gulfs, I launch myself in the air for several seconds at a time, resuming a break-neck speed on the other side, and trying to avoid the faint, wind-sculpted spines of salt. As I speed along, the pits become broader and a beckoning blackness swallows the bottomless bottoms. I'm running faster and faster and spending more time in the air with each jump. I remember thinking, at this speed, my lungs should be pyroclastic coals four sizes too big for their collapsing pleural cavities. It's a little aggravating that I'm managing these speeds with such minimal cardiovascular effort. So I run faster. How do you know how much faster you can go without that feedback?

The weird part <<weirder part>> is that I can see a figure falling from the sky a few miles ahead. It's just a silhouette, really, in steady descent. I know it's a woman. I know that I know this woman. I'm bounding over these seemingly bottomless chasms toward a woman falling from the sky, but for some reason I know that she's not why I'm running in that direction. Different levels of my consciousness are trying to reconcile this conflict. My dream consciousness knows what I'm doing there, but some nagging, moralistic consciousness is framing its obligations as foregone conclusions. Since the dream consciousness is clearly the dominant, intercepting the woman isn't a serious consideration, even though I don't immediately know what I'd be doing there <<or what she'd be doing there, for that matter>> if it wasn't to intercept her.

Every several seconds, a thin film of what feels like a dense, electrically-charged plasma <<I could feel it moving upwards through my body>> rises steadily in a sheet from the ground, ascends a couple hundred feet, and blows a deafening exhaust from its periphery at the distal circumference of the scaly flats. Then it violently collapses from whence it emerged. Upon each arrival it discolors the depth of the pits like a reflective surface of water casting ripples of light off its settling irregularities. When it reaches the terrestrial surface, it rises as a contiguous plane, though paper thin, like the surface of a deluge flooding the entire valley at a depth of some hundreds of feet. Then it roars a blast of fata morgana that deforms a 360-degree arc of distant mountains and horizon and crashes through the ground. This phenomenon is noticeable but doesn't result in any significant distraction. I just know it's an expected element of this environment and don't pay it much mind.

I'm running so fast the resistance is deforming my face and the wind is cool and encouraging. Hurdling chasms, trying to detonate my lungs with unreachable speeds, glancing at this falling woman . . . I can see that she's going to fall straight into one of these pits, but I'm undeterred. I clear the pit with my arms wheeling like a triple jumper and rocket beyond her. I don't look back; I assume the pit prolongs her descent. I feel like the woman has her place there, but I know my objective, and it's far more structurally relevant to my purpose and presence than attending to the woman. Bizarrely, I remember her saying, "Not fast enough," as she drops behind me. Not fast enough? I'm like Usain Bolt in Hermes's shoes! So I run faster. My feet are hardly touching the ground, but I can hear booming cracks with each barefoot fall. I can feel pressure from my speed building up under the tamping storm clouds. It's limiting any further acceleration, but the objective is rapidly approaching. The low, black mountains in the distance are now imposing walls as black as the Earl of Hell's waistcoat <<stole that from Patch>>. A blast of icy light elucidates my closing distance. I'm going to run through that mountain. That's my mission. This seems perfectly reasonable in dream reality, and the thrill of it, the thrill of doing something so determinedly impossible, makes me think I might be the lightning itself. Everything about my consciousness is sinew and twitch and invincibility. At the last possible microsecond before impact, the obsidian wall seems to lunge at me.

I don't even remember waking. My conscious analysis of the scenario is seamless with the impact. I lay still for a while in a sort of weightlessness.

There's no getting back to sleep after a somnothrashing like that, so I don't bother. I feel like I'm viewing the world from thirty thousand feet—the sharp focus of whole road-cut counties swallowing the microscopies of self-pity and apprehension and busyness and listlessness. My lungs and shoulders have tripled in size and I'm evaporating in some stratospheric ebullience. I want to know what broken knuckles feel like from hitting a stainless steel refrigerator door.

So with all this distension uncorking, brewing, brimming, I decide to exothermize with a long run. Well, long for somebody that hasn't run in ten years.

It isn't the cleverest thing to do when you can't sleep, but there went up a smoke out of my nostrils, fire out of my mouth devoured; my lungs felt like clouds carried by a tempest and my fingers were the bow of Jonathan and the sword of Saul. I'm a Mean Joe Jack Ham Lambert chimera and I can feel my skin sizzling. I need a healthy release of this energy so I don't find out how far I can throw my coffee table.

Life has veered so far to the left over the past decade, I have to take a minute to determine if I even have the means to go running. Other than my typical attire, I just need . . . nothing. I guess I'm always dressed as if I'm about to go for a run. I feel like this should be a source of shame, but I'm too proud of being exercise-ready.

I open the front door. A breeze as sedating as slushy Mountain Dew spools around me and settles on my neck and ears. It's only upper forties, but being outside in a depopulated darkness, in a deep-sea silence, in a wind suffused with the bouquets of oil refineries and pasture land is electrically apocalyptic. Then the roar of an airliner departing from Salt Lake International litters the whole valley and the effect is ruined. But my hands are biblical weapons and my skin is still sizzling, so at least there's that.

Earbuds in. Player set to shuffle.

I've never seen much use in stretching out before a run, so I walk to the end of my driveway and just start running.

Something distinctly classic rock or alternative rock plays <<I use keyboards to distinguish, so this must be alternative rock>>. It's telling me that the chemicals between us lie in this bed. It has a good tempo for running.

Why running through a mountain is an intuitive reality keeps my mind occupied for the first few minutes. <<Patch is backhanding me on the shoulder: *Your mind is a megalopolis; would you rather be having a colonoscopy or a massage?*>> "Not fast enough," she said. She's falling from the sky to what would seem a grizzly death and she's concerned about my speed? Maybe she was just as interested in me running through that mountain as I seemed to be.

I turn left onto the Legacy Parkway Trail, relieved that, for the remainder of my run, the excursion is likely to be humanless. People outdoors at this hour are always up to no good. Unless it's me out for a run.

Patch was an avid distance runner. Not marathon distance, per se <<claiming that the human body was not meant for such distances>>, but he covered nearly six miles at a decent clip daily. He was always extolling the virtues of distance running, declaring that it was a metaphor, *the* metaphor, for every aspect of life and living. The more you run, the more you understand who you are and what you're doing here. It was the great paradigm for reaping and sowing, hedonism and asceticism, good and evil. He would say that fasting and distance running were the most instructive of all heavenly gifts, the greatest means of understanding our full power as beings of intent and will, the greatest means of studying the volume of our capacity in relation to experiential extremes. As an energetic teenager, I didn't fully appreciate a lot of this old-world wisdom. I actually enjoyed running. But today, all two hundred and seventy lung-crushing pounds are acutely attuned to the analogies.

My lungs are making that transition from getaway to gotaway and are trying to flee their costal cage. Suffocation is flooding the streets of the megalopolis and I need another distraction . . .

I get to start the Manuscript today. I can't tell if I'm afraid or excited or annoyed. I am resigned to the disruption in my life, but Patch is an overhauler. The payoff will be exquisite, for sure, but it will be commensurate with the investment. And I'm not sure I have the energy. But here I am, running. Like Patch always said, *Anticipating is a waste of resources.* And I know that getting fit now won't have any effect on my sixteen-year-old fitness, but I might as well forge my mind in that fire so I don't waste any time when I get there. <<Get then?>>

I feel like I'm in the bog of an asthma attack. I'm forcibly huffing clods of carbon dioxide into the path of the already unbreathable, forty-five hundred-foot, inversion layer-compressed, oxygenless brown air. My auxiliary breathing muscles are pushing shattered ribs into my collapsing <<collapsed?>> lungs. I'm looking around for landmarks to both motivate myself to keep going and to stop. *Leave it all on the road! Pacing your pain is just another way of giving up!* Another song plays. It sympathizes with my condition. *I have been guilty of kicking myself in the teeth* . . . The bottoms of my feet catch fire. Get back to the Manuscript. The pain keeps pulling my chin back to make eye contact. My mind finds some forbidden paths and I formulate a regimen of linebacker drills. If my mind goes back with me, I'll need to pack some of this mental luggage for the trip. Patch looks right, I float to the left, he tucks the ball and moves forward, I converge, he pumps his arm, I watch his eyes . . . I can feel my body slightly misaligning itself and the pain is only half registering. Why was I wearing a parachute? It didn't occur to me that I might not be able to clear those pits. But I knew the parachute was there for a reason. What if I hadn't awoken after making contact with the mountain? There's broken glass in my hip joints. This time I hear my dad in one of his rare army moments, "Pain is weakness leaving the body!" Weakness is pouring out of my screaming knees. Another song plays. I can keep going for one more song. *Life is pain! The pain from the disgrace of quitting is much more acute than whatever pain is meted out by endurance!* It's getting harder to distract myself; the pain of the bone marrow biopsies in my sacrum and ischium keeps pushing my head under. I'm still breathing, I'm still alive. I'm still alive, I keep running. *The greatest teacher is the moment! The most insidious anti-teacher is the kill switch!* I know all of this pain will sublimate ten seconds after I stop. I can pull the plug any time I want. Come on, Elliot, would you rather douse this fire or breathe it and learn something about yourself?

I keep running in case Patch is watching me from a drainage ditch or one of these park pavilions.

I cross 500 South and a dim violet scar cuts across an outline of rumpled mountains to the east. The sky seems to open up. Woods Cross becomes almost discernible and my pain is mixed up in the derelict and the discarded and the rusty and the simplicity of its grazing horses. Its contours and shadows and layers are gorgeous in the ash of this plum laceration scoring the outline of the Wasatch heights. I feel like an unnatural element of this scene, like this moment is somehow significant because I'm here—not necessarily significant to me, but significant to the universe, like my presence here is some frameshift that will be referenced as critical at some future time. There's no reason why I should be here. I'm so out of my element, only impossibility could have enticed me here.

Lodged in the reeds of my swampy reflection is the realization that I have already run well beyond my intended mark. So I keep running. Only the prospect of a well-lit world and, with it, pesky human types turns me around. My diaphragm feels like a blazing filament, but my breath is regular and inaudible under the funneled music. The ineffability of this darkly beautiful world enriches the oxygen, expands my thorax and numbs all the mind-body superhighways. My mind relaxes into the distance of sounds, the drawing of the dawn's blade across the northern sky, and an untraceable reassurance.

Step after step my body inhales life and exhales rot. I'm vaulting chasms. Not fast enough. I accelerate. My knees are bound up. The shattered glass in my hips dissolves into a frictionless lubrication. The biopsy needles are nudged out by flexion. The bottoms of my feet are breathable nylon. *It's not a second wind, it's a victory of the mind.*

CHAPTER 14

"If everything seems under control, you're just not going fast enough."
– Mario Andretti

I'm sitting at my dining table in a post-run euphoria, forged and flushing blood quieting my mind on its Circle of Willis scaffolding. Venous sinuses are sweeping toxins from permanent residences and they drain into my muscles like an elegant paralytic. I'd forgotten how good this feels. It's the parasympathetic spooning following a sympathetic pogrom. I am still and comfortable and in need of nothing. The morning sun is finding breaches in my blinds and exaggerating its inroads with trapezoidal smears that look like corporate branding on my bare walls. A cold shower has seemed to wash away my sins and the volume of my conscience is turned way down. It's rare that I experience calm, but I think I've leapt clean over *calm* into a deep tank of *sedate*. This is what I always imagined happiness feeling like: settled, transcendent contentment.

Most notably, I don't have a headache.

The Manuscript is opened to today's entry and its Rose-gnarled, solicitous fingers are tapping me on the forehead. Patch has concealed himself in one of the viburnums and is peeping through a window. I swear I can feel this. His impatience is making the nape of my neck itch. *Thou art my battle axe and weapon of war: for with thee will I break in pieces the nations, and with thee will I destroy kingdoms; and with thee will I break in pieces captains and rulers . . . so get on with it, ya wee dafty!*

I know there's no preparing for something like this; I just hope that when it's all said and done, there's not a recognizable shred of me left. I mean . . . I think I hope there *is* a recognizable shred of me left. Or maybe I did mean for it to be negated. My whole life seems a parapraxis-prompting dislocation these days. Up doesn't look as up and down is only obliquely down. I've circled back to the point in the ouroboros where my life is fusing its end with the beginning.

Page one <<it looks like we're back to old-timey typewriter font>>.

Forget absolutely everything you know, or think you know. All natural laws, all physical certainties, all unquestioned realities, all scientific springboards, all foundational premises, all dictating physics, all measured and predictable motions, throw them all out. They are all actual and theoretical stumbling blocks. You have been dropping quarters in this virtual massage chair long enough. What you have been programmed to accept and embrace is a womb so confined, confining, and convincing you may go mad without its amnion and umbilicus, and for this I am sorry. Nobody handles this cesarean section well. At best it will infuriate you. Rage is a good reaction to this extraction. Denial and dismissal is the reaction of worst case. Rest assured, I will be your eyes to the blind and feet to the lame throughout the entirety of this transformation. Just stick to the manuscript and you will discover that you have become the epicenter of stability as everything else stumbles around you.

Please don't say anything about a red pill . . .

Since nothing I am about to unfold is based on the pretexts of accepted knowledge or assumptions, there is no way to make it simple or linear or give it a logical progression. Entire layers will be ignored, dazzling attractions will be bypassed, gold bars will be left on the side of the road. Questions will invariably outpace my explanations. It will sound like I am repeating myself, frequently summarizing, backtracking, getting ahead of myself, and jumping around, because I am. It is a loose narrative that does not lend itself to cogency, cohesion, or coherence; just entertain all possibilities until you experience them for yourself. From your perspective, because you are largely (not a fat pun, though you could stand to lighten up a little) a product of government schools, mass media, and spoon-fed pop science, everything I am about to reveal is, in all ways, impossible.

This is already sounding much bigger than putting someone back in their sixteen-year-old body to play football. Either the walls of the world just fell away or I somehow got a lot smaller.

This manuscript is not going anywhere, so you can return to these explanations any time, but I want you to focus and try to comprehend through the first reading. Drink some of that super-sweetened bile if you think it will help.

Every one ten-thousandth of a second, a facsimile of that prick in time is created as a topographical, three-dimensional, semi-holographic, retrievable record of the entire diametrical breadth and depth of the earth. Each of these facsimiles is called a frame, *much as you would consider a single photographic frame. It is the archived, dehydrated (you will see why I use that word later) representation of a specific ten-thousandth of a second. Once a frame is generated, it drops (do not get snagged on the directional references used in this treatise, they are more for conceptualizing and less for precision) for a period of one hundred and twenty years, in a state of freefall, more or less, until it comes to rest atop the accumulation of frames that have completed their one hundred and twenty-year descent. The series of frames presently in the course of their one hundred and twenty-year descent constitutes the* frameset. *The frameset is composed of what we call the* apical frame *(the frame that represents our physical world and is neither technically created in this process, nor considered a frame as such), and every other, called* archived frames. *All frames in the frameset other than the apical frame are dropping at the same rate, so they are equidistant. With a frame created every ten-thousandth of a second and a freefalling stack of frames one hundred and twenty years deep, there are, at any given moment, 37,765,440,000,000 frames falling within the frameset, the apical frame being the point from which the archived frames fall. At the termination of that one hundred and twenty-year descent, a frame comes to rest on the accumulation of aged-out frames that preceded it. This settled stack of ever-accumulating frames is called the* petram. *It is a bedrock of immutable, inaccessible, permanent, irretrievable frames, and constitutes a fixed record. Since the petram is an accumulation of thousands of years of frames, its depth exceeds that of the frameset by exponents and multiples.*

Imagine a snowfall. <<Story time! He does this—extols my intelligence and then fable-izes his point.>> *A snowflake crystallizes at a height, it falls for a period of time, drifting steadily downward in a lag behind its older siblings at a distance, and eventually comes to rest on the snow that has already accumulated on the surface. In the context of this analogy, the crystallization of the snowflake represents the generation of an archived frame, an exact replica of the apical frame (physical world) at that particular ten-thousandth of a second. The snowflake (archived frame) then begins to fall. The totality of snowflakes (frames) in the course of their descent is the frameset. Any given snowflake (frame) falls for a period of one hundred and twenty years. The depth of the snow (frames that have completed their one hundred and twenty-year descent) that has accumulated on the surface is the petram.*

That was quite helpful, actually. He started losing me at 37,765,440,000,000.

Unlike the virtual nature of the archived frames, the apical frame represents our hard, physical reality. It is the knuckles, the clocks, the brick walls, the train whistles, and the things on which we stub our toes. Despite its ten-thousandth of a second lamina (if I can conflate depth and time), it is impenetrable and unyielding. It is the veneer that prevents us from backsliding through those virtual, semi-holographic, ethereal archived frames. Though it is not technically true, as far as humanity is concerned, we only exist at the apical frame, the now, the most current ten-thousandth of a second.

So, there's an apical frame that's technically our physical world, and every ten-thousandth of a second it is copied and becomes an archived frame, like a big photocopy diorama registering a particular ten-thousandth of a second of the whole earth. Then that archived frame falls for one hundred and twenty years, at which point it becomes part of the petram and can't be changed anymore. Does that mean the archived frames can be changed? Does that mean someone can change anything in the last hundred and twenty years? Seems arbitrary. So, if it was 2000, everything preceding 1880 would be unchangeable? What happens to the rest of the frameset if something is changed fifty years ago? I should probably write these questions down. I'm curious to know how they figured all this out.

Though each frame is separated temporally by one ten-thousandth of a second, it is also separated spatially by a function of frame drop speed. Because our corporeal experience renders this space incomprehensible, we will say it is as big as it needs to be, and big enough for our purpi. <<Like Patch's modified plural of *purchase, purpi* is his now-correct-sounding plural of *purposes.*>> *The space between any two frames in the frameset is called a* Gontlet *for reasons upon which I will later expound. These Gontlets are populated by entities that do and do not, should and should not act upon our corporeal reality. They are worlds in and of themselves, full of perishers and articles (as your Nan would say), confusion, peril, and, unfortunately, crisscrossed by toll roads we cannot circumvent in our itinerancy. As an archived frame reaches the end of its one hundred and twenty-year lifespan, it becomes fused with the petram and the Gontlet below is compressed and squeezed out of existence. It ceases to be an occupiable space. Now take a big swig of your diabetes poison and dig in . . .*

Come on . . . I'm not that predictable. <<I take a big swig under the surface of the table so the Manuscript can't see. The frigid delectability arborizes into every capillary and my attention becomes voracious and capacious.>>

When Gontlets, which are actual, physical spaces, are compressed and eliminated, pressure builds up in the system. To relieve this pressure, the system uses vents, *vertical columns of exhaust that circulate as cylindrical ports at varying depths throughout the frameset to release this accumulation at the apical frame. Vents are initially formed at the geographical center of the earth, the North Pole, the first ten-thousandth of a second of every new moon. Generally speaking, they are about thirty meters in diameter and reach frameset depths of about twenty years, roughly one-sixth the depth of the frameset. No single vent spans the entire depth of the frameset. A newly formed vent is referred to as a* nascent vent *and immediately commences a spiraling, southeasterly, counterclockwise course from the North Pole at a swift, constant speed. This widdershins, north-south maiden voyage is called the* nautilus. *The duration of this widening, southerly nautilus is about twenty-nine and a half days, the period between new moons. The thirty-meter diameter exhaust aperture of a nascent vent remains affixed to the apical frame throughout the entirety of the nautilus. It would not be much of a vent if it did not reach the surface. There is only ever one apical frame-affixed nascent vent circulating at any given moment. When the nascent vent has spiraled southward to approximately eighty degrees south latitude, completing its twenty-nine and a half-day nautilus, the aperture of the vent abandons its connection with the apical frame and becomes affixed to the archived frame representing the first ten-thousandth of a second of the next new moon. Now an* archived vent *whose aperture is affixed to a falling archived frame, it begins to sink into the frameset in a south-north course called the* anti-nautilus, *a mirror image of the nautilus it took to the south. Whereas the first twenty-nine and a half days (the nautilus) are a static, two-dimensional spiral, the next twenty-nine and a half days and beyond are similar to involvement in the formation of a whirlpool—both corkscrewing laterally and descending. I know I am describing multi-dimensional, multi-directional movement, but it is important that you* *are able to conceptualize these basic motions. <<Basic?>> Archived vents move in this twenty-nine and a half-day northerly anti-nautilus, twenty-nine and a half-day southerly nautilus, back and forth and back and forth, sinking all the while, until time's advance, like a wood chipper, begins to take its legs out from under it, and it is pressed entirely out of service following the hundred and twentieth year. As a nascent vent is created every twenty-nine and a half days, and archived vents are circulating at varying depths, intersections within the ventosphere, in aggregate, release the accumulating pressure from its one hundred and twenty-year depth.*

No fable? If any explanation could be groomed by a fable, it's that vent madness. A fable and some Dramamine.

To complicate matters, nautiluses cycle through initial launch directions (in this order: east, south, west, north) with each new moon, like a quadskelion. Due to these variations, the interchange of nascent vent adhering to the apical frame to archived vent beginning its anti-nautilus to the north occurs ninety degrees to the east with each cycle. This affords a tidy lot of eight tracks to monitor throughout the depths of the frameset: nautilus-east, nautilus-south, nautilus-west, nautilus-north, anti-nautilus-east, anti-nautilus-south, anti-nautilus-west, anti-nautilus-north. Since these events are so regular (and have been for millennia), the entire ventosphere has been mapped, including its constellation of intersections, going back one hundred and twenty years.

Mind you, though the superior end of a nascent vent is fastened to the apical frame, treading water during its maiden circumambulation, so to speak, the nascent vent does not create a void on the earth's surface as it circulates. Vents are, for the most part, ethereal constructs that do not disrupt the physicality of the terrestrial surface of the apical frame. They do release an indiscernible, barely measurable exhalation, but have no noticeable effect on terra firma. It is why they have eluded human attention until the relative recent.

Perhaps it is more useful to consider archived frames as placeholders that can be reconstituted with physicality if they are revisited, and that vents are punching deep holes (roughly 6,294,240,000,000 frames deep) in the frameset at varying depths (a function of their age) as they circulate. We can drop through these vents to occupy any archived frame less than one hundred and twenty years in the past.

So, time out. A little discrepancy here: If it creates no actual opening at the surface of the earth, at the apical frame, how can you access the vent? I'm assuming you can't dig to it. Though, why I think this won't be answered in the next sentence is *pure deed macaroni* <<Patchism>> on my part.

We are not yet in the weeds, so take a sip. <<Oh, that can was gone after the third sentence. I get another and hurry back.>> *All other features are predicated on this design, so it is important that you can model this in your mind for mental manipulation.*

Just carry on, old man. I'll keep up.

You may have already arrived at the impasse: vents do not disrupt the tangibility of the earth's surface in their maiden and anfractuous ramblings; we use these vents to reach provisionally archived frames. Seems a hopeless business . . .

Yes, yes, way ahead of you. Read on, Lizzy!

I have been a regular in the machinations of this system for decades, riding its elevators, charting its horizons, tumbling down its stairs. I have found death and resurrection on every continent. And yet, pithy summaries of its phenomena still elude me. Its vastness swallows all of my attempts to reduce it and all that remains is an unrecognizable tsantsa. My only consolation is your brilliance. If I give you enough, I am confident you will flesh it out and give it armor. We have found some vexing aberrations, so, plainly, we do not know everything.

You will not encounter anything paradigm shifting about this next aspect, but you will need to understand its applications to the broader system. The totality of your entity, from the organism that interfaces physically with your environment to the consciousness that processes that interplay and creates its own domain, comprises two components, one tangible, one intangible (it may be vastly more complex than that, but for the purpi of our paradigm, we can suffice ourselves with the two for now). The tangible is referred to as the hull *and the intangible as the* umbra. *A vent will only accept the umbra. However, the apical frame to which the aperture of the nascent vent is affixed, upon which you presently find yourself, prevents the hull from accessing the vent. Thus, the only way the umbra can access a vent is to be separated from its hull. The only way the umbra can be separated from the hull is death. The only death that will qualify an umbra for the vents is a punctuated one.*

I no longer like where this is going.

Put simply, the umbra is the aspect of the duality to which we would, perhaps with seeming paradox, attribute life. It is the rarified substance that animates the hull, powers consciousness, and manages the mind. The hull provides the depths, the wind, and the sea monsters, but the umbra is the unimpeachable helmsman. True, the captain can release his grip on the helm and let the storm steer, but that is ultimately the prerogative of the pilot, not the squall. <<I love maritime metaphors, if that was a metaphor. Is he talking about some spirit-body interplay?>> *It is difficult to speak of the hull and umbra beyond the context of one another because it is such an integrated entity that, when the umbra pauses its occupancy with the hull for any span of time, the umbra does not quite function the same. Though there is not anything inherently alive about the hull itself, it seems to square the umbra in ways we do not fully understand. Whatever its components, the umbra is indestructible, and exists bound to, or free of, the hull. It can be shrunk, dimmed, and polluted, but on it will persist with no threat of annihilation.*

The umbra with which you are born is termed the native umbra *and is permanently integrated with its hull until death. They can separate briefly, but death is, by definition, the prolonged and insurmountable absence of the native umbra. The umbra is anchored to the hull via* moorings *located in various parts of the body. These moorings are much like a receptor specific to the particular domain of a particular molecule; an umbra uniquely dovetails with the moorings of its native hull, providing the most secure connection. This mutual specificity is an important aspect of what we do as pikirovateli (or trouplongeurs, if you prefer the French).*

I remember that term from the funeral audio. Hole divers. I wonder if those are the ones that drop through the vents.

As with the tolerant specificity of all receptors, any umbra can bond with a non-native hull. Any umbra not derived from the native umbra (this excludes lendemains as they are native umbra derivations (more on that to follow)) is called a xenoumbra. *In large part, xenoumbrae are uninvited guests and more parasites than symbionts. They are messy squatters. The attempts of xenoumbrae to stitch to the moorings of non-native hulls, though possible, and possible for some duration, are only ever successful intermittently and ephemerally. Nativity, in this regard, will always trump determination, practice, and concentration. However, a hull with viable moorings can accommodate any number of umbrae at any given moment, to include multiple lendemains and xenoumbrae. This is the core principle upon which we capitalize in this venture.*

Once the hull's moorings can no longer secure the native umbra, whether that be a result of degradation over time, congenital misfortunes, trauma, dissolution, dissipation, etc., the umbra is released to inhabit the Gontlet directly subordinate to the frame created the moment the umbra was released. This manner of death is simply referred to as Gontlet death. *For our purpi, this manner of death is, though occasionally tragic, irrelevant. I will expound on the nature of the Gontlets shortly, but death independent of contact with the vents is just death and does not further our discussion along.*

As I said, death is necessary to access the vents. As far as we understand, this is non-negotiable. But, as previously mentioned, in order to access the vents, not any death will do. If an individual, hull and umbra intact, is able to impact the $707m^2$ $((30m/2)^2 * \pi)$ of real estate <<which is a postage stamp when you take its square root>> *over which a nascent vent is passing below at a rate of speed sufficient to cause the moorings to sever violently, ripping the umbra from the hull, the umbra can be propelled through the vent's apical frame lid, leaving the lifeless hull at the surface.* <<Lifeless? Like the dead kind of lifeless? You save me from suicide to subsequently stage my suicide?>> *The vents act as valves that push the exhaust in one direction, apical-ward, so velocity against its current has to be relatively substantial. The higher the rate of speed at impact, the deeper the umbra descends into the vent; thus, the earlier the umbra arrives.*

I know we are dealing primarily with space here, but this is, in effect, the essence of time travel. It isn't particularly sexy, but, there it is.

As a disengaged umbra descends through a vent, it is, for simplicity's sake, traveling through a twenty-year void in the frameset (I'm not happy about using lengths of time as linear measurements either). As mentioned, velocity at impact determines depth of descent. If a speed sufficient to cause death is not achieved, you are simply maimed; though reversible, it is highly inconvenient. As a relatively high rate of speed is necessary to ensure death, the system seems to impose a minimum depth corresponding to that minimum speed. Not many wish to experiment with what this minimum might be, but we have had reports about receding as few as two months. It is commensurately difficult to achieve a high enough rate of speed to descend to depths that constitute decades. The density of lower levels of the atmosphere, we have found, are quite prohibitive. Besides, there are reasons why reaching such depths is inadvisable.

It will come as no surprise that this community is composed largely of pilots, skydivers, and owners and operators of airfields. It just simplifies things.

Ah, died from a *flying incident*. Right.

As an umbra descends through the vertical channel of the vent, it is plummeting past archived frames and Gontlets of the frameset. Descending through a vent is something like jumping into water—once the density of the water overwhelms the density of the object descending, buoyancy enforces an equilibrium and the mass slows to a stop. The buoyancy in this system tends to eject laterally rather than vertically, and, once the umbra reaches that density-equalized depth, dictated by speed at impact, it is ejected into its associated supra-frame Gontlet. This jerking from the vent into the Gontlet is, in great measure, due to the magnetism the native hull exerts on all derivations of its umbral nativity within the welcoming archived frame.

A hull's moorings have a powerful affinity for its native umbra. If those moorings are healthy and intact, the native umbra will always be coupled with its hull. They are till death do they part, as it were. But the moorings' affinity is not exclusive to the native umbra; it extends to all of the native umbra's versions and derivations. As today's umbra will not be the same as tomorrow's, we use the term lendemain *(a brilliantly apt French designation meaning the next day) to refer to any other iteration of the native umbra. Every instance of* Pik-ing *(our industry term for the use of a vent to reoccupy a native hull in an archived frame, pronounced* peeking*) introduces another lendemain into the system. The more you engage in this enterprise, the more lendemains you stand to accrue. The nature of this accrual and its arbitration with the native hull is a crucial fundament of our exploitation of the system.*

If a lendemain shares a frame or Gontlet with its native hull, at whatever depth, there will be a strong mutual attraction between the two—the native hull will attract the lendemain and the lendemain will seek the hull. The closer the lendemain is geographically to its native hull when released into the Gontlet and its associated frame, the less time spent in the Gontlet and the less time needed to couple. This is significant because the Gontlets are bazaars of nastiness, and the allure of their seducements is every bit as attractive as the magnetism of the native hull. As a disengaged umbra, you are hyper-aware, hyper-sensory, hyper-alive. Everything is boldfaced, capitalized, and has three exclamation points. It is a level of consciousness we are not accustomed to in this soaked, weighted blanket of a hull. You retain full capacity of all mental faculties in this state—consciousness, choice, will, autonomy—but it is something like a disconnected, disorienting dream state and, as it is an utter abolishment of the gating principle, it is easy to forget what you are doing there. It is much like the screams of your conscience hushed by the kill switch of your curiosity; you have all your faculties, but some voices seem to be louder, more beautiful, and more insistent for a moment. Much of the manuscript is designed to help you navigate the gauntlets of the Gontlet to your hull.

Okay, so . . . okay, hold on. Let me stir this a little more; I think it's starting to separate. And I don't need another drink! So, when I . . . what did he call it . . . Pik, when I Pik, I have to die at my present. I have to use the ground to separate my umbra from my hull because the vent will only allow the umbra. But I have to be going fast enough to both die at the apical frame surface and to propel my umbra into the vent. Once my umbra is in the vent, and depending on the speed at which I'm shot into it, I sink through the frameset as another version of my native umbra called a . . . lendemain. So a lendemain is just an older version of me since I'd be going *back* in time. Then my past hull sucks this lendemain out of the vent, across the Gontlet, and into that past hull, assuming I can make it through all the nastiness of the Gontlet. While I'm travelling as an umbra in the vent and the Gontlet, separated from my hull, I experience everything sharper and louder, but also like I'm in a dream. Am I getting this right? And I can do this again and again since an unlimited number of lendemain can occupy my hull? It seems like things would quickly become confusing in there. So, the native umbra will always be in the hull, and you can stuff lendemains in there, and xenoumbrae can also fit. But the hull prefers and secures the native umbra and the lendemains over the xenoumbrae since the native versions sort of fit in there better. So how do you determine who does what in there? Is it just whoever got in there last? Or are they all just observers of what the native umbra is doing? But what would be the point of that? And can I just shortcut the Gontlets by jumping into a vent twenty feet away from where I was at the time I want to get back to? Seems simpler than spending a lot of time trying to get me through the Gontlets.

If the lendemain does couple with its hull at a deeper frame, it will secure itself to the moorings and share occupancy of the hull with the native umbra (and any other associated lendemains and xenoumbrae). Remember, only death can extricate the native umbra, so the lendemain does not displace it. Once a lendemain couples with its hull, that frame becomes the apical to that entity, its present. We call these archived-now-apical frames reconstituted apical frames to differentiate them from the principal apical frame, the topmost apical frame that represents the objective present. In effect, now and present are relative terms as pikirovateli have occupied archived frames and restored their apicality throughout the frameset. The same traversability rules apply to archived vents coring reconstituted apical frames deeper in the frameset—hulls are prevented entry to the vents by the restored physicality of any reconstituted apical frame. It seems that a lendemain recoupling with a younger native hull rehydrates that corresponding frame and restores its terra firma. If you traverse a vent via Pik-ing and descend through a reconstituted apical frame (or several), it will have no effect on you since you are only an umbra until you recouple with your hull.

Every different choice an individual makes from its recoupling with the hull at a reconstituted apical frame and onward is updated to the principal apical frame (the most present present), which could be a considerable distance into the future. This update is a daily occurrence. Depending on the magnitude of any changes made, some people may cease to exist, others will exist that did not in the previous iteration of the frameset. Some changes matter very little, others fell civilizations. We have discovered, though, that there is very little that one individual can do to push broad timelines off their tracks. The weights and balances are quite resilient, and people and populations are not as mercurial and suggestible as we like to think.

Though not frequently reaching the threshold of substantial derailments, these daily changes create warps and wefts of byzantine complications. Time, it turns out, is more chiffon than it is wool, and all changes made, from the just-petram-fused frame to the principal apical frame are registered in a ghastly, cumulative manner. A change made thirty years in the past incorporates in its update a change made twenty years in the past, which then incorporates in its summative update of the previous changes a change made ten years in the past, and so on until the principal apical frame. The update is simply the frameset reconciling billions of probability matrices in (very) fast forward to incorporate all changes made from earliest to latest. The update runs strictly through native umbrae and has no effect on lendemains, giving those that have Pik-ed the advantage of being conscious of all changes made and all iterations (to a degree). Not knowing any better, the native umbrae accept these changes as their own history, their only history.

I wasn't really exaggerating—everything I remember happening yesterday may not have happened the way I remember it except as part of a fast-forward update. That's bleak. And a little deterministic. Or is a fast-forward update just as historical, just as *me*, as a version that unfolded at a natural pace? After all, if it's a function of probability matrices based on what I've shown the frameset of myself, I guess it's as much *me* as anything. What about the people that exist after an update that didn't exist before it? How does the frameset determine their likely outcomes without any previous exposure? *Byzantine* seems like an understatement.

The totality of the aforementioned is to provide context for the following important principle, and the reason for the content and order of the manuscript.

The umbra will end up being the dusty, elusive horizon of man's last frontier, I am sure. What we do know is that the umbra has a size, a density, and a luster (it also has color, but the particulars are well beyond the purview of our paradigm). In aggregate, these attributes are referred to as the mreg *of the umbra. Of all the intricacies and variables inherent to this machine, the mreg is our primary consideration. And though the Subverts have introduced an element of competition into this enterprise, all are keenly aware that helping each other across the street is infinitely more productive than running each other down in the crosswalks. It is a concept the Subverts had to learn the hard way. Mreg is, more or less, an equalizer.*

When we speak of the mreg, it is only useful in the context of an individual. Mreg can certainly be compared one individual to the next; they are measurable attributes, after all, but it would be like observing that Arnold Schwarzenegger is more muscular than Bobby Fischer. The comparison is only practical in a discussion of the native umbra and its future iteration(s), the lendemain(s). As previously noted, a hull can accommodate any number of umbrae, but the right and left limits of this arrangement are strait and unforgiving. The moorings to which an umbra attaches secure all qualifying umbrae, including variations of the native umbra—the lendemains—to the hull. Other umbrae, the xenoumbrae, have the ability to occupy the hull, but these are always just tolerated, fugitive arrangements, and they easily slip from the moorings. This first position is determined by the magnitude of the mreg of any umbra occupying the hull, including the native umbra. All umbrae affixed to the hull are, at all times, vying for control—control of the hull's physical abilities, control of activities of the mind—and the mreg determines which umbra wields that scepter. The more pronounced the difference in magnitude, the more control it exerts over the other occupants. It is, of course, preferable to have the Pik-ing lendemain wield total control of all faculties, but this is only attainable if the mreg of that lendemain significantly outweighs and outmuscles all other umbrae occupying the hull. This is achieved by development of the mreg, a process known as kwazants *(derived from the French croissance, which means growth or increase, but the Subverts didn't like how much it looked like croissant, so they mauled it with transliterations until kwazants came about). We rarely speak of the mreg independent of kwazants, so you will hear reference to the developmental term (kwazants) much more frequently than the construct itself (mreg).*

I have nothing against the French, but I'm already disposed to like these Russians. Their contrariness is hilarious.

Kwazants is the gasoline of this engine. Kwazants is the airbags. Kwazants is why you have this manuscript before you. As with all courses of development in the human experience, exposure breeds capacity. Whether it be academic, physical, musical, mental, the more you do, the more you can. Beneath the surface, this increased capacity is simply expansionary—synapses multiply, muscle cells enlarge, neuromuscular junctions specialize, bones thicken, tissue is repurposed. We are quite familiar with these phenomena. And while these changes occur at a physiological and morphological level, they are also recorded on the umbra. We call this imprinting gravure. *All exposure and experience is dual-routed to the hull and the umbra (as, conversely, is all degradation and atrophy). But we are not quite to kwazants yet. Learning how to play the oboe or speak Tagalog is useful, but has little effect on kwazants (depending on the motivation for learning how to play the oboe or speak Tagalog). The umbra has its own sinews, viscera and neurology, all subject to the same expansionary effects, but whose cells have been differentiated to respond to slightly different stimuli. Without getting too philosophical, kwazants is a function of, at its center, integrity. I'm not talking about that cliché doing-the-right-thing-even-when-no-one's-looking bromide that corporations use to keep employees from stealing pens; I mean the full and honest remittance of the conscience's taxes to remain unburdened and unaudited. It is a tenacious deference to that disapproving glance, a reverence for the folded arms of the third rail. Since a composite of values, morals or ethics, to some degree, is as individual as the architects that design them and the storms that mold them, it is more about one's adherence to that composite than about absolutes, hence integrity as the precipitate.*

Even individuals that share a persuasion or a parish or a household differ so vastly from one another in what constitutes fair or honest or benevolent, the virtues themselves are not worth necropsying. To one, alms is a lifeline; to another, the insulting bloodletting of self-reliance. To one, meekness is a vulnerability that invites exploitation and abuse, to another it is the grandeur of restraint and civility. The umbra, the mreg, is more responsive to the obeisance made to these inherent impositions than to a wholesale, blunt force attack of charity or sympathy. Its muscle cells hypertrophy (kwazants) in the bosom of a guileless Golden Rule. But though the crystalline structure of these composites is infinitely distinct, there is so much overlap at the core, it is only individual at the edges. Nobody abides having a secret betrayed or being wrongly accused or having their property assumed by others; the nuances are in the weeds. There are some duplicitous sophists and relativists that like to bleach black and soil white, but these artifices are always laid bare when they are not the beneficiary of the dissimulation. When they're Robin Hood, theft is virtuous; when they're King Richard, it is, toes to teeth, an abominable immorality.

This reminds me of when he would always say, *Principles do not belong on a palette!* He never mumbled or equivocated, so everything he spoke was exclamation marked.

This general concurrence does not necessarily preclude hypocrisy, only that if the fringes were burned away, it would be an admission of all the same gears in the same arrangement. Most drift tempest-tossed through life on rafts of unsubstantiated dichotomies, live-and-let-live unaccountabilities, rules-for-thee-but-not for-me hypocrisies, and not-my-brother's-keeper slips. We all know this is self-serving poppycock that only works in an unindictable bubble and with a short shelf life, hence the force of integrity's lever as a purifier/putrefier. It matters not that we condemn our conscience to our mind's perdition to prevent whispers from slipping through—we know in our evasive eyes and dorsiflexed feet we are always accountable. Like the bloated dead, liability is difficult to keep submerged, even with cinder blocks. Walking casually past a screaming conscience, notwithstanding the effluvia of eloquent excuses, is atrophy. When the impurities of rationalization are boiled out, the distillate is just a black gum of selfishness and fear, to neither of which kwazants responds. All in all, morality is not as subjective as some promote.

Imagine hearing paragraphs like that thirty times a day—that was my childhood.

This whole enterprise is impossible and improbable on all levels. It is one-hundred percent risk and zero percent reward, and yet here we are. I will leave the Gontlets alone for now, but I feel it might be useful to impress the criticality of this process of kwazants upon you. Walking away with the perception of self-help book will dull the teeth needed to crack these bones. The only way out is through, and since I have dropped you into the thick, I want you to have a sharpened scythe.

This is red letter and worth repeating: all umbrae occupying a hull want full access to, and control of, all faculties—physical, mental, executive, and actionable. Bad things happen when this control is disputed. Kwazants must categorically settle this dispute. The consequences of uncertainty in this regard can be plotted on a continuum from concentration problems to self-control issues to full-scale disconnection from the tether of the apical frame. And you cannot play this game dangling in a Johnny Jump Up that resembles schizophrenia.

Holy. Raging. Headache. You'd think I'd tolerate this better, doing research for a living. This is like talking someone through high-level math without being able to write anything down.

Remember, supplanting all occupants of a hull is a function of an elevation of moral character; those attempting to change things in any significant regard are bound by this premise, and the all-seeing eyes of the premise cannot be deceived. Of course, this eliminates the possibility of receding in time to kill someone, have someone killed, convince someone to kill themselves, sabotage another's life or prospects; steal; etc. Foul intent is atrophy no matter how utilitarian the motivations are on paper. So don't spend a lot of time worrying about your fellows.

A brief word about your fellows. No doubt my memorial service exposed you to the vertebrae of the industry. These are the watchmen who have guarded gates and patrolled byways for the past few centuries—the Merovingian, largely, but the Subverts have well-deserved seats at this table.

The Merovingian are an old European family whose lineage persists in modern-day France. As far as can be traced, at least back to the mid-1750s, the Merovingian discovered the vents, though serendipitously, and have erected a fortress of oaths and vows around what has become an impregnable subculture. Their position is that access to the vents should be limited to those properly trained in their use in order to spare the world incorrigible directions. In other words, they believe only the Merovingian should be allowed to use them to guide the course of history. They have the most experience, after all. Though this may sound self-serving, and we have only a shallow understanding of what they have modified over the past few centuries, the earth marches on relatively intact.

Unfortunately for The Merovingian, in a most improbable manner, a group of Russian skydivers stumbled onto the vents in the mid-90s. Cold War Soviets in the 1950s knew of the vents, but it does not appear that they used them, and that knowledge seemed to have gone underground for a few years until after the collapse of the Soviet Union. It didn't take long for these two communities to become aware of one another. The Merovingian dubbed these Golden Youth the Subverts, as they were bent on exposing the circulation of the vents to a much broader field of participants than the Merovingian thought advisable. The Mero could see a fault creeping through the foundation of their principality. The increase in the number of Russian proselytes was accompanied by an increase in abject consequences (irreparable insanity, unintended deaths, vanishings, suicides, etc.), a phenomenon that buttressed the Mero's argument that they alone should be the gatekeepers. And I appreciate the merit of the Mero's argument—those raised in indigence struggle with the management of sudden wealth. The Subverts have not relented, but they have since retreated to consolidate in their growlery. This is the essence of the face off: the Merovingian want locks and keys, the Subverts believe that opposition for opposition's sake is its own virtue. I am the lone, neutral party in this scheme, and have become a broker, arbiter, and buffer for the Merovingian and Subverts as they reconcile their idealisms with their pragmatisms. There seems to be an element of tribalism in the two sides' approach to the issue, so I have become a valuable, anational intermediary. There's much more to this dynamic than can be reasonably explained, but it is slightly less relevant to your purpi. Just know that these two parties are a permanent fixture in your life now, and that your involvement in this industry will prompt a cold shoulder from the Mero and eagerness from the Subverts. Since the Mero are such an insular society, I have spent considerably more time with the Subverts. Hopefully they will eventually consider you my replacement, but, in the meantime, you should not worry much about them. They are relatively harmless in a tornado full of machetes sort of way.

Yeah, they weren't horrifying or anything. Least of all my own mother. And how did he know he was going to need a replacement? He must have seen his death coming, or orchestrated it somehow. I guess a meticulous planner would plan his death as well.

That may have come across as lugubrious, but this is the whole game. Taper the undisciplined, fractious, unbridled, libertine, and capricious into a tempered scalpel and two-dimensional becomes three-. Since you haven't spent the last ten years engaged in pursuits of self-mastery, there will be some need of physical therapy to rehabilitate these muscles. The manuscript will serve this purpose. It is concentrated, codified kwazants. If you heed ad verbum, when the time comes you will be fit for the gallows.

You're a curious little spanky, I know, but shelve your questions for now. When the sun sets on this morass you will have your answers. Perhaps by then you will have some of the answers we lack.

I hope you tucked yer wee britches into yer wellies, laddie, because now we get to work.

You don't think getting through that was work? Did you really have to pack that with fustian <<I see the irony there>> and metaphor? If there's more, I need another drink. Life rises and falls on what you do with withdrawal symptoms. Along with all that other stuff.

Chapter 15

"The highest tribute to the dead is not grief but gratitude."
– Thornton Wilder

I feel like I just spent the last three hours challenging myself at an all-you-can-eat Chinese buffet. And on I read . . .

Assignment #1: GRATITUDE

Gratitude is seeing things as they really are. It is seeing the ripped seams as the stitches in your deliverance. It is perceiving the bifocality from individual monofocalities. It is the acknowledgement that all the weights and measures are calibrated to both justice and injustice, fairness and unfairness, and that they tend to neither cosmic accommodation nor malign targeting. It is the understanding that every moment, whether catabolic or anabolic, is creation. It is the realization that your harvest exceeds your planting. It is an appreciation for a mathematics that balances even in the presence of only variables. It is the humility to concede that even the failure of fortune is a fortune itself. It is an acknowledgement of your powerlessness, and that all your force and intent and design gets you no closer to your objective than trying to steer a ship on land. It is that black, nitrogenous richness in which all of morality is rooted, and it is the irrigation. It is the beginning of kwazants, it is its end, and it is its weekly massage. As long as you remember that you are not doing any of this and that none of it is being done to you, you can maintain a modesty that is neither diffident nor sanctimonious, and you come to perceive everything in its true nature and context.

Now sit your restless self down and list, with pen and paper, and exhaustively, everything for which you are grateful.

See, this is what I was afraid of. I knew this was going to turn into some self-help program. Right after rewiring the universe, he slams on the breaks with some meaningless chore that will take all of five minutes. On second thought, I see now how this might be necessary.

And don't gimme nunnayer sass and crib milk! I know introspection is anatomizing contumacious closet skeletons, but you either trust the process or end up the disregarded squeak in the subconscious of a sixteen-year-old whose stability is dictated by testosterone.

When you feel like you are done, post it somewhere accessible so you can add to it as needed.

Fine, fine, fine, fine, fine. Whatever. Gratitude. Whatever. I fish a notepad and pen out of a kitchen drawer and sit back down in a miff. He's playing mushy games with me now; he knows I wasn't feeling a lot of gratitude a few days ago and wants to teach me a dirty, diaphanous lesson. Like an idiot, I'm looking around my house for ideas of what I'm grateful for. I know that's not what he's asking for. There's a hatch somewhere that leads to this rabbit hole and I just need to find its half-buried handle.

A full minute has passed in defeated silence. Seriously, am I that entitled that I can't think of a single thing I'm grateful for? Okay, my mother. I am genuinely grateful for my mother. Though, as I'm brushing the dirt away from the edges of that answer, I'm not sure exactly why I'm grateful for my mother. She gave me life and all, yes, but I feel like I need more to justify that answer. This is truly sad. I keep thinking things like, She did the best she could, given the circumstances, but that seems more like an exoneration than a reason. My mom was always available to me and supported everything I ever wanted to do, regardless of the sacrifices she had to make. That's it—that's the hatch.

I'm grateful that I had a dad for as long as I had a dad. I'm grateful that my parents loved each other and showed it, so much so that I knew they were more important to each other than I was to either of them, that their love for each other felt like a force field around me. My dad would always tell me that they had the means of replacing me—he couldn't replace Mom. I'm profoundly grateful to Patch for snatching me from what was sure to be some bleak teen years. And I'm not just saying that because I think there are cameras in the light bulbs. My dad was in Afghanistan so much, I don't think I would have noticed a huge difference after his death, but Mom's putrefying sullenness would have pulverized under the weight of its crushing gravity anything light or happy, or any attempts at such. Patch dynamited that gloomscape, and not only did I have a replacement dad, I had a dad that was present, truly present, and engaged and interested and demanding and wild. I truly felt like I knew my place in the world when he was around. I'm grateful for the security of this house, and that I have a space to create and destroy, animate and decimate, without judgment or interference. I'm grateful for the job that allows me such a liberal and untethered tether. It seemed like a dream as everything was drifting down in soft-landing blocks that fit together squarely and evenly—educated by a mustachioed magnifying glass, that PowerPoint book, a few curriculum samples, a little networking, some word-spreading, and I was self-employed and handsomely compensated.

This may sound disingenuous, but I am grateful to be alive. Especially now. I feel like I know my place in the world again. We shouldn't only be remembered by what we look like stumbling around in the dark, looking for the light switch. And no man has more gratitude for any grace than I do for the over-sweetened, celestrus <<that's a combination of *celestial* and *citrus*>> nectar of the throne room of the eleventh heaven. It is a confection after the art of the apothecary, tempered together, pure and holy. Yes, I am talking about Mountain Dew, and, no, I am not kidding about this. The only thing better than Mountain Dew in this life is Mountain Dew with two packets of Splenda. Hard fact.

I spent the next two hours in a sort of mind diarrhea. Ideas were invading as grasshoppers for multitude. I didn't realize life, even an un-itemized life, could be so gold, silver, brass, and titanium. That magnifying glass brought my schmuckiness into sharp focus. I did some surgery with tape and hung the eight-page, finished-for-now product on my fridge. It couldn't look more ghetto, but it's there and it's done.

The house is still echoingly quiet. I can hear the engine of a commercial jet roaring in the distance. Or maybe that's not such a distant engine. I can hardly tell in the throat of this valley, swallowing, suppressing, regurgitating every sound from Hill Air Force Base to the Salt Lake Airport. The flanking mountain ranges bat these sounds back and forth like a pong board or suck them into endless slot canyons.

Now I can't look at something without feeling some degree of gratitude, like its effect, its utility, its convenience is somehow responsible for all of my good qualities. Curse you, old man! Like my mind isn't already skipping six ways to Sunday! I tape a couple of blank sheets to the bottom of the list hanging from a fridge magnet like a third-grade school project. It was a mild summer. I haven't had a flat tire my whole life. I was born in America. I've never been seriously ill. I've never been mugged. You have to cut it off, Elliot!

Okay, what else . . .

I know you startle easily, so I'll try to ease you into this next part. <<Ah, shiggity briggity . . .>> *And this isn't an affront to your masculinity, but I find your predilection for cheery-colored, economical vehicles that are barely broader than your shoulders a wee bit jessie.* <<How is that not an affront to my masculinity?>> *This is a matter of credibility, so don't be wroth with an old man who just had your car stolen.*

I feel an almost tangible tug at the wire connected to my right elbow. It isn't the manliest of motor carriages, but I like that car. I swear, Patch, you better not be messing with my stuff! It better be safely tucked into its garage-swathed covers, I mutter as I swing the garage door open. Yep, it's gone. How in the hot hoarfrost of Hades did you manage to steal a car that has been no more than thirty feet from me all morning? And from a secured garage! I think to make better use of my doorbell camera and review the footage from the past hour. Doorbell cam, click. Minus one hour, click. Fast forward, click. Whoa. That's impressive. That is art. They're not even that clever in the movies. These operators even make the saccadic, keystone-copish twitches look pretty smooth. Uh . . . you forgot something, guys . . .

The footage overtakes real time and a vehicle I assume belongs to the car thieves sits majestically, reflecting the world with buffed wax in my driveway. I watch for several minutes in case they come back for it. Or it blows up. I don't know why I think the peephole will give me a better view than the doorbell camera, but I look through it anyway. Everything is as serene and unmoving as it has sounded all morning. I make an unwarranted racket unlocking the front door in case that discourages an ambush. I tiptoe to my driveway like a monstrosity of stealth.

This black machine is devouring the autumnal blaze of its backdrop. The olive of the prairie grass flattening to the north is washed out to a cooling white; the rivers of purple tipped grass coursing like veins hither and thither are bled to a graying drab; the shadows of the clouds burrowing into the cracks in the mountains look more skittishly mauve; the horizon melts into the clouds, or vice versa maybe, in a haze of browns, purples, and grays with no discernible hue one way or another. This vitreous demon of a Dodge RAM 3500 mega cab seems to pulse and heave as it sucks color and light out of the world.

I make three full laps around the beast, hoping that marking my territory will actually make it mine. Maybe I should pee on it. It's a distorted representation of the absorbed vibrancy of vicinal landscaping, blinding chrome, tinting, polished rubber, and a black and silver Pittsburgh Steelers logo where you'd typically see the ram on the tailgate. It's something I could see Jack Lambert, Jack Ham, and Joe Greene piling into to get a burger after beating the pudding out of the Denver Broncos. It's flexing, screaming, bone-crushing virility.

I accept your trade, you wily Scot. Between that wired Godfather spy suit and a machine that chuckles at small mountain ranges, I feel like I've been officially inducted into this Mero-Subvert mafia.

Don't hurt yourself trying to unwind all this waggery. I prefer things go as planned. The keys are in your nightstand. <<My nightstand? Seriously?>> This gratitude list is important. Keep it accessible, keep it visible, add to it often. It is a reliable check against runaway egoism and the misapplication of merit. Before it came to pass I shewed it thee: lest thou shouldest say, mine idol hath done them, and my graven image, and my molten image. What you are about to accomplish is bigger than the measurable universe; signposts, grunts, index fingers, vigilance, and intuition will get you much of the way. Make sure you recognize and acknowledge these ministrations. Supplanting them with your brilliance is ruin and atrophy.

I will not often crowd your life with these assignments. Today and tomorrow will be a rare exception. I have to preface tomorrow's today because you'll need to give yourself time tomorrow morning to read the day's assignment and be at the Bonneville Salt Flats by first light, 6:44 a.m.

Yikes. That is early. Early is bad. Satan is in the dark. And what about that weirdo dream I had last night? I dream about the Salt Flats, then I'm to visit them the next day?

Elliot, I know I am but a memory, but I'd prefer not to be. I know I am putting hooks in your jaw and upending your life, but I fear conveying the appropriate level of urgency will elicit an exaggerated response. I just need you on pace to destroy the Walter Paytons and O.J. Simpsons of Columbia and Richmond County high school football programs, to eat the flesh of the mighty, drink the blood of the princes of the earth, be filled at the table with horses and chariots, with mighty men, and with all men of war. Just be strong and quit yourself like a man and you will be all buckler and shield.

Now stop reading.

CHAPTER 16

"I believe the game is designed to reward the ones who hit the hardest. If you can't take it, you shouldn't play."
— Jack Lambert

Schools of fish are making sharp, broken columns in my brain. I think they're showing a protein how to fold. Scratching or massaging my scalp does nothing to settle their futzing about. The moment I have a thought, they nibble at it and excrete the bits elsewhere so I can't address it as an intact musing. I remember this feeling, sitting in biology or history or trying to make sense of my inanity-fuzzed teammates at lunch—sharp, broken columns of linebacker drills were always superimposing themselves on everything in my foreground. But . . . but now I have the option of walking away from my foreground and indulging the superimposition.

I *am* going to be a linebacker soon. And I do need a break.

I'm changing into workout clothes <<putting on sneakers since I live in workout clothes>>. I grab an agility ladder and jog the two miles down Legacy Parkway Trail to one of the many green cutouts in suburban Woods Cross. The sign reads Mountain Valley Park. *Mountain Valley* is as clever as *Land with Grass* in this vast mountain valley. The park, like ninety percent of these parks ninety percent of the time, is empty. I claim the corner of a soccer field and stretch the agility ladder out. Despite a decade pause, my feet brains and their perfect recall are already halfway down the ladder, my arms pumping like a train's crank rod. I can hear Coach Caterwaul as he follows me down the ladder: *Knees are too high! Faster with the arms—the arms drive the feet! Ickey Shuffle, go! Riverdance, go! Carioca, go!*

As a teenager, I'd rest with my hands on my hips. Now I'm on my knees, ears ringing, my chest doubling in size with each gasp, pulling the grass up so I don't lose consciousness.

Bunny hops, go! Foot exchange, go! I'm one of those idiots who, if he's taking the time to exercise, tries to murder himself or he feels like he's wasting his time. *Economize your motion! Tighten it up! Eyes straight ahead!* I'm tracking Mike Pruitt on a sweep from Brian Sipe as I'm doing lateral in and outs.

I know I'll say this every time I go outside, but I forgot how good it feels to just *be* outside. Fifty-eight degree air, even at four thousand feet, is way better than indoor air. <<Remember to record *outdoor air* on gratitude list.>>

I survey the length of the crumpled Wasatch Front from north to south and try to conceptualize a frame. It seems like a lot of data to catalog ten thousand times every second. I wonder if there's a way to slip under the apical frame and get into one of these vents with the hull intact. I don't like all this quick-stop death talk. Do these nascent vent nautilus tracks get close to Salt Lake City? If it corkscrews around the Earth in a counterclockwise track from north to south for nearly a month, it would have to.

Reverse crossover, go! Hip twist, go!

DAY 2

Chapter 17

"Go to heaven for the climate and hell for the company."
– Mark Twain

Mornings are Satan's tongue-rot morning breath. My alarm heralds a doped fuzz that's like regaining consciousness after a face-bruising, rib-breaking beating. Wake up at 4 a.m., 8 a.m., noon, it doesn't matter; it takes just as long for that soupy anesthetic to wear off. And trying to roll out of that sandbox of a mattress at my size doesn't help matters.

I figure it takes about an hour and a half to get to the Salt Flats from here; I'll give myself an hour to read this next assignment, twenty minutes to eat something, sixty seconds to dress and groom, and I have to be there by 6:45 a.m. <<6:44 a.m.>> So here I am at 3:45 a.m. cursing the cupboards or the cameras in the light bulbs or that eavesdropping suit or wherever that sadistic Scot is keeking from. I don't even have enough energy to raise my fist and shake it. Just know that you're being cursed, old man!

Let's see how much damage you're going to inflict today . . .

Assignment #2: CONCENTRATION

To the Gontlets!

Great. I don't think my stomach can handle Dew this early.

Heaven, hell, purgatory, paradise, prison, perdition, underworld, waiting room—all of them and none of them quite serve our purpose here. Each is gorged with prejudice and preconception, so to settle on one would be misleadingly lazy. And if you were able to poll the entities of the Gontlets, their descriptions would vary so wildly you would wonder if any of them knew quite where they were, or if they actually shared a common location. Which, in many senses, they do not. Though I previously defined the Gontlets as the spaces between frames, the space above the principal apical frame is also an inhabitable Gontlet, by far the most *inhabited Gontlet. A variety of beings reside, some temporarily, some permanently, in these spaces. It is a multi-generational, multi-phasic, multi-dimensional playhouse.*

I'm smooshing my head at the temples to see if I can squeeze this morning katzenjammer out of my eyeballs.

A full taxonomic catalog of the beings inhabiting the Gontlets would exhaust you in one sitting, so I have spread the designations out across the length of the manuscript. <<There's a full taxonomic catalog?>> *For the purpi of this assignment, all the entities of the Gontlets are there for a specific, albeit different, reason. Some know the reason, some do not, but all occupants are a hazard—those that do not know why they are there (or that they are there) only slightly less so. Though some are engaged in an objective reality, most are mired in a subjectivity that is played out independent of every other entity in the Gontlets. They are in their proverbial own little world. This stew of knowing, knowing but not knowing what to do, and not knowing has the effect of muddying your own calculations of the Gontlets. You will invariably be stirred into these clashes of collateral, intentional, and intentionally collateral.*

Though some will see you and some will not, you are visible to every entity in the Gontlets. Some will interact with you directly (and promptly) and have an explicit and scripted agenda, some are officiously and disingenuously helpful, some are of ancient date and will know you from beyond the compass of your memory, some will attempt to coopt you as an extra or even supporting cast in their mind's production; for some you will be a confusing vagabond in their delusion, some are lonely and simply want company, some will contend with you as though you were an existential threat, some you will recognize because they were famous, some will recognize you because they knew you when they were living, some will know precisely what you are doing there and will make genuine efforts to help you on your way, and some only want to blind you, snare you, and devour you. It is not always immediately apparent which is which.

Sounds a little like high school. So, are we talking dead people here or are there other entities in the Gontlets? Some know they're there and some don't? Some know they're there but don't know what to do? Sounds more like hell than heaven. And some *can* see me but *won't* see me?

The only way out is through the broad avenues of these interactions. There are no vacant alleyways or country roads in the Gontlets.

As previously mentioned, as archived frames are generated from the surface of this construct, Gontlets fall for one hundred and twenty years toward the petram at the depths before they are pressed out of service. Any occupant of the Gontlets is free to move throughout the entire one hundred and twenty-year frameset, anywhere there is a functional Gontlet. Though some know this and some do not, most are urged apical-ward by a capitulating buoyancy dictated by a less reality-jarring sequence of advancing motion. To some, the Gontlets are contusing enough without the world standing still, or worse, moving in reverse. But remember, the principal apical frame is not the only active apical frame in the frameset, and these entities are fine keeping pace with any apical frame (including reconstituted apical frames) as they all mimic a familiar progression of time.

So, as I'm falling down in a vent, will the world appear to be going in reverse?

As you will be laterally traversing a single, static frame once you enter the Gontlet, any attempt to engage you will result in that entity's cessation of forward (apical-ward) progress through the frames. The world around you, the frame, will be a moment as frozen as the single page of a flipbook animation, but the Gontlet will be like a well-attended job fair with aggressive recruiters vacillating in tone and manner between saccharin and insistent.

To think, I'm one of those statues on a freeze-frame hologram all this madness is maneuvering around . . .

There are those that are preoccupied with the entities of the frames (frame direction and speed being a primary concern) and those that are preoccupied with the entities of the Gontlets (frame direction and speed being nearly irrelevant). You will mostly concern yourself with the latter, as they will mostly concern themselves with you. The former will be virtual blips as they try to keep pace with the advancing frameset, and, commonly, the aftermath of their veiled demise—that is, unless they are so distracted by your presence they are willing to endure the confusion and agitation of the sputtering frame into which they have debarked. Which is less likely. Just know that the majority of this category will follow standard frame progression at or near the principal apical frame and you will need not contend with them.

Though the Gontlets are a strobe-lit haunted house on a Gravitron full of Raiders of the Lost Ark *booby traps with fire raining down from heaven, it is not the external elements that pose the most proscriptive obstructions. The most proscriptive obstruction is your mind. I do not know if preparing you for this state will make it better or worse, but I would be remiss if I did not say something.*

You will be a disengaged umbra, emancipated from the bridles and dictates imposed by the hull. A tar-soaked hood will be pulled off all sensory organs—the volume, the brightness, the sensitivity, the peripheral angles, the proprioception, and the reception will all be enhanced and fine-tuned. Your mind will be trying to reconcile the near lawlessness of the Gontlets with the inviolable strictures of physical law. It will feel like a super-charged dream but you will know you are not dreaming. You will not notice the consummate timelessness of your circumstance until you recouple with the time-governing sprockets of the hull. It will be such a saturated experience; your attention will be pulled to the margins and tangents. You will have the tendency to slip from the stage to a seat in the audience, like your exploding consciousness is something to be excitedly observed, and you will be less inclined to act purposefully. When I say virtual blips, it still amounts to a landscape of multiplicative double takes raised to powers. It's like sprinting through a corn field filled with swarms of gnats.

That sounds pretty cool. I've always felt like a million colors just doesn't do this world justice.

The xenoumbrae of these spaces will exploit this enhanced and compromised consciousness to redirect, weigh down, and overwhelm. These are tenured

residents of the Gontlets who have spent millennia retooling fairness and cour-
tesy and compassion to cajole. Some of these entities find you more useful in the
Gontlets than in a hull. Some just want you to be lost and miserable because
they are lost and miserable. Some have designs for you. Earlier, I mentioned
the magnetism of the native hull for any lendemain sharing an archived frame.
Magnetism is a little misleading here (there are no good analogies in the Gont-
lets!) since there is no actual, physical pull. A lendemain does not have to go
searching for its hull, but it does take a degree of focus to clear a path through
the Gontlet, like trying to do math in your head while some cheeky arsewhistle
is yelling out random numbers.

Which brings me to your assignment.

Finally. I don't think I could have lasted much longer at this hour. Filthy, rat
poison, rotting flesh mornings!

You will encounter many such exercises throughout the manuscript, but
I'll keep the warm up to basic mental calisthenics. You need to develop strate-
gies to vividly and firmly hold images, sequences, and dialogues in your head
regardless of the intensity and intimacy of external stimuli. Because few have the
discipline to develop this ability, it is more a superpower than a parlor trick. You
have developed superpowers before, so this should be a snap. You will need to
be that linebacker tracking the ball like a circling shark.

Go to the Salt Flats Rest Area just off of I-80 westbound. Dress warmly.
Bring a pen and notepad. Bring a head lamp. You will need to hear, so no head-
phones, no music. Bring a camping chair. Park on the east side of the parking
lot and walk straight north two hundred yards. Be seated and facing east by
6:44 a.m. Record in the notebook what you see and hear as expressly and as
explicitly as your morning-fogged mind allows. Pin your mind to a composition
of the incremental alterations that accompany the lapse in time. Do nothing else.
Think about nothing else. Just watch, listen, and write until the sun is full twenty
degrees and the variations cease to be significant.

At least it's sitting.

When you're done, proceed to Papelbon Security Solutions on East Broad-
way, Suite C, in Salt Lake. Mr. Papelbon will assist you in completing the assign-
ment.

Now stop reading and go!

CHAPTER 18

"Here comes the sun."
– "Here Comes the Sun," The Beatles

Camping chair, head lamp <<how did he know I had a head lamp?>>, pen, notebook, keys to that acid-spitting black dragon in the driveway. Dress warmly. And I'm off to the Bonneville Salt Flats at this wretched hour.

I turn the key and hear the growling displeasure of an entire firmament of tumbling thunder. My heart is warmed. That rich floor mat-leather seats-vinyl new car smell . . . only the smell of bacon rivals it. The tread on the tires is making a flapping hum as I travel south on 1100 West. Everything is displays and menus and symbols and buttons. This is truly the first-class of automotive experiences. Did I mention the glorious new car smell?

Salt Lake City is a metropolis tightly flanking I-15. A fifteen-minute drive to the east or west and you're on a mountain or in a desert. Ten minutes of westbound I-80 and I'm in a land of brimstone and salt and burning. Even in the daylight, the colors of this desolation are washed out versions of olive and flax and beige and gray; the crops of mountains moving away to the west are indistinguishable browns and shadows; the only color is the black of recently shredded truck tires.

But at this hour, even with my high beams, the only color I get is shapes. It gets impressively dark outside of the city. I can tell I'm getting close—even in the dark everything is white when you approach the Salt Flats.

It's 6:34 a.m. My timing is impeccable. I park on the east side of the parking lot, grab my gear, and hike two hundred yards north. *It's cold as a witch's tit* <<Patchism>> out here. Somebody must have opened a window in Tooele, and one in Wendover; *by what way is the light parted, which scattereth the east wind upon the earth.* How am I supposed to write in this vortex? I snap the chair open, strap on the head lamp, tuck the notebook in one drink holder and a bottle of water in the other, fold myself in my trusty blanket, and plop my fluffy <<Mom's polite term for *fat*>> self down, facing east.

First light, 6:44 a.m. Focus now.

I was hoping the moon would be visible to illuminate anything, but it's not. The heaven that is over my head is iron and the earth that is under me is brass. Or salt, in this case.

A thin, dark blue anti-serration begins to separate the heavens from the serrated edge of the low mountains emerging from the void, like teeth from the half-buried key to Hell's gates. The anti-serration pales and the segregation spills to the north and south—a bolt of cerulean lightning streaking <<inching>> left and right across saw blade channels from its central cauldron. The dark blue blinds are pushed up in softening waves pulsing from the yet faceless serration. A dark, rusty haze is draping itself across the teeth and the eye shadow of this closed eye of color shifts impossibly from fire to heat to smoke to the sea to gunpowder. The eyelid broadens and retains mostly yellows and blues, revealing disruptive, dawn-obscuring eels and egrets sweeping their charcoal bodies across the darker blues of the heights. The glory low-crawling to the eastern horizon fires its first salvo and the pinks and purples of the veins and arteries of eels and egrets are splashed across the morning. <<I think I just told the sun to slow down a little too loudly.>> Blues and grays both soften and harden the lines of the clouds as the light skirts around their contours. Washes of indeterminate color blossom across the surface in anticipation of the low-crawling glory cresting the horizon. Forms and shadows are sliding down the mountains like a glacier and . . .

Okay, that's weird. Has he been here the whole time? He's got no shirt on! It's freezing out here! About a hundred yards to the east is a guy doing kata without a shirt on. Is he just doing kata in the dark? On the Salt Flats? Where is this guy coming from? There are absolutely no other cars in the parking lot. You can't walk here from anywhere. The Bonneville Salt Flats are quite literally nowhere. Strangest thing I've ever seen. I feel like I'm going to tire of hearing myself say that pretty soon.

I don't remember Patch specifying what I needed to record, only that I record explicitly and expressly what I see and hear. I see a lunatic doing kata in the darkness of cold, nowhere Utah.

The spectral skin of this prone and sprawling crocodile is emerging at the borders of its scales. The termini of the karateka are snapping and repositioning so fast it seems like I can see through his silhouette-defined negative to the light of the arrows and shining of the glittering spear beyond. The demi-sun bobbing on the horizon burns away the karateka's edges and all that can be seen of him is the limbless dance of a dark torso. How is it that he happens to be directly between me and the rising sun? That can't be coincidental. As I scan to the left and right, the brackish scales move like the cellular reorganization of light at the bottom of a swimming pool. The sun is pressed between the horizon and a fry of bleeding eels decomposing in the lower morning altitudes.

Okay, now what? I hear a weak hissing sound and this expanse is half echo chamber, half soundproof booth, so I can't tell where it's coming from. I struggle to shift my tree trunk of a body to the left and I see someone a couple hundred yards to the north. It looks like he's trying to mow the Salt Flats with a large bottle rocket. No, that's one of those paint wands they use to mark utilities and stuff. I wonder if that has to do with something going on at the raceway. But this early in the morning? In the dark? There is weirdness at the Salt Flats today. Although, to the karateka, I may look a little weird sitting in the middle of the Salt Flats at dawn's crack with a headlight. And now Mr. Painter Dude is running away at a full sprint . . .

So, was I supposed to focus all of my attention on the sunrise and the karate dude and the brine landscaper were the distractions, or was I just supposed to focus my attention on whatever I saw or heard? It implied the sunrise, but I don't presume to know the mind of the magi. Maybe I didn't understand the assignment—

SHIT! Shit! Shit! Shit! Shit on a dairymaid's doily! Both of my arms are enshrouding my head and I'm sprinting with reckless abandon back to the truck, my vestibular organs trying to keep up with legs outrunning their feedback. When I make it back to the truck, my lungs are like peach pits and all they let me do is cough. Man, two hundred yards is a long run at that pace. I'm hands on knees until the pharynx-crowding urge to puke passes. At least I'm two hundred yards farther from whatever that was. I want to collect my thoughts and composure in the truck, but the key is still in one of the chair's cup holders. I was already half way back to the truck before I realized I'd left everything behind.

I can't get all the connection points to my torso to stop shaking. It's reassuringly quiet, so I bravely emerge from my defilade. A hollowed plume of salty powder hangs like a stent in the pink air. It's right where that spray painter dude was a little while ago. And that karate dude is still doing kata, like nothing happened. Maybe he has headphones in, but there's no way he didn't *feel* that. It felt like a bomb had gone off. From the dimensions of the plume, maybe not a bomb, but there was some power in that percussion. I don't know what you'd call an explosion whose crunchy barbs were filed down by a boom with a breathy peal, but it was like Atlas stomped his foot <<I understand the absurdity of the logistics of that prospect; it's just for emphasis>>. I felt the ground sink a little beneath me. How can that guy carry on without any pause for curiosity? I was half way to next week before it registered that I was at a full sprint! He's even facing the freaking plume! I would go ask him if he felt that, but the whole situation feels so unnatural that I'm sure he'll just end up being a hologram or something. Patch is in this somehow. This has a distinct Patch feel to it.

Why am I just thinking of that now? Oh, crap. I think I just failed the assignment.

I storm back to my chair like a bratty toddler. Oh, I'll watch, listen, and write, all right. I grab my notebook and march my sassy self directly to the crash/detonation/impact/whatever-that-was site <<hoping I'm not walking into unexploded ordnance>>. I'll play your game, you baby-snatching dingo. As my stride lengthens with determination, I'm tempted to stop and record the novelty of these little parapet-bounded countries I'm passing too fiercely. It really does look eerily reptilian.

I'm looking left and right as I speed walk with pouty hips just in case there's a genocide or bio-attack I should also be paying attention to. I can't get past the strangeness of the situation. *With the soles of my feet have I dried up all the rivers, out of my nostrils goeth smoke, and the streams thereof shall be turned into pitch, and the dust thereof into brimstone, and the land thereof shall become burning pitch.* This scene, this place, it has a very familiar otherworldliness.

As my height begins to offer me a clearer view of the devastation, I can see a circle of glittery black paint about thirty meters in diameter framing a shallow crater. I stop walking and consider that observation. Thirty meters . . . oh, no. Oh, please, please don't tell me . . . I start step-dragging sideways towards my horror.

You have got to be kidding me. Patch, this is too much! What am I supposed to do with this? <<I think I said that part out loud.>>

Watch, listen, and write . . . I circle the paint <<I've seen forensics shows; I ain't gettin' that jive on my shoes>> so I have the best view of my subject. I try to shake the discombobulation out of my head. Holy heights of heaven this guy is so disgustingly dead. If my hands were free, I would be wringing them. Hopefully Patch has accounted for the fact that standing near a dead body could implicate me in his death. I look back at the karateka in case I need an alibi. And wouldn't you know it, he's gone. Great. I start to write, neglecting to record the part about me running away: a tangle of unnatural contortions collapsed the reptilian skin in on itself and a dark mud has coagulated beneath the puncture. The puddle of disjointed, yellow and black jumpsuit is face down. Much of his head is buried in the mud, but it's clear he's not wearing a helmet. Very little blood for an impact that moved the earth. Some has pooled at a knee joint that has violated all the laws of the patella. I don't know a lot about skydiving, but that's definitely a parachute, and it definitely didn't open.

I get it—it's a prelude. Come to think of it, this spandex warp of chiral symmetry could very well be me. Though it might take some time for me to work out if that's possible. I haven't Pik-ed yet, so I should exist at the principal apical frame, right? Maybe I have Pik-ed, but . . . no, I don't think I can have two hulls on the same frame. I should probably be mulling this over somewhere else. I know it's just in my head, but a puffy self-consciousness is projecting sounds and noises in every direction. As I turn to hightail, I notice something I hadn't before. Aside from the circle, there's an arrow painted in the southeast quadrant of the circle that's pointed in a south-southeasterly direction. I write that down. Then hightail. More accurately, I shuffle my feet to erase all comings-to and goings-from shoe prints from the scene.

The sun is full twenty degrees. The variations have ceased to be significant. <<I'm not actually looking to see if any of that is true.>>

CHAPTER 19

"You can fool some of the people all of the time, and all of the people some of the time, but you cannot fool all of the people all of the time."
– Abraham Lincoln

That was the first time I've been around death in person. Human death, anyway. Come to think of it, I didn't check to see if he was actually dead. Again, forensic shows—I know better than to cross-transfer. But the karateka . . . the karateka I'm sure was either a hologram or was somehow a ground controller for these improbable histrionics, so I'm sixty percent sure I don't need to find him and snuff him out. <<I'm mafioso now; I need to sound the part, right?>> So, first time I've seen what looked convincingly like human death. I feel innocences suffocating in the mud with that faceless pulp, and the bubbles of their last breaths are moving through the thickness with a fatal wheeze. I'm a little disappointed the matter didn't elicit a more softhearted seizure. My emotional venesection almost seems passive, like someone's reading it to me rather than experiencing it myself. I guess when you suspect that every unlikely thing swirling around you is flimflam, you're less inclined to be fragmented by it. Something like, *there is no spoon*. And this is a puzzle. Patch knows I can't resist a good puzzle. Puzzles, even puzzles cluttered with dead bodies, are still puzzles.

I enter Papelbon Security Solutions, Salt Lake City, into the navigator, whose display is nearly as big as a standard iPad. I swear I'm in the cockpit of a B-21. And the median of apricot-banked white sand rivers wedged between the opposing directions of I-80 is the perfect bombing run.

Once I get up to speed and let the dashed center line hypnotize me, the house lights of my mind dim and the curtains are drawn. The parachute didn't malfunction, the skydiver never released it. The skydiver meant to die. He got up to a certain speed that would ensure death at the apical frame and propel his umbra into a vent. The paint circumscribed the position at which a passing nascent vent would be located at the very moment the skydiver needed to impact the ground. Good hell, the timing of that intersection would have to be surgically precise if the nascent vent has to spiral the face of the Earth from North Pole to eighty degrees south latitude in twenty-nine and a half days. I'm assuming the arrow indicated the direction the vent was travelling. He said it was a counterclockwise movement, so the vent would have to be moving south-southeast. The body was fairly close to the arrow, so maybe it's advisable to position yourself closer to the head than the tail of a vent. While the skydiver's body is violently barred entry to the vent by the inflexible physicality of the apical frame <<the ground>>, the umbra falls <<I'm using Patch's directional scheme since it appeals to my logic>> through the shaft of the vent to a depth determined by the speed at impact. The umbra is falling through a hole punching through archived frames where greater depth equals farther back in time. When the umbra reaches the prescribed depth, it is ejected into the Gontlet where it kind of worms its way past buskers, knaves, and devils-may-care until it rejoins its native hull and reactivates that archived frame as its new apical frame, and the clock starts ticking again for that individual.

Miles of distribution centers and industrial parks backdropped by a berm of brown mountains backdropped by a berm of black mountains welcome me back to civilization.

I roll up <<grumbling through jugular acid glands>> to Papelbon Security Solutions and park on the south side of the street. I immediately recognize this façade. As I cross the street, I notice, to my left, a familiar storefront: the Proper Gentleman. A street with a Patch shell company theme—this is definitely *turf*. I stop on the sidewalk and see Vivian looking at me through the window. Rather mournfully. Then she's gone. I *am* feeling a little stubbly . . .

Suite C, Papelbon Security Solutions. This guy must get his office furniture from the same catalog as that automaton lawyer because . . . there's no office furniture in here. I'm standing in a fifteen by eight foot nothingness with a single door on the wall opposite that has an Employees Only placard. I just stand there and wait for the punchline.

Then the door pops open.

"Mr. Dillinger! I hope you haven't been waiting long."

"Just arrived."

"We've been waiting for you! Come in. Come in."

I look around for the *we*. He ushers me into another fifteen by eight foot vacancy and closes the door behind me. A foldout table with some equipment and a laptop separates two simple office chairs. One, the one I'm sure I'll be sitting in, has a thin black pad on the seat and faces perpendicular to the other. I introspectively observe that this company clearly didn't exist until this morning.

"Have a seat, Mr. Dillinger. Let's make sure you're comfortable."

"So . . . what's going on?"

"We're just going to run you through a few mental exercises. Nothing difficult, promise."

Again, I look around. Does he not know that *we* is plural?

I take a seat. Something around my torso, clamped on my finger, blood pressure cuff, a pad under my feet. "This is a lie detector."

"No," he corrects. "Lie detectors are fictional. This is an *emotion* detector. It's important that you know there's a distinction."

"You're saying lie detectors don't exist?"

"I'm saying lie detectors do not exist, and never have. The term *lie detector* is only used to perpetuate the myth that a machine exists that can read people's minds. I have been a polygrapher for thirty-five years and I would rely more on the flip of a coin to out a liar than this machine. This is just a tool to scare you into thinking we've caught you in a lie so you spill your guts. Most of the time I tell people the machine says they're lying, even though the test results are clean, just to scare them into giving me something. It's all a bluff. And it always works. People have a lot more faith than they give themselves credit for."

"So why am I here? I haven't done anything." As I say that, my conscience is bashing a puddle of Lycra with a hammer. A warming head and cracking knuckles tell me my tattletale limbic system is lighting up like the Rockefeller Center on Christmas Eve.

"Whether you have or not is irrelevant. It's an emotion detector, remember. If you give me appropriate emotional reactions when I ask for them, you will walk away with conclusive results."

"Are emotions that easy to create . . . or suppress?"

"That, too, is irrelevant. We're not here to create or suppress emotion, we're here to overwhelm the machine with emotional noise. But, yes, emotions are easy to create. With a little practice. You just won't be using the emotions the tester is looking for. I hear you're a fast learner so this shouldn't take too long."

"Are you saying I'm here today to learn how to beat a lie det—a polygraph?"

"Beat? I don't know about beat. I'm just helping you use your mind in a way you probably haven't spent a lot of time developing. It will result in conclusive polygraph results, yes, but that will be incidental to our primary task. Now shut up and sit still."

After the morning I've had, I could use a good sit still.

"Since your experiences this morning are still fresh, we'll use those." <<My experiences? What does he know of my experiences?>> "And they provide a useable contrast. I want you to look straight ahead at the wall. Don't close your eyes, just stare at the blank wall. Your responses will be limited to yes and no. Do not say anything else." He pauses and emphasizes his point with direct eye contact. "I repeat, do not say anything else. You will lie to every question I ask you. Some will feel like consequential lies, some won't. I don't want you to pay much attention to the content of the question, only enough to know what your answer needs to be for it to be a lie. We need to practice something first, so stare at the wall, listen to my voice, and secure this image in your head: You are sitting comfortably. You're outside. It's cold out, but your body is wrapped in warmth and the wind is cooling your face. It's a wide-open space but it's quiet. Nobody's there but you and nobody can ever get to this place but you. The light is breaking over the mountains and turning the clouds brilliant colors. Now hold as many elements of that narrative as you can in your mind for ten seconds."

The wind *was* nicely counterbalancing the rolling effectiveness of that blanket. And the clouds were stretched taffy rainbows pulled from hot pink to lilac and glazing—

"When I ask a question that would elicit a more consequential lie, this is the experience you hold in your mind. Not just the image, but all sensory facets you can incorporate—sounds, sights, smells, sensations—the whole experience.

Keep staring at the wall; here's the second exercise. You're standing over a mangled skydiver—"

"Hey—"

"Quiet!" he barks. "I'm not interested. You're standing over a mangled skydiver in the middle of the Salt Flats. All of the limbs are bent in unnatural ways. It's dark and it looks like things are crawling out from under the skydiver. There's more blood than mud in that crater. You turn the skydiver over and see your grandfather's blood-soaked face, his eyes wide open. All of his teeth are broken and his jaw is cocked unnaturally to the right. You know at that moment he's dead because of something you did. Now hold as many elements of that narrative as you can in your mind for ten seconds."

The entitlement I've developed by virtue of my size has been nipped and my reflexes are rattling their cages, demanding that their proxies strangle this disrespecter of persons with the folding table. Reflex notwithstanding, I know, not that deeply, that this polygrapher is really Patch. I know that everyone I encounter from now on will, more or less, be an agent of the Marionettist. I turn the skydiver over . . . I turn the skydiver over and it's Patch. I can feel black pitch burning the walls of ventricles and aortas and intercostals and freezing my ears. I'm a whorl of rage and pity and penitence. Why did he have to add those details about the teeth and jaw? That's disturbing.

"I will be asking you three specific questions that won't evoke a significant response when you lie. For those questions you will hold this scenario in your mind. Those questions are, Is your name Elliot Dillinger? Are the lights on in this room? and Are you in Salt Lake City? Do you understand all of these instructions?"

"Yes, sir."

"Good. Let's get started. Breathe steadily. Don't move, don't sniff, don't yawn, and most importantly, don't talk unless you're saying yes or no to a question. Again, do not say *anything* other than yes or no. Clear?"

"Yes."

"I'm going to let the equipment calibrate for thirty seconds and then start. Just sit still, stare at the wall, and focus your mind. Is your name Elliot Dillinger?"

"No." Cadaverous snakes wind in weaves, blood slipping from their lime-tinted, moonlit scales. I know he said crawling, but this is just what popped in my head. I reach my hand into the shallow puddle of blud <<blood mud>> and turn the body over from the front of the left shoulder. Oh, Patch. The constriction of my heart feels like a dying sort of weeping. Gossamers of blood move in arched filaments across his open eyes. Larger drops are festooned along the curled ends of his musta—

"Have you ever had sexual intercourse with your mother?"

You foul sod! My mouth <<and much of the rest of my body>> is forming the word *no* and it takes some effort to force a *yes* out. Remember, Elliot, it's an emotion detector. Just play the game. "Yes." For a split second my paranoia hopes this isn't being recorded. This could be pretty damning out of context. The eyebrow-raising eyelid of color captures more bumpy streaks in the deep swipe of its eyeshadow. The wind sweeps the warmth of the gurgling light out of the valley. I'm warm and the stillness has the effect of Vivian running her fingers through my hair. The rust of the serration crumbles into—

"Are the lights on in this room?"

"No." Larger drops are festooned along the curled ends of his mustache. His Brylcreem-sculpted hair is matted and gritty. I can't get his eyes to look at me. How can something with so much life be so heavily lifeless? What did I do to—

"Have you ever Pik-ed?"

I feel my body jerk a little.

Well that's odd. Why would he do that? Now I have to consider that this guy might be a spy for the Merovingian. Wouldn't they already know the answer to that question? He said that lendemains aren't affected by the update, so anyone that has Pik-ed would know that I haven't. Or wouldn't they know? But Patch had me come to this address at this time, so this must be his guy, no? But anybody could have known that this was going to be happening <<supposing with all this time jumping they could know anything>> and liquidated Patch's guy. But this guy just taught me how to subvert a polygraph, so I could just tell the truth and make it look like a lie or lie and make it look like the truth. He would have to be Patch's guy; who else would know that I even knew what Pik-ing is? Again, this has Patch's fingerprints all over it. This is definitely a punch-counterpunch blender he'd throw me into . . . to *assess*. Well, if you want to play games, White Man Whitman, let's play games.

"Yes." The rust of the serration crumbles into a white powder and the light seeps into alluvial crevices. The parapets of the sallow scales brighten at the horse road. The clouds bleach except at the floor and corners where they work light grays into fainting pinks—

"Have you ever stolen a car?"

"Yes."

This went on for another hour. A soul waxing hour. At the conclusion, he showed me all the graphs. It didn't take me very long to exaggerate responses to the controls and tame the consequential deception. By the end I was convinced that this is one of Patch's guys. Just based on gut. And I have a substantial gut.

I'm both asking and answering why I just had to depose the supremacy of the misnomered lie detector. I now understand that no man has the ability to discover what is going on in my head unless I explicitly tell him. And even then, can those words be trusted? How many situations have I avoided because I was sure direct eye contact or a quick scan of my body language or smelted intuition would lay my thoughts bare without a word, without consent? If their darling truth-exposer can be dethroned in twenty minutes, I am an impregnable fortress with ravelins and murder holes and arrow loops. I feel my eyes widening, my chin lifting, my scapulae pulling my shoulders back. I suddenly feel my size.

DAY 5

Chapter 20

"I fear not the man who has practiced 10,000 kicks once, but I fear the man who has practiced one kick 10,000 times."
– Bruce Lee

I'm marveling at how much this past week has chucked me around. It's like being on the end of a frog's tongue in a business of flies—snapped out and jerked back until I'm sick. I've been to a funeral filled with kamikaze time travelers, to a libratory I didn't even know Patch had not twenty minutes away, I beat a lie detector <<*emotion* detector, whatever>>, I saw a freshly dead body, I started running again, I got a bitchin' new truck, my tailored suit spied on Russians <<and the French, I guess>>, and I was groomed by the hands and blades of a goddess. Keratin is filling the dead and dying cells of deeper and deeper layers and I'm feeling bulletproof. Or at least bullet absorbent. Yes, I considered what thirty pain killers could do to my heart, but strength answers weakness in kind. I'm no less for any of it.

Kwazants is aggravating the seams, I can feel it. Punch me and see.

While this is all well and good, my mind has become a whirling dervish and I keep forgetting about my daily Dew. I'm eight steps ahead of all my expectations and trying to keep up with a galloping reality. A beckoning backcloth of evenly mowed green fescue ascending in converging five-yard lines to the horizon is pinned to my fovea and I'm wrenched into that pre-gladiator fight apprehension that frosts everything with a get-on-with-it impatience. I try to work, but I can't sit still for more than an hour without taking to the agility ladder I replaced the coffee table with. That Manuscript is pretty thick. I don't know if I can survive an assignment a week for that magnitude of heft.

The world isn't wound to your watch, ya wee loon! Fine. I get it. Patience is virtue, virtue is kwazants. But if you wanted patience, you should have used something other than the linebacker angle. That's just mean. Cruelly, life rises and falls on how much you let people use your dreams against you.

I haven't had any Mountain Dew in two days and still all my juices are Adderall and Apple Jacks. What can I use as Narcan for excitement?

Day 7

Chapter 21

"Sometimes the questions are complicated and the answers are simple."
– Dr. Seuss

I figure it would be better for my marbles if I sweat out my impatience rather than pace my carpet threadbare. It's productive pacing, but my house is shrinking and the air is becoming too carbon-dioxidized. If I'm going to walk a line and pull my hair out, I might as well track-sprint-track Tony Dorsett to the sideline while I'm doing it. And who doesn't love a cloudless forty-four degrees?

I'm jogging down Legacy Parkway Trail with bottles of Gatorade, cones, an agility ladder, cleats, cash, and a football packed in a backpack secured so loosely to my person I must look like a big bolo bat to the truckers and soccer moms barreling down Legacy Parkway. For what do we live, but to make sport for our neighbors, and laugh at them in our turn?

You're welcome.

I reserve the same corner of the soccer field and erect the manageable parameters of the vaults and velaria of my coliseum. This time I'm in rare luck—four ten- to twelve-year-old boys are playing soccer at the other end of the field.

This is why I bring cash.

I wave a flabellum of bills over my head and bellow, "Who wants to make thirty dollars in one hour?"

Of course I have takers. They cover seventy yards in eight seconds with gaits so wild I'm afraid they're going to hurt themselves. Or each other. Or take flight.

"Here are the rules, you knuckleheads:" <<I need to get on their level>> "you have to have a quarterback, at least one receiver, and at least one running back. The quarterback has five seconds to throw the ball on my count. The quarterback can run as well. You have to commit to a single play—no flea flickers, double passes, or hook and laterals." They all look at each other with a single eyebrow raised.

"It's me against all four of you turd burgers. No first downs—you have to get a touchdown in four downs or you lose like loser-faced losers. You don't need a center, the guy that snaps the ball, but you have to announce the start of the play by saying go. I'm leasing you, so you get the money either way, but you have to try."

I intentionally narrow the field so I have a fighting chance <<covering four spider monkeys amped with Fiiz soda is a coronary on a field a hundred and sixty feet wide>>. Practicing with cash-driven boys is way better than drills, and these kids are at the perfect, pre-swagger age. They are just boys wringing every drop of unsoiled and unscripted fun out of their minutes. Girls will ruin all of that for them in a couple of years, but for boys, true boys, that lust for citius-altius-fortius will always rival that lust for girls. Or maybe it just becomes the means for that end.

Even after ten years of office chairs and Mountain Dew, my reactions and reflexes emerge from a perfect embalming. These kids are no match for this fat-sloughing tower of power. All I get is grumbling, "It's no fair, you're too big!" and "How do you know where we're going to go?"

I get to unholster a few Patch staples, like, "Looking for fair in life is like looking for love in a laundry basket!" and "Less whine, more shine!" I throw in a few of my own that have to do with bras being on too tight and panties that keep riding up. All I get in return is head shaking and whatevers. It occurs to me that they might not know what a bra is.

I toss them each a Gatorade with as much Coke commercial Mean Joe Greene cheese as possible, hand them each thirty dollars, and watch them Eeyore their way home. Sore losers.

As I'm doing this, my eyecorner catches this Dick Butkus-looking guy <<everyone looks like one or another football player to me>> walking two dogs veer off Legacy Parkway Trail and walk unequivocally in my direction. The dogs don't look big enough to do any damage, but my default is *on guard* <<read: DANGER ZONE HIGH ALERT!>> when I'm approached by any living thing anywhere at any time of day or night for any reason. And with all these other layers of frames and Gontlets and xenoumbrae and vents, who knows what you can trust. I furtively unsheathe a full bottle of Gatorade in case I need to unleash havoc on the legendary Maestro of Mayhem.

"Don't worry about the dogs, they don't bite." <<I've been bitten by dogs whose owners used those very words.>> "My name is Nathan Blackgoat." <<Coolest name I've ever heard.>> "I'm the defensive coordinator for the Salt Lake Stingers."

"The arena football team?"

"Right. Just from watching you for three minutes I know you're a better linebacker than anyone we have playing for us right now. Do you play college ball?"

"Oh, I missed that window ten years ago. And with the shape I'm in, I'd be lucky to make it up the stairs to the field after suiting up."

"You don't move like you're out of shape. Frankly, I don't care about age and fitness if you can move like that for a couple hours. Here's my card. Why don't you come down to the Ute's soccer field next Thursday at noon and you can work out with us. Maybe it'll suit you. Just text me when you're on your way. Number's on the card."

Then he's gone.

This is the only thing I've ever wanted in my whole life. I don't think I cared so much if it was NFL or the Rocky Mountain Football League or an arena football team, I just wanted to wear pads and weaponize my body.

But why now? Seems like luck more favors the visible than the prepared. Can I short circuit this whole forging process with all the Pik-ing and kwazants and whatnot and just be an arena league football player? The outcome is basically the same, is it not? Is this just another Patch-administered test of my resolve and my trust? Is this guy a Mero spy trying to heave me off the tracks? I feel heaved.

Or is this just an unrelated, random encounter with a defensive coordinator for a local arena league football team that just happened to see some guy working out with some kids on a field in nowhere Salt Lake City? This all seems so unfair. *Looking for fair in life is like looking for love in a laundry basket!* Right. *Calling something unfair assumes an elevation sufficient to survey the full landscape of fair.* Yes, I get it already!

Okay, think, Elliot. Think. Things like this don't happen to me. They've never happened to me. This week has been nothing but hooey and hogwash; why would I suspect this would be anything but the next line of crashing waves? Because that's all it is. Nobody walks up to a has-been that's clearly out of shape and flatters him with, "You're better than anyone on my professional football team." No one! That experiment they did with the kids and the marshmallows to prove something about delayed gratification, that's all this is. I won't even pick at the marshmallow and try to hide the little gouged depressions with other parts of the marshmallow. I will *disappoint the devices of the crafty so that their hands cannot perform their enterprise*! You're always calling me brilliant, Patch; well, here I am being brilliant!

I tuck the business card safely in my backpack.

CHAPTER 22

"Sorry, I'm a bit of a stickler for paperwork."
– Sam Lowry, *Brazil*

On the way home from the park, a thought shot its hand up and waggled its fruit snack-fueled fingers like a hummingbird wing. Most of my less directed thoughts are just subversive, Sharpie-scribbled-on-cardboard road signs that pry me from a steady course and create more work. I have learned to pass them by without as much as a No? Nobody has any questions or comments? This waggle persisted throughout subsequent worksheets and even into recess, so I felt like I had to call on it.

I thought it would be useful to consolidate this entire effort within the physical pages of the Manuscript itself, to make it a comprehensive account rather than trying to incorporate islands of pocket litter and somehow coordinate their contexts with paperclips, tape, and dog ears. I'm averse to clutter as it is, but more than hating clutter, I love compressed, high-density, space-saving, white dwarf mega-libraries I can carry in a shoulder bag. I'm going to record all of my observations and experiences on the backside of the Manuscript page(s) they correspond to. It may be a little more time-consuming, but I'll thank myself for the investment in easy reference. I may even affix sticker tabs with keywords to the pages' edges. I'm just fun like that <<an effigy to pathological anality>>.

It's only been a week, and every event was such a face-slapping photo flash I don't think I'll have any trouble recreating them. Most of these memories are bullies anyway, shoving my idle, between-class moments into lockers.

I grab the third to last page of the pre-assignment explanation from the Manuscript and flip it over. Just minding my own business <<I'm clearing my throat>> and a lawyer calls. Patch is dead. Go to lawyer's office. Will. <<I'm expounding on all this, of course.>> Patch's apartment. Manuscript. Boxes. Pictures. The Proper Gentleman. Vivian. Broken tailor <<getting seasick picturing that pitched gait>>. Funeral. Speech. Translating audio file from spy suit. I transcribe the entire transcript on the Manuscript. Weird dream. Running.

The print is becoming micro to maximize space. Three pages is barely enough. My cramping wrist reminds me to pour myself a Mountain Dew, settle it on a Steelers coaster, and slide it to the appropriate carbon dioxide-sparking radius. I put those pages back in order and flip the manuscript page for Assignment #1 over. Gratitude list. I transcribe the whole list and add *intuition* and *bitchin' new truck*, though that's probably on the list three or four times already. On the back of Assignment #2: Bonneville Salt Flats. I transcribe all my notes. Dead dude, yada, yada. Polygraph. Salt Lake Stingers recruitment.

The clicking of the end of the pen on my teeth snaps me out of the stupefacient whirring and snapping at the end of the reel.

It feels like there should be more, though that was an exhausting, week-long lifetime. So this will be my modus henceforth to eliminate any lapse in memory and to record a faithful narrative of all my dealings with Manuscript's directives.

When I'm done, I can send it to a publisher. Lunacy sells.

DAY 8

Chapter 23

"Everyone should be able to do one card trick, tell two jokes, and recite three poems, in case they are ever trapped in an elevator."
– Lemony Snicket

The curmurring of morning flights from SLC to the world's ends rattles from the belly of the earth. I've never been awakened by them before, but I'm anxious to gallop through the Manuscript, so any old drag race or howitzer fire would stir me from my much-needed beauty sleep.

I deterge my dining table with Mom's secret table cleaning concoction of equal parts water and vinegar, twelve generous drops of dish soap, and peppermint essential oil <<woops . . .>> and wipe it with a microfiber towel <<paper towels leave shrapnel>> until the residual holms consume themselves. The Manuscript is placed ceremoniously on a surface fit for surgery, its southern face parallel with the edge of the table, its walls an engineering marvel of streaked verticality.

I'm ready for anything <<I cringe every time I hear myself say that>>.

I feel like I should be wearing an ephod and a mitre. Shouldn't the blueprints for time travel be approached with some reverence, a washing and anointing maybe? As it is, I've lost enough weight in the past week to feel a sort of sagginess in my big top T-shirt, and these basketball shorts are just a profanity. Maybe it is time for some new clothes. *Rewards in increments are just celebrations of failed restraint!* Yes, thank you, Patch.

Assignment #3: BAG OF TRICKS

You're on a train. It's quiet. It's warm. You're comfortable. Hills of country green slope in and out of a powder blue sky as you mumble across the countryside. A stop is announced and the train slows. It is your stop. You crowd the doorway in anticipation of your departure. Instead of those green slopes and that blue sky, a strobing, salty screech of discordance and assault greets you as the doors open to a battering rookery. You try to shrink back into your sanctuary, but the tracks are bare, the train has deserted the platform. An instinctive preservation of personal space herds you into a closed, meandering circuit bounded by inquiry and accusation and suggestion. You seem to be in a street market with loudly aggressive vendors, but nobody knows quite what they are selling. The resounding blast wave elicits a reversion to pushy politeness and you try to attend to each individual, but everything is simultaneous and awkwardly stuttered at the same time. You only understand every third word. Everyone is needlessly prolix and frustrated and they express everything in terms of only hopes. Individuals approach and recede like lightning in all impossible directions and they are circumfusing you like a cracking roulette wheel. Some seem helpful, some officious, but you cannot distinguish which are which. There is an overpowering smell of everything from freshly baked cupcakes to gasoline to microwaved salmon. Brightness and darkness are suffused and it is more a flickering than a neutral amalgamation.

Such is the state among the Gontlets.

You're a horrible salesman, Patch.

Upon further dissection, there is perfect soundness to this untidy gallimaufry. Though some have gone mad in the brief, welcoming frenetics of the Gontlets, we have had the great fortune of pikirovateli so steeled in their minds, so centered in their purpose, so immune to inane influence, that they have been able to spend extended periods of time in the Gontlets before re-coupling with their hull. They have collected intelligence so vital it has changed our approach to every phase of the enterprise. To you I relay this intelligence that the Gontlets may become a brisk stroll rather than the woebegone quicksand for which it has a propensity.

Fearmongering aside, the Gontlets are, sure as shortbread, the most fascinating environment you will ever encounter in your existence, at least as you currently understand it.

The occupants of the Gontlets lie on a continuum. There are good and there are bad. Yes, there are those that are neither, but though the neither are not inherently bad, they are just as poisonous to your purpose as are the bad. So, essentially, there are good and there are bad. The distinctions are more or less immaterial as, for the most part, it is not always apparent which are which. I will restrict my comments to the nature and identity of the occupants; you will need to parse out intention according to your own discernment. You may find this itemization supererogatory, and this it may be, but I find that having the option of ignoring information is always preferable to being ignorant of it. Besides, this may assist you in devising strategies to outwit the devices of the different classes of entities.

I will begin my accounting at the most obstructive end of the continuum and work my way to the ushers-by-noninterference, so to speak. This, like all attempts to characterize the demographics of the Gontlets (or, furthermore, any aspect of the Gontlets), will be looped, knotted, and branched. It is an ecosystem that defies simple explanations, much the same as an elaboration on our own apical frame existence. Besides, this is just a summary of the Gontlets from a personal observational perspective and an interpretation of second-hand accounts. What we know is only what we surmise, and you will eventually contribute to the convolution of this cannon.

In other words, you don't really know that much.

Among the Gontletians are a race of Exiles, banished to the frames and their intermediate spaces for an attempted coup against their king. The kingdom from which these beings were expelled is beyond the purview of this exposition, but the manner of their banishment to the frameset allowed them to retain all memory of their, and, consequently, your origin. Don't sort your mind on that for the nonce, just know that our system of lateral and vertical closed loops is a part and not a whole. In a sense, the frameset and its respective Gontlets are the Exiles' kingdom, as much as unattended teens squatting at their parents' vacation home would consider it their kingdom. However, these Exiles are more like bullies than governors, as they were never born into the frameset and do not have, nor have ever had, a hull. They exist strictly as umbrae in the Gontlets. Without a physicality to engage in physical destruction, their weapon of choice is luring their wards off cliffs.

They sound fun.

The umbra may be a super-entity, and the hull may be a sensory silencer, but the war between monster and mettle, the occasion for kwazants, as it were, can only be waged when the two are merged. It is a schoolhouse like no other. Since the Exiles have no hull, they understand only half of what it means to be human (maybe sixty percent if you count their lodging as xenoumbrae), and, as such, are underdeveloped entities. They do not care about the constructs of good and evil as hypothesized, philosophized, and fretted over at the apical frame; they only do that which antagonizes the king and subverts his purpi. They are patient students of human nature. They are cunning and perspicacious. Behind the plasticity of their pleasantries are teeth so cut that greetings are garrotes, compliments are contempt. They want nothing for you but what has been their lot for millennia—comprehensive anguish—and they will employ all their devices to achieve it. Their acquaintance and familiarity with you predate your memory, even your amnesic birth <<amnesic birth? Huh?>>, so, more than just proverbially, they know you better than you know yourself. They are extraordinary beings in the greasiest and most execrable ways, and they should never be underestimated. Your presence of mind to cleverly disarm them will never surmount their presence of mind to menace you with lip-licking doggedness. They are the princes and generals of this principality.

Other than the crawling sort of malaise choking my acini and spilling exocrine vinegar into my blood, they don't sound so bad. If I can talk my way out of my aunt's ex-husband, Clark, luring me into a carnival porta-potty with the promise of free ride tickets so he could diddle me, I can smooth talk these clowns.

The vent ejects you into a Gontlet spanning the space between two frames, static facsimiles that represent specific ten-thousandths of a second; the Exiles are not mystified by this immobility. The discovery of a trespasser they can delay is much more tantalizing than keeping pace with frame progression to harass other, more permanent residents of both frame and Gontlet. This proves particularly problematic for pikirovateli as this class of entity tends to throng them in greater numbers, and their numbers are tremendous. So tremendous, in fact, they have the resources to focus efforts on both the dead of the Gontlets and the living of the (apical) frames. The Exiles' influence is not confined to the residents of yesterframes' Gontlets; they follow all active segments of the frameset, to include the Gontlet comprised of the supra-principal apical frame. It should go without saying, then, that these entities, the Exiles, are, at this very moment, and at every other moment, swarming everyone, all the time, past and present. To fan the flames, your mreg will be considerably more noticeable than your peers in the Gontlets. A substantial mreg exposes you as an agent of the king and the Exiles will ensure that you receive an extra special welcome.

Okay, hold on. <<My brain is resisting the absorption of this caffeine for some reason.>> Every time a pikirovatel Pik-s and recouples with his native hull, he is reactivating a dormant archived frame—I think he called these *reconstituted apical frames*—and this initiates the ascent of that archived frame as a new, deeper apical frame within the frameset. If enough pikirovateli have gone back to different times, this reanimates multiple segments of the frameset. Could the majority of the one hundred and twenty-year frameset be active at this moment? Are all changes made by all these pikirovateli at every depth in multiple regions accounted for by the update? Have these questions already been answered? I don't remember. I may have to reread everything; this is becoming too much to keep straight.

For now, keep it in the back of your mind that they exist and that you will encounter them. Rather, they will encounter you. They are there to assist you, as it were, in losing your way. Most entities in the Gontlets cannot see the Exiles, but they are able to manifest themselves to any they choose and many will manifest themselves to you.

The next two specimens are really just one class, but I will treat them separately as their engagement with you will be noticeably different. The entire class is simply called the Dead, but the first division I will address are referred to as Lifers. Most of the individuals that are relegated to the Gontlets following their mortal demise (I will, hereafter, refer to this as Gontlet death as not everyone makes their abode in the Gontlets upon termination of mortality) prefer to take up residence with familiarity. Whether they know they are dead or not, they become the disregarded prisoners of routine. As all Gontlets older than one hundred and twenty years are squeezed out of existence at the petram, and are, therefore, uninhabitable, those who perished greater than one hundred and twenty years ago are forced to ascend with the rising tide of the frameset (as it would seem from their perspective). Initially, they try to homestead, but all eventually see their home, their community, their entire civilization slowly replaced by another, and then replaced by another again. The Lifers are the veterans of the Gontlets. Some have been dead for thousands of years. They are homeless, purposeless, and embittered. They have developed a stony acceptance of their reality, and do little to improve their situation. If the Exiles wish not to engage you directly, they will most likely suggest that the Lifers do their bidding. But this is rare as the Exiles know they have but a spot of tea with the pikirovateli (especially those with a monstrous mreg) before they are on their way. In this regard, the Exiles are of the if-you-want-something-done-right-do-it-yourself mind.

The Lifers actually sound *less* pleasant than the Exiles. At least the Exiles are social and interested and have purpose.

The other entities constituting the Dead are the Blanc-Bec. We attempted to defrancify this term, but thought it would be like vandalizing a Da Vinci. The French is just too elegant and befitting. I will, hereafter, pluralize Blanc-Bec with an s (Blanc-Becs), but the s is not pronounced. The Blanc-Becs have died in the last one hundred and twenty years. Some know they are dead, some do not. Generally speaking, the longer they have been dead, the higher the probability they know they are dead. Though some remain in denial for extended periods of time, when you are unable to physically interact with the elements in your environment and your screams and pleas are ignored, you tend to question the terms of your reality or slip into lunacy. For most Blanc-Becs, as long as their familiar physical surroundings remain intact, they will be a fixture of that geographically-contained environment. It is what they know. It is their solace. Those that know they are dead are qualitatively similar to the Lifers, a little less rancorous, a little more despondent. For our purpi, we are more concerned with those that do not know. Most of the Dead (Lifers included) prefer to accompany the standard progression of frame creation, as this is the only environment that replicates their accepted understanding of the world's movement. Though this is most simply done at the principal apical frame, ascending at clock's pace within the frameset at any depth will achieve the same effect. Remember, reverting in the direction of archived frames (descending in the frameset) will, depending on the speed of that reversion, slow, stop, and eventually reverse perceived motion. However, some are willing to tolerate a welter, to include an inert world, to lock eyes with a source of potential information. Unfortunately, since the vents are not closed cylinders penetrating the frameset, their contents are plainly visible to all residents of the Gontlets. As you descend, you can see them, they can see you.

Well, that foils all of my plans to tiptoe, unnoticed, through the Gontlet.

Some of the Blanc-Becs will follow you to your point of departure from the vent, Exiles will converge on you, Lifers may loiter out of interest. You are like a celebrity in a glass elevator and everyone wants a selfie. The Malcolms (what we call the umbrae that do not know they are dead, from Dr. Malcolm Crowe of Sixth Sense *fame) will accost, pester, insinuate, berate, implore, be pitiful. You will appear slightly different to them (being freshly dead, having a substantially larger mreg, being deposited from a vent rather than melting into a Gont-*

let at death) than their fellow Gontletians, so they will approach you as if you are some kind of emissary. They want updates and explanations and messages relayed. Some will be diverted enough by your unnatural arrival and the prospect of communication that they will be unruffled by the fact that their world has slowed to a bewildering state of torpor.

Why does he think I'd just stand around and gawk at these waylayers? I'm a man-mover by trade! If I've got places to be, I'll part the Red Sea with my shoulders and a grunt. I am the *sword without and terror within!*

You're thinking like a linebacker; I can hears the gears. <<Crap . . .>> You are looking for gaps in the line, like you're going to muscle your way through the Gontlet. You can think that if it gives you comfort. At least you're thinking. Let's discuss a couple of impediments to this approach. First, umbrae do not use muscles and oxygen to impede or pursue. They know too well the capacities of the umbra to resort to such inefficiencies. They move by intention, irrespective of space and distance. The hull does not enjoy such faculties, so it is not a simple explanation. Without raveling you in Gontletian physics, it is more or less a think-and-you-are-there actuation. But if you can do it, they can do it, and, again, at least the Exiles know you better than you know yourself, so do not suppose you are going to outmaneuver them. Secondly, I have mentioned this before but it bears repetition—your hull is a powerful sensory suppressor. Loosed from this sensory censorship your umbra registers all stimuli as if you had a giant alien head cortex devoted to each sense, including the hundreds of dormant senses suppressed by the hull. Colors multiply and vibrate at a frequency that creates distinct sounds. Distance has no effect on volume. Stacked, dimensional attention replaces linearity of processing. Vision decrypts all wavelengths at every reflective depth. It is like, after having your pupils dilated, walking into a high-end strip club that smells like motorcycle exhaust with free Mountain Dew on tap, arcade games lining the walls. This fuzz of super-consciousness is not to be dismissed when strategizing inroads through the Gontlets.

I hope you've been hydrating with that fat-happying yellow meth drink 'cause ah'mnae done here, ya wee skippy!

Mountain Dew! Holy butt balls, why do I keep forgetting to drink my beloved? That's why the caffeine isn't working, I haven't even had any yet! Patch would be flattered; it's a testament to how enthralling this all is.

The last two species of the Gontlets are more aptly classified as visitors than residents. You will always see them there, but they are always on assignment and you will rarely see the same ones twice. They have established permanent residence in an unknown elsewhere so they are there and then they are not. These two classes are the Dovolniya and the Inscrutables. Dovolniya comes from the Russian and means the contented. The French have their own term for this class that breaks out to something like eyesmilers, but only the French can pronounce it correctly so I stick with the Russian. The Dovolniya, as their namesake indicates, have broad strokes of serenity and cheerfulness, almost rapture, brushed in the muscles of every expression. They do not run around like happy idiots but their eyes are a relaxed understanding and they are always ready to laugh. They clearly have purpose, but they are never annoyed by impediments. They are busy but not hurried. The Exiles exert great efforts to mimic the Dovolniya but their impatience and malice restrict them and it comes across more as a transaction than an encounter. The Dovolniya do not make deals and do not have an agenda for you. They may not agree with your presence in the Gontlets, but they want to get you on your way as quickly as possible without seeming officious or facilitative. They are more subtle plows than salesmen. They know who you are, what you are doing there, and understand the perils of loitering and delays at the whim of the Exiles. Because your mreg will reflect the true nature of your character, they will treat you as a peer and be as helpful as they are authorized to be, but you are not their responsibility. As they are umbrae like the Exiles, it is difficult to distinguish between the two by appearance, but the Exiles vastly outnumber the Dovolniya, so if you are not sure, probability favors Exile. My general approach has always been to avoid interaction with any of the Gontlets' entities, but when it becomes inevitable (which it will), a fairly reliable distinguisher between Exile and Dovolniya is how they say what they say. The Exiles tend to speak faster and make everything sound urgent. The Dovolniya tend to out-listen their words. Again, not hard, fast rules, just know that the Dovolniya will try to avoid you in the main. Another reliable distinguisher is that the Dovolniya always travel in pairs. The Exiles are so intolerant of each other that watching them force this arrangement is like watching people in couple's therapy.

I'm heedlessly exhibiting this obsessive floccillation as I read about my fate. I feel like I'm gearing up for a horrifying self-infliction of pain that people will talk about for generations.

I'm not entirely convinced that mention of the Inscrutables is necessary or useful. <<That's never stopped you before.>> *True, they are entities you may encounter, but in all my time wading through the Gontlets, I have never had any interaction with them. I am not sure I would even hazard the effrontery to make such an attempt. Nobody knows where the Inscrutables come from, where they reside, why they make forays into the Gontlets, or why they collect certain of the Gontlet dead from the realm of the Gontlets. They are, as they say, inscrutable.* <<Why are we focusing so much on the bounds of the frameset? This unknown somewhere sounds way more intriguing.>> *They are both easy to spot and difficult to look at. They are beings of light, the intensity of which is only known or appreciated outside of the hull, in the courtyards of the Gontlets. Getting close to them is like getting close to the speaker through which the microphone you are holding is being amplified—the feedback is instructive. Umbrae interact physical-*

ly with umbrae in a similar manner as a hull interacting with a hull at an apical frame. Umbrae and hulls cannot achieve a comparable physical interaction. Given these observations, we assume that the Inscrutables are somehow occupying the Gontlets while in their hull as umbrae cannot interact tactilely with these entities at all, and the Inscrutables interact with the environment of the Gontlets quite differently than all other entities. They move as quickly as light itself and shake a decade of archived frames when they speak. They are spectacular and terrible. Aside from their effortless brightness, they will never engage you. To the Inscrutables, you are a rogue entity and they do not want to validate your presence by acknowledging or assisting you. They know who you are and what you are doing there, but you are perceived as an uninvited guest. And though the Exiles and Inscrutables can see each other, their only observable interplay is Exiles scattering like rats at the approach of Inscrutables. Like the Dovolniya, the Inscrutables are always in pairs.

Lastly, uncharacterized entities exist in the Gontlets for which I have little intelligence. You may encounter other pikirovateli, of course, and lendemains occasionally slip from the moorings of their hull, but there are others, arcane beings, that have power and influence. No pikirovateli has reported any interaction with them, but the consensus is that they are not there to make friends. They are dark-black men in black robes with a ferocity in their hood-hidden eyes. As far as has been observed, they seem to enforce the laws of the Gontlets, though I can't give any clarity to that supposition.

So the Exiles see everyone from their curtained shadows, can be seen by whomever they choose, interact with all entities whether ostensibly perceived or not, but for the Inscrutables. Lifers are nomads in the Gontlets, isolated from all family and familiarity, preying on the Blanc-Becs, preyed on and puppeteered by the unseen Exiles. The Blanc-Becs are one foot on the frames, one foot in the Gontlets, and commonly puzzled. The wayfaring Dovolniya move in and out like a cool breeze and warm wind, proselyting insurrection with their smiling eyes and placid gestures. This minacious chaos of disconnectedness will descend upon you like an air mass, and as there is no linearity in the Gontlets, all stimuli is processed as tiered machine gunning spates.

When your lendemain falls to its equilibrium within the vent, it is deposited into a Gontlet. At that moment there is a brief card catalog search, if you will. Your entrance through a back door may be an infiltration and a violation of the order of the Gontlets, but you are still there and need to be registered in the system, even if for a vanishing moment, according to rigid protocols. Assuming residence in the Gontlets via the vents is puzzling to all the guardians and gatekeepers, but before objections are registered, your antecedent hull senses and summons you, more or less. It is as if your hull is awakened to the possibility that it might be missing something. The further away you are geographically (remember, the frames are indexed replicas of the world's breadth) from your hull, the longer this sensing takes. Once the connection is made, a beacon, a humming maybe, is added to all other layers of stimuli. If you attend to this signal and follow its directional prompts, your native hull will assimilate you in short order (though that phrase is virtually meaningless in a realm where time is an unrecognized construct). The system seems to promote this connection since it places you and clears the interloper from its books. If you avail yourself of the counsel of the manuscript, kwazants will forge a great and terrible mreg. This both speeds recoupling with the native hull and attracts a lot of attention. The benefit is worth the cost.

It is this meantime, this card catalog search, for which you must prepare so you are not washed away by the levee-defying surges of the cannibals and carnivores of the Gontlets. The beacon does not hum forever. You will need to have ready diversions that can be employed to turn the tables on the table turners. Your hull, from whence you came, the apical frame point of impact, is dead, and your native hull already has an associatively cataloged umbra at the archived frame to which you are traveling, so if you get stuck in the Gontlet, it is, ultimately, of no consequence to your existence. You simply become a de facto ward of the Gontlets. For this reason, it is vital that you keep it together. I would prefer you manhandle the Gontletians like that bone-crushing, quarterback-retiring thug of a linebacker that once possessed you, but I see the years have curdled your majesty, so we'll take it one fragile step at a time.

I didn't know you were supposed to be funny, Patch. So these Gontlet types can be manhandled, huh? Interesting.

Retrieve the deck of playing cards from the unsealed box. Do it now!

What, are you going to time me with your pretend stopwatch? Charlatan!

For this assignment, you need to learn three card tricks to effortless execution and with the dexterity of a nanosurgeon. Yes, yes, it seems as rote as the other assignments. Just do it and thank me later. Card tricks stun everyone, the living and the dead. It will buy you time while Gontlet administration and native hull sensing are reconciling. They are also useful for when you recouple with your native hull, as your lendemain will not know the day nor the hour of the depth to which you Pik. <<Maybe that's why it's fruitless to target geography when you Pik—you'd have to know where you were at every when.>> *It is useful for that segue from refamiliarizing stupor to reestablished composure. You will need a minute to figure out where you are and what you were doing; your native umbra will have a mini-revolt and you'll look and sound like you're having a stroke. Just express epiphany with your face and ask for a deck of cards. They're never that far away in the industrialized world. You know this is a marked deck, so you shouldn't have any problem swiftly mastering the first trick.*
Now stop reading.

Card tricks, huh? Hang the Gontlets, I can see how card tricks could be pretty useful in all unpleasant social situations <<*unpleasant* was probably a redundant modifier there>>. I lay the cards out face down and study the backs. Sure enough, they're *all* marked. That foul scapegrace. To this day his wizardry with these cards has vexed me. Your burnish is blistering here, Patch! Or . . . Sir Manheim Beetleskeech, or whatever your name was that day. Was any element of my life as it seemed? I feel like I stood up too fast and my world is collapsing into a deckle-edged, unfocused postage stamp. And I'm to carry on this legacy of legerdemain.

I'm rereading the census of the Gontlets. Every few words prompt eight more questions. I don't know if I have the patience for this to unveil itself a few teasers a week. He said I couldn't read ahead, but there has to be something else, some way to tear this thing open without violating the spirit of his instruction. But then I don't develop the patience necessary for kwazants to explode my mreg <<said with a cadence of plaintive resignation>>. But surely I can patiently hold the hand of the Manuscript while engaging in a little self-study on the side? I need to find my key to that code we devised; the notebook in that box might have free information. And I need to get into Patch's apartment. What would be the point of showing me that place but for me to mischievously wile my way back in?

CHAPTER 24

"If you could kick the person in the pants responsible for most of your trouble,
you wouldn't sit for a month."
– Theodore Roosevelt

I'm teaching myself how to shuffle with one hand. You never realize how fat and paralytic your fingers are until you try to get nimble with massaged face cards that move across each other like water and river rocks. They feel like balloons, stuffed in mittens, dipped in shortening. The fingers that is, not the cards. I think I might have suffered a corpus callosum injury on the playground when I was a kid—my mind is very clear about what my thumb should be doing, but it seems to have developed a pathological case of either catatonia or stage fright.

I don't know why I didn't think of this before. What social malignancy <<again, *malignancy* can be replaced with *situation* or *interaction*>> can't be cured with a card trick? It's a magic show you don't have to pay these third-party extortionists a so-called convenience fee for. Though, come to think of it, I've never actually seen somebody doing a card trick in any workaday setting. It occurs to me that since I don't look or speak Russian or French, this might give me away as the Cartographer's ward. Certainly, card tricks are an Exile-stalling industry staple. I guess if it exposes me, it exposes my nemeses. <<Can you have nemeses in a war of out-chivalrying your opponent?>>

As I fill up the room with exasperated teeth grinding and the first syllables of grade school profanity, there's still a sort of teeming, Swiss-cheese quiet coagulating and thinning around me. I'm starting to feel undone in these quiet rooms all alone. It's one thing to academically acknowledge that forces of good and evil are buzzing about in the universe somewhere, but I'm starting to *feel* them. Almost *hear* them. The same way the totality of obstruction-sculpting soundwaves and vertiginous air pressure in a room creates a three-dimensional, subconscious map, and the slightest variance pricks at all your diffused senses, I can almost *track* them. I would chalk it up to the power of suggestion at this point, but I think it might be the other way around. That tour of the Gontlets gave the ghosts skin and a surname. This may not seem like a reasonable conclusion to be drawn based on that observation, but hosting ghuests <<ghost guests>> thin enough to slip into your mind changes a man. I think my hour of mental sogginess has passed. Patch would always say that the risk of being the direct object for a split second is being the direct object for eternity. I don't think I appreciated the weight of that claim as a teenager, but the electricity of my present has given it some breath. I don't think I can afford the exploitability of passivity in the midst of this experiment. Henceforth and forever, I must be a man at all times about his wits. I don't want to open <<or leave open>> any doors. And it's not just the salmagundi of squatters that want to ride me like a Ferrari or move my dishes around for shock value <<which is a little disconcerting, for sure>>, but the hooks in my cheek I thought were tugged by bored, fun-loving brigandmirths are feeling more like tire irons backstitched into my muscles by masked faces under garish lights. I just think there's more at stake now.

Maybe if I tried some lumbricular calisthenics this would be easier. I need Buckethead's nodose, spider-leg fingers that seem to move independent of minds.

Self-possession, itself, is *sharper than a two-edged sword, to the dividing asunder of both joints and marrow.* David of Goliath-killing notoriety was history's ultimate badass. If he was a contemporary, he'd be a linebacker for the Pittsburgh Steelers, no question. But I always loved Saul's reaction when he saw David behaving himself *very wisely*—he was afraid of him. Being big is an easy intimidation, but I remember encountering little guys with prefiguring eyes that seemed to survey life's vistas from a position of elevation or futurity. They seemed to know the end from the beginning and would coolly behave themselves wisely. Being a mesomorphic mammoth is a useful curtain wall, but the kind of fear I always wanted to invoke was in the strategist, not the battering ram.

Oh, hey, I did it! Well, the easy part anyway. Now I just have to feather. Heaven help you, thumb, if you don't exhibit a little autonomy, *there will be hell to pay! And you can't afford it!* <<It's hard to forget that threat when it was roared with a lot of ham thirty times a day.>>

I write *thumbs* on my gratitude list. I've been witness to the fruits of perseverance in my life; I know they'll eventually come around.

DAY 9

CHAPTER 25

"It is by no means an irrational fancy that, in a future existence, we shall look upon what we think our present existence, as a dream."
– Edgar Allen Poe

Another weird dream last night. That Manuscript is becoming a powerful hallucinogenic, I think. Normally my dreams are like watching a *Bad Lip Reading* in a sandstorm, but these dreams have a spectral, hyaline clarity to them, and they breathe more like an open-air gallery than a smoke-filled pool hall. It's clean, and though the venues are never recognizable, I don't feel misplaced or wonder what I'm doing there. Everything is as it should be despite nothing being as I would expect it to be. I'm standing at the doorsill of an undefined expanse, though I keep calling it a room. Everything is a depthless, coconut sort of white which gives the illusion of walls, floor, ceiling, though I can't actually make any of those surfaces out and no shadows aid these illusions. It has vague dimensionality, but there are no visible seams between height and width or depth. The only thing I can see with any certainty is this sumptuous, delicate milkiness gathered at the edges of the expanse and lightly, but not obtrusively, filling its space. It wasn't a cloudy or misty kind of whiteness, it was a pervasive plasma kind of white which, I know, is even more unpicturable. This is why it reminded me more of a room; the white was submerging but pellucid in the center and seemed to gather structurally at the perimeter. I'm talking in circles now. Dreamlands are lawless that way.

You know how you just know things in dreams, even if what you know is not at all intuitive or its appearance contradicts what you know it to be in the dream? Well, I know that I am standing at the threshold of Eternity, capital *E*. I just know. I always assumed eternity to be a span of time, not an entity or construct or a room, for that matter, but that's where I am—Eternity. Even at its apron, I know the voluptuous whiteness indicates no real boundary, only the tree-rimmed promenade to another Eternity. *Another's* Eternity. It isn't so much that I am in Eternity, but that I am fully aware, despite the ethereal, LED glory framing the frameless room <<expanse>>, that this is *my* Eternity, that this was and is my home, and has been for ages and eras immemorial. I'm standing at my own front door. It's that sensation of the first sip of gelid Mountain Dew after a long run, cold shower, and ensconced in a trained couch cushion in sweats you've worn basically every day for seven years. <<Right, now I've turned Eternity from a span of time to an expanse to a sensation. I get it when Patch says there are no good analogies in the Gontlets.>>

I'm claiming a big, white expanse <<room?>> as my Eternity, I understand this. But, again, things you just know in your dream even if they don't make sense—this is my Eternity's canvas. There's definitely somebody standing next to me in this dream, available for questions? Making sure I don't get too creative? I don't know. I don't know what this person looks like; I never think to look at him. Her? I just know the person is there specifically for me. We communicate throughout the entire dream, but it's all in my head. I don't speak, I don't hear voices, my lips don't move. I think and the individual understands. The individual thinks and I understand. It's the way things work at my home.

We stand there at the doorsill for what seems like a revolving ever, like every time I have a thought, time begins again. It's a never-ever-forever sort of loop that I don't give much thought at the time <<at the time, ha>>. I know what I'm there to do and I don't discern any blackjacking from my companion to get on with it. We're there until we don't need to be there anymore.

The pearly iridescence has a giddiness about it, like it's jostling on the front lines, waiting for the command to run screaming into an historic battle. It's hard to describe senses in dreams, but in this sterility, everything has its translation— concepts had smells, abstractions had voltage. I know that fate is here because of the rich, agricultural smell of damp, fertilized topsoil after a heavy rain. I know that death is here on a long trigger from the bouquet of bubonic lymph and dried blood on Ankou's cloak, and the refraction of his unsharpened scythe glinting like flames in the seams of the distant apron. It's a moment of generational conquest or a thousand years of slavery.

And then I see it . . .

It's as easy to see as a fly in milk. Which is kind of what it looks like, a fly in milk. The same woman from my previous weirdo dream is falling through the sky into my white-room Eternity. She's flailing this time, like she's trying to flip onto her stomach. In the preceding dream I knew I was supposed to ignore her and run myself straight into a mountain. Not this time. I know exactly what I'm to do and how this will end, I'm just not sure how to get from one to the other. And then, with a clap of realization, I communicate to my speechless sidekick, "Holy shit, I know kung fu." I didn't really know kung fu, and this had nothing to do with fighting, but the solution did seem like an unprompted download.

From the floor's enamel, homogenous purity, from the vanishing walls and indiscernible halls, I mobilize that giddy whiteness and give it the command. Urbanity blooms like a blast radius—towers are erected in ascending stacks; complexes and structures bound across the fallow sea of trampled opalescence; green signs preside over their avenues; planters and park strips chromatize the neutrality of the smoky grays of construction, mostly as an afterthought. I focus more on upwards than outwards since I'm going to use my blanched confederates to catch this girl in freefall.

My self-consciousness tries to lure my focus to the margins with the thought of using my arms like a conductor or magician to dramatize this creation of worlds, but a water break-taking tract in my brain sort of laughs it off. All the while, my companion is advising, encouraging, admonishing with the savage honesty of one of those yes/no Bits on *Tron*.

The floors of a particularly soaring edifice are stacking from the inside out like the blossoming of a mutant weed with balconies. Once the ascent of my sky-scraping snare greets the descent of its catch, I start to deconstruct from the apex at a rate just slow enough to gently catch her in the squibs of its exploding palm. Then it is controlled demolition from the base, floor by collapsing floor, until she can be seen strutting from the already-cleared rubble <<even my subconscious is fairly tidy>> like Sylvester Stallone on a backdrop of fireball that used to be a bus or something.

As smoldering as that strut is, the moment I realize she's safely grounded, she immediately appears not two feet in front of me. Again, I don't look <<or need to look>>, but dream me knows that her appearance has replaced my companion, or maybe that she's absorbed my companion, like it was really part of her the whole time and she's just gathering up all her bits.

We just look at each other.

Her hair is in a messy bun, a color as black and glossy as a Murgese, that moves like the very billows of the sea. Her lineaments are neither striking nor unexceptional, but the composite is devastating beauty. The raven black of the surging swells of her hair spills over into the tidepools of her eyes. She's dressed in a zip-up hoody and a lot of stretchy clothing. Her hand is resting atop her belly to draw attention to the fact that she's pregnant. I know it's a dream, but that scene was truly dreamy.

I've never seen this woman before, but it's like looking in a mirror where the reflection is clearly not me. Dream Elliot knows he shares an identity with this woman, but I'm just a jaggedly ripped half of that complimentary whole. Whatever she has ninety percent of, I have ten percent, whatever I have sixty percent of, she has forty percent. I don't want to say anything like yin-yang <<mostly because I don't know exactly what that means>>, but we are an indivisible, asymmetrical duality. Though we look nothing alike, I can see my reactions and expressions surfacing in her features. Her hungers and thirsts are passing on the shoulders of my umbra's highways. Echoes of our Eternities are covalently bonded in our inter-helical space like elastic nitrogenous bases. She's a superior me and I'm a superior her.

As I'm marveling at this phenomenon, she points to a mountain in the farscape that, though I don't remember creating, was stamped into the milk like a county seal. It was *the* mountain. It was *my* mountain. Its towering, rocky face was as still and beckoning as an offensive line, and you know how linebackers feel about offensive lines. I can see neither my hand nor hers, but the sensation of grabbing her hand is mentally tangible. The corners of her mouth slide approvingly toward the cockled rim of adorable dimples and we start running like a bullet train. We're running so fast I can hear the dairy white making a straining hum, almost a groan.

I look over at my eighty percent and she has, at first glance, this expression of intensity and determination, but as I study it, it's more like the all-in parlay of laying one's life at the feet of another's confidence. She looks intense and determined, but it's adumbrated by hesitant and hopeful.

Then I wake up.

I don't know why I always feel like running after dreams like that. Fresh air and distance from furniture I could throw and things I could punch has always been a sort of glue for things wanting to burst out of me. Even the reach of the open sky seems confining after visions of such vastness and infinite power, so you can imagine the coffin my bedroom walls were feeling like. Running outside is the quickest way to ascend to the gods, dine in your collective omnipotence for an hors d'oeuvre, and then have them kick the living hauteur out of you so your frangibility is never again in question. Until the initial several minutes of your next run.

I go through the garage on my way out so I can admire the thews of the beast caged therein, running my fingers across its burnished obliques.

The orange clouds make pink valleys of the darkly-veined slopes of snow, and the rest of the sharp edges of the Wasatch Front are a gloomier, grayscale adaptation of the fatal faces of *Guernica*. The Bountiful Temple sits like a light-house on the bench, cutting its marble blade into the sloping, russet hillside. The air <<if I can call it *air* at this altitude>> is like Mountain Dew to my lungs, flushing all of the appliance-circulated slosh out with a prolonged, forty-one-degree draught.

I just start running so I can push the ceald <<the nominal form of the adjective *hot* is *heat*; the nominal form of the adjective *cold* should be *ceald*, especially since *coldness* is stupid and *cold* being both the adjective and the noun //and sometimes an adverb, for the love of stupid language// is confusing>> as deep into my extremities as possible. The discomfort of my pace isn't registering through the billowing night sea and black eyes of that woman, so I keep accelerating. My breath and footfalls are so far away I'm not even sure I'm the source of those sounds. I'm a big person, but I'm becoming gigantic and the ground is moving farther and farther away. I feel like tipping a car on its side. I feel nothing but an unquenchable power. Where's a running back in the flats when you need one? Who is this woman to me? How or why would we be two halves of a single person? It is a dream—so maybe it means nothing at all. But this didn't feel like a dream; this was a crisper, brassier reality, like how Patch describes the unleashed sensory of the Gontlets. It may not have been reality as I experience it, but it was in some parallel, and I just know it had a fatidical significance.

I'm nearly sprinting now.

CHAPTER 26

There is nothing more satisfying than the harvest of repetition <<other than the acid bath given all the muscles of my hands and fingers every time I flex, extend, or oppose>>.

I can, with the help of a little acetaminophen, aspirin, and caffeine, cut and shuffle a standard deck of playing cards with one hand, and I only have to gather the far-flung fragments of failure from the table every third attempt. That's in less than twenty-four hours! I think this is the coolest thing I'm currently able to do. Imagine shuffling a deck of cards with one hand . . . But enough of the side games; I better get on with the actual card tricks.

By this time next week, I'll be the pied piper of wowed chicks wanting a piece of my magic.

DAY 11

Chapter 27

> "At the tone the time will be 11:59 and 50 seconds. (Beep)."
> – Audichron

My parents used to have a cordless landline phone when I was a kid, one that you plugged into one of those little rectangular wall jacks. I remember using it. It hadn't yet become an antiquated novelty, but cell phones had picked up a little steam by then. I don't know who I would have called <<probably Jane Barbe>>, I just wanted to feel like a punk pre-pubescent talking to his parent-proscribed girlfriend in an 80s movie. It's funny that the ringtone has never changed. I wonder if that was an unshakable relic that was a function of the infrastructure, or if they carried it into the digital age because it's such a collectively understood sound—not broken, don't fix it sort of thing.

"Hello?"

"Hello, Mother."

"Well, hello, my Elliot. What a happy surprise."

"Just being a good son."

"Oh, yeah? Since when?"

"Good one, Mom. I probably deserved that."

"I'm teasing. It's always lovely to hear your voice. I miss it."

"You're too kind by half. Did I catch you at a bad time? Do you have a minute?"

"I always have a minute for my only son."

"What about the son Dad always said graduated early from our family because he was so much better at making his bed than I was?"

I can hear a snicker trying to make its way past a hard break on a seawall of sadness.

"Your dad . . ."

I've always been spellbound by how fissile my dad's death was to Mom. It was as if the entirety of her hope and happiness and overall well-being filled the spaces between all his structural components and his death dragged all of her pulp out with it, and she was just this dial tone with a perpetually fresh burning crater in her soul. Not the most fortuitous investment when you're married to a soldier whose second residence is a war zone. Sorry—Arkansas. Some move on. Some go crazy. Some give up. Mom was embalmed with gloom. Anything that had the propensity for eliciting happiness just drained out of that crater before it could be enjoyed. She's a good woman, albeit badly broken. I have to avoid topics like men, fathers, family, society, life, death, politics, religion, happiness, sadness, etc. or I'll have to watch whatever happiness she had accrued that day sour, and feature by feature is gorgonized until she's that insensate dial tone staring through me. It's why I generally avoid her. She's good with the weather, when I'm going to give her grandkids, and, strangely, the newest action movies.

"Would you be interested in having lunch with me on Friday?"

"Of course I would. That sounds nice. What inspired this happy occasion?"

I can tell by her voice that a guarded suspicion is nudging through the flattered inquiry like a slow-moving bowling ball sluggishly toppling pins. I could be better about catching up with her. She does live a mere twenty minutes away. And I am her only child. Only family, I guess.

"I miss my mother and want to spend time with her."

"Yeah, try again."

"You are becoming a hard and cynical woman, Mom."

"Taught by the best, I'm sure. In your words, I'm just being a realist."

"Well said. Fine, I want to talk about Patch."

"Patch?"

"Grandad."

"You know I don't know him by those names, right?"

"I forget."

"Why did he have you call him that anyway? Of all the names . . ."

"He said it was a common nickname for somebody that wore an eye patch."

"Your grandfather never wore an eye patch a day in his life."

I start giggling. "I know. I thought it was weird too. You know how he is."

"Is? Oh, boy, we really do need to talk. I hope he hasn't got you chasing after all his humbug."

"I guess it depends on what you mean by *humbug*."

"He was involved with some weird people, Elliot. You'd do well for yourself to not get all jury-jumbled with that crowd. To involve yourself in a caste of little beauty and no breeding is giving bad connections to those who have not been used to them."

That's Jane Austen channeling herself through my overexposed mother. "You're so funny, Mom. I'll be fine. I'm a very big boy."

"I know you can handle yourself, but I think these people might be dangerous. You saw them at the funeral, they're like a band of splashy rumrunners."

I pause to pore through all the Jane Austen-related screenplays to see where the term *splashy rumrunners* came from. No way she came up with that on her own. But after her behavior at the funeral, I don't believe for a second she's not the *queen* of this band of splashy rumrunners, as she so knavishly puts it.

Persuasion, maybe? That has naval officers in it, right?

"Okay, Mom, you have two choices: Kneaders or Zupas. What'll it be?"

"Please don't make me choose. Either one is great."

"Which one did you go to last?"

"Kneaders."

"Zupas it is. I wouldn't want you to have to have Kneaders twice in twenty-four hours."

"Very funny. I hate cooking for myself and everything else is so greasy."

"Your mom is greasy."

I can hear her shaking her head. "I don't know what that means."

"I'll meet you at 2 p.m.," <<minimizing my fragile stomach's exposure to Utahans who are notorious for chewing with their mouths open>> "at the one downtown, the one on 600 East. I'm sure you know the one."

"Elliot . . ."

"Yes'm."

"I saw his body."

"Sorry?"

"When they brought him back to the States, I was the one that identified the body."

"Okay?"

"I just wanted to make sure you didn't think this was another one of his schemes or more of his role playing. I want you to have closure in all this. I know you two were close."

"Are you implying that I thought he might still be alive?" <<Body or not, he's totally still alive.>>

"Yes. But just because we had a funeral, it doesn't mean he's not still with us."

My blood drops three degrees. "Maybe I misunderstand the whole point of funerals then."

"You know what I mean."

No, you crazy, cryptic coot, I have absolutely no idea what you mean! You tell me you saw the body and that a funeral doesn't mean he's not still with us? What is that? I tell you what it is, it's the exclamation point at the end of a week of maddening equivocalities. Being a pathological literalist, I don't like ambiguity, I don't like *doesn't mean he's not still with us*, I don't like locked caskets, I don't like my mousy mother scolding splashy rumrunners in their native tongues, I don't like *we want to take care of you in a way that makes sense according to what we know*. Is he not really dead? Is he still with us in some post-mortem, spiritual sense? Is he still with us in some other abstract sense? Gontlets! Vents! Frames! Exiles! Dovolniya! *Doesn't mean he's not still with us* could mean virtually anything now. And I'm the kind of person that will always claim he understands even if he doesn't to avoid looking stupid.

"Yeah, I get it."

"Elliot."

"Mother."

"You know your mother loves you, right?"

"I never doubted."

DAY 12

Chapter 28

"I command you as King of the Britons to stand aside!"
"I move for no man."
– King Arthur and the Black Knight, *Monty Python and the Holy Grail*

The case's leather has the appearance of a diseased dog. Not so much due to age <<Southord didn't start making lock pick sets until the nineties, I think>>, this particular case was prematurely mottled from excessive handling. Patch and I spent a great deal of time picking locks. Legally picking locks, that is. Picking our own locks. And though the case looks like a flakey ringworm rash, the guts are made of full-hard spring stainless steel that shows its bruises as polished discolorations at the functional ends.

Being a teenager, being a boy, being a football player, I always preferred the rakes. Blitzing, rending, click. Goring, rocking, snap. Quicker than retrieving nasal spray. Muscling counterpins to the shear line is what Jack Lambert would do if he picked locks. That or just bite through the shackle. With molars, that is; he didn't have incisors. It was part of his charm. Patch preferred to make love to each pin and coo and coax the driver pin to the shear line. He was more a Renoir than a Lambert, but, then, he was like that with everything—all finesse. Needless to say, he was way better than I was. Locks just seemed to warm to him. And he was never pleased with himself when the lock would finally yield, like it was just a natural expression of gratitude for his gentleness and polite request.

I think he used picking locks as a truth serum of sorts, the same way the self-preserving rigidity of your mind melts when you're doing a jigsaw puzzle and your macerated mind and loose lips are draped over branches and decomposing fish-horses, saying any old thing before you realize it's out. It's a mindfully mindless activity and you get stuck in the middle somewhere. He would tell me stories about my dad when he was young and then go quiet. Silence is evil, so I would always reciprocate with whatever was dripping from my limp inhibition, and my honesty and secrets and doubts would swallow the heavy emptiness. He would just grunt at all the right punctuation and sentence breaks until I'd run out of all of my mental fragmentation. Then he'd reassure me and tell me what my dad was doing at that moment, always reporting it as though he'd received a letter from him recently. I think it was a switch-role-switch therapy that healed us both. Between his extraction and my extract, my dad was resurrected, brushed off, and animated in memoriam every bit as much as when he'd follow Mom around the house after returning from a deployment, madly jabbering about the craziness of warzones while she cleaned. Or madly caressing her with solaces because he'd distressed her with talk of warzones he'd eventually be going back to.

Mom could have benefitted from the mental maceration of picking locks, but she was always too busy cleaning something or doing Sudoku or at the Bingo Palace.

I grab a padlock. Rake, rake, click. Re-lock. Rake, rake, click. Boring. I pick the garage door lock. No problem <<and now I have to replace all external door locks with something an amateur can't pick in thirty seconds>>.

I need to be sharp if I'm to hack Patch's front door with low relief. For more complicated, rake-resistant locks <<which Patch is sure to have employed as his apartment's watchman>>, picking locks is as much whispering sweet nothings as it is technique and mechanics. The subtleties of the binding pin or the sensitivity of the springs or an overset pin are discerned by a neuromuscular nanochoreography that's more a proprioceptive ballet than a fine motor skill. I need to remind myself what it *feels* like. However, I don't think I have anything more complicated than that building grade doorknob that basically picked itself. Maybe I should do some recon so I know what I'm working with. If it's a cipher lock, all this fuss will be for naught. But I do remember the lawyer using a key. And why would Werner Von Spazziweasel teach me how to manually bypass locks as a teenager if it wasn't to pick this very lock on this very day?

Having said that, this moment now has a very familiar tincture to it. It's like one of Captain Cataplectic's numbered scenarios. *Dillinger! Scenario 17! Hiding in plain sight you must infiltrate my headquarters with a Bogota Rake, a tension wrench, a cover story, and your wits! Urban setting, moderate foot traffic, high visibility. Nobody is watching and everyone sees. Go!*

Let's start with an ensemble from the Fall Salt Lake City Camouflage collection—any low-numbered University of Utah football jersey worn over a black hooded sweatshirt; a red University of Utah baseball cap; darker colored, boot cut jeans with tasteful scars and bleached thighs; dark, overpriced hiking boots; a two-month accumulation of facial hair <<minus the grooming>>; and a ten-year accumulation of Five Guys and Mountain Dew <<minus the concealing>>. I'm a single, anonymous drop in a Great Salt Lake of conformity.

My little red cheerleader car was way better for being inconspicuous. It *was* anonymity. That truck is like driving a lane-gormandizing middle finger down the road and parking it is like parking a cruise liner. However, Utah is a land of trucks, and for a downtown, Salt Lake City is dwarfingly spacious. I think I'll be okay.

I'm glad I opted not to drive to the apartment with that lawyer; I still have the address logged in my maps. Now I'm noticing a curiosity in my maps' search history: his apartment is also on East Broadway, right next to the polygraph place and the Proper Gentleman. That's not weird. How much of that street does he control? Patch was just a grandad that visited a lot when I was a teenager. Could he really be the mustachioed swashbuckler he seemed to be? Interdimensional time portal cartographer? I'm going back and forth with my belief of all this. He's a rascally card player, for sure, but could the gilding of omniscience not be gilding at all? Could he really be this godfather of breadths and depths? I can hear him now, *Your belief or disbelief has no bearing on the truth of a thing!*

I settle into a parking space on the south side of East Broadway and just sit. I need to case my target. <<I love using all this tradecraft speak!>> Scenario after scenario, instructions always started with *look*, just stop and *look*. Are there aberrations? Is something egregiously out of place? Are items there that shouldn't be there? Is there an inconsistency in the environment? Just *look*. He wanted me to recognize dead drops that hadn't been established, alternate ways in and out, demographics that didn't match locations, etc. These last couple of weeks have been an inconsistency and I've been on the defensive. Time to *look*, Elliot.

It's your typical late-1800s brick apartment building with an old bruises color scheme—dirty reds, chalky purples, dusty blacks. Voussoirs of a dark, beaten purple are arched between the cream springers and keystones atop each window on the top floor. Even if I hadn't been here before, I would've suspected that to be Patch's place. Stubby, Spanish-tiled eaves slope from the roof and over the complex's entrance. Wrought iron sconces, capped merlons extending from the roof, a downspout running like a glazed ureter down the side of the building, solar panels anachronistically sunbathing on the roof—otherwise it's just a stout cube of sturdiness perched in a nest of browning concrete and deeply inset egress windows. It was boring and venerable at the same time. Very clean, very tidy. There doesn't seem to be anything amiss on the . . . nope, there it is. That's what I'm looking for. Halfway up the access ladder mounted to the east side of the building, just under the second-floor platform, there's a brick, a single efflorescing brick. Every brick in the structure has retained its deep bruising but for this single brick. And you don't normally see single bricks efflorescing.

I look both ways before crossing the street <<Utah drivers>> but I'm really more interested in avoiding the watchful eyes of Vivian and that broken Mariner. I'm sure everyone on this block is an agent of the Pied Hyper somehow, but I *know* they are. I don't know if it really matters, but better safe than noticed, that's what I always say.

I walk my invisible self to the alley on the building's east side and climb the ladder. Sure enough, the leprous brick is just set into its position. I dislodge it and discover that it is about a quarter the weight you'd expect for a brick its size. Looking left and right <<since I'm no longer invisible on this ladder>>, I hook my left arm under one of the rungs and use both hands to inspect the brick— bending, twisting, crushing, sliding, pressing. Ah. Here we go. I find and press a small depression on one side and out of the other side pops a small drawer with a key in it. I have no earthly idea how he expects me to figure this stuff out. Maybe I am as brilliant as he thinks I am. Or maybe he has ten thousand keys hidden all over the building and just hopes I find one. Well, I found one, ya wee scamp!

I take the elevator to the third floor. It clearly doesn't like my weight. I can't find a certificate stating the last time this herniating elevator has been serviced. That makes me nervous. I'm pretty sure I used the stairs last time I was here, but I didn't see access to a stairwell downstairs. I think I would have remembered the eternal punishment of riding an elevator three floors with that soul-sucking lawyer.

I'm very excited. I love field trips that don't involve other humans. My breathing settles beneath the swift current now that I'm home free. Patch's apartment is the only reason to be on the third floor and the landing is an open, empty aisle lit by begrimed seventies bulbs whose waxen light can barely reach the corners. Plenty of time and privacy to pick that lock, in case this isn't actually a key to his apartment, and the sound of an elevator will alert me to any unlikely visitors. I check the kangaroo pocket of my sweatshirt for the loose lock picking tools I stored in there. I flex my chest and shoulders to make sure the backpack filled with twenty-ounce bottles of Mountain Dew and assorted goodies hasn't slipped off. I may be here a while and I don't want to raise my profile by frequent trips to the Maverik not a hundred yards down Broadway. Hopefully his power is still on so I can keep these bottles of rapture and rhapsody chilled in the fridge.

The elevator coughs, wheezes, and rasps a throaty, mechanical death rattle at its grave on the third floor. With no life to retain the muscles' rigidity, the elevator's lips part and I can feel its dying breath swim around the contours of my neck and shoulders.

And, of course it wouldn't be that simple . . .

They say it's not really fight or flight, but that it's freeze, and then fight or flight. I'm working through the *freeze* part.

This is awkward. I'm standing in an open elevator, staring at a security guard standing by Patch's front door, his face aglow with congeniality. He's looking right at me. I can't be unseen. Why is he smiling? Shouldn't he be on his guard with a stern look and some pointed questions? I could be anyone! I could be here to pick that lock and illegally gain entrance! I feel like Alice <<Herbert>> casually scribbling a note and firing it from a bow as guards with flowered halberds nod and grin approvingly at my mischief. I know, I'll tell him I just have the wrong floor.

Life rises and falls on the adjustments you make to curveballs.

"Hi. Sorry, I . . ."

"Good afternoon, Mr. Dillinger."

I look behind me in case Patch just crawled out of some hidden panel in the elevator. Certainly he wasn't talking to me. Ah, yes, certainly he *was* talking to me. Elliot, Elliot, Elliot, you muttonhead. Why foreseeth not I this? Pawn and puppet, Elliot! Pawn and puppet! Glad he cut me off before I could say anything about having the wrong floor. How weird would that have looked?

"Hello." I walk purposefully from the elevator and shake the guard's hand.

"How can I help you today, sir?"

"You're guarding Patch's apartment?"

"You call yourself Patch?"

"Call myself . . . no, I mean Mr. Dillinger, you're guarding Mr. Dillinger's apartment?"

"I'm not sure where this is going, sir. You're referring to yourself in the third person and it's confusing me."

"I'm sorry, third person? No, I know that I'm Mr. Dillinger. I'm talking about my . . ."

The more I talk, the deeper his glabella collapses onto the spine of his nose, and it dawns on me that he thinks this is my apartment. Why would he think this is my apartment? When that sleepy sandman smoke grenade of a lawyer said everything, did he mean *everything*? But, hey, why not proceed with that understanding? Maybe in time I'll be the Godfather and won't have to skulk about.

"Am I able to go in? I have a key." I hold my key up with a toothy smile.

"You don't need my permission, sir. It's your apartment, you can come and go as you please. Give me a minute to clear out the cleaners."

If he thinks this is my apartment, does he think I hired him? Isn't he a little suspicious about my hobbled inquiries? And seriously, Patch, picking locks, finding the key, what was that all about? I should just learn my lesson and expect greased skids when on Patch errands. Embrace the godfatherity! And if this is, indeed, my apartment, maybe I should vet these clowns. For all I know, these guys could be Merovingian stooges. I know I have no idea what I'm talking about, but I feel like I should start thinking about stuff like this.

"Do you happen to know who hired you?"

Gaiety stretches across the guard's face in all directions. Every feature is perfectly still in its flexed cheerfulness. He doesn't answer of course, just drapes his emerald, blinkless eyes over my curiosity and speaks through the stretched gaiety into a radio clipped to an epaulet. "Mr. Dillinger needs the room, boys."

I can hear movement in the apartment. Within ten seconds, three individuals in beige, industrial overalls with patches that read AAA Cleaners <<gimme a break>> emerge with totes and buckets pullulating neatly arranged bouquets of squeegees and brushes and squirt bottles half-filled with a spectrum of solutions. It all looks and smells legitimate.

The last of the three men is slightly obscured by the second until he passes me, but there's something, one of those aberrations Patch tuned me to, and it dumps a snapping outrage into my blood. It couldn't have been more than a wisp or a thread but for some reason it sets me off.

"Hey!" I bark it as an accusation of foul play and notice I'm pointing at him.

The three spin their heads around with some alarm. That's what it is. That mustache. He has a curled handlebar mustache. He's the same height and weight and stature as Patch and he has a curled handlebar mustache. What kind of game is this? I take a step toward him and dip my head to take a closer look. It's definitely not Patch, too young, but his unflinching tolerance of my close inspection is eerily Patch. Now you're making it awkward, Elliot. "Sorry, I thought you were someone else. False alarm. Sorry about that. As you were. Thanks for all your hard work with the . . . uh . . . cleaning the apartment."

They forgivingly resume their day.

The guard has relaxed his face to a more natural smile. I point at the front door to solicit his consent. "May I?"

He gestures me past.

"Merci beaucoup, monsieur."

He huffs out a chuckle, commending my artfulness. "Well played, sir. Enjoy your visit."

I really think I can get some good information out of this guy, but he knows I won't bother. And he's right. I have trust issues when it comes to humans, and when they talk to me, I can feel my whole body shaking its head and chanting, "Lies, lies, boring, lies, nobody cares, lies, hyperbole, lies . . ." This is a character flaw, I know, but I'm still alive and not institutionalized, so I translate that as dubiety with merit.

"Oh, and you can't remove anything from the apartment."

"I thought you said this was *my* apartment."

"Patch's orders."

This cloak and dagger crap will be the death of me.

"You'll understand when you have a look around."

As before, the door reads, "Who would cross the Bridge of Death must answer me these questions three, 'ere the other side he see." Patch and I watched *Monty Python and the Holy Grail* quite frequently, at least monthly. I think he appreciated something so lithospherically native to the mother country. And, aside from *The Princess Bride* and *Napoleon Dynamite*, it's the most quotable movie there is.

Everything is exactly as I remember it: the domed vestibule, the archways, the satellite dish farm, the chalkboards for heaven's sake, the welcome mat <<ASSUMPTIONS DIE HERE>>. It's right out of a Poe story <<appropriate, too, because there's a good chance people are buried in these walls>>.

The incisive edge of detergents and disinfectants blunts the sinfonietta of old, masculine musks. It smells more like a dead Patch now. Mom said she'd seen his body. Though I don't believe he's actually dead <<that wily rat>>, I felt myself dragged up the side of a cheese grater at that admission. I wasn't ready for that degree of finality. Still not. He was detonation after detonation and it would take much more than death to defuse him. I know the first stage of grief is denial, but if you knew Patch, you'd agree that death is not believable. Death is for mortals.

Oh, good, there's power. My afternoon is redeemed.

Okay, let's get to work.

I remove my name brand hiking boots that have never seen an actual hiking trail, place them next to the welcome mat, and tiptoe through the inner court. I start thumbing through notebooks fat with loose, handwritten notes, pocket litter, and brochures. *Botany, Botany, Botany*; *Card Tricks*; *Neo-classical Architecture for Equinoctial European Latitudes*; *Improvements on Swimming Strokes* <<?>>; *Genetic Mutations*; *Neural Mapping for Sensory Replication*; *Transparent Plasteramic Alloys for Everyday Armor*; *New Concepts for Home Flooring* <<?>>; *The Rolling Soldier Concept* <<man, this guy's tirelessly tiresome

mind>>; *Botany*; *Snap Magnetic Reversal for Ballistic Weapons*; *Axel-Mounted Intermittent Electromagnetism for Propulsion*; *The Nautilus and Anti-Nautilus* <<bingo!>>.

I find a raised trivet in the kitchen I can place my phone on, and the notebook under, so I can take sharp pictures. I'm making good time until some of the diagrams muddy my pace and I spend too much time indulging my immediate curiosity. Ah, shizburgers, some of these pages are written in our code. I really need to find that key. Where on earth would I have put what amounts to a decoder ring for a cipher I was sure I would never see again? In the trash, that's where! But if I know an undead Patch, it will somehow show up in a most unlikely whereabouts. I should probably check my pockets.

The guard was right, I understand why this information needs to stay put.

More notebooks on a table by the windows with strips of dyed fabric, hanging with weights clipped to their ends, from a large wooden frame. I wonder what was going on there. *Alternate Circulating Hemoglobin Vectors and Underwater Breathing* <<I wish I had time to photograph everything; this stuff looks interesting>>; *Gene Design and Nucleotide Rephrasing*; *Bliquelines and the Native Thread* <<bliquelines?>>; *Apical Frames*, there he is. As I'm page flipping and photographing, I'm realizing that this isn't a rabbit hole, this is a Kola Superdeep Borehole. No, this is Tartarus. How on earth does he have time to figure . . . <<I catch myself before the thought finishes itself. Time is all he has.>>

I'm already down one bottle of Dew and two Tiger's Milk bars.

I pop my head out of the apartment with another bottle of Dew and a Tiger's Milk bar. The guard's stretching gaiety accepts both offerings and he solicits a fist bump. I'm just glad he didn't do that exploding thing. So obnoxious.

More notebooks on a drafting table with unrecognizable equations etched into one side. *The Book of the Courses of the Heavenly Luminaries*; *Botany* <<again>>; *Ideas for Card Games*; *Mega-Helium Pocket Fly Suit* <<why does that sound familiar?>>; *The Starfish Suspension Bed*; *ПИКИРОВАНИЕ Math* <<I run a translator camera over that one and get *Diving*, so I photograph>>; *The Disposition of Umbrae* <<photograph>>.

Dozens <<maybe hundreds>> of uninventoried notebooks are stacked here and there. For another time, I suppose. I finally stand up straight and my back is telling me it's time to go. Have I been here for three hours already?

I gather my effects and head toward the door, only to be turned around by the dialogue and hominess of this sanctuary. There is debate and discovery in its stillness that I don't want to miss. Surveying such an archive, I am surer than ever that there's nothing dead about him.

"I'm done for the day." I don't know if I need to report this, but I feel like I should say something.

"When you get to the exit," he studies his watch, "wait forty-four seconds, then you're free to leave."

These games . . .

"Will I ever find out what that's all about?"

"Hopefully not. Have a nice day, Mr. Dillinger."

"Thanks, you do the same," I pause to read the name stitched on his uniform, "James."

I see the turnstile to the stairwell I used when I was here with Garrett Sanborne, Esq. on the other side of the landing, the west side. I use it so I'm not crushed under the pressure of making useless chitchat with James as I wait the ten minutes for the struggling elevator. Although, I could have probed. Maybe next time <<but probably not>>. I'm at the exit. Forty-four, forty-three, forty-two, forty-one . . . forty-four seconds is a long time. Games, games, games. Games from James. James's games. Blames James for lame games.

Low mountains and a sprawling valley to the west make Salt Lake City one of the great sunset cities. The evening sun is Bob Rossing a heaven-drawn canvas of clouds pinched at the horizon. The clouds roll like the swells of an inverted ocean and powdery-pink, evenly-spaced ridges cradle the darkly lavendered dead furrows of the deep sea. Fingers of pill-bottle orange flame from a softening inferno caress the roiling surface of the great ocean as they collapse into a retreating sun. Colors are never so beautiful as those played by light and sky.

CHAPTER 29

"When you go looking for something specific, your chances of finding it are very bad. Because of all the things in the world, you're only looking for one of them."
– Daryl Zero, *The Zero Effect*

I add *puzzles* to my gratitude list. I add *guardian angels*. I add *Mountain Dew* again.

Being a practiced people mover, it's not my character to work smarter than harder, but there's just too much to turn over in this house to go scavenging. So I sit on my couch, eyes closed, and trace a dipping, weaving thread through my history with that cipher. The decryption is clear as water in my head—it's a piece of typing paper folded in quarters with the symbols and their translations scribbled in mechanical pencil. I'm such an accomplished sip-taker, I don't need to open my eyes. I would fold it up and put it in a lime green, suede-textured notebook with a tree stamped on the front. I'm a methodical and theme-driven hoarder of life's bits, so it would be with . . . with other figures and . . . representations and symbols . . . and it would probably . . . holy hell for Hannah, I know exactly where it is.

I dash to a forgotten desk drawer and withdraw a clear storage bin filled with my autobiography as account registers. Digging, digging, digging, voila! There she is, buried under fill dirt of ledgerized debits and credits ten years deep <<expressing linear measurements in spans of time is kind of handy>>. Can you believe that? Why would I have kept this? And how would I have connected those dots so quickly? <<Answer: Mountain Dew.>>

It pays to be a maudlin packrat sometimes.

I add *epiphanies* to my gratitude list. I stand there for a moment wondering how absurd it would be to add Mountain Dew again.

I unfurl it gently from the corners like a disintegrating treasure map. A bit busy, but just as I left it. It was always a sort of work in progress. We must have been picking dial combination locks at the time because the margins are filled with its math. And I have some nasal spray retrieval times in the bottom left corner. Eleven point three eight seconds, not bad. Too bad they're all times with asterisks! That four-toothed, weasel-eyed, red mercury-peddling mountebank. It wasn't even a stopwatch! But man was that fun.

I quickly scan it into my computer and e-mail it to myself before the ether steals it away again.

I get the tedium out of the way first by allocating a PowerPoint slide to each digital image recorded at Patch's apartment. I may not be able to remove anything, but I'm disciplined and determined enough to recreate it. *Apical Frames, The Disposition of Umbrae, The Nautilus and Anti-Nautilus, ПИКИРОВАНИЕ Math.* There were several dozen notebooks I didn't get to, but this should keep me plenty busy.

Apical Frames. I study the diagrams as I format each slide. My fingers are feathering and squaring the paper's deeply inscribed drawings and captions. I do remember him mentioning the plurality of apical frames, though the explanations in the Manuscript are lite versions of what's depicted here. Okay, so, every time someone Pik-s and recouples with his native hull in the past, wherever he recoupled becomes another reconstituted archived frame, a now apical frame in the past, that is experienced as a present reality to all involved in that segment of the frameset. Everyone in that segment would be sort of swept up in that apical frame which is progressing through time at its regular pace and would be . . . consciously *living*, I guess is the best word, at that time. And that deeper reconstituted apical frame advances <<ascends?>> at the same rate as the principal apical frame, the *objective present*. I guess it wouldn't make sense for it to advance at any other rate as it would either lag or overtake.

So any individual, at any moment, could be experiencing multiple, nay, dozens of fragments of his life, all as a *relative present* to that individual, at different apical frames in the past and one at the present <<if that individual was still alive at the objective present, I guess>>. How is that possible? What happens if apical frames are active at ages four, eleven, nineteen, twenty-two, twenty-six, and twenty-seven and I make a slightly different decision at the eleven-year-old apical frame? Does it affect all future apical frames? Does it affect the whole frameset from there on out, apical frame or archived? Does anyone on these reconstituted frames other than those with lendemains know they're concurrently living different parts of their lives? Do they sense something is off or unnatural? Is this what the update reconciles? If somebody suffered a Gontlet death in 2000 and a pikirovatel Pik-ed back to 1998 and changed something that ended up preserving that dead dude's life, would the umbra of that dead dude be sucked back into his hull from the Gontlet at the update? Could he possibly live beyond his previous 2000 death date? I feel like I should already know the answers to these questions, but a drain is clogged somewhere in my head and the information hasn't slipped far enough down yet.

Okay, here's my answer. This shows that all changes are, relatively speaking, incorporative and additive, back to the first instance of <<all of this is mathematically notated with deltas and sigmas and such, so it takes a minute to interpret>> deviation from the original frameset. So, if I do something different <<or if some element of my environment is changed so that it makes what I originally did an impossibility>> at my eleven-year-old apical frame as well as at my twenty-two-year-old apical frame, the eleven-year-old change will ultimately influence and shape how the twenty-two-year-old change is modified and recorded, or overwrite it completely. If I'm interpreting this correctly. So maybe there is an advantage to going back as far as possible—you maximize the changes effected. If that's what you're after. But here it says that all aspects of self, namely personality, self-perception, character, exposure, experience, dispositions, temperament, one's umbral totality <<what he calls gravure>>, dictates the nature of the deflection of the summative change. So, the established and establishing *me* is more or less a buffer against any wild alterations? My nature is like those lane bumpers in bowling alleys against guttering my life? Or guttering it, I guess, if my nature is destructive. There's a note that says, "We are as we are as we ever were."

Maybe extrapolating from 500-level textbooks cold cod isn't such a good idea. I feel like I'm already getting ahead of myself and that all of my questions and musings are going to lay my stupidity bare when the full compass of this scheme is understood.

Okay, here's something: this says there's a worldwide, daily update to the frameset at 0000 hours Paris time beginning at the earliest <<earliest depth of the frameset, that is>> instance of *any* deviation from the original frameset. He has a smiley face next to "0000 hours Paris time" and a note that says, "Carcassonne, France." In all cases, these deviations are attributed to changes effectuated by trouplongeurs <<pikirovateli>> inserted into established, previously unmolested archived frames. There is no other cause for changes to archived frames, as far as he knows. It seems like Pik-ing is a substantial disruptor of time and requires a lot of wrinkle-ironing. There's a diagram that looks like a train station split-flap display board standing on end that depicts a change setting off a series of modifications up the frameset at the time of the update, all the way up to the principal apical frame. I'm just getting my bearings here . . . okay, good, yes, I get it. So, if a pikirovatel goes back to 1940, say, and changes something <<or influences a change; I guess he doesn't have to explicitly elicit the change himself, but something must be different for some change to result>>, it will rise as a bubble through the frameset and pop, if I may, at the next instance of change <<the bubble and pop stuff is my own metaphor here for illustrative purpi; I'm not quoting anything from the notebook>>.

That second instance of change will then be pressed into the context of the initial change. For instance, if a pikirovatel <<now a lendemain occupying his native hull and supplanting his native umbra>> decides not to have the child she originally had, any subsequent change further up the frameset related to that child never-conceived will, naturally, be irrelevant. Some second instances of change will be unaffected by the initial instance of change because they have no connection to one another. But, as Patch notes, the Mero are very clever, and their intentions are constellations that multiply up the frameset to effect policy broadly and deeply. No, shallowly. Vertically? I don't know how to express upwards from a depth. This becomes exponentially complex when you factor in dozens of pikirovateli/trouplongeurs evincing alterations at a variety of geographical locations, up and down the frameset, sometimes at cross purpi, sometimes inter-generationally coordinated, all with a professed and avowed utilitarianism. Since all apical frames move at a steady rate, no change will intersect with another <<unless two pikirovateli happen to Pik to the same frame, no?>> and all is left messy and discombobulated until the next 0000 hours Paris time <<Carcassonne time>>. At that moment <<ten-thousandth of a second, I'm guessing>>, the frameset, from the initial change to the original frameset within the last twenty-four hours, is updated to reflect an incorporation of all modifications, the outcomes of which are based on what *did* happen, not what *would have* happened, if events were subject to an unfolding at the standard progression of time. He writes, "NOT PROBABILISTIC, CHARACTERISTIC!!" in the margin. Apparently the system has built into its belts and pulleys a mechanism to withstand deep wounds to its infrastructure by resetting every day with imperceptible scars from a scalpel of acquiescent re-wiring. He is insistent that this split-flap display update is idiosyncratic and not deterministic. But that the frameset has as much right to self-preservation as any individual umbra or umbrae collectively. <<Huh?>> Is he saying the frameset itself has its own mind and will?

This is just smashingly sensational. I am much more easily convinced of things I think are too strange for a fellow human to contrive.

Apparently, any changes made to the frameset that incorporate the native umbrae of deceased Dovolniya or Inscrutables into reconstituted frames is . . . I'm not sure I understand this. It looks like their death is at the exact same time in every iteration of the update, like the update can't spare them from the moment of their original demise regardless of changes made to effect or prevent it. <<I'll save pondering that at greater depth for a long run.>> But he does answer my previous question, at least with regards to the Blanc-Becs. For the most part, this doesn't affect the Lifers because their Gontlet deaths predate a Pik-able depth, but for the Blanc-Becs, if a change is made in the frameset by a pikirovatel that obviates their original Gontlet death, their umbra will absolutely be reintegrated with their hull at the update. That's insane. So they can resurrect people and extend their lives? I wonder if they'd done that for Patch and that's why they referred to him as the Immortal at the funeral. I wonder why they didn't do that for his most recent death. Maybe his one hundred and twenty years expired and there's nothing they could have done.

I'm starting to get a headache. Between hunching over notebooks for hours and trying to crack this chicken scratch, I think it's ibuprofen time. I lay down on my stomach on the carpet and stretch my limbs out like a bloated starfish. How would he know that the Dovolniya are associated with frames outside the frameset? I guess you could talk to the Dovolniya in the Gontlets. I wonder how long you could last in the Gontlets getting information from the Dovolniya before you got stuck there.

So this is why I would have no idea if I've lived a different life every day, because I'm still just a native umbra, with no lendemain, unknowingly getting swept up in the daily update. And when I Pik, my umbra, a lendemain, will be disconnected from the plumbing of the update and I'll know what changes every day. I don't know if that's better or worse. Seems like it would get frustrating being aware of a new reality every day, if that's really how it would be. I see now why this requires a patient and disciplined mind. Minds <<at least like mine>> are most bent by unrealized expectations and having no control over your life—there'd be a lot you'd have to get out of your head about.

My curiosity is chastising my indulgence in this headache. Gut up, Elliot! Only three notebooks to go.

The Disposition of Umbrae. Code, code, code. I'll have to translate all that later. Now this is interesting—since only your umbra Pik-s, you will never appear to be a different physical age than you were at any given frame. If I'm seventy in 2000, I will always appear to be forty in 1970 since hull and frame are archived associatively. I may have a seventy-year-old umbra, and, commensurately, the wisdom <<kwazants in general, I guess>> that attends the additional thirty years, but I will appear as a forty-year-old. That means the Patch doppelganger I saw at the apartment could *not* have been Patch. Patch could only be the age he's supposed to be at this frame, seventy-something. That is, assuming I have the whole story. Which I'm sure I don't and can't rule out that being Patch. If he somehow figured out how to Pik with both umbra and hull <<what the Russians at his funeral were concerned about>>, then there are no knowns, givens, or certainties.

Half of this page is code. The other half talks about the longevity of the umbra being capped at one hundred and twenty total years. There's a grid with dates and ages. So, if you're sixty and you Pik back to twenty, then live until you're sixty and Pik back to twenty again, and repeat that one last time, you have exhausted all one hundred and twenty years of your umbra's lifespan. He says there's no way around this expiration at one hundred and twenty years. If you're only thirty years old and in perfect health when the hundred and twentieth year is reached, you drop dead. One hundred and twenty is the limit. He doesn't offer any explanations for this limit. Then there are all these dire warnings about Pik-ing to a time before your birth. It's apocalyptic, apparently.

The Nautilus and Anti-Nautilus. I don't think I fully grasped his explanation of these concepts in the Manuscript. I have a little more Mountain Dew in me now, so maybe my brain soil will be more fertile this time.

Okay, here we go. Nautilus. He has the Earth as a flattened disk in all these diagrams where the center is the North Pole and the outer rim is Antarctica. Oh, yeah, the routes are much easier to conceptualize like that. The nascent vent is a . . . what? Are there mountains at the North Pole? This shows a giant tree at the top of a mountain at the North Pole that sort of molts <<probably not the best word>> a cast of its shadow that slips down the mountain where it's funneled into its cylindrical shape by a pool that circulates counterclockwise at the base of the mountain. It looks like a page from the portolan of fourteenth century voyagers. The course of the nautilus looks like, well, the cross-sectioned interior of a nautilus, spiraling from the North Pole outward to a fairly southerly point, I think he said eighty degrees south latitude. The anti-nautilus, the vent's track back to the North Pole, looks like a copy of the nautilus, just flipped over and joined together at the nautilus's starting and ending points. I see, so the nautilus and anti-nautilus are a mirror image of one another and the trip out is a reflection of the trip back, but the origins and termini are at the same points. So a new vent is *nascent* for its initial nautilus to the south for a new moon cycle, anti-nautilus for a new moon cycle to the north after losing its connection to the principal apical frame, nautilus for a new moon cycle to the south, anti-nautilus for a new moon cycle to the north, and on and on for one hundred and twenty corkscrewing years until the petram has shaven it down entirely from the bottom and it is officially retired by time. With the creation of a nascent vent at the beginning of each new moon cycle, the direction the vent begins traveling rotates ninety degrees clockwise. I guess I should have looked up the word *quadskelion* when I read it the first time; it is an apt characterization. So between the nautilus and anti-nautilus, the four cardinal directions, depths of about twenty years, and a new vent popping up <<popping down?>> every month or so, there are significant occasions for intersect. My heavens. The concept is simple enough, I guess, but when you add counterclockwise to spiraling to downward to new paradigms to new vocabulary to new concepts to new realities, it just makes me want to nap. And I know this is just the fondant. All the new rules and realities are hurting my brain and I haven't even hit the sponge and ganache. I don't know if that's weakness or strength.

Just glancing at the images from the last notebook, the one about Pikirovaniya math, I just know I'm going to need a full night's sleep and something from Carl's Jr.

DAY 13

Chapter 30

"Distrust and caution are the parents of security."
– Benjamin Franklin

I'm not a battle-scarred mischief maker, but when there is something I must know, I feel like mischief is the only polished, Blackthorn shillelagh <<Patch owned one of these>> that will crack open the pretenses and expose the truth. Blackgoat's Butkus-baked praise of my athletic prowess was flattering, to be sure, but the sharp slices of light glinting off the tripwires cordoning this improbability are too nettlesome to disregard. I have a natural distrust of anything with lungs, but the timing, the location, the scale, it was all tied in too tidy a bow to break the bulwarks of believability.

I'm on the sixth floor of the John A. Moran Eye Center, loitering in what is supposed to be a café but with no food, no staff, and a view that comprises much of Salt Lake County, including the university's soccer field. My eyes aren't great, so I brought my trusty monocular to extend the field of focus. Utah is full of weirdness, so an oversized man peering across the valley through a monocular from the heights of a derelict café on the research floor of a medical building is really not that strange. The mumbling to myself part might be a little odd, but not the monocular.

Even though it's not raining, everything about the steels and irons and chromes of the sky portends rain. I should come up here more often just for the view. You usually have to pay for a view this awesome.

Some guy in scrubs comments on the view. I agree and hope he stops talking and goes away.

Between the slightly elevated softball field, some obnoxiously placed ever-stupid trees, and a forest of light poles, only parts of the soccer field are visible. There's a group of football types gathered around one of the technical areas of the soccer field. These must be my homies. There he is, that Nathan Blackgoat character, the Maestro of Mayhem, the Robot of Destruction, with his jellying falsiloquence and rolling forehead and neatly trimmed mustache, pacing the soccer field, appearing and disappearing behind the light poles. I'm waiting for his tell—flaring of the nostrils, flushing, maybe some knuckle cracking. I mean this universally, of course, not literally. I know this is a bluff, but the proof of the pudding is in the tasting. And I intend to taste that pudding. <<That didn't come out as sinister as I was hoping.>>

All his players are suited up and on the field, but they're just standing around. Would they be waiting for me to get started? They don't even know if I'm showing up, so it doesn't make sense that they'd be waiting for me. Maybe they're just waiting for the rest of their guys to show up. I've never been to a football practice where everyone is just standing around. Football players of all ages are like little kids—if there's a ball around, they're throwing, catching, or kicking.

These guys are all just shuffling about in Butkus-Blackgoat's changing directions like an uncertain school of fish and nobody's saying anything. The mask is already cracking a little, Blackgoat. What are you up to? Now he's communicating with someone on a hand-held radio. His players are getting fidgety. All right, time to add some leaven . . .

I text the number from his business card: This is the guy from the park last Friday. I'm on my way. Should be there in five or ten minutes.

I know texting in full sentences makes most people twitchy, but Blackgoat looks like a boomer. When in Rome, right?

I do love saying that name: Blackgoat. Blackgoat. It sounds like something that had very specific rules for sacrifice under the Law of Moses. Red heifer. Blackgoat.

He is . . . checking his phone. And here we go. Now he looks like the Sorcerer's Apprentice, his arms circling, pushing, waving, animating the fidgety, dispersing the loiterers. The players divide and fold around a line of scrimmage. Now they're running plays. These are legitimate plays, that's a positive sign. Blackgoat is scanning his surroundings and checking his watch like he's cautiously anticipating the arrival of a mistress with promise of . . . a pleasant conversation over good steak. He's back on the push-to-talk radio. Who are you talking to, Nate and your spate of fate?

I watch the dough rise in its richly-colored, gray-walled proving drawer.

Blackgoat. I'm trying not to say it out loud. The monocular is drawing quite enough attention.

After ten minutes of surveilling, politely smiling at curious onlookers, checking my phone, and julienning Blackgoat's patience into ribbons, it's time for the poorly-kneaded dough to collapse: Very sorry about this, Mr. Blackgoat, but I got in a car accident on the way. Won't be able to make it today.

He's checking his phone. Now he's baring his teeth. He looks as happy as a Doberman whose food has been taken away mid-meal. Now he's on the radio. He barks an order to the players and they all file by, taking something handed to them as they pass. My monocular isn't as high-powered as I hoped and I can't make out what he's handing them. Money? Is he paying them? Then the field empties. Everyone disappears behind the everstupid trees but Nate and his great plate of hate. He looks around, shakes his head, checks his watch one last time, and he, too, disappears.

My phone grumbles: NP had to canx anyway reports of <<lightning bolt emoji>> <3 mi. here every tues and thurs at 10 see ya soon

I can't stand this punctuation-less era.

So, that's it.

Centuries of inter-generational coordination, eh? *Am I a dog, that thou comest to me with staves?* I may have been hibernating for a decade, but I'm clever as a dragon and patient as a spider <<I'm neither of those things>>. And I thaw out quickly. Clearly, I have been underestimated.

My smile nearly stretches out of the bounds of its muscles and out of the sides of my mouth spills this guttural, diabolical chuckle. I'm so pleased with myself right now, I don't even care that my growling glee has caused a passing researcher to distort her face into something between horror and contempt.

This may appear a trifling observation, and piffling in its consequence, but much has been denuded, and with only a monocular, a little elevation, and an unwinnable yarborough. This community, this enterprise, of which I now seem to be a shareholder, is already cracking under the weight of its haste. Now, I say *haste* with the realization that decades may have gone into the planning of this ruse. Neither here nor there, though, because this disclosure suggests, at least from what I can hold down until 0000 Carcassonne time, that there is a structure, there are schemers, and I am somehow, for some reason, considered enough of a threat to orchestrate these flytrap hijinks. As of 0001 Carcassonne time I may have no recollection of this, but I am liberated at this moment. Is there a way to subvert the update? Can I use dead drops the same way those Frenchmen at the funeral alluded to, or do I have to be a lendemain for that to work? I probably have to be a lendemain—if things changed, I wouldn't even remember that I established a dead drop, let alone where it was. My things-to-ponder-on-a-long-run list is growing. I need to add *long runs* to my gratitude list.

I text: Thanks for your understanding, Mr. Blackgoat.

I peek through the monocular one last time. The empty field looks disappointed that all its football left. Maybe that's just me projecting—I love watching football, even if it's just small market semi-pros practicing.

Blackgoat. I think I may have said that one out loud.

DAY 14

Chapter 31

"Give the people what they want and then go have a hamburger."
– Judy Garland

I'm not a fan of overpriced rabbit food. Some people are tricked into thinking they're doing themselves a favor eating a 1,400-calorie salad rather than a 1,200-calorie burger, but I'm not one of them. And to add insult <<the sweet savor of fat-saturated, grilling beef>> to injury <<a colorful display of garden scraps>>, Tonyburgers is right next door. I have to remind myself that this is about my poor mother. Holy haymakers, that smells like the hot breath of burning beasts. I would ask how Zupas competes with the smell of actual food pouring in, but this place is empty, so clearly it doesn't.

I walk into a thankfully post-lunch rush dining room and see my mom sitting alone, hunched over a plate of greens that more whet an appetite than sate one.

"Did you already pay for that? The person that extends the invitation pays!"

"I'm so sorry, son, I got here a few minutes early and everything looked so good."

"You got here early so I wouldn't be able to pay for you, didn't you?"

"Hogwash in hand towels, El, from what your grandfather left us, psh, what is money?"

"Yeah, about that . . . maybe I lost consciousness during the part I was instructed to give you something. As the executor of that will, I want to know how you ended up with money without it coming from me? And why didn't I end up with any?"

"Oh, yes, I remember Mr. Sanborne mentioning something about that. I'm sure it's on its way. But money in the bank is so much nicer than all your grandfather's treasure maps and Easter egg hunts. Who has the energy? I just swipe this card and everything is magically paid for."

"You are really mean. For real."

Mom lets leak a quiet and rare chortle. Maybe these get-togethers are good for her. I haven't heard her laugh in . . . I don't remember the last time I heard her laugh. Maybe unbounded wealth has put her in a good mood.

"But look at you, you little bean pole! You look like you're wasting away! What's that all about?"

"Oh . . . about fifteen pounds."

"You are so much your father."

I can see little spasms in her neck dimple, like she's choking on inaudible sobs. I quickly grab her hand <<because this has needed to be said for a decade plus>> and try to preempt a scene with a little reality. "Mom . . . dear, dear, Mother . . . I had a father. You had a husband. We had things good for a while. It's okay to just . . . relish in that. Nothing lasts forever. It's the way of the world. Everything falls apart disastrously. All we can do is appreciate when things go right. You guys did a fantastic job of making things go right." <<I have no idea who just said all that.>>

She's looking through me again. "You're right. I'm sorry." She takes another bite of appetite-accelerating food and chews <<with her mouth closed>> slowly. She sips her water. "It's just that . . . I spend most of my days trying to figure out how to let him go. I've spent the better part of fifteen years trying to figure out how to let him go, and I think I'm struggling more now than the day that frumpy army colonel came to our door and ruined our lives. I loved your father so much because he loved me so much. And he loved me so much because I loved him so much. And somewhere along the line we got ourselves mixed up in each other, so much that it felt like we were just . . . some kind of tempered steel. Every mile farther from me he'd travel, more of me would go with him. Do you know what it feels like to die and continue living? Do you know what it feels like to live as half a person?" All of her faculties are languorous and still, but tears are accentuating the deepening lines of her face and magnifying the green of her eyes. She has to lean away from her greens so the salt of her tears doesn't season them.

I've had my fair share of crying recently, and I certainly feel like it at the moment, but I don't want to compete for sympathy so I put on my brave face. "How can I help you, Mom? There must be something I can do."

"Let's just keep doing this. This is good. Maybe someday this will be an acceptable substitute. You are your father, which makes it very difficult to be around you sometimes, but it wouldn't be fair to avoid you for that reason."

"Excuse me, I'm way cooler than Dad ever was! That guy took baths and wore sweaters and made bad puns and mowed the lawn in his uniform and made bread for the neighbors. He was a dork!"

She's crying, but she's beaming as she chokes out, "He *was* a dork. Oh, he was such a great dork."

"I'll try to stop being like him. I'll make better puns."

"You just be you, sweetheart. The only person you should ever change for is your wife. Nudge, nudge."

She takes another bite of her compost pile and it gives me an opportunity to repurpose the conversation. "So, Mother, tell me what you know about Patch's, Grandad's, whereabouts for the past decade. Did you know he had a place in town?"

"Of course. He would visit every now and again until a few years ago, and then he just stopped coming around."

"Why didn't you say anything? Why wouldn't he visit me?"

"I guess we just got the impression that you didn't want to be interrupted."

That was probably a reasonable observation. I have been a bit of a Unabomber recluse the last many years, only emerging from my extended pity party to restock.

"Do you know what he was up to for the last decade?"

"Not sure. He's very clever about steering conversations away from himself. Your dad was the same way. He'd make you feel like you were the most fascinating thing in the universe and you didn't want to disrupt his amazement by turning the focus back on him. I'm not sure your grandfather ever had a job. I think he might have been an inventor for a time, but who knows. He's a very private person. I gave him your address. Did he really never visit you?"

Everything she's saying sounds believable; I don't see any breaks in her narrative. And still, I don't believe a word she says.

"No, never. So, what about all these splashy rumrunners, as you call them? Where did he meet all these characters?"

"Oh, jeepers, right, that motley lot. What a side show. Your grandfather travelled an awful lot. There was no telling where he'd be from week to week. I think he actually visited your dad in Afghanistan a few times. What a harebrain. Absolutely nothing scared or intimidated that man. He was a god among mortals. So at ease, so genuine, so confident. I wish I had his moxie. I hope he's keeping your dad company until I can join them."

I'm so sure he's not dead that her comment stuns me a little. My incredulity almost erupts into thunderstruck denials.

"So why the closed casket? I heard one of those rumrunners mention that he'd tried to open the casket but that it was locked. Why would he do that?"

"Elliot, I think you're overthinking things. He picked up some strange associates over the years. Strange people do strange things."

"Okay, but why lock the casket in the first place? Did he suspect somebody might try to open it?" <<I.e., me.>> "Why didn't he just have the casket buried before the memorial service and have the service with no casket?"

"Again, son, overthinking things."

"I don't know, am I? I know he was a strange guy, but he was always so deliberate and every subtlety of every syllable had such specific purpose. There was no waste with Pa—Grandad."

"Well, then, maybe there was a reason for all that. But if there was, I'm sure it was meant for you to figure out. You guys always had your puzzles and riddles. Maybe it's your final exam."

"So you know nothing more than I do about him and what he's been up to for the last ten years . . ."

She won't look up, just sits there raking her rainbow mulch with the back of her fork. Then she stabs at eight different colors and takes an unusually large bite. I watch her chew like she thinks I'll get up and leave if she doesn't make some immediate comment.

"Are you happy, Elliot?"

Her eyes are now so fixed and steady it gives them the illusion of vibrating.

The question unbalances my voice a little. "What?"

"Are you enjoying your life, Elliot?"

I don't like how she keeps using my full first name. I'm still waiting for her to blink. Maybe it's *my* eyes that are vibrating because her irises are jumping all over the place now and she's sitting there like a young Drew Barrymore trying not to blow cars up. It seems like the overhead lights are flickering. I've never been afraid of my mom before. I'm waiting for her lips to split and a forked tongue to push wickedly through. For the love of all that is unblinking, woman, blink!

"To what do these questions tend?"

She knows what I'm trying to do there and points her fork straight at my face. The tine-directed death ray is shrinking my ethmoid bone and her last two questions are howling like wolves in the center of my head.

"Why would you think I'm not enjoying my life?"

"That is not an answer, son, that is the avoidance of an answer."

I have no more privacy. A prickly breeze is reporting all of my exposed parts. Everyone knows everything about me and they're laying mines along all the routes of evasion in and out of my confined platform of naked truth. I pull my head sidelong and lower my eyelids. "What's with the inquisition, Mom? It's been a while since you've expressed this level of concern for me."

Her eyes don't move. The fork doesn't move. The lingual bifurcation is peeking through tightening lips. "I want you to take some time to seriously evaluate your life and what you honestly want from it. You've been putting off living for too long now. If I'm going to let your father die, you're going to start living. I can't bear to see you hiding in that house all alone and pretending it's making you happy. It's just not you. No more wallowing in this bog of missed opportunities and football fantasies. You're a grown man; act like a grown man."

I'm gutted, of course, but it's not my habit to emote. My minesweeper clears an overgrown path of escape and I facetiously ask, "Is this about grandchildren?"

I can tell she isn't humored by my ironically puerile response to her request. The fork comes down, her lips loosen, and the corners of her eyes slump into helpless disappointment.

"Okay. Okay, I'll get out more. I promise." She's shrinking me with her sobriety. "I promise, Mom. Patch's. . .Grandad's <<I still can't believe she doesn't know these names>> Easter egg hunts have already gotten me out a dozen times!"

Game played.

The filaments holding her concern in a creased sort of line don't relent. Her voice takes on a melody of desperate pleading. "Regrets are terrible demons, but trying to reshape your history never really works. Things don't ever really change the way you think they can. Just live your life right the first time around and you'll never have regrets."

I am more focused on her tone and the contours of her grimace, but something feels horribly unwell about those words. What did she just say? I heard demons and reshaping history and regrets. The whole theme felt very Pik-ish, but I don't think I heard enough of it to justify alarm.

"I'm sorry, I think I just had a mini-seizure and my brain was . . . farting." <<That wasn't what I wanted to say.>> "What did you just say?"

The scorn is back. She holds my concentration with the fork again and lectures, "Think very carefully about everything you say and do for the rest of your natural born life, young man. I mean it. You only get one chance at this life. That's it. There's no going back. There are no do-overs." The fork is blasting its death ray in all wild directions now. "You do it right the first time or you live in regret. And you don't handle life's disappointments very well. And I'm not talking about football here. And don't look at me like that." <<I might've had a look.>> "If you want me to accept my reality better, you have to accept yours. We both need to pull ourselves out of this funk before we do something reckless. Do you understand me?"

I was listening that time. Everything about what she just said demands a reluctant solemnity. I can't process all of it quickly enough to make a reply. I'm sitting here with a blank stare, not just stunned by the content, but wondering who in hell's heart attack this woman is. Why, in the midst of my study of do-overs, is she emphatically insisting that there are no do-overs? *Coincidences were invented by the statistically idiotic to avoid accountability!* Yes, right, Patch, absolutely right!

I still can't think of a reply.

"Elliot?" Her solicitude sounds genuine.

"Mother, I promise not to do anything reckless if you don't. Everything I do henceforth and forever will be with measured intent and noble purpose." All the muscles of my brow and forehead felt tight upon that oath, so it must have been made in earnest. She appears convinced.

DAY 15

Chapter 32

"There is a saying in the Neverland that, every time you breathe, a grown-up dies."
– Peter Pan, J.M. Barrie

Saturdays used to be a finish-line, a decompressing exhalation. Now I spend Friday nights holding my breath. Other than a skydiver using the Salt Flats to make sweet, horrifying music with his body, it hasn't been as feverish as I feared. Oh, and my car being stolen. And the spot polygraph. And the deconstruction of my reality. And the funky dreams. I know electricity will soon be running unbroken through all the circuits of my life; until then I hold my breath.

My house is a fluent translation of the morning sun and it's dictating that naked warmth in my dining room. I knew I'd be enchaired <<I was going to say *butt-bound*, but enchaired sounds more professional>> for who knows how many hours with the next assignment, so I woke up at the devil's hour to go for a long run. My savage hatred of waking up to alarms is only smothered by the oppression of the valley's dusky tranquility, the enormity of its glabrous muttering, and, best of all, its post-apocalyptic desertion. I've always envied those characters in movies that wake up from a coma to a world without people. How gloriously peaceful. I was so distracted by the image of that girl in my dreams that I forgot to think about all the things I was going to think about on my next long run. I didn't really get to see her face in the first dream, but it was etched pyrographically onto the insides of my corneas in the second. I know there's no way to gauge fair and unfair in this world, but if anything approaches unfair, it would be putting the image of a gorgeous, fictional girl's face in my head and implying a preternatural and intimate association between us. And to twist the knife, I know her name. Well, I don't know her name, but it's sailing across all the distal extremities of my hypoglossal nerve. It starts with a . . . agh! Piper? Allison? Hayden? See, it's right there! I may pine, it may seize, but that image does take the sting out of running. Now I sit, showered, purged, purified before the newly dedicated maternity hospital of seraph-hand hewn marble, the apricity of the edging dawn reading its transcript through my radiating walls.

Assignment #4: INVINCIBILITY

To the Gontlets! Yes, we must revisit the Gontlets for this exercise. <<I already don't like the Gontlets. They sound like a big, never-flushing toilet.>> *Once the vent has discarded you, you will, in many respects, be processed. The administration of the Gontlets will register your arrival, your native hull will begin its summons, and the welcoming committee will press. The registration of your arrival will sidestep your cognizance and you will faintly detect the magnetism of your native hull's beckoning beacon. Again, we are mostly concerned with the candied carousels and carnival workers of the welcoming committee; they constitute recoupling's most prominent encumbrance.*

Trouplongeurs have been devising strategies to ford the Gontlets for centuries (pikirovateli only decades, technically). Those with the greatest navigability have developed a certain degree of transcendence in their forays, the same transcendence you will need to develop. I have systematized the influences that will prey upon you in the Gontlets, but I have not adequately impressed upon you the humanity-pealing pandemonium that will shear and tear at every hairsbreadth of the spectrum of human proclivity, especially the first few times through the Gontlets.

First few times? What in hell's happy hades do you mean by *first few times*? I thought this was about going back to sixteen to play football! This better not be some Janus-faced bait and switch to install me as a wrench in the machinations of a centuries-old mafia of time governors! <<Though I know perfectly well that's exactly what I'm being primed for.>>

We steady ourselves against threats, demur at flattery, bleed from our hearts at unmitigated torment, bristle at enmity, defer to confident expertise, stand in lines upon direction, stall at comedic banter, and cower when multiple entities compete for our attention simultaneously. All of this will be multiplied and folded into your perfect perception. All of your instincts will be standing on edge. You must understand that, though all of this attention is directed towards you, nothing is happening to you. You have the right to remain silent, as it were. You have the right to remain flat and unreactive. You have the right to remain motionless and unaffected. You have the right to sing and scream. All entities of the Gontlets, including your umbra for its hopefully brief sojourn, are autonomous beings. You do not have to let the novelty and babel of the Gontlets chew you up. It will, at first, but this exercise will help you quiet your mind and meet hellfire with hearth fire. The interplay between umbra and umbra is much the same as that of hull and hull, but the pain of any physical assault in the Gontlets is an anticipatory sensation based on expectation and your experience with the hull. It is like the aching, cold sizzle of your legs as you walk across gravel barefoot—it is more artifact than fact. This is to say, the prospect of any material assault is feigned and not worth the presentiment.

Well that's disappointing. How am I to use my size to herald pain if it's an illusion?

We have a tendency to politeness when we are addressed in any civil manner. We assume politeness begets politeness and most of civilized humankind grants benefit of the doubt. In general this should be suppressed in the Gontlets because it is a counterproductive convention in a country of peddlers and solicitors. The good opinion of any entity in the Gontlets, including the Dovolniya, is not worth incidental intercourse. The Dovolniya will forgive any brusque brush. The rest are inconsequential.

By saying that, I am not promoting a discourteous posture. Certainly that would spike strip kwazants. There is a substantial difference between malevolently uncivil and concentering tunnel vision, and you will need to gather your forces on the side of the latter. Though it will not be immediately noticeable, there is a life to save (your own) and you will need to temper the temptation to small (or any other variety) talk with a breaststroke of determination that cuts through a sea of else and extraneity. This transcendence will look more like an athlete emerging from a tunnel, ignoring all the hands outstretched for a high five as he is dialing in psychologically rather than an affront of callous and spiteful snubs. Omitting the Exiles, these entities are not vindictive counterforces, so there is really no reason to be curt. Just be dialed in.

Today's assignment will collapse your attention, soften your surroundings, and be so internally distracting that externality will recede into a distant and recessed plane of indistinctions. It will depressurize your mind, at the same time pressurizing everything external. The essence of this exercise is pain, but it will be self-inflicted, self-sustained, and forthwith relieved at your whim. This ensures that willful resolve will be the sculptor of your centered attention. As you dim the roar of the throng, the tinnitic hum of the native hull will be more discernable and more magnetic.

Reactivity is the natural byproduct of your size, strength, and programming to physically contain, and you will need to declaw those impulses so you are not mired in the quicksand of confrontation and toplofty debates. Proverbs does not have great things to say about pride and haughty spirits, and I know what a sucker you are for an animated row. So calmy doony, ya wee twitch, and remember that though this attention is directed toward you, nothing is happening to you. Hopefully your polygraph experience adequately convinced you that your mind is an inviolable vault and that you alone grant tours of that space. I will remind you that one of the Gontlet's entities, the Exiles, has familiarity with you that predates your birth and memory, but it does not follow that they are privy to the contents of that vault if it remains locked from the inside. Based on this pre-memorial association, they will know what buttons to push to engage delay, but they can have no signature save that which you betray. It may feel like they are in your head, but it is only an intimacy of extensive exposure. No matter how hard you try to de-youify yourself, at the marrow, you are always you. Your impulse to correct and clarify will be preyed upon. Reduce your faculties to half an ear, no mouth, and a beautiful woman sashaying across the stage of that whetted mind's theater. Kwazants will blunt these blows, but you will need an ace in the hole, at least for the first few sallies.

Not fond of these references to multiple incursions into the Gontlets.

The most logical vehicle for developing this transcendence from a tellurian, hull-based experience is long distance running, but I'm sure that has been on heavy rotation from the very mention of the word linebacker. I rely on your tempestuous predictability, my boy. As a modification, this drill will have you holding your breath. Development of this capability is more unflappable finesse than hammering, but, I fancy, according to your deranged, demolitionary ways and means, you'll just randomly hold your breath until you nearly pass out at convenient moments throughout the day. I have always admired your never-the-bullfighter-always-the-bull pluck, but, though you're certainly welcome to take that approach supplementally, it is not maximally profitable. This exercise is less about holding your breath than it is about exploring the landscape and architecture and weather patterns of the chimerical province to which you flee in your mind. It is the world that is superimposed upon your open-eyed world to escape the strangling realities of dying. This version of breath-holding is designed to engage the whole consciousness and will require at least twenty uninterrupted minutes each day. So noan ya girnin' and greetin', ya wee quean! Just do it and thank me later.

I read two full pages of breath-holding methods, philosophy, and instruction, which reads like a Wim Hof textbook. For some reason I thought this whole regimen was going to be more like obstacle courses and mixed martial arts and Patch-style scenarios. This is more like tai chi in the park and meditating in lotus while balancing on your index fingers. Who would have thought that time travel was so cerebral? Maybe not cerebral, but . . . I guess transcendent is a good word.

How your mind must disengage while holding your breath for extended periods of time is comparable in all respects to the elevated, attributive dissociation you must achieve while surfing the Gontlets. And since you cannot speak while holding your breath, this will train you to bite your disputatious tongue. As a disengaged umbra, you will not experience any of the pain associated with panicking lungs, but you will experience all of the structural sensations attending that thrashing hysteria. It is similar to anesthetized teeth being extracted—the sensation of pressure is an illusory shadow of the pain. It is important to marry the sensations with the transcendence so the psychological echoes of the enterprise are retained. Eventually you will swim through the Gontlets with a talk-as-you-walk confidence, as it were, but for the first few rambles, <<stop with this first few macaroni!>> this will bridge the gap.
Now be gone! Go and do!

Holding my breath . . . how hard could that be? I empty my lungs and take a deep breath, my cheeks rounding out my face. I'm checking the wall clock. Twelve, fifteen, twenty-two, twenty-five, thirty-one <<my head is heating up already>>, thirty-four <<holy monkey this hurts>>, thirty-six <<I can feel the entirety of my diaphragm>>, thirty-nine <<my throat feels like it's cramping>>, forty-one <<ice or hot coals are topographically mapping out the terrain

of my alveoli>>, forty-four . . . okay, that's it. I look up the breath holding world record. Twenty-four and a half minutes. Great. That's insane. I guess I can only get better from here.

Seriously though, Patch, it's a good thing you rained down that elastane-clad death upon my head or I'd think this whole thing was an elaborate ruse to get a good posthumous laugh out of Elliot's gullibility. That mangled skydiver was pretty convincing.

Life rises and falls on presentation.

Chapter 33

"People say conversation is a lost art; how often I have wished it were."
– Edward R. Murrow

Well, that kind of petered out. I allocated an entire afternoon to reading about windows in the firmament that could propel me into the future or something. Now what?

I sit very still so I can pick out all the different instruments in the symphony of silence blaring through the house. It seems a paradox that my new appreciation for silence was born of chaos and uncertainty. I guess it's just as well that I swapped distraction for distraction—music-choked wallowing was just my way of extinguishing a fire with gasoline. At least being manhandled by the Manuscript is a fire I can starve by sucking everything audible out of the house. As profoundly halcyon as that silence is, it does have the effect of amplifying the rumbling of the storm fronts moving into my head—the questions, the musings, the reconciling, the anticipating. Patch's version of life and death <<and everything in between>> has made my mind bubbly and my many thoughts are dashing pillar to post.

Bubbly . . .

I know exactly what I need to do right now. Need? Maybe not need. But *need*. What good is life if you're not always looking forward to something?

Due to some recent weight loss, my jeans are fitting better, so maybe I'll wear jeans for this junket. It doesn't hurt to overdress every now and again. Should I shave as well? No, Elliot, come on, you're getting a gallon of diabetes at a gas station whose patrons are wearing either reflective vests or pajamas. Jeans are enough pomp and pageantry.

I grab a forty-ounce refill cup whose clown-faced Holiday logo has been abraded by years of a dishwasher that apparently has something against print. I like it this way; I never have to remind them it's a refill. I used to try to limit my interaction by using a Maverik cup at the Holiday, but I was getting some fairly wry expressions.

Pocket knife, phone, wallet, key, cup. All set. When my cheerleader car was stolen a couple weeks back, about thirty dollars in loose change was stolen with it. Or so I thought. When I explored all the truck's lidded compartments for a new Dew-change home, I discovered that he'd replaced my thirty dollars with about one-hundred and fifty dollars in quarters <<never doubt Patch's punctiliousness>>. I was so excited I just sat there and did the math. One hundred forty-one and a half refills! Then I thought, crap, this just means that the next assignment is going to be something about never drinking Mountain Dew again. He's punctilious, but he's a rat.

My paranoia is muttering that I should adopt a degree of variability in my routines. After exposing Butkus-Blackgoat as a Merovingian hack <<this is

my working theory>>, I've gone from trusting nobody to distrusting everybody. Screw you and your French morality! I take 500 South to the west and Redwood Road south to the Holiday. Ambush averted. Booyah! <<But can it really be classified as paranoia when old young Frenchmen are actually spying on me at regular intervals of my lifespan //though I probably wouldn't word it like that to a clinician//?>> I should have tried that breathing exercise before I ran this errand.

American convenience stores with soda on tap are the pinnacle of progress and the crown of civilization. They're better than the combustion engine, air conditioning, and ballpoint pens. Combined. <<Add *convenience stores, combustion engine, air conditioning*, and *ballpoint pens* to my gratitude list.>> I'm feeling lordly in my jeans, my laced-up shoes, and my now two hundred fifty-five-pound, shoulder-squared frame as I strut to the bank of life-enhancing flavors. There's a guy, tall and square like me, already at the Mountain Dew tap. I'm immediately suspicious. I need to get him to say something to see if he sounds French. He looks French with his nose and his hat. <<Actually, he doesn't look French at all, and I can't see his nose yet.>>

He glances at me sizing him up and says, "You waiting for the good stuff?"

My heart curls up behind my throat and my brain screams at itself to say something. Something clever! Don't be stupid! You're dressed formally for goodness' sake! "If it's not Mountain Dew, it's stupid." See, that wasn't so hard. Though I don't think it sounded all that cool.

"Ain't that the truth."

I can see he's wearing a Toronto Blue Jays cap. "Now there's a team I cannot figure out. How do you have that lineup and not win every game?"

"Good question. They won two World Series with a shittier lineup than that."

"I remember that lineup. Are you from Toronto?"

"Buffalo. I lived there with my mom, but would go to my dad's in Toronto on the weekends and he would take me to games. It was back in the early 2000s, so it wasn't their glory days."

"Well," <<I hold my empty cup up>> "to another World Series and the return of glory days."

He nods.

"And if not, at least there's Mountain Dew."

He chuckles. "That does take the edge off. Take it easy."

And he's gone.

I just had a full conversation with a complete stranger in a public place. How did I do that? I feel like I just won a spelling bee. I'm staring through the store's opening and closing doors into the shrinking horror of the big, bad, scary world beyond. It must look idiotic, but I'm stuck in the undertow of this wash of accomplishment. But when I see him leaving the store, I quickly attend to my drink business. I don't want him to think I'm going to *Cable Guy* him or something.

Cube ice to the cup holder ridge. I hold my cup against the tap and watch the sweet blood of golden unicorns rapidly top me off with its sparkling, xanthous fluorescence and foaming meringue head. Pause for the effervescence to settle. Fill. Pause for the effervescence. Fill so full I have to focus to make the four steps to the counter. Straw in first, then the lid, otherwise the depression of the lid when inserting the straw creates a fountain through the peeled open flanges of the X-slot and you waste precious unicorn blood that will, without fail, spill into the inaccessible abyss between the seat and the center console.

I'm second in line. I have no intention of engaging in conversation for the rest of the day, but I wonder what I'd say if I was such a person. I can't think of anything beyond vocabulary pertaining to the transaction. This is really sad. The weather, Elliot, really? How his weekend is going? No, lame, he's at work at a convenience store; clearly it's not the greatest of weekends. I get distracted by the display of cigarettes behind the clerk. I wonder what percentage of customers buy cigarettes. I wonder what percentage of customers come here *specifically* to buy cigarettes. I wonder what the most common item purchased in conjunction with cigarettes is. Other than a lighter, I guess. I'm at the counter.

"Quick question," <<I guess I'm doing this after all>> "when somebody buys cigarettes and some other item, what is the most common *other* item?"

The clerk doesn't even pause before answering, "Either soda from the fountain or donuts from the case."

"Really? Not chips or nuts or something?"

"Nope, soda or donuts. Or a lighter, maybe."

"Interesting. Thanks, sir. Have a good one."

"See you tomorrow."

"Most likely."

Wow. People are a lot more civil than I knew they were *not*. Could I have had conversations that painless every time I've come here these many years? The prospect is still a little repulsive but those two instances weren't debilitating. I don't want to be that guy everyone dreads encountering because he publicly embarrasses or won't let them get on with their day, but maybe I can probe a gentle medium that is much closer to attic salt and absquatulation than solicitous therapy, say. Nothing I strive to be or do has anything to do with the world at large, but I really should be, in some way, connected to my species. If people are murdered in my neighborhood, I don't want to be considered a suspect because I fit the profile of a reclusive serial killer. Which I do, I think.

I sit in my burnished citadel feeling very much superior to the townsfolk on the lower planes. I take a fifteen milliliter sip <<I have devoted extensive study to the optimal delivery of Mountain Dew for maximal delectation and it turns out to be half an ounce through a 0.219-inch diameter //jumbo// straw per sip; a milliliter more and there's too much air in your mouth, a milliliter less and it triggers the swallow reflex too quickly>> and let its citrusy sweet death roll off the sides of my tongue. My brain, in its dowsed refreshment, is telling me that everything is now right in the world. It's telling me that even if everything was toppling down around me and the earth was opening up below me, everything would be right in the world. I don't know how I'd become so depressed this past decade with daily reminders of how right everything is in the world. Sometimes multiple times a day. Maybe it was the Mountain Dew that was keeping me alive.

<<Add *Mountain Dew* to gratitude list. Again.>>

I have this curse . . . correction, I have many curses, but one of the more obnoxious ones is that traffic lights can see me coming and they turn red, I think out of spite. Although, now that I've been introduced to the concept of kwazants, it might be Cavendish Crookshank fiddling with me for my own good. This used to annoy me immensely, this red light curse; I'm more about the destination than the journey. And Utah drivers make me hate driving in general. But I've started obliging these thimblerigging, ineluctable delays. There's a lot to take in at any individual intersection, wherever you are. I try not to pay attention to the drivers or the cars because that's just blood-boiling, but the cloud-capped mountains, the landmarks, the groomed entrances to housing developments, the industry, the sun-stained weeds of vacant lots, the general capaciousness of the West, it has its rugged beauty. There's so much you'll never know about your own city when you're always consumed by the destination and you get pissy when somebody grabs your head, yanks it left and right, and forces you to look around.

A half an ounce. Everything is right in the world.

The west side of North Salt Lake is a bedroom community serving the megalopolis from Ogden to Salt Lake City to Sandy. Redwood Road carves a straight line across its north-south length. My curse <<opportunity for growth!>> halts me. Customer-less businesses, industrial warehouses, parking lots framed by rock beds of sage bushes and ornamental grasses. The north end of Redwood Road is a polygamist ghetto eyesore to the west and, to the east, an auto body shop that converts traditional vehicles into monster trucks. Including a bus. It's fantastic. With farms and distribution centers and horses and golf courses and sheep and puddle jumper airports and fast food joints and parks just to fill space, it is rurally urban. And other than the occasional roar of commercial airliners, and rarer roars of F-35's tearing the blue of the sky to shreds over Hill Air Force Base, it's pretty quiet.

This anodyne in Yellow #5 may be contributing to my nostalgia, but, Dew or not, this place is awesome. <<I really wanted to say, "I Dew love this place," but I self-censored. You're welcome.>>

Chapter 34

"But in the end one needs more courage to live than to kill himself."
– Albert Camus

I have a clock hanging on the wall above the front door, a digital clock that has all these settings I can toggle through: an analog version with the moving hands and such, a standard numerical mode, a display that scrolls like a sinister hourglass, a world map setting with the time at each time zone, etc. It came with a remote control which is somewhere around here. It was on the analog setting when I misplaced the remote, so that's what I'm stuck with. There's probably a way to change it manually, but who has time for that? Besides, I'm probably one of the few of my generation that can translate the hands of an analog clock into numbers, so it makes me look super world-wise to all my visitors <<that guy that delivered the file boxes>>. The analog setting is furnished with not just the hour and minute hands, but a bonus seconds hand as well. It isn't one of those smoothly tracking motions that make it look like the hand is dipping in and out of the clock between each hash mark, it is a jerky snapping from second to second. I hate it. It makes time look angry, like its cadence is a goose-stepping march to an execution.

Each half-ounce of Mountain Dew is jamming all the switchboard's circuits and I'm just sitting here on my couch watching the seconds hand slap the seconds away. I get stuck in this mental eddy occasionally and I've learned to just go with it since it tends to open up into velvety vortices. Twenty-six is yanked to twenty-seven. Twenty-seven is shoved into twenty-eight. Twenty-eight is jolted to twenty-nine. I can see the span of twenty-nine to thirty as a blow-up diagram of Patch's improbable reality. Ten thousand frames are falling away like a card spring. I'm spiraling around the perimeter at the speed of descent, even with a frame-bound, Gontlet-frosted sandwich cookie the height of one ten-thousandth of a second, the width of the world from pole to pole to pole. Let's say I'm an umbra falling through a vent and I'm expelled into this Gontlet. Assuming I'm at a frame within my lifetime, I'm now younger. I'm younger but I know everything I've . . . I retain all the information I accumulated up until the day, hour, minute, second, ten-thousandth of a second that I recouple with my native hull at this frame. For what that's worth, since all that information could be for naught if things change every day. But being a lendemain, at least I'd know what was changing every day. For better or for worse, I guess.

Okay, so I'm younger. I'm younger and that's it. I just go on living life again from that point. So how do I get back to where I was in the future other than just aging at the same pace I've ever aged? There's no way back. I just have to wait it out? Is time travel a one-way street—backwards? Why would someone do that over and over? Sounds like just as much a hamster wheel as the hamster wheel

I'm trying to get out of. I'd be tweaking my future just to have it un-tweaked. And I'd have no idea from what depth in the Frameset these changes originated. Are these even realistic considerations if I know that I'm changing things and things are changing me every day? If the total lifespan of an umbra is a hundred and twenty years, in theory somebody could live to a hundred and nineteen, Pik back a hundred and five years or so, and wreak all kinds of domino-tipping havoc for a year before they expire. The iterations of our history must be in the thousands. If this has been going on for centuries and the update is daily, I suppose each daily, place-holding iteration could be in the hundreds of thousands. I wonder if there's much jockeying going on to amend things at that minus a hundred and twenty years mark before it's sealed into the petram. Would it matter what is cemented as immutable history that far back if the intervening century plus remains an erasable white board? It seems to me that the majority of these battles would be fought within the last couple of decades. The logistics, according to Patch's explanations, don't seem to favor deep frameset diving. And Pik-ing deeper than your own birth is right out.

There must be something more to it than just Pik-ing to herd world events into your side's pen; there's no way all these people are okay with reliving the past decade or two over and over as campaign staffers. The thrill of permanent youth, world domination, secret agent life, whatever aside, wouldn't you want to grow old with someone? Have annealed, collective memories? Be surprised by something every now and again? Fall in love artlessly? Is this really a war like Patch says it is and the expectation is that foot soldiers fall on their swords? And then fall on their swords? And then fall on their swords?

Again, what do I know? Being a high school linebacker sounds pretty bitchin', but would I want to do it over and over? And, if I'm being honest with myself, I don't think Patch has any intention of me becoming a high school linebacker again. There's no way he'd expose me to these clockworks for something so metaphysically picayune. What would you tell me to do here, Patch? Is this really what you want from me? For me? *You're always free to stiff the piper, but don't blame choice when you're childless!* No, Patch, that's not helpful. *Most people cannot open their minds to new ideas unless a mind-opening team with a peculiar membership goes to work on them. A genius working alone is invariably ignored as a lunatic.* Now *that* I remember. That's a quote from Vonnegut's *Bluebeard*. Patch had me write a paper detailing the five individuals from history I would use to staff that mind-opening team and why. I can't remember the exact composition of the team, but I do remember him peaking an already peaked eyebrow at my inclusion of Adolf Hitler. Or maybe it was my inclusion of both Jesus Christ *and* Adolf Hitler, I don't remember. But why would that particular quotation come to mind? I'm not working alone, I'm working with you, Patch. Oh . . . Now I get it. Maybe I'm supposed to be part of this mind-opening team. Irrespective of all his references to my brilliance, my mind isn't big like that. Wallowing in quicksand isn't one of the marks of a big mind, and I tend to wallow in quicksand.

Whatever. I'm more or less expecting the Manuscript to put everything in its place. Patience, Elliot.

I go to the sink to rinse my cup and notice a corner of that polluted dusk plastic behind a KitchenAid that's more for accessorizing than for baking. It's the pill bottle. It's my suicide, if I can call it that. I threw away the pills but not the bottle? What kind of masochism is that? I try not to heed its self-loathing siren song, but it's sitting there in my open hand and as beautiful as that song by that band: 1-2 tablets every 4-6 hours as needed. Do not exceed 8 tablets in a 24-hour period. Of all the things to forget to throw away, why that? Even the clutter of essential, clean, and geometrically arranged furniture bugs me; how would I overlook a haunting disembowelment of phantasmal orange? I roll the bottle a quarter turn. No hoplites, no battle cries, no knells, no mandates. Just a shell of undone suicide. Stitched at the seams of anger, regret, and embarrassment is a poorly-ventilated burlap hood being pulled over my head. I can hear a lamenting moan scraping its fingernails on stone walls and a croaking spleen emerging from a discarded <<or so I'd hoped>> darkness. The sphacelus of the cartilaginous rings collapsing my trachea is creeping like an infection into my crackling lungs. As if the stony inanimation of the past decade wasn't debriding enough, now my overreaction to it is the night falling on that stony inanimation. I can feel my shoulders quaking and the canker is like a threatened porcupine pushing quills through the skin of my arms and face from the inside. All of my musculature is a tetanus-locked rigidity and I'm surprised that the bottle hasn't shattered in my hand. I have to brace myself against the ceald of the stone countertop and wait for voluntary control of the muscles of my torso to return.

The loudest voices are loud because they want to force your failure. The voices you don't hear are quiet because they want you to succeed on your own merits, from your own preparation, of your own will!

There were, are, and always will be choices, but this one is the most consequential!

Okay, you're right. Get it together, Elliot. It's over. I'm heaving disappointing and disappointment out of my poker-stoked lungs. All my running lately has made that a lot less uncomfortable.

I confront the pill bottle again. It did crack a little at the top. Deserved. I considered ending my life for mortifyingly shameful reasons, like sixteen-year-old girl reasons. It happened and it's over. People do reckless things sometimes. I'm still here and better for it. Forewarned is forearmed. Now stop this, Elliot; there are things to do.

The non-sensory layer of my consciousness is watching the light of an oranging sun pour down the western face of mountains and spill across a salty wasteland, and my breathing settles on the crest of that rolling wave. I place the possessed prescription bottle at the <<geometric>> center of my dining table as an imprecation, as a plague, as a memento, as a trophy. I have the prescription label facing south so I can stare it down while I eat cottage cheese and pineapple chunks in the mornings. I am not afraid of you, you impotent crucible of causticity.

Speaking of breathing, maybe this is a good time to do something while I'm doing nothing . . .

I lay supine on my LoopLinked Iron Loft <<trademarked>> Berber carpet that, in turn, lies supine on DoughCloud <<also trademarked>> carpet padding. I'm a good student, so I memorized Patch's breath-holding sequence. Twenty minutes. No problem. <<Famous last words, I know.>> It's a good thing I'm lying down—after a minute and a half of near hyperventilation, I would be lying down anyway, unconscious, with a head injury. I'm already eating those famous last words; this isn't as no problem as I thought it would be. I feel like my whole body is swelling up and everything is supersaturated. Ten minutes in and I'm up to a one-minute breath hold. I feel both high and nothing. My fingers are stretch tingling, like they're overinflated. Fourteen minutes in and I think I'm hallucinating. I don't try to distract myself with that sunrise anymore—it's getting boring. What can I think about that pulls me out of myself? I need something wringing, something that inundates. I need something that . . . oh, I know. I don't know why this wasn't a thunder-clapping afflatus. I haven't been able to stop thinking about Lana for days. No, Penny. It's not Penny, but I'm so, so close. I know it has a vowel in it and starts with a consonant. There's no reason why I should know her name, but somehow I know her name. Penelope? Okay, I'll stop.

Sixteen minutes in. I'm back to forcible, deep, rapid breaths. The swells of a black sea fold across the two dark stars lighting the night-lit sand of zygomatic and buccal dunes. Last breath hold. An off-shore breeze smooths the sand of the windward slope, but the leeward slipface is wrinkled into a knowing smile. The moonlight cuts voluptuous vermillion folds into the sand. This woman looks nothing like me, nothing like any relative on either side, paternal or maternal, but she's my twin. Half <<maybe her eighty to my twenty, really>> of all the corpuscles and sinews and viscera used to create a single entity in the beginning of all beginnings was somehow shuffled into separate molds, and the singularity became an inextricably concatenated duality. How do I know she's my twin?

When I'm able to stand up without falling down, I add *dream twin I hope is not related to me by blood* to my gratitude list and am entertained by its risible Rubik's Cube of absurdity. I add *physical reminders of life-defining moments*. I cross out *life-defining* and write *folly-averting*. I cross the whole thing out and write *deliverance*. I don't laugh at that one.

Chapter 35

"Or as though you struck one man and he fell and as far as you could see other
men rose up all armed and armored."
– *For Whom the Bell Tolls*, Ernest Hemingway

November rain doesn't make sense to me. It's a drought in the summer when every-thing's growing and needs water but flooding when my grass is basically dead straw? All summer my grass is a pale scorching, and now it starts to green up. What a dumb climate. It sounds like war out there—low-altitude jets rending the skies from east to west, the stentorian cracks of munitions throwing earth up with lingering growls and showering the windows with its debris and destruction. I've heard half a dozen different explanations for why we don't get much thunder and lightning in this valley, which signifies to me that they don't know or aren't willing to say they don't know because the indomitability of science might be called into question. These phenomena are age old, after all, and should have ready and reliable explanations in all the annals of antiquity. All that to say, this storm's thunder and lightning are a rare treat for this area. And a hypnotic treat—I could sit here for hours swimming in the clatter and clangor of this bathed Battle of Bull Run.

I'm getting pretty good with these cards. I told you my thumbs would come around. I don't want to show my hand <<pun intended ex post facto>>, but I have mastered some pretty cool card tricks. Mr. Bicycle would be proud of what I've done with his brand, I think. They're more scratch your head kind of tricks than run away screaming because your brain broke, but not horrible for a rookie. They're sure to dazzle a bored eight-year-old kid in a waiting room someday. Or a Blanc-Bec want-ing news of her nephew serving in the Great War.

I'm managing the pace of this Manuscript scourge tolerably so far, but I need to start erecting levees so the rising tide doesn't wash away all aspects of my life that aren't somehow nailed down. And this tide will rise. It is the Elliot way <<both Patch, because he is a human deluge, and me, because I am the embodiment of a plague of perfectionism>>.

Twenty-minute breath hold routine, practicing card tricks, one-handed shuffling <<and various other flourishes>>, working out, adding to my gratitude list, making money to support my Mountain Dew addiction—all of this has to be worked into my every day. And there will be more, for sure, but I'd like to at least assemble the bones so I can just attach the meat as it's heaped on. I'd also like to start learning Russian, just to preempt eventualities. I'm a planner <<i.e., I don't do well with surprises>>.

A Davis County Government entity sent me some work a few days before the Manuscript supplanted my attention. They didn't give me a hard deadline, but if I want to preserve a reputation of dispatch and distinction, I should probably knock that, and all other projects outstanding, out before things involute. It's this *sure as shortbread* <<Patchism>> involution that makes me nervous.

I add *didn't have to dig up Patch's body and somehow get it to Morocco* to my gratitude list.

DAY 16

CHAPTER 36

> "I don't think lamination is the end of the world. I mean, I'm not laminated and
> I'm having a great time."
> – Noel Fielding, *The Great British Bake Off*

The line rings three times, then:

"Hello?"

"You know, Mom, I programmed my number into your phone myself. I know my name pops up when I call. You don't have to pose your greeting as a question."

"How do I know somebody didn't jump you and nick your phone?"

"Nick my phone? You've been watching British crime dramas, haven't you?"

"You better have called me for something other than to just muck about. I will not be . . . chuffed to bits if you don't let me crack on with my day."

I feel like she's reading these from a list. At least she migrated in time from the Victorian Era to modern-day Sussex or Liverpool.

"It's that baking show you're watching on the tele, isn't it!"

She chuckles. It's good to hear her laughing. Maybe she was serious about her efforts to let go of Dad.

"I just called to say I love you. And I mean it from the bottom of my heart."

She made a little squeak after the first half of my statement, as if to express some heartfelt appreciation for the sentiment, but the second half ruined it.

"Just because you speak the words doesn't mean I won't figure out that you're quoting lyrics, young man. I grew up with that song, you know."

Now *I'm* laughing. I don't joke around much with Mom because my attempts are usually sucked into a vortex of black, matte-finished woe, and instead of mirth and merriment, it's a dead space where I question all the decisions I made in my life. She's not a killjoy, she's a slaughterjoy and then she'll set joy on fire and watch it burn with the expression of a no-blinking robot.

"But for real, I just wanted to thank you for going to lunch with me. It was good catching up. If you are not otherwise engaged, let's do Thanksgiving dinner at Chuck-a-Rama next Thursday."

"I am not otherwise engaged, sir. I would be well-chuffed to accompany you."

"I'll call you early next week to plan since your generation struggles with texting. And lay off the BBC!"

"Ha ha, you wheelie bin."

Nope. Epic mistranslation there.

DAY 17

Chapter 37

"My religion consists of a humble admiration of the illimitable superior spirit who reveals himself in the slight details we are able to perceive with our frail and feeble mind."
– Albert Einstein

I don't know why, but I started praying today. I guess my thought was, if I was going to be grateful, I might as well err on the side of being grateful to something, somebody, who or whatever the source of all this benevolence and deliverance might be. A shrine of gratitude to the ether seems a little impersonal, and almost a little ungrateful, as if luck or cosmic stardust was more likely responsible for statistically impossible . . . disentanglements than somebody preventing doom at every turn. The more I add to this gratitude list, the more I realize how little control I have over outcomes, and how often things go right when they could just as easily <<why not fifty percent of the time, if it's all chance?>> go horribly, devastatingly wrong. In my estimation, this has really only occurred twice in nearly three decades. Maybe three times. And when you fixate on the three bad days you've had in your life, it's harder to notice the thousands of entropy-defying, self-repairing gratuities, and the cruise of oil that never fails. I don't want to be statistically idiotic to avoid accountability, so I'm dismissing the possibility that this recent shrapnel blast of providence could be coincidence. When you multiply probabilistic denominators, the number just gets too low.

There was this girl in high school that was infatuated with me. She was like a high school football groupie—at every practice, at every game, staring starry-eyed and slack-jawed at me. It was a good thing I knew very little about the ways of the world <<sex>> in high school because I probably would have had three kids with her by the time I graduated. She was gorgeous, but she was vacant, the kind of girl horny jocks like to take advantage of. It was fortunate for her she was enamored with a guy that wouldn't know how to take advantage of her even if they were taped together naked. Before every game she would say something like, "Sending happy thoughts out into the universe for you!" Huh? Did she think there was a deep space canyon wall that was going to reflect those happy thoughts back to me in time for the game? It was such a weird thing to process for me, especially at a time when I was regularly reading about a God that was grabbing everybody by the scruff of the neck and throttling them. I realized that, in essence, everybody was a person of faith; some concentrate it in institutions, like government or science; some in a laissez-faire sterility of fate or karma; some in a nameless, faceless, nebulous universal energy; some in humanity; some in nature; some in the laws they believe govern their experience; and some invest it all in themselves. In each case, without wielding the scepter ourselves, we're all just interpreting. I guess it's just easier for me to be grateful if I can direct that gratitude toward a conversant, receptive entity rather than any construct external to my skin. I guess I'd be talking in circles if I said that thanking nothing feels weirder than thanking something, more specifically someone. Gratitude, it seems to me, is more a function of acknowledgement of favor than affirmation, capitulation, or self-congratulation.

If I broadcast gratitude to a something or someone, whether there is a something or someone or a nothing or no one, I can't really lose. I doubt the nothing or no one will take exception. If it's the converse, I'm liable to incur some displeasure from a something or someone for the misattribution.

I remember walking in on Patch praying one time. I had never seen anyone pray in real life before and I asked him what he was doing. He didn't move, he didn't answer. I thought he might be crying, but I didn't dare approach him to find out. He was Scottish, and citizens of the motherland have funny ways of sending messages to children. Not that I feared him, I just feared the shame and embarrassment that might have resulted from that correction. So I just watched him. He must have knelt there, his interlaced fingers pressed into his forehead, for another five minutes with absolutely no regard for my presence. Of which, I'm sure, he was aware. Nothing escapes the attention of that man.

When he finished, he got up, walked over to me, punched me in the chest and said, "We were just discussing you."

DAY 18

Chapter 38

"Deep into that darkness peering, long I stood there, wondering, fearing,
doubting, dreaming dreams no mortal ever dared to dream before."
– "The Raven," Edgar Allan Poe

I had another dream about what's-her-name <<Mabel? Paxton?>> last night.
This morning, I guess, since the sun was turning my black blackout curtains
the color of soot <<not a perfect science, apparently>> when I was snatched
violently from my Shangri-la by a knock at the front door. Dream front door, that
is, not my actual front door.

This was a much longer dream than the part of it I recall. So long, in fact,
that I was exhausted when I woke up because all my sleep was hijacked by these
protracted and mystifying sequences. Howbeit, I would take these dreams every
day of the week and thrice on Thursday to be in her company <<Grace? Kaylin?>>,
even if she is just the midnight <<8 a.m.>> manifestation of programmed channels of action potentials, nodes, and neurochemicals. My subconscious happens
to be heaven's court portraitist, and the Eves and Marys are not unpleasant to
look at.

In the earliest part of the dream I can recall, everything is black. This isn't so
much a darkness from the absence of light, it's a darkness from the absence of
eyes and an occipital cortex. It's a blackness you could feel, like moving your
arms through a water stripped of every other molecule. There's no fear or uncertainty or threat in this blackness. I know I'm supposed to be there and that I'm
in no danger of any variation. It's like a womb—a deep-earth fortress of liquid
latency.

She's there as well. I can't see her <<unfortunately>>, but I know she's there.

All around me <<us>>, I can hear, almost feel, this sort of pressurized howling that sounds like we're traveling at light speed in a metro tunnel with the
window rolled down just a little bit. It isn't a loud or painful sound and it's more
exhilarating than worrying. All of my spatial and proprioceptive sensory corrob-
orates a tremendous rate of speed.

As we move like photons through this atramentous duct, what's-her-name
<<it's two syllables, I'm sure of it, and it's *right* there!>> speaks. As she speaks,
whatever organs or cerebral structures that process voice in this element indicate
to me that the voice is coming from my own mouth. This time it isn't think-con-
versing though, it's an audible voice, distinctly feminine, internally processed.
She <<we, I?>> says, "We're dead." There's no panic or melancholy in its tone,
just an objective observation.

"We *are* dead, just not how you think." This time it's my voice, my mouth,
but it comes from the same place. "But we'll only be dead for a minute. If I did
the math right."

Dreams are confounding enough without all the alterations to the fabric.
It's so distressing hearing myself saying these things without any way of

determining its context or impact or meaning. I'm sure I'm sewing together all of Patch's Manuscript madness, but these dreams are so high-definition, so much like the super-sensory characterizations of the Gontlets. I rarely dream about people I know <<I know I don't really *know* her>>, and even more rarely dream about the same person twice. I dream quite frequently, but rarely remember what I dreamt about once consciousness makes fusion stew of my brains. And they feel like they're making a point, a point I should be paying attention to <<sorry, Patch, for the all the preposition-ending sentences>>. Jumping over pits, ignoring the girl, running into a mountain; catching the freefalling girl in a white Eternity; this one—they feel like they're telling a story.

So I say, "But we'll only be dead for a minute. If I did the math right." At that moment, a white pinhole appears on the horizon of the void <<I acknowledge the difficulty of horizons in voids>>, lightminutes away. It's so noticeable because it's the only thing that could be noticed in this inky pall of pitch. As we speed along like tenth-generation cruise missiles, the pinhole starts to expand until we're upon it, and it becomes a doorway at which we find ourselves standing at the doorsill of that white expanse <<room>> of Eternity, all milk and coconut and bare.

I keep saying *we*, but I haven't actually seen her yet. I know she's there, and that seems to be enough for me at the time. However, real me is kicking dream me for not at least glancing over to further tattoo that image onto every tract of my neural pudding.

We stand there for anywhere from a minute to a millennium <<time just seems to lose all its bearings in these dreamworlds>>. I can hear us thinking. It must be more millennia than minutes because there are lengthy, complex collaborations stacked one upon another and stretching into an infiniteness that's buzzing with . . . I don't know, design? creation? It's like a reenactment of Genesis—light, water, land, life <<minus insects>>, free Mountain Dew on tap, etc. With some mutual intent, we synchronously take a single step, not a figurative step, but an actual step. As in my previous dream, civilization seems to blossom in every direction with each footfall, but this time the composite is a hybridization of our separateness, our individualities. It's my world with all the gaps in perfection I might have overlooked or couldn't conceive filled in by her contribution, and vice versa. There seems to be overlays of possibilities, like several different versions of events are happening simultaneously, but they're being compressed into one summative reality. Everything we want there is there. I don't know if everything we *don't* want isn't there as well, but it feels like we achieved something monumental and it's time to relax in an environment of perfect safety and comfort.

My house is just where it is with no remarkable differences <<better landscaping, maybe>>. I'm lying on the couch with my head resting on her lap. Strangely, I have no book in my hand, but I know I'm reading Joseph Conrad's *The Heart of Darkness*. I know she's reading, too, but I still haven't looked at her. She's running her fingers through my trellised tangle of hair. If I hadn't had the recent Vivian experience, I probably wouldn't have appreciated how good that felt. And there was something else, something I'm sure I knew while in the dream, but can't make sense of now—someone else was there, a third person. I don't think they were supposed to be a significant actor in the events, maybe an auditor or a referee or something, but no one we spent any time appeasing.

I can feel all the non-heart attributions of where my heart is supposed to be swelling to an unreasonable size in this beatific family room, a swell of reunion and relief and resurrection, as if contentment is going to explode like warm light out of all my pores. I want to say something, something grateful or appreciative, but I don't want to run a pin through this idyllic inflation. So on I read, "They shouted, sang; their bodies streamed with perspiration; they had faces like grotesque masks—these chaps; but they had bone, muscle, a wild vitality, an intense energy of movement, that was as natural and true as the surf along their coast. They wanted no excuse for being there. They were a great comfort to look at. For a time I would feel I belonged still to a world of straightforward facts; but the feeling would not last long. Something would turn up to scare it away. . ."

Then there's a knock at the door.

It drubbed me so cleanly from sleep that, before I knew it, I was standing at the gratitude list on my fridge. I'm not sure what I was doing there because I had no idea what I was intending to write. I was just feeling grateful. But now that I'm here, I should write something: *happy dreams.*

Chapter 39

"Blessed is he who expects nothing, for he shall never be disappointed."
– Alexander Pope

It's Tuesday, 10:15 a.m. I'm on the sixth floor of the Moran Eye Center again. I just can't help myself. Maybe I'm drawn here because rectangular grass fields remind me of battle. Maybe it's the view.

I didn't expect anyone to be here, but I needed to see for myself so my paranoia didn't jeopardize my lucky break in case last Thursday was an anomaly. I know there are a lot of reasons why they wouldn't be here today but weather isn't one of them. There are no field reservation conflicts. Salt Lake City isn't under attack by a foreign power. All seems to be well in the world.

Oh, that's hilarious. I just got a text from Mr. Blackgoat himself: Just warming up if you're interested in coming out.

They must be at a different location this time; there's no warming up going on here.

I reply: Same place?

Then the response: Same place just txt me 10 min before you get here so I can have our equip guy get ur gear ready.

Blackgoat, you scamp, I'm not wasting another minute on your jackhammery. I'm tempted to tell him I'm already here, but to what end? And I may need to exploit this subterfuge in the future, so I should probably keep it on life support for now.

Life rises and falls on dashed hopes.

Blackgoat . . .

DAY 20

Chapter 40

"All you can eat buffet not mean all day buffet. You no come stay 4 hour. You eat—you go home."
– Chinese restaurant marquee board

I'm not a big fan of buffets for many reasons. For one, I don't like watching people eat. Their standards of etiquette are low, especially in Utah where chewing with one's mouth closed is out of fashion. Also, I can't eat a lot in one sitting, so I never get my money's worth. But I have this pathology that requires me to eat a volume of food commensurate with payment rendered, so I end up overeating and spending the next several hours wrangling with my posture so I don't die of positional asphyxiation. And then treating the ensuing headache. Misery all the way around. Like Patch always said, *Your pain is self-inflicted!* Not that he was ever wrong, but he was especially right about that. *Is* especially right about that.

I don't know if Mom is working on her happiness or if I'm just really funny these days, but she is laughing a lot more than normal <<an annual, stifled chortle is more than normal>>.

I miss mashed potatoes and gravy. Most home-style foods, actually. Why do I never think to eat at Chuck-A-Rama? <<Because I'm not seventy-eight. Also, see buffet grievances above.>>

I had an agenda for our feast this afternoon, but Mom appropriated the conversation with more of her weirdness.

"Your dad would be very proud of you, you know."

"Proud of me for what?"

"For what you've become as an adult."

"What? Fat and pasty?"

"Elliot!" Her suppressing hiss backfires and alerts the patrons she's attempting to spare. Her face is all pinched in the middle and her lips disappear in their compression. It looks like somebody stuck a big screwdriver in her face and turned it ten degrees clockwise. Each blink separates a glance at me and a glance at hopefully unsuspecting eighth-platers.

I realize that I'm sitting in a sea of obesity and might have said *fat and pasty* with more bass than I intended. But, come on, these are my people. Can't the obese talk about the obese? Besides, since when do the obese have enough self-awareness to pick up on that? It's why we're okay with public trough-feeding, right?

"Believe it or not, El, though you were a football superstar, your mind is the superior faculty."

Superior faculty? Do people talk like that when they're not quoting a movie? Oh, wait, maybe she is quoting a movie. Scrolling through Jane Austen adaptations again . . . *Emma* maybe?

"Are you quoting a movie?"

Oh, no. She's not blinking again. Said I something amiss <<*Persuasion*>>?

"I know what you think of me, Elliot. You were a boy, so I let your dad take the lead in raising you; I was a mess for a spell when your dad left us." <<Spell = decade.>> "I haven't seen hide from you" <<this was an expression my dad used frequently to indicate a middle ground between absolute and relative, a vitiated version of the more superlative *neither hide nor hair*>> "in the past ten years, so I get that you don't know that much about me; but there may be more substance than you give your old mom credit for. So don't patronize. Just because your intellect is on your sleeves doesn't mean everyone's is."

Wow. She is becoming quite effective at chastisement. I take a bite of mashed potatoes and corn and pretend that didn't sting. I was going to back out of that insinuation slowly and play dumb, but I think the better of it. Maybe she is smarter than I give her credit for. For which I give her credit? I'm trying to think of how Patch would say it; he made everything sound so regal.

"Well, then . . . since we're starting down this new and strange path of sideways honesty, if I asked you something, Mom, would you be straight with me?"

"No, Elliot."

"No?"

"No. You need to start figuring things out on your own now. You're a big boy and you like a good puzzle." She shoves some livestock feed into her mouth and doesn't look up.

What is going on? Why is my mother starting to talk like a . . . like a mother?

"You don't even know what I was going to say!"

"Clearly, you're integrating into your grandfather's world. He has always had more influence on you than I have, so what's the point?"

There's my in. "What do you mean, integrating into his world? What do you know?"

"You don't ask your mother to lunch twice in a week's time without it being a checkpoint in one of his gimmicks."

The hinges of my mandible loosen as the accusation progresses. "Oh, Mother, the impudence!" Her face is stale doubt. "This has nothing to do with Patch . . . with Grandad!" <<It really doesn't.>> "The temerity! This is mother-son bonding time! I feel genuinely bad that the only family you have has basically ignored you for a decade. It is unpardonable. But now you ask, it puts me in mind . . ." <<*Pride and Prejudice.*>>

She doesn't like it when I commandeer dialogue from her beloved Jane Austen films for casual use. Mostly because she knows I'm jabbing and not garnishing. She stops blinking *and* chewing now.

When I finish chuckling <<for the most part, I take Mom as seriously as I would a precocious four-year-old>>, I ask, "What do you make of all Grandad's passions, his pursuits?" <<*Sense and Sensibility*, but it's an honest question.>>

"I'm not answering any more of your questions if you're going to besmirch fine cinema."

"Okay, I'll stop. But, in my defense, it's hard to avoid when those screenplays are the backdrop of my childhood."

"What is your question, smart aleck?"

"Grandad seemed like a brilliant man. All his research, his associations, his projects, what do you make of all that? Was he just a garden variety Renaissance man, or is there something to his work?"

"I'm sure you would know better than I would, but I will say this, we don't always want what we think we want. Some things are better left undiscovered. Your grandfather, I think, was more like an Eve, weighing boons against banes. Anyone else in his position would be a . . ."

What? Is she a philosopher now? I think this is the first time I've ever seen her pensive. Dad's death wasted this woman. Now I want to have lunch with her every week just to see what comes out of her mouth.

I finish the thought for her, "Victor Frankenstein?"

"Victor Frankenstein. See, I did raise a smart kid."

"Gratuitous, low-hanging fruit, Mom. But what do you mean by weighing boons against banes?" <<I've never heard her use the word *boon* or *bane* in my life, nor any higher-level word that wasn't in a Jane Austen movie.>> "Do you know what he was into?"

"Elliot. Dear. I know you're just toying with me now and that you already know much more than I do. Just be very careful and make sharpwise sure his is a world you want to be involved in." <<In which you want to be involved, per Patch.>> "Forbidden knowledge is always accompanied by the direst of consequences. Victor Frankenstein . . . how your mind works. It makes me miss your dad just a little less sitting here with you."

Patch was a virtual nimbus of praise and compliments, but I think that one excelled them all. It makes me feel like I came from somewhere or I belong to something.

"Your grandfather was smart, but he wasn't perfect. Imperfect conclusions come from imperfect minds. I'll say it this way, just because you find something perfect, doesn't mean you know how to wield it perfectly."

She just keeps getting stranger and stranger and stranger <<*Kung Pow: Enter the Fist*, not Jane Austen>>. I really want to know what she means by that, but I can tell she's getting tired and fading into a sluggish sullenness. Maybe I'll pick up there next week.

She perks up and finally answers my question. "From what I could gather from eavesdropping and sneaking peeks, he was trying to tunnel to another world. Crazy, huh? Or he was trying to figure out how to cheat death. One or the other."

She knows something. I know she knows something. She's trying to sneak the truth in by making it sound absurd. He's trying to tunnel to another world <<whatever that means>>. I'm going with that. Would the frames and Gontlets be considered another world or was he looking for another other world? Maybe it's in the Manuscript. Curse you, Patch, and this weekly slow-roll! Let's kick this skank into high gear! But for the kwazants!

I get home and I don't feel like I'm going to split open lengthwise. I write *self-control* on my gratitude list.

DAY 22

CHAPTER 41

"Sometimes you have to let the me machine idle so you don't smash everyone
in the crosswalk."
– Elliot Dillinger (Patch)

Assignment #5: SELFLESSNESS

*It has arrived, ya wee warmer—the day you have dreaded for some time,
I reckon, the day your house is no longer home. You mastered the role of king
and courtier, now it is time to be a crusader. And hiding in your dining room
to vanquish vehicular casualties maketh not one a crusader! I know how that
vulpine mind of yours maneuvers.* <<Bummer. I was thinking more along
the lines of a crusade against crusades, but even still, I think he's on to me.>>
*Fortunately for you, I'm pernickety enough to have machined the nuts and bolts
myself.*

A week ago, those words would have sent me into fits and starts, but I think
the arrival of this hour has been baked into my anticipation and I've become a
little more calcified. So eat that, old man!

*One of the greatest contributions to American literature, any literature for
that matter, is* The Green Mile *by Stephen King. It is the story of a man awaiting execution, wrongly convicted of the murder of two young sisters. His name
is John Coffey (like the drink, only not spelled the same) and he has an extraordinary gift which he uses unassumingly and sparingly throughout the story. It
could well be said that John Coffey, himself, is the gift, as all the benefit from
the use of this gift is realized by the beneficiary and not the benefactor. In fact,
it is a contract of inverse proportions, and the extent of the benefit realized by
the beneficiary is commensurate with the extent of the agony experienced by the
benefactor. There seems to be no incentive for John Coffey to ever share this
gift, hence an economy of use determined by a careful selection of beneficiaries.
The deserving are few and Mr. Coffey is astutely discriminatory. It is this careful selection and its maximization of consequence that vindicates the sacrifice.
Though it is occasionally based on imperfectly calibrated scales, it is human
nature to reward merit and satisfy genuine need.*

*The following may sound hardened and captious, but so it is in the strata
of human proclivity. There are many in the world, fault of their own or not,
who cannot do for themselves. In this condition, some pity themselves to solicit
sympathy, some broadcast it to solicit charity, some blame to justify bitterness,
some brand themselves with it to be hailed as a martyr, some do anyway because
they cannot be inconvenienced by the fact that they cannot, and some simply do
without because they do not want to impose on the goodwill of others. Because
you can, yours is the goodwill of others.*

It is one of the many paradoxes of the mreg that self is only improved when the self gets out of the way. The self, it turns out, is a dumb and cumbersome construct, and the greatest obstruction to objectivity, hyperopia, and clarity. To madly philosophize, one cannot improve one's self by improving one's self—rectitude is more a tennis match than a robe. Like I have belabored on many an Elliot-centered moment, "If you want to make the image clearer, look through a lens and not in a mirror." That is not to say that one should disregard development of self, but kwazants, again, paradoxically pivots on the development of other selves, often at the self's own peril, and all efforts should be within the context of sharing that gift of inverse proportions. Something must be lost for something to be gained. To magnify the cliché: what you give, you get back with interest.

Yes, one should moderate and de-escalate and exercise restraint and be merciful and make peace and have compassion, and all these improve the capacities and functions of the self. They are the essence of kwazants. But is the effect of all virtue not cinched up in the Celtic weaves of a fabric that dresses societies? Is not the interface the only true judge and jury of intent and character? Are our wounds dressed by private and unspoken pardons? Is unfeigned commiseration convincing as an entry in a journal? Is benevolence proven in a role-play of the mind? Forgiveness and grace and deference and magnanimity are pointless in a vacuum. I dead horse beat this point because the criticality of a robust mreg cannot be overstated. It secures the lendemain, it firmly subordinates the native umbra and all coincident lendemains, it creates a muscle memory, so to speak, which establishes elevated baselines. True, kwazants stretches all surface area, including the bullseye on your back, but, as you know, with magnitude comes intimidation. A prodigious mreg may identify you as an enemy of the Exiles, but a prodigious mreg will identify you as a great and terrible enemy of the Exiles. The Lifers will avoid, the Blanc-Becs will admire, the Dovolniya will respect. Besides, the greatest obstacle to presence of mind, situational awareness, and quick reaction time is dwelling on one's own thoughts and emotions. You will need to stay frosty in the Gontlets.

I don't mean to kick a man in his salty wound, but your vacuum living will no longer do. In order to reap kwazants, one must sow the best seeds of the self in fertile soil, and to reap this harvest, there is no more effectual sickle than a grip of innovation, a blade of ownership, and an arcing slice of talent. It has to be as personal to you as it will be to the recipient. There has to be a profoundly human synthesis involved. It must obscure the boundaries of selves. It must transcend the crudeness of words and speak with a tongue of immortality.

I remember Patch saying stuff like this all the time and, as a teen, I had no concept of what he was trying to convey. Well, even as an adult I admit that it doesn't make that much sense to me. He would say things like, *I may not be infinity or eternity, but I am a million years,* and *Spend less of your life trying to save time and more of your life refining time.* I could tell that it meant something to him, but I thought he was just trying to sound mysterious and sophisticated. He would eponymize with names like *The Centennial Sentinel*, which, given my current understanding of his context, might be gloriously apropos; I just liked the alliteration. Despite his ceaseless commendation, I'm really not that clever.

Steer your mind around the stale and unimaginative. No picking up trash off the shoulders of freeways or baking cookies for neighbors or ladling out soup at homeless shelters or donating $6/month for a Filipino orphan to have school supplies. All of those have their place, but that is not what we are about this time. This is about transplanting your quintessence so there will be an interest in the long-term effects of the donation. As I said, it is the careful selection and its maximization of consequence that vindicates the sacrifice.

For this assignment, I want you to create a program incorporating all afore-mentioned elements and that will require your participation at least week-ly—your personal participation, to wit, not an administrative, managerial, or oversight role. Make it explode with Elliot goodness and brilliance. You have a lot to offer. Now offer it!

Return next Saturday. There is so much more, and I am greatly looking forward to seeing you tossed about by this convulsion of nature.

Innovation, ownership, talent . . . <<I already know exactly what I'm going to do.>> I can innovate. When it comes to implementing my own ideas, I'm a control freak, so ownership is a foregone, get-your-filthy-mitts-off-my-idea. I may be a little short on talent, but I make up for it with size. All deprecation aside, though, for this, I do have a talent.

I was contracted a few months ago to create some presentations and instructional material for patient advocate programs at Primary Children's Hospital in Salt Lake City. In order to get some background information on how the staff envisioned these programs functioning, and its ideal implementation, I visited a few departments. As I roamed, I could see that parents were weary and stretched thin, kids were bored and restless, and many were babysat by devices. I remarked to my escort, offhand-edly, that they should have a reading corner a couple of hours a night, like they do at libraries, someone dramatizing stories to groups of kids so they can be para-screen entertained and the parents could attend to other responsibilities <<it's no secret that most families in Utah have more than one child>>. My escort nodded her head and said it was a good idea, and that was that. It's not a brilliant idea, but it checks all the boxes. I don't know how to talk to women my age, but I can relate to kids like they're blood brothers from another mother's blood brother's mother-brother. <<I'm still a little disturbed by Patch's explanation of *mother-brother*.>>

Chapter 42

"Every body allows that the talent of writing agreeable letters is peculiarly female."
— *Northanger Abbey*, Jane Austen

I'm sitting on my couch, tilting my head all the way back so everything splenius and obliquus and capitis is pinched and aching. Sequences are playing out on the *Illustrated Man* that is the skip trowel texture of my ceiling. I don't know what it is about staring at a ceiling, but the disfigurations of the negative space somehow bridle my cerebralizations and hold them steady until I can get to them.

I have all these unanswerable questions circling their answers like bugs in the light. How old was Patch? Was his death really the result of a flying incident or did his one hundred and twenty years expire? <<This assumes that he's dead. Which he's most certainly not!>> When he would come over during my teen years, had he already Pik-ed by then? He must have. People don't become swashbucklers of renown without a little time travel under their belt. Sash.

Once you Pik, you lose connection with the objective present, the principal apical frame. It bugs me that you can't resurface. It would be Groundhog Day. Groundhog decades. How would you not lose your mind? What matters at that point? I know that my present is wherever I am conscious at the moment, but without a lendemain, I must be an unwitting consciousness at other reconstituted apical frames as well. Am I only those consciousnesses for twenty-four hours at a time? Am I then resorbed into a singular Elliot consciousness at the update until some meddling jackhole misaligns my integration and my timeline, again, splinters into a schizoid frameset and history is poly-me until the next update? As I presently appreciate my own consciousness, since I haven't Pik-ed, am I Elliot Dillinger's consciousness at the principal apical frame or am I conscious at some reconstituted apical frame, as an extra in the cinema of the timebrokers, or a pawn in a Sicilian Defense of lendemain vs. lendemain? The more I think about it, the closer I'm pushed to an edge of unpredictability. Indeed, it angers me <<*Persuasion*>>. I really have to stop being affected like this. *Anger is a loaded weapon you hand to your enemy grip side out*, Patch would say. And, according to the books <<no books, just the Manuscript>> anger is umbral poison. Anger is kwazantsial thwartation. What's the line, *help me to accept the things I can't change*? I just don't like being the sagebrush in Wild West shootouts. It's lame. I may not be conscious of it, and I may not have made the greatest use of my time and choices the past few years, but now that I know that plunging into my youth through laundry chutes is a thing, I want to find some plate mail and a broadsword and go medieval on this scheme. I need a lendemain; I need to subvert the updates.

Now I have a headache.

I'm writing an email to the woman who escorted me around Primary Children's Hospital a few months ago. Her name is Annie. I love the name Annie. There was a girl in high school named Annie Mott who was large in all the right places and wouldn't give me the time of day. Every now and again I would catch her looking at me, but if I ever cut in with the unspoken you-must-admire-me-be-cause-I'm-a-high-school-football-god opening and winning smile to cajole her into conversation, she would say something epigrammatically dismissive and walk away with a garish and exaggerated air of snobbery. Man, was that something. It's true what they say about girls playing hard to get. I spent the last year and a half of high school playing this game with Annie Mott. Then high school suddenly ended and everyone ceased to be.

Not all stories have a eucatastrophe.

I hate writing emails. It's like sculpting a masterpiece blindfolded. Every word is a giant dog that will either lick your hand or bite it off depending on how you approach it, and you have to tiptoe through this minefield of obsequious obeisance or your program hobbles limbless into consideration <<I know *limbless* precludes hobbling>>. It's really kind of degrading.

I spent the better part <<all parts of it were horrible>> of an hour writing a dozen different drafts of this email, and all I can think about now is Mountain Dew on ice. I have a drinking problem.

After all that, I just saved it as a draft. It's Saturday and I don't like goading people into weekend work. I'll send it Monday morning.

DAY 23

Chapter 43

> "I felt very still and empty, the way the eye of a tornado must feel, moving
> dully along in the middle of the surrounding hullabaloo."
> – *The Bell Jar*, Sylvia Plath

At first I thought it was birds, but birds don't drone. The sky dimmed like it might when a veil of birds is drawn across the face of the sun, but this was a curtain, not the spinning rod of vertical blinds from capricious flight. There are a lot of single-engine Cessna's buzzing around here, but this sound was panoramic; it was everywhere. My house was the centerpiece of acres of cross-legged monks in humming meditation. Metaphorically, that is.

Turns out, it was an alien invasion.

Sometimes my ears start ringing when I'm holding my breath, especially when I approach the minute-and-a-half mark, so I thought it was that. But the sound started filling out and the whole world got stuffier, like I was in a womb with all the sounds of circulation and digestion amplified in its immersive medium.

In my life before the Manuscript <<BM>>, I would have spent some time on my security camera app and armed with a machete <<I'm the last house at the end of a dead end street with no neighbors for fifty yards>> before venturing into extra-drive-wayal territory, but since I'm in an up-down-up-down-left-right-left-right-A-B-A-B <<or whatever the Nintendo cheat code was for infinite lives>> Patch-hardened biome, I just busted out there with my phone and voracious curiosity. Voraciosity. I think I might have left the front door open as well.

I don't even get to the end of the driveway before realizing there's a darkly polluted river in the sky. About fifteen feet above my head, coursing like the Mississippi, broad and flat, is a channel of gigantic bees. They're the size of small Cadbury Eggs. There must be millions of these bees cutting a gangrenous scar into an already ashen, bloodless sky. I can't really see the margins of the river banks but the cloud-cluttered day seems to be uninterrupted fifty feet to the left and right of me. They seem to have an established hard deck at a fifteen or so foot elevation, and there are no violators. The river bottom was the river bottom and there was no fighting that hard reality. They didn't think a thing of my presence, just went about their business, whatever that business seemed to be. <<Migrating? Do bees migrate?>> I know Utah is the Beehive State, and SLC's minor league baseball team is the Bees, but I don't think I've ever seen a bee here. And certainly not biblical proportion monster bees like these.

I stared up from the river bottom for nearly twenty minutes, everything splenius and obliquus and capitis pinched and aching. I'm hypnotized by their loudly animated conversation. And by the size of these beasts! I'm only marginally exaggerating with the Cadbury Eggs comparison.

As minatory as this current of fat death monsters is, it is a great comfort. It's the first time in weeks I don't feel like I'm in one of Patch's petri dishes. I believe Patch capable of commanding rivers of bees, but I don't see why he would. Though, I rarely understand why Patch does what Patch does. Maybe this means something. Something to ponder while holding my breath.

DAY 24

Chapter 44

"The act of treachery is an art, but the traitor himself is a piece of shit."
– Mike Tyson

This is too good. I sent Ms. Annie that email this morning and got a response back within ten minutes. She thanked me for taking the time to think of ways to improve the lives of the kids and their families. She praised the merits of the idea. She even wished me success in my future endeavors. Then she signed it, "Annie" <<which is a stupid name>>. But even after I clearly explained that it would require no internal resources or manpower, and that I would be willing to manage and administer the program myself if the time commitment was in any way burdensome, she said they weren't equipped to implement such a program and didn't have the necessary staff to run it properly. Equipped? Equipped with what, a book? I couldn't have been clearer that the program is fueled, oiled, and powered by volunteerism. No staff would be required to run it, let alone run it properly. *I'm* the staff! There's no reason why this . . . <<all this invective is splattering off the walls of my reactivity like an unflagging vomit, so I fix what's-her-name's image firmly in my mind, with the dark swells of her hair washing onto its olive coast, and I breathe, all the way in, all the way out>> overworked and underappreciated young lady shouldn't want such an enterprise adorning her already strapping resume.

I can feel my umbra dissolving in these gurgling pools of venom. I need to let this stuff go. This is not an affront worth lendemain subordination.

In its essence, is goodness mental or behavioral? If, in my head, I want to murder someone, but behaviorally I'm always showing them patience and forgiveness and love and kindness, am I still a bad person? Are decencies still poison if poured through a sieve of dormant murderous inclinations? Does thought have to bear fruit according to its seed? Or can my actions betray my intentions? I would imagine it would just make it more difficult for a crop of kindness to sprout from a field of fury, but can it be done? If it can be done, does it make one an unstable dichotomy whose harvest will eventually be cankerous? Are actions only virtuous if they are manufactured in a factory of virtue? Can a good tree ever produce bad fruit? Should virtue be developed from the outside in or from the inside out? The very act of thinking about these things is probably a good start.

I'm not much of a grudge holder, but I do tend to scrape people off that I perceive have wronged me, and I don't think that's going to be a healthy way to approach relationships from here on out. My head is clearing and my breathing doesn't feel like volcano exhaust. I'm back to equanimous problem solving. Annie was a speed bump, so what. Nothing is truly a single point of failure if you're willing to take the long way around.

I like resolving matters of all species at the lowest possible level. But I don't like insecure, mid-level manager control freaks who view every good idea as a rain of trebuchet-launched fire on their kingdom. I gave Annie her chance; now I climb the ladder. And the real sting for Annie is going to be her eventual involvement in this program. She should know by now that these endeavors slip through the grates of corporate levels, and when I approach her superior with it, she will become his program-implementing pawn. Superordinates are all about padding their resumes with the success of programs they had nothing to do with. With which they had nothing to do.

My reputation for quickness and quality took a circuitous route to Brian Pettiman. I developed his very embryological idea for these patient advocate programs into a bouncing baby behemoth in short order and he was, with a lot of eyebrow-slumped glowering, skeptical of my quick quality. He even implied that such work generated that quickly was improbable. I just said, "You're welcome." Then took his money. He is a director of something or other, but he was pretty chill. He seemed like he had a pretty good handle on his work flow so interruptions were easily tolerated, if not welcomed.

I copied and pasted the text of my email to Ms. Annie into an email to Brian, took a moment to consider all the awkwardness I'd have to endure from the fall-out of my treachery, then hit send. Confident in my thirty thousand-foot vision for this program, I think Annie and I will be a dynamic duo once all her rage finds its way into the ground water. Until then, I keep an eye on my six.

It must be a slow day at Primary Children's; I already have a reply from Mr. Pettiman. Oh, this is priceless. This is not going to be one of Annie's better days. He says, "This is brilliant! You must have spies in the halls because I've been approached by parents and staff voicing this very concern. How soon could you get this going? Do you need anything from me? I cc'd Annie Ketterling on this email. Work with her to set this up and she'll make sure you have space in the wards every night, any materials you need, and she'll notify parents and staff that this will be an option. Please copy me on all communications so I can relay progress to stakeholders. I was really struggling with a solution to this problem and you just laid it in my lap! We'll just need to get you and any other volunteers properly onboarded (vaccines, orientation, BLS certification, parking pass, etc.) Let's discuss offline, Annie. Thanks for thinking of us, Elliot! Let's make this work!"

Lots of exclamation points. That's a positive sign.

Sorry, Annie. The moral of this story is: never poo-poo Elliot's ideas. Life rises and falls on having enough humility to knock the king over when you're in checkmate.

DAY 26

Chapter 45

"Appear weak when you are strong, and strong when you are weak."
– *The Art of War*, Sun Tzu

I am officially certified to break ribs under the pretense of saving a life. Now I just need to find somebody that looks like they're not breathing <<even a labored wheeze will do>>. The best part is, they don't even have you breathing for them anymore. I always had a problem with that. It's interesting how controvertible incontrovertible truth is. If you went to a CPR class twenty years ago, you would be looking for a pulse and establishing an airway and pausing compressions to give breaths. And if you were to question that approach, you would be assured it was supported by indisputable truth, facts, science. Now you don't bother finding a pulse, establishing an airway isn't a primary concern, and you don't pause chest compressions at all. And if you are to question this approach, you would be assured it was supported by indisputable truth, facts, science. I wonder at what point they'll just say, "Our general opinion today is . . . " and leave it at that, so truth, facts, and science aren't one day the tarot cards of inquiry.

I'm heading up to the Salt Lake Clinic to have blood drawn for a QuantiFERON test. Apparently, they don't want me around sick kids if I have tuberculosis. At least it's not a flu vaccine. I used to get the flu vaccine every fall religiously until I realized that every time I got the flu vaccine, I got the flu. I would go get my flu vaccine, then stop off at the store on the way home and stock up on flu medicine. I always felt like they were Trojan horsing me to teach me a lesson about the dangers of Trojan horses. And yet I kept coming back. I haven't gotten a flu vaccine in the past five or six years, and I'll give you three guess what disease I have mysteriously been spared for the entirety of that same timeframe. Okay, two guesses.

The Salt Lake Clinic is typical of updated medical buildings—strange protrusions and angles, unnecessary artistic and architectural elements, clashing bricks and stones and metals and glass. It looks like the newest architectural vogue was added to its face every few years, regardless of whether it harmonized with the existing style.

I have to park in north Timbuktu so my truck can snack on three parking spaces without a lot of sneers. It's a glorious driving machine, but it isn't very parking-friendly. As I approach the building, I notice these two racially ambiguous men <<maybe man-boys, since each weighs about as much as one of my legs>> taking a keen interest in me but making failed attempts to look like they're not taking a keen interest in me. When I glance at them, they stare quietly at each other. It's weird. I can tell by their static-driven dialogue as I pass that they haven't developed their plan past *look at him without looking at him*. I figure, if they won't look at me while I'm looking at them, I'll take the opportunity to catalog everything about their little lady hands, the mustaches they've been growing since they were fourteen, the black, astronaut puff jackets that are so prevalent among Utahans, the shorter one's black-rimmed spectacles, the gray Mazda next to which they're loitering, and its Utah State license plate number. That's all I have time for.

Don't mess with me and my cataloging speed. Functional paranoids have skills.

Other than all the sick people, medical buildings are some of the pleasantest places to be with their helpful staff and airplane hangar lobbies and plastic vegetation adorned concourses and their cocci print art deco furniture. Healing is in its tidy air. And, of course, this would happen as I turn the corner to check in at the lab . . .

"Lord tunderin' Moses, if it arnt da feller wit da suit. 'Ow's she cuttin', b'y?"

I understand, "Lord thundering Moses" <<at least I'm eighty percent confident that's what he's saying>>. All the other syllables are hitting a breakwater. He's seated and the room isn't pitching aslant with every other step, but I would recognize that coastal patois anywhere. I get that attributing anything nautical to the Mariner is a supposition, and that he may have never stepped foot on a boat or lived anywhere near the water, but everything about him screams fisherman. He just needs a yellow sou'wester hat and matching mackintosh and the image is complete. When his identity strikes that funny chord, all I can think is, what are the odds of seeing him here? Oh, yeah, everywhere I go in the Patchiverse now, the probability of improbability is one hundred percent!

I don't think I ever got his name at his shop. I got Vivian's, for sure, but did he ever mention his name? "Hey . . . it's the master tailor. Thanks again for that suit. I don't know much about cloth or stitches so my compliments are going to be pretty hollow, but I'm sure I jumped to the top of the social food chain when I put that thing on."

"Ya knows yerself, b'y."

I can't tell if he's misunderstanding me or if his comments are appropriate responses in his language.

The unbroken half of his body pops out of the chair and he jams the webbing of his right thumb into the webbing of mine. "Dey calls me Jack Janes, they dooz." If I wasn't as strong as I am, his grip might have done some damage. Definitely a fisherman. I look back and forth at his face and his hand and can't shake the impression that he's somehow carved out of wood. With a clear lacquer finish. His face is etched like a ploughed field with all the furrows radiating along the grain of each separate facial muscle. He's either a thousand years old or thinks a whole lot about life is funny.

"It's a pleasure, Mr. Jack Janes."

"I takes it all, b'y, da pleasure and da rest."

"How's Vivian?"

"Ah, best kind, b'y. Come by fer a shave dis half or dat, dat ducky gets a long face sittin in deyr wit just her toughts. She could use a good yarn from a feller."

"I think I might. I am due for a shave."

A woman across the waiting room drops her phone and it tumbles into the leg of a table. The concourse's acoustics let everybody know. Not three seconds later, the gentleman sitting across from her does the same thing. The woman who first dropped her phone said with a hangdog sort of apologetic smile, "It's contagious." Then, as if desperately wanting to avoid inclusion in this scene of gaucheries, the gentleman sitting nearest the Mariner flails about with a half dozen attempts to snatch at his fumbled phone before it eventually finds its way to the floor with a flat plop.

They do say the Salt Lake Clinic is haunted, but I start panning the waiting room, the hallways, the lab staff, to catch what I'm supposed to be catching. This feels like one of those for-those-who-have-ears-let-him-hear type parable moments. There's a conductor with a baton close by, I know it. Certainly Patch wouldn't have wasted three phones dropped in succession. As I'm scanning, almost unconsciously my mind dumps, "A lot of gravity in here today," out of my mouth. <<It's a phrase my dad would use any time somebody dropped something.>>

Mr. Mariner Jack Janes flatly corrects, "Density, b'y."

"I'm sorry?"

"A lot of density in here today."

I'm trying not to be condescending with my eyes or my tone as I respond, "No, I meant gravity."

"G'wan, b'y. Me nerves rubbed right raw wit da gravity and its rotten fisheries. William of Ockham, he beez somersaultin' in dat grave of his. 'Entities must not be multiplied beyond necessity,' he writes. Got me drove wit dem gravity pickles."

Did he just summarize Ockham's Razor? Is everybody in this industry a closet philosopher? I feel like I'm back at that funeral watching my mom scolding the splashy rumrunners in their native tongues.

He is visibly miffed or disappointed or something so I tread lightly. "I'm not sure I follow. What does that have to do with gravity?"

"Density."

"What does that have to do with density?"

"Some chummy falls to da floor and yer invokin' some mystical force dat poofs into bein' at some magical mass. Ya drops yer helium balloon, beez ya still invokin' *gravity*? If yer divin' and bubbles beez floatin' to da surface, still *gravity*?"

I don't know if it's his argument or the fact that it's percolating through that accent, but I can't think of anything both cogent and respectful to say. It is reminiscent of one of Patch's electric fence arguments—the moment you get close, you realize your error.

"Movement is density differential, enda da stories, b'y."

"Mr. Janes," <<I'm venturing into incredulous>> "are you implying that there is no gravity?"

"Aye, me ol' cock, iffenz ya wants ta know a ting about da world, ya gots to unknow all yer knowins. Starts yer learnin' from da first bricks, and only reels in what beez happenin' directly ta *you*. If yer fallin' troo de air, always trust density over gravity. Nar'n of us beez livin' in a vacuum."

Ah. Now I see the connection. But maybe not; I did start the gravity talk after all. Or maybe Patch knew I'd absentmindedly say what I did in that situation because I'm hardwired to say it. Things are getting too theoretical these days. I feel like I have to consider the butterfly effect every time I try to make heads or tails of some oddity. Dissecting the preeminence of chickens and eggs is tiresome. What happened to the good ole days of isolation and predictability and Mountain Dew and a whole genre of music I just refer to as Pearl Jam?

"Der's a cataract as black as da Earl of Hell's waistcoat" <<Hey, that's Patch's phrase!>> "cloudin' yer—"

"You've been avoiding me."

My attention is yanked to the left. Blackgoat. In any other context, this improbable reunion would have stumped me, but I just smile, more so from the limpidity of these designs and confluences. I almost feel like I'm behind the curtain *with* the Wizard now. Though face to face with a known fibber, and knowing that my half of the duologue will, more or less, be reciprocal fibs, I'm more at ease than I thought possible for me. I'm about to introduce the two to soften the interruption, but Mr. Janes preempts me.

"Aye! T'da buddy wi'da big mout, I beez talkin' to da feller. Maybe learns yer manners and waits yer turn!"

I can see anger and embarrassment filling Blackgoat's head like a carafe, and all that remains of his countenance is the unnatural, waxy vestige of a polite smile.

Something very strange is happening right now. They look like two boxers, unblinking, ignoring the ref's instructions so they can just get to the clobbering each other part. I may be totally reading in to this, but this is what's going on in my mind: They know each other, or at least know good and well *about* each other; the Mariner outranks Blackgoat in whatever social order dictates these things; the interruption is intentional, meant to draw me away from the Mariner's homily; the Mariner isn't concerned with kwazants, so is not one of the pikirovateli; Blackgoat's emotional containment indicates that he *is* one of the pikirovateli <<maybe trouplongeur>>. My stream of consciousness is either brilliantly percipient or absolute madness. I can see it going either way.

"My apologies, sir. You're right, I had no right to intrude on your conversation like that. I'll be sitting over here, Elliot, whenever your conversation with the good gentleman is done."

"Aye . . . da manners of da youngins deez days. Rubbin' me nerves right raw . . ."

"Sorry, Mr. Janes, Mr. Blackgoat, but I should really get checked in. It was nice seeing you again, Mr. Janes. Mr. Blackgoat, I'll text you. Promise."

As I walk away, Mr. Janes sticks his foot out to trip me. He's unsuccessful, thankfully, but as I turn to see from whence the attack came, he winks at me. What is it with people winking at me?

When I check in at the desk, at the mere mention of my name a big display is made about taking me right back, in full view of a grumbling waiting room crowd. They're throwing around, "VIP," and, "Director's orders," and, "These people don't mind if you cut in line" <<they clearly mind>>. I need to start volunteering in all industries that are notorious for long waits and crappy customer service.

I glance back, almost to apologize for the special treatment, and I notice that Blackgoat and the Mariner are still staring at each other. Okay, then. There are definitely sides in this enterprise.

Venipuncture is fascinating to me. The fact that my entire circulatory system can be emptied with this millimeters diameter tube is just astounding. From vigor to gravedigger in seconds. I always ask the phlebotomist how often people watch the needle go in. About half. What gender handles it better? Always women. Who passes out more? Men. Usually the more muscular men.

The whole event of bleeding me takes all of three minutes, but as I walk out, Blackgoat and Mr. Janes are both gone. It makes me think that they were just there for me, they made their appearance, they had their exchange, no reason to hang around. What weirdness. This would all be simpler if there wasn't that one percent of my brain that thinks all of this is just tea leaves and I'm reading meaning into the meaningless.

I turn down the parking lot aisle, anxious to get to the Holiday where my precious Fountain Dew awaits and . . . come on! I just want to get on with my day! I'm starting to think that the Manuscript is just the textbook; the rest of this rubbish is the clinical experience. I so don't feel like doing this right now. But the nice thing about reading the Bible so much is that you come to the realization that goodness or probity or righteousness, whatever, is situational. It's not a one approach fits all kind of application. Love, patience, kindness, peacemaking, they all have wardrobes full of different outfits for different occasions. So if you weirdo timejumpers want to play some games, let's play some games. I can be terribly good.

Those two man-boys are standing close to my truck at the northeast end of the parking lot. I can tell they're pretending to admire my vehicle to kill time until I get there. Finally, they devise a plan! I walk, my eyes fixed on them, and stop about fifty yards from the truck. You can't miss me there in the road, standing, staring. They're still pretending they don't see me, crouching down near the wheels, pointing to things on the truck. I stand there, invisible apparently, for a full thirty seconds as they continue their charade. I reach my hand in my pocket and hit the fob's panic button. The one crouching nearly falls over trying to get to his feet. The other almost gets airborne. One has his hand on his chest and they both look down the aisle at the guy standing in the middle of the road staring at them. Now I have their attention. They stand there, stunned, watching me. I am unfazed, statuesque, staring, patient. I don't think they were prepared for the upper hand to be usurped. They put their hands in their pockets and watch me. It's an epic stare down, but since this is my life now, I might as well grab the bull by the horns. Or the malnourished boy-men by the proverbial scruff of the neck. I'm just assuming this is a Patch-orchestrated scenario and I proceed accordingly. I don't feel physically threatened since I can consume a Carl's Jr. meal of comparable caloric value as one of these kids, so I just wait and stare. The situationalness of my life is quite entertaining when I treat it as a role play or movie scene. And this is a nail biter. No accountability, no consequence, just good theater, where I take off the bowler hat and fake mustache and go home.

This goes on for another thirty whole seconds. I'm counting in my head.

And . . . victory. One goes, the other follows. I'm motionless until the parking lot is clear of them.

Virtue's application must also be tempered by the edict: *Be ye therefore wise as serpents and harmless as doves.*

I get settled in my truck and a rogue wave of weirdness sweeps me off the rocks and back into the unsettling depths of vagueness, like treading in a dark ocean where you can't see what creatures might be circling and lurking. Why am I struck so? What was it? Was it the loiterers? The Mariner? Blackgoat? That's it. It was Blackgoat. Blackgoat called me *Elliot.* I scroll through my text thread with Blackgoat <<such a fun name to say!>> and there's no mention of my first or last name. Did I tell him at the park, where we first met? He was there and gone so quickly I don't think there could have been a proper introduction. I was more worried about his dogs biting me.

The more I think about it, the more I'm convinced I should take Blackgoat up on his offer—not so much to play for the team but more so to keep my enemies closer. I don't trust that yoyo and his cool name and perfect mustache.

When I get home I add *probity's wardrobe* to my gratitude list.

DAY 27

CHAPTER 46

"If you want your children to be intelligent, read them fairy tales. If you want them to be more intelligent, read them more fairy tales."
– Albert Einstein

I've been going over how this is going to work in my head. I'm a planner, remember. And I don't like looking stupid, being unprepared, or relying on others whose standards of excellence are so decidedly below my own <<*Pride and Prejudice*>>. I know I'm just a volunteer reading to kids, but what e'er thou art, act well thy part, right?

Instead of any of the weird arrangements that allow both the reader to see the text and the audience to see the pictures, I settle on a slideshow. I am a PowerPoint wizard, after all; I may as well play to my strengths. Now I need to figure out a way to get the pictures of the greatest children's book of all time, *Edward Fudwupper Fibbed Big*, on to PowerPoint slides so I can run the slide show on a TV while I read the text. Maybe I'll just scan them.

As I pull up PowerPoint, my mind imposes some nagging, faded afterimage onto the slide's bewitching blankness. I've been wanting to do this for a while, but just haven't had the time. Thinking I can whip this out in a flash, I start developing a pictorial depiction of Patch's scheme with the frames and vents and Gontlets and native hulls and umbrae and recoupling and updates. I wanted to fit the whole scheme on one summary slide, but was made to understand <<by my mind's roommate, the one with the uncompromising, compulsive tendencies>> that it was more manageable on thirty-eight slides.

It's a work of art, like an anatomy textbook would be a work of art with labeled needles exploding from every illustration.

And now I'm out of time. My flattery has a horrible definition of a *flash*.

Okay, well, I'll work with what I have, I guess. I'll just add a few cartoonish elements, some animations . . . done. This will either immortalize me or kill the program straight out of the gate. Embed my super awesome fonts in the file <<only unimaginative morons use default fonts>>, email it to myself, grab the iPad, and I'm off.

You would think it goes without saying, but the evenings are dark these days. In the summer, you equate dark with light traffic, but as winter approaches, the safety of visibility is stripped from already lethal traffic. And the University of Utah, built on tiered benches, one complex per tier, as many patients as students, isn't your most navigable of campuses <<Patch would say *campi*>>.

I'm not as nervous as I thought I'd be at this stage. This *is* my element, after all. I'm like the Pied Piper, except that my wardrobe is pretty monochromatic and I don't play a pan flute. Just in the sense that I can get kids to follow me out of cities. Pathetically, the thing I'm most nervous about is the nurses. It's hard to look cool when you're entertaining children. I have to remind myself that I'm not a linebacker trying to impress the chicks this hour, I'm a merry-andrew trying to impress six-year-olds. But if one of the byproducts of being a goof is a cute nurse wanting to make out after, that's cool.

I have no siblings; the only kids I was ever around were friends and peers; I've never even held a baby. I don't know why I'm so comfortable around kids. It probably says more about *me* than kids. Kids are just . . . real. I don't mean innocent per se <<I've met some bona fide demon seed before>>, they just haven't accumulated all the sludge, the neuroses and cynicism and insecurities, that colors adults' humorlessness and steeps their fearless curiosity in vinegar-soaked rags. And I'm a sarcastic person; kids think sarcasm is funny. Adults think sarcasm is condescending, especially those that don't get it.

A couple of AV-savvy nurses set me up with a large screen TV in a room called Sophie's Place on the third floor. It's like a music studio filled with shapes and colors that give me a headache. Apparently, they use it for music therapy. Hopefully not for the kids in the neurosurgery wing.

Sophie's Place is just a room off the main hall. It is centralized among several in-patient wings, so it is accessible to patients from a variety of pathologies. My presence must have been announced among the corridors of the sick and afflicted because I can hear them congregating through the open door, just out of view. Nurses have successfully summoned the chance consumers of a fine-spun yarn, but I hear coaxing to get them past the threshold. Now I hear parents coaxing. Oh no. Now they're begging. This isn't good. Lucky for me I'm a planner. I'm prepared for a duel with trepidation. This pied piper <<minus pied, minus piper>> stuff is no exaggeration.

I've been holding my breath a lot lately and have deepened, enriched, and expanded all facets of my voice's sine wave. My words are coming out of the left side of my mouth as I bellow, "My grandfather was a pirate!"

All the chatter in the hallway stops.

I take advantage of the pause. "His name was Patch. You want to know why his name was Patch?"

Now I wait. I hear some shuffling. And, behold, my first victim.

"Ah, you must be Caleb!"

"My name is *Hudson*."

"Yes, yes, that's what I said, *Hudson*. Finally! Come in, come in. I've been waiting for you, Hudson, for hours!"

The right side of his face crumples into that benefit of the doubt giving I-think-you're-lying-but-I-don't-know-for-sure expression kids use until they develop more sophisticated responses <<eye-rolling, head-shaking, the ever-genial *whatever*>>.

Hudson looks to be five or six. Clearly, story time is a staple in Hudson's life—he climbs right up on my lap and wriggles his body comfortably into my mass.

"Oh, okay. Welcome to story time, Hudson. Since you're the bravest of the brave, with the heart of a three-headed lion with eight rows of shark teeth, you get to run the slideshow. Whenever I say, <<I cover his ears>> 'Do it, Hudson!' I want you to swipe this to the right. Got it?"

An exaggerated, voiceless nod.

I pull out a dozen eye patches I picked up on the way over and put one on myself and Hudson.

I cover Hudson's ears and yell out, "Because, says he, it's a common nickname for someone who wears an eye patch! Why, you ask, would this pirate need to wear an eye patch?"

A girl not much older than Hudson peeks around the corner.

"Harper! Come in, come in!"

"I'm *Olivia*!"

"Of course you are, Olivia! Harper is just Latin for Olivia. Here's your eye patch. This is a pirate story, so we all need to wear eye patches."

She quickly puts it on and starts looking around the room, like the eye patch was supposed to be a 3D monocle or something.

Two ten-year-old boys, overhearing talk of eye patches no doubt, stand in the doorway.

"Owen! Henry! Welcome!"

They look at each other with that eyebrow-raised acknowledgement of an old man's lunacy.

"Whatever, you're now Owen and Henry for the purpi of this splendid chronicle of pirates and insurgents and time travel! Eye patches, boys!"

Owen and Henry <<not their names>> have reached that age where a consciousness of self-image wars against unabashed fun, but after bellowing <<I cover Hudson's ears>>, "How do you expect to be a pirate if you can see out of both eyes, matey?" they slip them on and take their seats on chairs shaped like slices of pie.

Four's a good start. More will follow. Hudson is quite proud of his position as first mate, though still trying to make himself the cold cuts of my doughy guts.

My first slide is a picture of Patch, half-doubled over laughing hysterically at something. I tilted him supine, photoshopped an eye patch on, removed the photo's background, and have him freefalling on a high-altitude backdrop. Thus begins our tale . . .

"This is my grandfather. He is a pirate. His name is Patch. He is also a swashbuckler and a mapmaker and an aerialist and—"

Henry asks, "Did somebody poke his eye out?"

"Sorry?"

"Is that why he wears an eye patch, because somebody stabbed him in the eye?"

"Patch never wore an eye patch a day in his life! Do it, Hudson!"

Hudson swipes right like a champ. The next slide has a stack of frames and a miniature Patch suspended in the air just below a small airplane.

Four more kids appear. Owen taps on his eye patch and points to me. With limply contained enthusiasm, they retrieve their gear, put them on, and sit on a robin's-egg blue ottoman that smells like a migraine. I don't think I had any expectations about the face of my audience, but it's far motlier than the expectations I would have had if I'd had expectations. Various stages of hair going and coming, a fashion line of hybridized lounge and functional wear I would title Pajamafied EKG Lead Accessible, kids wheelchairing in, IV infusion pumps that rival Darth Vader's chest computer.

"You may be asking yourself, How was Patch a pirate? Well, you'd be asking yourself an excellent question. Do it, Hudson!"

Hudson initiates an animation of Patch falling through the air and into a vent.

"Patch found these holes that move along the surface of the Earth, these nearly bottomless pits that extend deep, deep below the surface. Finding these holes is very tricky and you need to do a lot of math to find out exactly where they are." Several kids mutter their hatred of math. "And it's even trickier since the holes are moving all the time. Falling into one of these pits is kind of like falling into water where the water stops you from falling too deep. What you find in these holes is not what you'd think. Patch isn't just a pirate; Patch is a *time-traveling* pirate."

My speech is affected; I'm gesticulating with the arm I'm not holding Hudson with, and my eyes are as bugged out as the sockets allow.

"Falling through these pits is like falling through a book back towards its first page, back towards your *life's* first page. The deeper you fall, the farther back in time you go. Do it, Hudson!"

The next slide is the perspective of the Gontlet from a vent.

"Once you stop falling, it's like you're shot out of the pit into a space between two of the book's pages, two of the book's *earlier* pages. So if you're on page two hundred and seventy-eight and fall through one of these holes, you could possibly be on page . . ." <<I'm checking comprehension.>>

One of the new kids calls out, "One hundred!"

"Yes, you brilliant little so-and-so, yes, one hundred maybe! Because one hundred comes before two hundred and seventy-eight, right? So, let's say he's shot out of the pit into the space between pages one hundred and one hundred and one. If he fell into the hole when he was sixty years old, let's say, maybe at page one hundred he's only twenty years old. Once he's in that space between pages one hundred and one hundred and one, he's not done. Now it's the hard part. Now he has to fight his way through all these people that live in the space between the pages. Do it, Hudson!"

Hudson initiates an animation of people appearing and disappearing all over the screen, crowds thronging, the slide's background flashing different colors <<hopefully no epileptics in the room>>, and an audio backdrop of a thousand geese.

"He's got to find his twenty-year-old self and jump in so there's not two of him roaming around! Crazy, right? If Patch's sixty-year-old self jumps into one of these holes in Romania . . . who knows where Romania is?" <<Nobody knows.>> "Okay, if his sixty-year-old self jumps into one of these holes in Provo, but he lived in Salt Lake City when he was twenty, he's going to have to do a little traveling, right?" The Provo-Salt Lake City connection is clicking.

"Everybody that ever lived on Earth is living between all these pages, so he has to use magic to distract everyone while he slips through the crowds."

Owen asks, "What kind of magic? Does he have a wand?"

"Mostly card tricks, actually."

One of the new kids in his early teens brings some depth. "Why did he want to go back in time? Did he not like his life here?"

"Name!" I demand.

"Grayson."

"That's a really good question, Grayson. There's something about this pirate story I haven't mentioned yet—Patch isn't the only one that knows about these holes. There are these French guys that know about them, too, and they don't like other people jumping into these holes. And there are these Russian guys that know about these holes and they want *everyone* to jump into these holes. So there's like a war going on. And Patch knows more about where these holes are than both the French and the Russians, so he's kind of stuck in the middle of this war. He's the mapmaker for these holes and they need his maps so they know how to find them properly."

I was too engrossed in my story to notice that the assembly had doubled; one of the nurses is holding up the door jamb with an absent grin and a fatigue that's pulling her shoulders forward. I've run out of eye patches, but some of the older kids give theirs up to the younger kids who eagerly slide them on and adjust them.

Olivia nearly murders the mood with her six-year-old innocence. "Maybe he was getting a divorce and wanted to go back to tell his wife how much he loves her so she doesn't want to get a divorce."

Grayson brings it back. "Maybe he fell in love with a girl and wants to go back in time to be with her longer."

What is going on?

"Good observations here, people. What else? Why else might he want to go back in time?"

A newcomer, Liam, adds, "Maybe he wants to win the lottery because he knows the lottery numbers."

"Ah, yes, Liam, yes! But that reminds me of something else I haven't mentioned." <<Now I have parents as well; the whole point was to give you a break!>> "Every time Patch, or some Frenchman or Russian or anybody else falls into one of these holes and finds their way into their younger self, time sort of starts again from that point. If any of them make any changes, it starts changing *everything*. So, Liam, why are you here, in this hospital, on this very day?"

"I fell off my bike and broke my . . . my . . . it starts with a *p*."

"Pelvis?"

"Pelvis, yeah." <<I'm relieved his crash didn't result in a broken penis. That would have been awkward.>>

"Okay, Liam busted his chassis falling off a bike. If you went back in time one month, would you make that same bike ride, knowing that you'd break your pelvis and end up in the hospital?"

"Nope."

"Right, no. So you wouldn't be in this hospital right now. You wouldn't be in this room right now talking to me. We never would have met, most likely. All kinds of things would be different without taking that bike ride. And all those differences would cause more differences, like the ripples moving away from a rock you throw in the water. And all those changes bump into changes that were made by somebody else that fell through one of these holes until changes are ricocheting . . . bouncing off each other at all sorts of odd angles."

The younger kids are more entertained by the slide show and my tone; the older kids have that concentrative grimace of trying to figure something out.

Grayson asks, "So why do these guys get to make all the changes? Can we make changes too?"

"I guess, yeah. We'd have to do the math and find one of these holes though. Or find Patch's maps, maybe."

One of the mothers keeps looking back at her husband in the doorway, like he should be intervening, but he seems too humored by the dialogue to notice her fussing.

A curious ten- or eleven-year-old still wearing his eye patch joins the conversation. "Does Patch remember everything when he gets young again?"

"Name!" I yell.

"Kutter."

"Ah, Kutter . . . Kutter with fadder and mudder and sister and brudder who makes all the hearts of the pretty girls flutter, that is a brilliant question. The answer: Yes! He remembers everything."

Kutter starts vocalizing his stream of mental processing. "How does he fit back into his younger body? What if he got fat? Is he like an avatar or something?"

Are kids really this smart now? I know it's not in the air or the water or Utahans would be better drivers. At the mention of *avatar*, everyone pays attention.

"Kutter, Kutter, knife in butter, you are far more brilliant than anyone tells you, even if they tell you you're brilliant all the time! Because when you fall into these holes, only your mind can fit into it. And it's just your mind that can fit into your younger self."

Grayson wonders aloud, "What does your mind look like?"

Yeesh. These kids are like the boogie boarders to my wave. I need to be careful what I say or I'm going to be giving flesh and bone to abstractions that will lodge themselves in under-myelinated brains.

It went on like this for a while. Which is great since I was wondering how I could stretch this material across an entire hour. This slide show will last me weeks at this rate.

Hudson has gone rogue and is advancing the slides and all the animations and the younger kids are laughing at double-time time travel. "Undo it, Hudson!" Hudson is giggling at his insurrection.

Henry asks, "Have you jumped into these holes? Are you from the future?"

"Nope. I've been right here my whole life. Well, not in this room, but in the present, yeah. And my congratulations to you parents for making unbelievably intelligent kids. Yep, I've been right here the whole time." I think my voice drooped a little into what might have sounded like disappointment.

Then a question from Olivia: "Do *you* know any card tricks?"

I know card tricks! Why did it not occur to me that children could be entertained with card tricks? "You know what, Ms. Olivia, I *do* know some card tricks. I have to practice for when I have to get through all the crowds in between the pages, right?"

Olivia asks if I can do one.

"For you, Ms. Olivia, I would do anything. Except eat peas. Peas are disgusting. It's not personal."

Cutting charges are severing the pillars of the congregation and they collapse layer by layer into the foundation that is me and Hudson. The spotlight is getting a little too bright for Hudson and he leans the back of his head against my chest. A nurse asks if I need a deck of cards as I'm pulling my Apollo deck from the pocket of my loosened jeans. I can see the hands of the older kids twitching as I'm single-handedly shuffling the deck, their empty hands simulating the motor movements they'll use when they locate a deck of cards afterwards.

Based on facial expressions, one-handed shuffling may end up being more impressive than the trick itself.

I have Olivia assist me with a trick called the Three Travelers. It's a simple trick that pushes my balloon fingers to the limits of their dexterity, but it's a real stunner. Even the parents look perplexed. Perplexed is a good sign for a novice with free-thinking fingers.

"Hopefully none of you are still here next week, but if you are, this is your homework for next Thursday: I want you to tell me what age you would go to if you could go *forward* in time, and tell me why you picked that age. Everyone clear?"

Everyone nods. Some are already thinking about it. Then they disperse, Hudson reluctantly.

These kids would definitely follow me out of the city. I need to get a pan flute and a coat of calico, just for effect.

The fussing mother approaches me. Here we go . . . I can already feel all my knee-jerks wanting to pick her up over my head and make a hole in the far wall with her body. Which I'm pretty sure I could do.

I superimpose what's-her-name's face <<I swear it's Reyna or something>> on the back half of Sophie's Place. The room falls away to an Eternity, white and woven from the top throughout. I'm sure my faded foreground thinks it strange that I'm looking through and beyond her as she confronts me.

"Are you sure it's a good idea to be filling these young minds with jumping into wormholes and alternate realities?"

From the cadence of her speech and her enunciation, I can tell this woman is educated. Patch would say, *Education, as the world defines it, is a basilisk that, with a wink, makes rigidity of creativity, complexity, and imagination—it turns everything lively and living to stone.* Her hands are on her hips, she's standing uncomfortably close to me, and she keeps looking back at her husband who clearly wants no role in this exchange. The whitewashing, the breath holding, the attention to consequence, it must be having its effect in widening the gap between stimulus and response because it takes me so long to respond, she's able to take one more glance at her husband before my eyes microscope back to the obstructing wall of ugliness.

I try to replicate Blackgoat's waxy smile in the clinic waiting room and speak with more scorn than I'm actually experiencing. "You're right, I should've been talking about eating green eggs and ham with goats and on boats. Don't worry, these kids will be force-fed plenty of the world's quote-unquote realities soon enough." Then I brush past her; stop at, nay, overshadow her husband; have a long, commiserative conversation with a brevity of eye contact; shake his hand without a word; and walk out of the room.

I'm not sure why I shook his hand. By virtue of my magnitude, I feel like I can take liberties with being a little weird every now and again.

Patch says there are numberless approaches to every situation and very few of them can be dismissed as wrong or lauded as right until all human history is shaken out. And, as a self-proclaimed utilitarian, I don't beat myself up too much about initial reactions <<I wish it wasn't, but that is so untrue>>. That being said, hard sarcasm rarely endears. Unfortunately, this is how I get when someone questions judgment I confidently consider sound. Something else to work on, I guess. I think to apologize to the <<clinically>> concerned mother, but I'm still tumbling in that riptide of brute reactivity and can't ensure that the wall will remain bodyholeless, let alone convince of sincerity. A more heady strategy next time will have to suffice. Actually, why? Why next time? Patch would say: Next time *is the* never *of the conscience masseur!* and *There's always a reason to NOT do something!* <<I end all of his quips with exclamation points because he always seemed to be either loudly emphatic or straight up bellowing.>> Things are never as dire as I think they're going to be. And if I'm wrong and it goes badly, I chuck her into the wall.

I go back in the room and the couple is in quiet conference. The husband has his hands on his wife's shoulders and is looking at her quite lovingly. With exertion, she uses her leaden limbs to express herself with some deflation. When she sees me looking at her, she looks away.

I'm looking <<because I really am this time>> inquisitive and sincere. I even try to sound sincere when I say, "I'm honestly not trying to be confrontational here, but out of curiosity, why did you say that?"

She collapses into her husband's arms and gets weepy. She slides her body to face me without leaving the embrace. Her whole body is crying but her voice is pretty steady. "I don't know. I don't know why I said that. I didn't need to say it. You're right, we read our kids nonsense stories all the time. They're raised on nonsense and I think it's great. I really liked your story and the kids were eating it up. I'm just so beside myself in this place. I don't know if you have kids, but there's no greater stress in life than seeing one of your kids in pain and not being able to do anything about it. It just tears away at all your good sense. I'm sorry. It was wrong of me to take it out on you. You were really good with the kids tonight. I should just be grateful and shut my mouth."

I'm thinking the following monologue, but only half aware that my mouth is making it into audible words. "Wait, I say some nasty, sarcastic thing, and *you're* sorry? I clearly need to work on my sensitivity. Of course you have a sick kid or you wouldn't be here. Why wouldn't I consider that when interacting with a parent in a children's hospital, for heaven's sake? I'll tell you what, I'll accept your apology if you accept mine."

Her face is buried in her husband's chest but she nods her head anyway.

"Which kid was yours, if you don't mind me asking?"

"It was Hudson."

My shame is squeezed out as a chuckle, like irony through a pasta roller. Of course it would be Hudson.

"Tell me what I can do. I'll do anything you want."

Her face emerges from her husband's chest. She glances at her husband again and asks, "Would you visit him?"

"You'd be okay with me visiting him?"

"He hasn't been this . . . playful in a long time."

"I will absolutely visit him. It's the least I could do for being such a brat. And I'll bring real children's books."

She returns to her sternal Wailing Wall. The husband mouths, "Thank you." I don't want to spoil their moment so I hand him my cell number and leave.

Patch would always say, *People reject the notion of miracles not because they're faithless, but because they're ungrateful.* He says that most people see outcomes as a summation of individual probabilities when they're really multiplicative. Setting my perception on these rails has helped a little with gratitude, so miracles are a little more pronounced than they otherwise would be. But that, to me, was a miracle—my return to an uncomfortable social encounter <<my presence at a social encounter at all, really>>, the misplaced apology, my defeated defenses, the leaked counterapology, the resolution, it was all a little too all Sir Garnet to shrug off as fortuity. This was impossible with every facet gemologist cut.

I'm back in my house, my fortress of decompression. It's dark and quiet, only a motion-sensing light in the kitchen undimming the darkness until my stillness renders me invisible again. My mind is just mindlessly treading water. I'm not the kind of person that attributes success or accomplishment much to his own merits, so I wasn't feeling smug or megalomaniacal or anything. I was just satisfied, pleased maybe, that it wasn't an abject failure. I was bracing myself for abject failure. And none of the nurses indicated any interest in making out with me so, in that regard, maybe it was a failure.

I reignite the motion sensor light with a trip to the fridge. I write, *I was eyes to the blind, and feet was I to the lame* on my gratitude list.

I may have missed the mark with this assignment; it's hardly selflessness when I'm the one reaping all the benefits.

Life rises and falls on unanticipated enlightenment.

DAY 29

Chapter 47

"Security is mostly a superstition. It does not exist in nature, nor do the children of men as a whole experience it. Avoiding danger is no safer in the long run than outright exposure. Life is either a daring adventure, or nothing."
– Helen Keller

Who knew there was a world outside the bank of fountain drinks at the Holiday, and that it wouldn't try to murder me at every turn? <<I have always felt a kinship with Captain Yossarian.>> In fact, I think I feel my umbral bones <<understanding the paradox there>> getting denser. My self-circulating ignorance is circling the drain with every seized opportunity. And with a renewed social confidence, a frame unburdened by twenty or so pounds, a more sophisticated fashion <<jeans, shirts with collars, shoes with laces>>, and a ride that propels me into the lower heavens of status, it's not so bad.

I haul the read and unread blocks of the Manuscript from my office to the dining table in separate trips. Based on my experience with this harlequinade, I have been made stronger by that which has not killed me. Why continuest I to doubt? <<Because it's Ace Quantrillitrain and his Venus flytrap ways, that's why!>>

Assignment #6: MORTALITY

My decision to resume long-distance running has been an auspicious one. I feel like my heart can better handle being impaled by things like *mortality*.

Concerning the frameosphere, there isn't much upon which I need to expound or philosophize for this assignment. This is a purely mechanical aspect of the enterprise, one with which you will acquire intimate familiarity. Hopefully this eventuality has been leaven in your subconscious and, consequently, baked into your expectations <<I don't remember Patch ever using that phrase, but I must have gotten it from him because I use it all the time>>. *If not, this day of reckoning will reckon more like the eschaton than simply taking the next logical step into the void.*

With superlatives in cost (lowest), profile (lowest), and efficiency (greatest), it is the pikirovateli staple for accessing the vents. Yes, the math, the maps, they illuminate the target, but if you're relying on Kentucky windage for accuracy, it will be a short and permanent journey to the shallowest Gontlet.

Today you're going to jump out of an airplane at fifteen thousand feet with only your wits to save you. Your wits and a parachute.

Please tell me this is just another dig-up-Lazarus-and-take-him-to-Morocco kind of knee-slapper. I hardly think it reasonable to make a Johnny Utah out of an Edward Scissorhands in a few weeks. Although, he's right, this eventuality should have been a foregone conclusion.

Don't worry, you survive this day intact. You can trust the all-seeing eye. Wendover Airfield. Now go! The team is waiting for you.

I feel like one of those dogs laying down on an electrified plate in learned helplessness experiments. In agony, I will drive to Wendover Airfield because I know it is my only real choice.

Chapter 48

"He is terribly afraid of dying because he hasn't yet lived."
– "The Metamorphosis," Franz Kafka

This is something I should be kidnapped and driven to in a windowless van with Hall & Oates B-sides blasting rather than willing what feels like an infected, swollen foot to keep a gas pedal depressed. <<I should learn how to use the cruise control in this thing.>> Despite the all-seeing eye's reassurance, it feels like a death march. Drivers are passing me with near-PIT maneuver aggression because I can't devote enough attention to keeping the truck up to the speed limit through the tenebrous doom laid thick by my mind's dry ice fogger.

I think I understand how it feels to be standing on the gallows, listening to a rabble of the ravenous gather, a Venusian atmosphere of hot breath greenhoused by a roughly-stitched hood offering a hashed preview of my imminent asphyxia. My eyes, my head, my shoulders, my lungs, my very existence: it all feels so heavy and catatonic. I keep having to take deep breaths because I'm too distrait to breathe in.

This was my mom for months after an over-dressed colonel came to our door with the bad news. She always had that far-away stare and gasped her forgotten inhalations.

I've been driving for hours <<twenty-eight minutes>> and nothing about I-80 is salty yet. I knew this day would come, this bug spray-tasting zero hour, the day the training wheels would come off and I'd be pushed down Canton Avenue.

Over the next twelve hours <<forty-five minutes>>, I keep telling myself all I have to do is show up. What could go wrong if I just show up? Then the mountains give way to a sky as open and clear as the vision of my mangled, X-marks-the-spot death. I can see a flailing black dot pitted against the sky's lone cloud, outfalling its deliverers who finally have to deliver themselves. Then the boom . . .

I'm reminded by patient and understanding Utahans that I'm going fifty-four miles per hour in a seventy zone.

Wendover on the Utah side looks like a seventies, small-town America set for a movie where a lot of people end up dead from drugs or gratuitous shootings. Quentin Tarantino would do brilliantly here. And this is where I die, where *Reservoir Dogs* meets *No Country for Old Men* <<not a Quentin Tarantino movie, I know>>.

I drive to the rear of a parking lot and see what is unmistakably my party gathered near a chain-link fence. Russian fashion is unmistakable. There are four of them and they seem anxious to get on with things. I don't immediately see a plane with its engine running, so hopefully I get a little time to work through second thoughts before surrendering all my legal rights and an untimely death.

<<Although, this *could* be timely. I'm not really sure what Patch has in mind for me.>>

My survival instinct is coiling around my curdled legs like a boa, but my propriety and testicles are shoving me out of the truck. I don't want them to have to wait on me, and disclosing my clutching, prehensive terror to men of men is absolutely out of the question. I'd rather the ground take me at terminal velocity than be responsible for portraying American men as milquetoast in the face of gritty Russian types. Gut up or shut up, Elliot. Time travel is clearly a man's sport, and if I'm to get any playing time, I need to quit myself like a man and fight.

Okay, now I'm ready.

I'm greeted by an impossibly jolly Russian, a sort of burlesque of the fatherland. He is undoubtedly the leader. This kind of social confidence subordinates.

His accent is thick, his vowels are long, and all his *r* 's bounce, "No worry, we take good care of heir. You live," <<leeyive>> "I promise. You are cash cow."

Actually, that was pretty pacifying. Aggressively happy is always smotheringly soothing. Wait, *cash cow*? Did he say *cash cow*? What in Cerberus's cracking colon is that supposed to mean? Am I suppo—

Before my curiosity can be planted and watered, the rest of the group approaches and a more convincing English speaker with hints of heritage in his *h*'s and *r*'s interrupts. "Elliot, I'm Yuri. This is Dimitriy, Ivan, and Sasha. Dimitriy and I know you from Kapatel's funeral." <<Kapatel?>> "We've known him for a long time. We were all sorry for his . . . passing. But he's like a cockroach—he never seems to stay dead. We have to get going. As much as we try to blend in, once Dimitriy opens his mouth, we may as well be wearing swastikas. His accent and need to high-five everyone start a timer."

Dimitriy has this troubling, can't-wait-to-slit-your-throat kind of grin, and he bumps through his English. "You live," <<again, leeyive>> "promise."

Yuri can see the pallor invading my face like a leprosy and he reassures me, "Don't worry about Dimitriy, he's Russian. At this moment, he's your greatest friend in the world."

I nod in mumness.

I'm jammed into the back seat <<herrings in a barrel, Yuri says>> of an outfitted Mercedes-Benz G-Class <<that makes my truck look like a rusted-out, taupe Pinto>> with four total strangers yelling at each other in Russian like they're disarming a bomb that's going to detonate in thirty-four . . . thirty-three . . . thirty-two . . . Dimitriy is the loudest, highest pitched, and most animated. The others are mostly shaking their heads. "Nyet, nyet, nyet, nyepravilnah!" I feel like I've invaded a dining room at a family reunion. Yuri incrementally summarizes the ordnance disposal pandemonium and it translates to content much less critical than the tones and volume would betray—mostly about soccer and how attractive Maria Zakharova is or isn't. The way Dimitriy draws out what is obviously the Russian word for *so*, it is clear he has a thing for her.

I never had a brother, but I can't shake the notion that I somehow grew up with these guys. There's something familiarly familial about this particular dynamic. Is this possible? Can artifacts of pre-update iterations persist through native umbral threads? Could I have converged with Russians, these Russians, at some juncture that created sturdy wisps of update-resistant memories? The fact that I would even consider such a thing leaves me in this weird, muddled guck, like I'm snapping in and out of amnesic stupors. And this after a sixty-second drive down Airport Way to the Enola Gay Hangar. I'm more fuzzy now than terrified.

I was starting to feel like a step-brother, a cousin at least, but now they're all in black and yellow jumpsuits with a sheen, not unlike that tangled mess on the Salt Flats, and I'm back to being the outsider in a solid blue suit with these goofy, white pads stitched into the arms and legs. I really thought we had something here. Dimitriy is teaching me how to skydive in excitedly broken English, as if he's explaining how all this rigging works when we're already in freefall. Yuri cuts the crusts off Dimitriy's pleonastic pidgin and makes digestible English of it <<thankfully, too, because Dimitriy has a gold crown on one of his molars and my brain resets every time the sunlight hits it>>. I'm on the ground, on my belly, limbs pulling my chest and thighs off the ground and luxating in an attitude of flight. I find the primary chute handle. I find the primary chute cutaway handle. I find the reserve deployment handle. Waving off. Chute handle, cutaway, reserve. Again. Again. Again. They're very good teachers and all four are taking a keen interest in fast-tracking my muscle memory. Dimitriy's making good on his promise that I will leeyive.

"This is a lot of information for a tandem jump. Will I need to remember all this for my first time?"

Dimitriy whips his head back and forth and corrects, "No hook to! We don't do hook to! Elliot like free bird first time!" It took me a minute to figure out what *free beard fierce time* meant.

Yuri puts his hand on Dimitriy's shoulder, which turns him off like a toy. He says, "We'll be right next to you the whole time. We teach you on the ground, then teach you in the air. We jump from fifteen thousand feet, so it will give us time. Dimitriy promised you'd live. You'll live. Remember, Dimitriy is your greatest friend in the world right now. You just worry about steadying your body up there."

I'm comforted. I feel diarrhea coming on.

I think I'm losing time because whole yards of my awareness are being folded over and sewn up. I remember taxiing, Runway 080, and now we're already at three thousand-feet altitude. Where did those thousands of feet go? Dimitriy keeps slapping me in the chest with the back of his hand and yelling, "You be like clay, we get you down, all of one piece! You got this, Elliot Dillinger."

"I got this!" I shout back.

"Da! You got this!"

"Da," I agree.

I should probably learn Russian.

I always thought skydivers circled back toward the airfield so they could land somewhat close to it, but we haven't changed direction yet and Ivan is opening a rollup door. We've been up for some ten minutes; we must be miles away from the airfield.

I'm trying to look cool and relaxed but my eyes are perfidious. I can't fix them on anything and it's making me look nervous. Dimitriy is on to me because he keeps reminding me, "Remember, you live!"

I smile that acquiescing smile and give Dimitriy a high-five as a reward for his encouragement. He's beaming bright giddiness on his comrades and brags, "He give me high-five, ya!" They all shake their heads in disappointment that he's so easily paid off.

This plane is much swankier than is reasonable for a vehicle whose sole purpose is jumping out of it. I thought it would be smaller and louder. Mercifully, however, since it is loud enough to obscure my booming, crashing, thundering systole that <<I swear I can feel this>> is jerking the plane a little with each of its hundred and thirty fulminations per minute. The world outside the window is islands of dark, puckered escarpments marring a vitiliginous profile staring at the north end of the Great Salt Lake. We must have headed northeast from the airfield.

I wonder if my cash cowitude paid for this plane.

Yuri's face occludes my view and my reverie is sucked out the open door. The volume of his voice competes with speed and engines and air. "You know everything you need to do. We'll be with you the whole time." Then, somehow, I'm nothing but a higher density mass falling through a lower density medium <<Mariner's words>>. It doesn't take long for the exacting resistance to shape me into an inverted arch and Russian bumblebees start swirling around me. Ivan and Dimitriy are flanking me to the left and right, respectively, adjusting my arms and legs. Ah, I get the goofy white pads now. Yuri is back in my face. Dimitriy pulls my right hand back to the bottom of the container to locate the handle. My left arm moves to the right for counterbalance. I repeat the sequence on my own. And again. And again. And again. I locate the cutaway. I locate the reserve. And again. And again. I give Yuri two thumbs up. The three of them drift to my ten, twelve, and two o'clock, though I swear we started with a fourth. Maybe Sasha didn't jump with us. I give Yuri another double thumbs up. The three drift yet farther. Yuri flashes ten fingers. I have ten seconds before deployment.

I don't think I'm the best candidate for activities that require life-preserving concentration in novel environments. This kind of curiosity will plunge more than the cat into the unforgiving salt lick below. Even over a dry lakebed blanched by salt and freckled with a topographical pooling of different shades of gray, it is clean and organized and distinct and beautiful. Airplane windows don't do this world justice. I look out at the horizon falling with me. Terrestrial features are blossoming like they're being gradually focused under magnification. My initial sensation of stepping through an absent stair has been replaced by a sensation of being launched skyward in a geyser of wind. I heedlessly admire the suspended cotton crop and the shadows it casts on its saline soil. I can't properly process this tsunami of splendor and I curse the inadequacy of billions of cells of specialized sensory. I think I get what Patch means by the hull being a heavy, wet sensory suppressor. If this view doesn't overload the system to cellular, light speed detonation, its translators are illiterate.

I shouldn't report this next part because I fear it will sort me into either the hallucinogenic category or the visionary one. Of which <<dreams don't count>>, I've had neither. Scattered across the sun-blanked sky I can see dozens of hazy versions of me skydiving, hazy like they were colored with pastels <<maybe charcoals since they all seem like they darken the sky a little>> and slightly smeared, distorted like I'm seeing them falling through a thick glass cylinder. I don't *see* a glass cylinder, but the effect gives the illusion of one. In all these iterations, I'm wearing the same black and yellow jumpsuit as the Russians, but I also have on a matching, full-face helmet. Right, I can't see my face in any of these iterations, so how do I know it's me? Well, it's me. I don't know what else to say. These figures are not identical iterations; they're all me in different instances. Some deploy parachutes, some don't. Some just disappear.

Movement from Yuri clears the sky. His fingers are three . . . two . . . one . . . I wave everyone away, reach back, and release the chute.

Then the strappado.

The aggregate has left me in a smoke and I manipulate the toggles with temerarious abandon while I consider the hallucivision, the fact that I'm traveling vertically through the open sky, and the enormity of a blur-bound world at four thousand feet. Dimitriy assured me that I'd live—I have some latitude up here.

But, true to Patch-fueled form, the breakneck bedlam never ceases. As I straighten out, I notice a blemish, a genetic aberration on the scales of the salten beast. It isn't a pool or a shadow or a rock. It's too symmetrical and even for nature. This is a perfect circle. My heart is seized in a fibrillating dread when I realize what this is. But, then, the paddles of pacification restore rhythm when it is clear that I have misread the symbol. This isn't a large black *X*, this is a large black lambda circuited by its circinate boundary. Oh, wait <<back to fibrillating dread>>. This isn't good. This is why I didn't see Sasha in the air. This means that—

I merely *register* a streak of plummeting bumblebee, then the impact, then a suspense-hoarding silence that stretches into the roots of my relief. Maybe that isn't Sasha after all. Maybe it's just some random, non-human, black and yellow object falling conspicuously in the center of a predetermined target. Then a distance-muted crack clarifies things and my skin gets frigidly hot and prickly.

The ring-bound black lambda <<it was upside down when reference points were available>> is Patch code for *highest state of alert*. We usually used it to indicate that Mom was having an especially crappy day and to be on our best <<well, better>> behavior.

I spend the next couple of minutes experimenting with the toggles so I can land as close as possible to the smoking meteor. Just as I get the hang of it, the others come into view. Then the Mercedes comes tearing around an earthen mound, starkly black against the barren, honeycombed achromasia. They land well before I frustratedly touch myself down and make quick work of gathering, bundling, and storing. I make nothing of the fact that I just successfully parachuted smoothly, coolly even, to the ground with no experience and mimic the Russians in their hasty tidying. I don't actually *see* a human body so I don't ask any questions. Besides, I'm in the company of strangers, of Russians, of daredevils, of time travelers, and I certainly don't want to end up biting the hand that feeds me. If Patch is right, if this is a gentlemen's war, and honesty and humility are its weapons of war, who am I to impose my unpracticed virtues on captains and commanders? I will have to draw from an arsenal of trust and benefit of the doubt for the time being until I have expanded my armory.

I pile my oversized body chockablock <<herrings in a barrel>> into the Mercedes and, wouldn't you know, Sasha is driving. Crap. Now there are six of us <<I may not have seen a body, but I'm pretty sure that was a body>> and one is suspiciously quiet, wrapped in a parachute in the boot <<I can't think of what the trunk of an SUV is called>>. I want to know, but I don't want to know. I think to raise my hand, but I don't think the Russians will know what that signifies. Damn it, people, I have questions! But before I can express any of my crowding curiosity, the vehicle erupts into loud, congratulatory happiness. I'm the man of the hour, apparently.

"You live, da?"

"I am alive, yes. I'm sorry, was that supposed to be difficult?" My after-the-factitude scolds my assumption of universal humor. It should be scolding humor, full stop; aren't Russians supposed to be humorless? Dimitriy seems to break that mold. I should get in the habit of cackling like a lunatic after all instances of sarcasm, irony, satire, parody, and mordancy. More aptly, I'm American, and they probably see me as a cowboy, so I should click out of the side of my mouth and wink.

Dimitriy guffaws with a series of *kh*'s, "This guy. . ."

"You're a man of your word, Dimitriy. I will never doubt again. Guys!" <<*Tovarishi*, Yuri corrects>> "Tovarishi! That was freakin' awesome!" <<*Chairtovski kruto!* Yuri corrects>> "Chairtovski kruto! When do we go again?"

Yuri glances back a little confused and says, "Kapatel didn't mention, maybe. That was just the first of four today. You'll sleep well tonight."

At any other moment in my life, that declaration would have been a coup de grace, *the* coup de grace, but here, shoulder to shoulder with these tovarishi, in this engineering marvel, forging roads out of suspended seasoning, jumping out of planes, Russian exultations breathlessly bellowed, probably a dead body within arm's reach, it feels more like a coup d'état. This is the nearest approximation to a family I've ever experienced. My parents were great, sure, but, in the smoldering cauldron of my being, I always wanted to be raised by brothers. Or wolves.

As we drive back to the airfield, I'm pretending to admire the bluffs of this alien planet while testing the frontiers of my peripheral vision. Whatever that is back there in the boot, dead or not, it's staring at me, I can feel it.

The sky is reset to its clean, boundless blue. I don't like it. It's missing something.

And then we go again.

DAY 30

"... for nothing contributes so much to tranquillize the mind as a steady purpose—a point on which the soul may fix its intellectual eye."
– Frankenstein, Mary Shelley

The house is silent <<as the grave, appropriately>>. It's a kneading kind of silent, a kind of silent that's growing on me. It's the kind of silent that amplifies whispers of *eminence* and *belonging* and *redemption*. It's the kind of silent that gives audience to the ordered arrangements of a rational mind. It's a mountainous kind of silent where stroking reassurances are distinct and unmistakable. It's a resurrection kind of silent.

I say silent, but looping in the trimmed hallways of my equanimity is the icy euphony and rhythmic cheerleading of some grunge ballad. The distillation of this euphony is massaging the coils and threads of my coronary arteries in a clutch of consolatory perspicuities. It's affirming the footpath I'm treading. It's easy to be objective when your horizons are in focus. Though, I'm not sure how the interpretations of a pacific grunge ballad will have any effect on the outcome. Maybe it's just supposed to be the song that plays when the hero vanquishes the enemy and gets the girl.

I won't change direction and I won't change my mind . . .

Sounds more like ratification.

Yuri was right—that was some good sleep. I don't think I've ever had two periods of consciousness bridged by a blackout reset that cleansing. It felt like I'd finished one stage of existence and was reborn to start the next.

DAY 31

Chapter 50

"If you go parachuting, and your parachute doesn't open, and your friends are all watching you fall, I think a funny gag would be to pretend you were swimming."
– Jack Handey

It turns out, I have those Russians on retainer. I went for another four-banger <<a construction my mother loathes and reminds me of her loathing by flicking the back of my ear when I slip>> today. I woke up, saw that it was clear and warm <<for December>>, and thought I'd pretty up the blue boredom with a plummeting Elliot. I have nothing to lose, right <<up-up-down-down-left-right-left-right-B-A-start>>? You have to take the good with the bad in the Patchiverse, but it's a generally good life when you can go skydiving any time you want with professionals for free.

I text Yuri and he calls back immediately. They're all shrieking in the background that I need to get my unmentionables down there totchaus! I interpret that as right away. Or it was just more profanity. They do seem to use a lot of profanity.

By the fourth jump <<eighth total>>, I'm untouched and unsupervised. The open sky accepts me as one of its own children and I'm initiated into a brotherhood of skysplitting swashbucklers. Soomashedshee, they call me. Hopefully that doesn't mean *pedophile* or *wife beater* or something. And I understand that the final exam is sticking these landings sans parachute deployment, but these little victories are delightful.

I'm under the canopy on the final jump and I can see the decomposing black lambda with its skeletal ring. As distance closes, it's evident that something more recent, less decomposed, is splayed across the vanishing lambda. Am I looking at another body? Are these cadaverous planes a pikirovateli graveyard? It's definitely the outline of a body. The closer I get, the more human it looks. I'm the first to land this time and wonder if I can catch a glimpse before they entomb him in his parachute and bury him in the boot of the Mercedes. But this one doesn't seem to have a parachute. I guess a parachute would be superfluous if the objective is to use the ground as an umbral colander. No cracked ground. No crater. Impact must have liquefied the body because he's awfully flat. Wait, there's no head. Where's the head? This isn't a body at all, it's just a suit. A rather new looking suit as well. It's one of the bumblebee suits, but has a slightly different pattern. I like this suit—it's shiny. What is a discarded jumpsuit doing out here? It wasn't here on the last jump. Did they just forget it? I wonder if they'd let me have it. I want to be cool like the Russians.

As I covet, the others start gathering around.

"Lay down, face down," Yuri directs.

"Sorry?"

"On the suit, lay face down. That was your eighth jump, training is over. This is the initiation ceremony."

The others look convincingly Russian—sharp features, unbreakable scowls, broken looking noses, and, of course, the humorlessness. I guess we're being serious here. As athletically and manly as possible, I lower myself onto and into the figure of the suit, face down. I can smell the salty earth despite the suit's sharp, synthetic smack.

"The suit serves as an optic that allows you to see through the apical frame and into the frameset below."

Really? See through the ground? How cool is that!

I can hear Dimitriy's uncontrolled laugh of *kh*'s.

"Dimitriy! Come on! You didn't even last one sentence!"

Dimitriy can't stop laughing. "He lays on dirt in his face!"

Yuri's still shaking his head. "One day Dimitriy will figure American humor out. Until then, the suit is yours, Elliot. This is the last time we call you *Elliot*. From now on you're *Naslednik*. Get used to it."

With a dignity aggrieved by my own careless disregard for good sense <<come on, this new reality makes anything possible!>>, I snap up as from my hundredth burpee and dust myself off. "Naslednik. Got it. Can I really have the suit? I like it!"

"It has always been your suit. You designed it, Kapatel improved it, we tested it. It has always been yours."

"What do you mean, I designed it? I've never designed a skydiving suit befo-hoho . . ." My voice starts languishing like it was hit with a tranquilizer dart. A wave of Patch electricity starts pulsing through my nervous system like a heartbeat. Holy huffing half-breed, I *have* designed a skydiving suit before. That scheming scoundrel, he was using me for his research. No wonder his assignments were so interesting; I was a time traveler's research assistant! I remember this assignment clearly. *That's* why I was so curious about the *Mega-Helium Pocket Fly Suit* notebook at Patch's apartment—I designed it! Mega-Helium Pocket Fly Suit is cooler than whatever I named it, but, Yuri's right, that's my design. Of all the weirdness.

"How did he improve it?"

"I don't know what it started as; I only know what he ended up with. That's what you saw on Saturday—we were using a dummy to test the suit. It's as accurate as an AK-47. You two must have really crunched the granite of science to get that thing to work. It will revolutionize pikirovaniya."

"Helium cells?"

"*Mega*-helium cells. They work perfectly. He added other gases as well. Automated delivery and resorption based on how you program all the parameters."

"GPS guided?"

"StratoNet quadrangulation at the suit's extremities, four points, incorporates towers at lower altitudes. We can slow belly-to-earth velocity down to nearly thirty miles per hour and hit four square meters, even on a slope. The wing's fingers open and close for precision guidance. We also use sensors on the lambda to guide the suit down to impact at the right moment."

How freaking cool is that. I designed a revolutionary skydiving jumpsuit as a teenager. Unbelievable. *Decrease my density,* he said. *Slow my descent!* My answer: fill a wingsuit with hydrogen. *I don't want to explode!* My answer: fill a wingsuit with helium. Man, oh, Manischewitz.

Now I'm thinking about royalties.

Since I've gone from not trusting anyone to distrusting everyone, I should question Yuri's claim about the use of a dummy on Saturday. But, now that I think about it, the dude I saw eat it on the Salt Flats was . . . actually, that was about twenty-nine days ago. The funeral was November 5 and the Salt Flats was a couple days later, the seventh, maybe. Today is December 6. Crap, are you serious? He said the nascent vent is created every twenty-nine and a half days and takes twenty-nine and a half days to circulate to its southern burial. I don't know if the quadskellion aspect would allow that nautilus track to end up at this exact location in the same timeframe, but it's a little fishy. Now I have hard math to do.

"Congratulations, Naslednik." It's Sasha this time. "Welcome to the club."

I'm in a club. I'm in a skydiving club. I'm in a skydiving club that will eventually become a time-traveling kamikaze death club. Which sounds way cooler.

I can see that Dimitriy is beaming so I run over and give him a high-five.

"High-five, ya! I got high-five! Booyah, Sooki!"

Yuri swallows a laugh as he's shaking his head. "You're pathetic, Dimitriy."

I can't wait for another cleansing, blackout reset of a night's sleep tonight.

DAY 33

Chapter 51

"Today's scientists have substituted mathematics for experiments, and they wander off through equation after equation, and eventually build a structure which has no relation to reality."
– Nikola Tesla

I thought I'd catch up on some banking today. Somehow $150,000 found its way into my account yesterday. One hundred and fifty thousand American dollars. Normally that would be panic about possible money laundering, then converting it into untraceable hard assets in smaller increments, but my faith in Patch is forming ice crystals. I'm sure Wainwright Witcherly has such a sum earmarked for something more consequential than a jukebox massage chair Mountain Dew fountain machine. Not that I'd ever squander a year's livelihood on such prodigal profligacy <<I just checked to see if that exists>>. Either way, I'm taking this as my cue to stop working and devote nine yards to training, study, research, etc. I know that's not explicit, but the more I roll down this Matterhorn, the more colossal this snowslip becomes. And I have a to-do list <<maybe a to-satisfy-my-curiosity list is more accurate>> that's growing and nagging and seducing.

This Пикирование <<Pikirovaniya>> Math notebook from Patch's apartment is at the top of the list. Most math isn't that interesting to me because I'm not clever enough to appreciate its applicability to my experience. Even when it's explained, my reaction is always, so what? It's like telling me what my adrenal glands did when that dog attacked me. Knowing doesn't change my reaction or the outcome. If it was made of predictive certainties that loaded internet pages faster or made a dishwasher that didn't take three hours to wash twelve dishes, I might give it more credence. Clearly we're not that advanced. And the nonsense rubber-stamp academics circulating in a maelstrom of government grants come up with is just eddying solutions to problems that don't yet exist. Nor are ever likely to. But this math, this is like watching the glowing green characters tumble down the face of the Matrix. This is wise council and a multitude of councilors. This is digital physiology. Drag coefficients, velocities through density differentials, calculations for fixed-rate transiting surface area on uneven terrain, buoyancy, nascent vent rate of acceleration from northern latitudes to southern latitudes. <<I thought he said the nascent vent moved at a steady speed.>> Finally, math with a little bioluminescence.

I thought I should go read to Hudson tonight, but it's already 3:30 p.m. and I still haven't worked out. Eh, I'll be there tomorrow anyway. Sorry, Hudson, you've been bested by an agility ladder and parallettes. See ya tomorrow, little buddy.

DAY 34

Chapter 52

"You are not supposed to like things. Only to understand."
– *For Whom the Bell Tolls*, Ernest Hemingway

The halls of the second floor have a conspicuously sad smell to them today. I don't know if I can disambiguate that perception; it smells like a funeral home, like someone has gone to the trouble of sweetening up the stench of death. I sniff my armpits just in case.

It looks like they've gotten me all set up in Sophie's Place like last week.

As I settle in, I notice the doorway become a nurse, stopped short, chewing on a thumbnail. She has a look of dismayed heartbreak in her eyes and posture, like I shouldn't have shown up tonight if I knew what was good for me. Apparently it's not just the smells that are sad. She turns to leave, but her heartbroken eyes get stuck on the door jamb and she sits there fidgeting with the lip of the strike plate.

Maybe I can snap her out of her vacillation; I interrupt her strike plate fascination with, "Where's my wingman? I need a swiper that swipes!"

The dismay shatters and all that remains is a goopy heartbreak. She tiptoes toward me while glancing back at the doorway. By the time she gets to me, she's wringing her hands.

"I'm so sorry, sir, you're talking about Hudson, right?"

"Right, Hudson, my eyes and my ears, my right hand and my left. The great slide advancer. Is he not coming today?"

The more I speak, the more agitated this nurse becomes.

"Sir . . ."

"It's Elliot. Are you okay?"

"Elliot, Hudson . . . passed last night."

"Passed what? Passed a test? Passed a stone? What are we talking about here?"

"Passed away. Hudson died."

I'm waiting for a punchline in the rigor mortising pause. I'm waiting for the beginnings of a smile to nudge the corners of her mouth, even just a little. My facial muscles are stuck in a politely smiling portrait of pain. Now she's crying. That pushes me beyond denial, and anger, bargaining and depression are a finger-painted swirl of cleverly designated shades of ebony smeared on my shallowed breathing.

"But . . . he was like . . . five years old! How does a five-year-old die?"

She touches the back of my shaking hand and consoles, "I'm so sorry."

And then, of course, the kids start filtering in, other children that will be dead by next week. Maybe all of them. Maybe all dead by tomorrow. Oh, Elliot, what have you gotten yourself into? Why did you pick a hospital? This is real life stuff! I'm not emotionally equipped for real life stuff. I can barely handle the emotional toll of a fraudulent charge on my credit card or someone in the cross-walk when my light turns green. What am I supposed to do with this?

In a trice, I'm Count Dracula in the sinking sun, Mr. Morris's bowie knife plunging into my heart, a dark reality holding the valves shut, my body crumbling into dust almost in the drawing of a breath. Everything that mattered in my life up to that moment felt offensive and shameful. This isn't a shallow pool of mangled felo-de-se I could objectify with detached observations in a notebook, this was Hudson! I knew Hudson personally! Hudson and I were pals for . . . okay, only for an hour, but it was a long hour and we really bonded! Those poor parents.

"Wait, nurse, ma'am, when did you say this happened?"

She whispers, "Last night, around midnight. His parents mentioned they were going to text you that afternoon, but his poor, little body started giving out and they were . . . well, you know . . . preoccupied."

She's diverting a pitchy river of tears into a cloth that looks more medical than standard handkerchief.

Of course it would be the afternoon. Couldn't go read to Hudson because you needed to work out. Just ridiculous, Elliot. There's something that'll stay with me for a while <<till my untimely/timely death>>.

The kids, some familiar, some new, are staring at me with the subtle smiles I wanted from the nurse with the repugnant report. Do it, Hudson! Nothing. I swipe to the next slide. I'm trying to hold it together, but every time I go to speak a stopper is pulled out of the bottom of the syllable and all the air is sucked down a drain in an abrupt puff. The nurse is back in the doorway, her body bent like a lightning bolt, damming the overrunning turbidity at their spillways.

Their patience is edging toward petulance in the muggy silence. I go to speak again but the nurse's heavying heartbreak sabotages my composure and I start crying. Not blubbering, but not whimpering.

One of the kids, maybe eight-years-old, says, "Does Patch die? Is that why you're crying?"

"Name!" You'd think, with all my yelling, they'd get the pattern.

"Miles."

"Miles, Miles and his sneaky wiles. Well, Miles, you'll be happy to know that Patch is like a cockroach—you can drop him from an airplane high, high in the sky and when he hits the ground, he just scampers away unharmed and unscathed."

"Then why are you crying?"

<<I'm crying because we're going to be pals and then you're all going to die! Run!>> I want to avoid the topic of death in a group of possibly dying kids, but kids don't like being treated like children, and I don't want to hazard the trust with which they're already cagey.

Grayson, who rescued the mood last time, plunges it into the abyss this time. "He's crying because Hudson died last night. Hudson was the one helping him with the slideshow last week."

I nod.

Their petulance slips back toward patience.

I can salvage this. "Thank you, Grayson," <<he's dumbstruck that I remember his name>> "the Freemason from Payson, that's a perfect segue. To the Gontlets! Hudson is going to help us with this slideshow after all."

I recover modestly and it goes okay. I give it a B+ for content and a C- for grip-getting. Given the hand I was dealt, those grades are respectable.

I'm standing at my fridge, staring at my gratitude list, wondering how to word this. I settle on *evanescent moments that engrave immortal memories.* Thanks for blazing the trail, Hudson, thanks for accepting me just as I am, thanks for . . . <<I'm back to crying.>> I have this feeling, like a golden fluorescent bulb running from my heart to my throat, that I'll see him again.

DAY 36

Chapter 53

"Good night, Westley. Good work. Sleep well. I'll most likely kill you in the
morning."
– The Man in Black, *The Princess Bride*

The nerve endings of my smug and presumptuous sense of justice are still a little
raw from news of Hudson's fate. My emotional survival instincts are starting
to align with the lugubrious Mr. Rochester's wisdom to Jane Eyre at the fire-
side: "If you do not love another living soul, then you'll never be disappointed."
<<When Miggs Jasper wasn't around, I often kept Mom company watching
period pieces, more out of boredom than interest.>> I know in all of my umbral
plumbing that's not the right answer, but instincts are stupid sometimes. For all
I know, Hudson could be an agent in Patch's grand design. In the final analysis,
people die. Some earlier than others. And it doesn't always have to make sense
to me, I get it. I know you're around here somewhere, Hudson, lurking in some
inter-frame Gontletian version of my family room!

Time for more pain . . .

Assignment #7: DISENGAGEMENT

*Through all my hyperbolizing, I have hitherto understated the Gontlets. Such
a society is impossible to conceive midst mortal glean, so you must stack your
quiver with arrows of all lengths for every species of peril. And, as you are
an alien in this environment, they will gape upon you with their mouths, as
a ravening and a roaring lion. Twixt the transcendence developed through
breath holding, the mesmerism of the card tricks, the scenes and images you
superimpose on the vista of the Gontlet, the taxonomic insider information to
which you have been made privy* <<he makes that look so easy>>, *and your
Smilin' Jack-inspired murderous determination, your survival is still a little
closer to possible than to probable. Lackest thou yet one device . . .*

*One cannot forecast the hour or day to which one will descend in a vent, and
if your native hull, at the depth to which you have descended, is geographically
distant at that moment, the duration of transit will be extended. Also, and you
needn't let this trouble you, the shortest distance between vent and native hull
is not always a straight line. Occasionally the elements, forces, and admin-
istrations involved in accommodating your recoupling will provide the most
unburdened route given the totality of the circumstances, even if that means a
more circuitous one. Sometimes the native hull is more amenable to recoupling
in certain emotional states. Sometimes the circumstances for recoupling are
disadvantageous or out-and-out perilous. Sometimes the population density of
the Gontlet itself is prohibitive. It is something like a network's use of packet
switching to find a datum's quickest course. Variables abound and the system*

seems to work itself out. As this passage is unaccompanied and of unpredictable duration, you will need to be fortified.

You will find that time is unsupervised in the Gontlets and minutes will seem like eternity and eternity will seem like minutes, but, be that as it may, the window for recoupling does not have an expiration. Rather, your mind has an expiration. Though it may be in subsequent incursions <<he's quite certain I'll be making a habit of Pik-ing>>, *as a Gontlet-rambling infant, discipline and willpower alone are no match for entities whose tactical training in ambuscades and subversions is as old as the Earth itself. The afore-enumerated stratagems for fording this jungle are vital, but they are not without decay. When its fuel is spent, the mind tends to seek respite under the shade of a tree. It is this switch from entertaining to entertained that lays vulnerable the umbra to two proton torpedoes. It becomes a water-walking Peter attending to the wind and the waves, filling the chasm of realization with fear, panic and uncertainty. At recognition of this decay, you will need to deploy a reserve chute, to draw from recent experience. This reserve chute will take the form of simple, rote memorization.*

Not that this is the silver bullet, but we have found that it complements the distractions you impose on the environment with an internal disengagement, if you like.

Granted, these assignments are not without tedium, but they have been proven in battle. They work. Treat them as you would our linebacker drills, only with air conditioning and your yellow venom. The difficulty and fatigue will be comparable. Every scenario, every exercise, every simulation to which I subjected you in those happy, humid years incorporated some element of memorization so this should be like riding a bike—a single-gear bike climbing a fifteen-percent grade.

Hilarious.

The Exiles are like sharks—if there is blood in the water, they will sniff it out, circle, and compliment your wardrobe until you have forgotten what you are doing there and the hum of the native hull is swallowed up in your volume-vaulted vanity. They know the eyes of a man holding his breath and reformatting his panorama; they know the eyes of a man who has become permeable to his immediate reality.

Personalizing this endeavor will facilitate proficiency, so I need you to handselect one movie screenplay, two poems, and two novels from which you can pull excerpts. And Ezra Pound's fourteen-word "In a Station of the Metro" doesn't count as a poem. Since your music preferences are like a child choosing what it eats for dinner, I have made those selections on your behalf. Again, trust now, thank later.

You'll need to retrieve file box #1 and unseal it.

Ah, what are you doing to me, Scurlock! You're just going to have me unbox the Stay Puft Marshmallow Man for goodness' sake! This is so humiliating.

Okay, Elliot, think. You can outmaneuver this cheeky cuss for once! Think, damn it! Okay, <<this is exhilaratingly futile!>> for the screenplay he thinks I'm going to pick *Monty Python and the Holy Grail*, so I'm going with *The Princess Bride*. For poems . . . for poems . . . I'm a masochist, so he'll presage "The Rime of the Ancient Mariner" and "Jabberwocky." I'll go with "O Captain, My Captain" and "The Raven." I ain't playin' the fool this time, old man! Okay, novels . . . what would Patch anticipate here? I don't really know. Outside the lines, Elliot, your hips need to lie! I used *Slaughterhouse 5* in several of my Patch-assigned essays and papers, so I'm guessing he'd pick that and . . . *The Strange Case of Dr. Jekyll and Mr. Hyde*. I always raved about that one. *My* picks will be *The Heart of Darkness* and *Fight Club*. Does he know I've read *Fight Club*? Maybe that's not fair. Hang it! All's fair in love and war and Patch-deposing book picking!

I retrieve the file box labeled #1, a box cutter, and a butter knife. I place the box on the opposite side of the dining table and defensively, gingerly, with the acetylcholine tension of uncertainty gripping my obliques, slide the blade across the securing lengths of tape. The lid heaves its freedom from the adhesive darbies with a chest-rising expiration <<acknowledging the paradox there>>. As anxious as I am for Patch to posthumously <<he's not even dead!>> slosh in the slain of this slaughter, I'm sure one of these boxes has a viper in it, just for *jolly rogery*. I crouch way down, so my head is below the table's surface <<distressing déjà vu>> and nudge the lid up from below with the butter knife, so its bottom edge is resting on the top lip of the box. Then I jab the side of the lid with the knife so it slides completely off the top of the box and on to the table.

I poke the side of the box with the butter knife just in case lid removal wasn't sufficient to stir his ophidian mischief. No hissing. No explosions. All clear, I guess. Time for your drubbing, you crestfallen clairvoyant! You think you're *so* clever. You think I'm *so* predictable. Damn it! Damn it! Damn it! Damn it! There's no way! *Fight Club*, too? No! That's not even possible! <<All things are possible to those that weave in and out of the warp and weft of time—cheater!>> Aha! You failed, old man! You picked "The Rime of the Ancient Mariner" and I went with . . . oh, come on . . .

It's a copy of "The Rime of the Ancient Mariner" with the pages ripped out and the pages of "The Raven" inserted. And a big, hand-drawn smiley face. That's not funny, Patch! You can't dragoon me into choices using my own choice to unchoose choices! This is a sort of nasty determinism! I take a minute to think through that protestation. My selections were uncoerced and unmanipulated; I, alone, with unmolested faculties, impudently championed my will by eschewing my will to stick it to another's will. It's like blaming a wallflower for forcing me to ask her to dance on a dare. The only honest conclusion I can draw is that someone knowing what I'm going to choose doesn't interfere with my capacity to make that choice. It does shrink me a little, but what can I do? Being Elliot hedges me about with an Elliotness that I can't seem to unravel from. <<From which I can't seem to unravel, damn it!>> When someone knows you this well, it's hard to argue that familiarity precludes will. Why didn't I ask him more about his life when I had the chance? How dare you use my own self-ishness against me!

My <<mostly good-natured>> rant is interrupted by the redolence of newness. I see a brand new pair of Fleet Feet brand Aftershocks running shoes. They still have the tag on them, and that is not English. Interesting. Those will be a nice feet treat. In addition to the copy of *Fight Club,* by Chuck Palahniuk <<clearly unread>> and the husk of "The Rime of the Ancient Mariner" incubating aged and abused pages of Edgar Allen Poe's "The Raven," I find a printout of *The Princess Bride*, screenplay by William Goldman, bound by a binder clip; a copy of *The Heart of Darkness,* by Joseph Conrad <<clearly read>>; and Walt Whitman's "O Captain, My Captain," handwritten in Patch's own pen. There's also some high-tech, alien-looking skydiving goggles which neither look new, nor have that redolence of newness. They smell like old sweat, actually, like my football helmet by the end of high school. One three-terabyte thumb drive. <<Do thumb drives come in three terabytes?>> And, of course, $10,000 in cash. It's always fun when you find heartbeat-skipping sums of off-grid moneys sitting around in unsecured boxes in your house. I wonder if all these boxes have money.

Excellent choices, those. <<Wretch!>> I taught you well. Memorize the entire screenplay and both poems. Find a half dozen or so passages in each novel and memorize the stuffing out of them, to the point of bored recall. Memorize them and always recite them in a particular order so the recitation flows as from a single source. Vary the pace of recitation so you can accordion completion time. Make the environment in which you implement this assignment as consistent as possible—sights, smells, sounds. You will find some music on the flash drive. It is not an extensive catalog, so I want you to listen to all of it and pick five or so records that resonate. I have included a medley of genres, but most is a tempo and depth for which you have already expressed some degree of predilection. Memorize the lyrics of these five records. Memorize the instrumental lines. Play them on a loop. Play them until you love them or hate them, then keep listening. Recall favors music above textual excerpts. Again, choose what resonates, not of what you think I would approve. Memory accompanies, and is enhanced by, interest.

Now be gone! Or whatever I have to say to get rid of you.

I load the thumb drive. Fourteen folders. Some are recognizable, some are just weird. Frank Sinatra, The Birthday Massacre, Destiny Potato, Matchbox 20, Big Wreck, The Beatles, The White Stripes, Led Zeppelin, Alice in Chains <<I love them, but I can't think of a single song they sing>>, The Dead Weather, Norah Jones, Wolfmother. That's manageable, I guess. At least it's not climbing a mountain. I should stop tempting those fates. I assure the ether, I love climb-ing mountains! Climbing mountains is awesome! My roused walls snarl, turn over, and settle back into their slumber. It *is* rather quiet in here. Let's do something about that. Let's see here . . . The Birthday Massacre . . . *Fascination* . . . play. Funky keyboards . . . very eighties . . .

I think you know why I'm here. I think I'm falling in love with fear. This is the moment of blind and sincere fascination . . .

DAY 39

Chapter 54

"There is no abstract art. You must always start with something. Afterward you
can remove all traces of reality."
– Pablo Picasso

The first thing about this dream that I'm fully conscious of is that it is, indeed,
a dream. Who dreams like that? And once it's understood that I'm dreaming,
why wouldn't some layer of my un-, sub-, hypo-consciousness wake me up?
The jig is up, right? So on I dream, knowing I'm dreaming, stuck in a beautifully preposterous outland I can't affect or correct. The frustrating aspect of this
dream is that it isn't linear, it's just a series of realizations and no way to make
sense of them individually, or in any context. It's like looking at a self-portrait
you don't remember painting.

I know I'm in my house but things are different. I'm not specifically attending to the differences, but it feels off. Everything appears to be in its proper
place, but it's brighter and happier. What's-her-name is there <<Petunia! Raven!
I'm so close I'm choking on it!>> but I can't see her for some reason. I think
I might be laying on her lap. I can feel her kicking me in the back of my head,
but I'm not interested enough to try to figure out how she's pulling that off in
the position we're in. It's noticeable but not irregular. Though I can't see or hear
him, I know there's someone else here. It's a familiar presence, somebody that's
supposed to be here. It's the same person in the white-room-Eternity dream that
is replaced by what's-her-name. My advisor? Foreman?

Is Dayton a girl's name? Dayton is reading *The Heart of Darkness* to me.
She hates that book. Every few sentences she stops to ingeminate her hatred
for his writing, his face, and even his stupid mustache <<though, that might just
be overflowing contempt from the hatred of the writing>>. I smile like a happy
idiot when she reads, "Between us there was, as I have already said somewhere,
the bond of the sea. Besides holding our hearts together through long periods
of separation, it had the effect of making us tolerant of each other's yarns—and
even convictions." And though she, again, follows the period with a philippic
about his use of the word *yarn,* that was us—tolerant of each other's convictions. I'm mauled by its brilliance, she's enraged by its grandiloquence. And I
couldn't love her more for it. Our oppositeness is our greatest strength and we
both know it.

There's a perfect peace in this place. It's bright and clean and quiet.
Disruptions are impossible and somehow we know it. Which makes what
happens next so . . . primal. Neither of us mention it, but I know we both hear
it. It's not necessarily a sound, but if it was, it would sound like someone trying
to twist a boulder in half. It was the Manuscript. The Manuscript was sitting on
my desk in the office at the back of the house screaming in its rock-wrenching
silence. It was a kind of variable noise <<not really a noise>> to which your

ears could not adapt <<now I'm getting it>> and tune out. For the nonce, this soundless sound is like a tapestry hanging on the dream's walls. It's just there, and making sure we know it's there.

Strangely, my mind starts compartmentalizing and it feels like an office building with glass walls, each room coordinating some different function. All the rooms are me, but the *big* me, the *executive* me, has ears in every room. Several of these offices <<if this metaphor makes any sense>> are planting monolithic climbing trees, their widths tripling their heights, in the endless expanse of my front yard. Root system architecture and radius, crown measurements, dripline to dripline—spacing them properly is its own discipline.

Everything starts impregnating, like I'm expanding in all directions. Time starts to abscess and my swelling consciousness engulfs more of the past and future. I almost feel like the nocking point of a bowstring being pulled away from the alignment of the timeline so I can see over the horizons of the present in both directions.

The noise that's not really a noise just stops. Then there's a knock at the door. My whole body is both agitated with excitement and sedated with a satisfaction of finality. I know who it is. I know what this means. It means that all omens, all forebodings, all dubieties are tied up in smart bows and set to rights. Loose ends are serger-stitched. It means freedom as a destination. I stand in the antechamber, exhale a lifetime accrual of apprehension, inhale a skyline's dawn of possibility, then I open the door . . .

That's when I wake up.

So my brain can't wake me up when it knows I'm dreaming, but dreambrain can snap me out of it right at the big reveal? What a stupid, useless head.

I've been listening to Patch's music catalog over the past few days. The first album from The White Stripes is my favorite so far. And everything from The Birthday Massacre. I never pictured myself as someone with whom music from the likes of The Birthday Massacre would resonate. *Captivate* is probably a better word.

I write *foresight* and *cool music I never would have found on my own* on my gratitude list. I want to add Mountain Dew, but I don't want it to get weird. It's already on there six times.

DAY 42

Chapter 55

"No good deed goes unpunished."
– Clare Boothe Luce

I just got back from lunch with Mom. I told her about my escapades with the kids at Primary Children's. This was her response: "What on earth would possess you to do something like that?" The words were just suspended over our table like an evaporated offense, sitting on her greens like an inversion layer. I just needed to breathe in to be offended, but her words were so instructive I couldn't bring myself to do it. There was more to the statement than a question mark—it was a commentary on my identity. It must be so contrary to my character <<at least the character I advertise>> to do something like that, that my own mother was astounded by the report. If any offense could be taken, it would have to be offense at my character, not my mother's observations of it. I guess I'm a person that withholds his goodwill to keep a low profile from roving and punitive neuroses and insecurities. At least, this is how my mother sees me. Instructive and depressing. <<Life rises and falls on brutally honest character x-rays.>> Then she went on to make sure that I was supervised because every-one's looking for a lawsuit these days. Then she told me not to read the kids any of those books where the artist tries to sneak phalluses <<she actually used the word *phalluses*>> in the pictures everywhere and it started getting weird so I changed the subject. She means well, I keep telling myself.

I sit down on my couch to recover from the exhaustion of society and conversation.

I have no friends, so every text I get is business. Other than the occasion-al, puzzling string of emojis from Mom. My phone's text notification chime usually elicits that deflating defeat of having my afternoon planned for me. Or falling further behind. Or disappointing somebody. Not this time though. My first, real, personal text <<other than Marci at the dealership stepping over the line into personal, but really just telling me it's time for my five thousand-mile service>> goes like this:

We just wanted to thank you for making Hudson's last week one of the best in his short life. He talked about you the whole week. When he knew it was time, he had me put his eye patch on. He left us a peaceful, happy pirate.

She includes a picture of Hudson, pirated, his jaw relaxed, his face already a little gray and relieved.

Twenty minutes have passed since I read that text. I can't stop crying. What a horrible thing to do to somebody! Horrible or tender. Or horribly tender. That image will haunt me until the day I join Hudson myself. It's absurd, but I feel I'm in some way responsible for his death. Did the happiness kill him? Was it too much fun for his beleaguered body to bear? Absurd, I know. And now I have to respond.

I've been trying to distance myself from thinking in terms of fair and unfair. It's an intellectual conceit that proscribes a healthy interpretation of the world. Every time I hear myself <<or anyone else for that matter>> use that word, *unfair*, it just sounds like they're exploiting some perceived unrequited favor to justify selfishness and laziness. I'm starting to cringe at the hubris of it because I sound like a tantrum-throwing brat who thinks he knows what bedtime is better for him than his parents do. I don't want this to sound like I'm growing up, but maybe Hudson's death is like fertilizer to the soil—I just need to figure out what to plant in it.

Didn't mean to compare you to poop, little buddy.

Chapter 56

"Life is pain, highness. Anyone who says differently is selling something."
– The Man in Black, *The Princess Bride*

I'm perfecting the art of being non-reactive while holding my breath. For years I've been a doting helicopter parent to my comfort, and even the prospect of discomfort would give me such tremblings, and flutterings, all over me—such spasms in my side and pains in my head, and such beatings at heart, that I can get no rest by night nor by day. <<*Pride and Prejudice.*>> Mrs. Bennett's drama is only mildly superfluous; I have been a fierce defender of my comfort zone's margins for some time. All for naught, really, because I've been having fun in the wastelands that involve that comfort zone. If I'm being honest with myself <<which I am much more frequently these days>>, discomfort is one of life's here-till-Sunday gratuities, so I may as well join what I can't beat with acceptance and awareness.

I pulled my groin playing football when I was a freshman in high school. I was laying on a gurney in an emergency room and it hurt so bad I was hyperventilating. I thought I was going to pass out <<from the hyperventilating, not the pain>>. A nurse came in the room and was fiddling with a vial of something. With a flatness bent toward irritability, she said, "Stop breathing so hard or you'll pass out." So, being the obedient people pleaser I am, I stopped breathing hard. Wouldn't you know it, the pain neither increased nor decreased. Then she put a needle full of meperidine in my left butt cheek. I'm using that experience to drive my approach to discomfort: I can be in pain, but nothing says I have to be so reactive to it.

I feel like developing this non-reactivity will help me keep my head out of this world. That didn't come out right. Maybe . . . help me keep my head in another world. Still not what I mean. I feel like our cultural and societal engineers have steered everything toward, and cemented everything in, rage and its derivatives. Our institutions, our architecture, our city planning, our laws, our patterns, queues, parking lots, waiting rooms, technological disarmament <<meaning the morons that try to steer their shopping carts with one hand because the other is having a loud speaker phone conversation in the open public>>, it is a paradox of *civilization* because it engenders incivility. By nature, I'm not an angry person, never have been, but my sensibilities are pricked in weird ways sometimes, and my reactions, especially behind the wheel of a car, can be positively savage. Sometimes I watch in awe from the bleachers of some third-person schism, wondering from what gland that venom was spit, wondering if that was really me. Every circumstance, every situation, requires all of my consequence-weighing deliberation to remain civil and <<visibly>> unaffected. There's a trick, I know there's a trick, and if I'm going to sufficiently subordinate sixteen-year-old Elliot, I'll need to discover that trick. Otherwise, I'm in jail for murder or trapped in the tower of a teenager fortress bellowing unheeded portents. Hopefully that trick is as simple as developing this non-reactivity. Like Patch always said, *If something's hard to quit, you know it wasn't good for you.* He would also say, *The tortoise of positive action will always beat the hare of negative reaction.* I think I finally understand what he meant by that.

I don't know if my parents had always planned on having only one child or if it just worked out that way due to circumstances beyond their control. I remember thinking to ask when I was in my early-teens, but decided I didn't really want to know. If it was always just me, I'd resent them for not giving me brothers; if it was never just me, I'd feel bad for salting wounds. <<You tend to grow up a little more quickly as an only child because you're always stuck with your parents, and they're always talking about adult things.>> Either way, somewhere around eight-years-old they started pitying me for it. In the summer of my eleventh year my parents flew me out to San Diego to stay with my aunt and uncle. They had four kids from eight to fourteen and thought I'd have more fun on a beach with kids my age than cloistering myself in the coolest parts of the house for a month. They were correct. I'd been to East Coast beaches before, and they were okay, but within minutes, I realized that, though I'd been to a beach, I'd never been to a beach. A beach isn't the sand, a beach is the waves. West Coast beaches are real beaches <<well, more real than East Coast beaches>>.

It took me the better part of a cloudy day to get the rhythm of the ocean, then we were best friends. My cousin taught me to body surf properly and that was it—I was one with the sea. The water was exquisitely cold. The clouds bedimmed the normally bedazzled surface of the deep-breathing ocean. I was transformed into this pale, aquiline <<I know I'm using that word wrong, but it sounds less highbrow than *ichthyic*, less ambiguous than *fishy*, less trashy than *piscine*, and more like a super buff merman>> torpedo that needed neither sleep nor sustenance. I was in the water ten hours a day and I don't ever remember eating. Taming the wild of nature ruins your appetite, I guess.

When I first got in the water it was so cold it felt like I'd been bitten. I must have looked like a real middle-country kid because I snapped my foot back and looked around to see what bit me. I hoped it was a jellyfish. After seeing three of my cousins charge the water and dive right in, I figured sissy time was over. Boys can't let other boys out-boy them. In I charged. I thought my heart would never start beating again, but man it felt good to be screaming and laughing with boys my age.

At first, I just wanted to feel the raw power of the ocean so I yielded to the circular motion of the shallowing waves as they turned me over and over. Feeling that uncontested <<uncontestable?>> power was fun for the first eight tumbles. And, though I wasn't too concerned about it in the moment, my skin was getting a little sand-worn. Once I learned how to body surf, I just wanted to get back out to the breakers as quickly as possible for another ride. Or attempt at one, anyway. My cousins taught me to surface dive under an approaching wave and dig my fingers into the sand until it passed, then launch myself to the surface at a deep ocean angle.

As the sun receded, I would find myself treading water past the breakers, my best friend heaving me gently up, lowering me softly down, so, for a moment, I could stand, flat-footed, on the sea floor. The ocean was this beautiful world, entity even, stretched like a mysterious impossibility to the sky's flat, delimiting limit. I remember standing there in a trance for hours, bobbing up and down, experiencing a single sensation: wonder. My mind was clear and the blue magnitude crowded everything else out. This is the sensation I want to bridle. This is how I want my non-reactivity to manifest, a sensation of crowding wonder, purged of prejudice and preconception, with eyes that see the fully-formed entity and not all of its transitional forms.

I add *Pacific Ocean* to my gratitude list. I add *brothers from another mother*. I add *awe*.

Chapter 57

"At times the whole world seems to be in conspiracy to importune you with emphatic trifles. Friend, client, child, sickness, fear, want, charity, all knock at once at thy closet door and say,—'Come out unto us.' But keep thy state; come not into their confusion. The power men possess to annoy me I give them by a weak curiosity. No man can come near me but through my act."
– Ralph Waldo Emerson

The card tricks, the breath holding, Thursday nights at Primary Children's, Friday lunch with Mom, the memorization, the music, skydiving, snooping about in Patch's personal effects, messing with Blackgoat, my self-imposed Russian study, working out, the Manuscript, it's all getting quite bloated. Wrapping up work projects was providential. Between prospective, self-inflicted projects and Patch-inflicted pain, my schedule is soon to be morbidly obese. Being a pathological planner may not be enough. I might have to start losing some sleep. I wonder if that's part of this kwazants-promoting scheme— to see how composed I can be under pain-pricked duress. I don't have a slumpy or humpy disposition <<what my mom calls people when they're *sleepy* plus *grumpy* or *hungry* plus *grumpy*>>, but I've never fasted from sleep or food for forty-eight hours either. <<Looking forward to that day, because I know it's coming.>> There's no challenge in being nice when you've got a good night's sleep and a belly full of Mountain Dew. *Goodness*, as Patch would say, *only counts when it costs something.*

It's nice though—my planner makes it look like I have a life now. Instead of a single word on each day's entry <<work>>, I'm actually running out of space.

I underline *foresight* on my gratitude list.

CHAPTER 58

"If I had my life to live over again, I would have made a rule to read some poetry and listen to some music at least once every week."
– Charles Darwin

Listening to the wrong music is like being raised on Miracle Whip—Miracle Whip is fine, it adds a tangy zip to an otherwise dry sandwich or salad. But one day your classmate is tired of eating the same mother packed and prepared sandwich day in and day out and wants to trade for your sandwich. Well, you're tired of your sandwich too, and you think, why not? You take a bite and the palate fairies pick you up by the scruff of the neck, thrash you about the head and shoulders, and chuck you down some stairs. You snap at your friend, more out of outrage from the deprivation than from any actual indignity, "What is in this sandwich?"

Your friend is glowering at you because he thinks you've played a low-down dirty trick on him and he shoots back, "What's in *this* sandwich?"

You clarify, "The white stuff! What's the white stuff?"

Now he's incensed. "It's mayo! What is this crap?"

Mayo? you muse. What is mayo?

Then you run away to finish the sandwich before he asks to trade back.

I understand now that I've been listening to Miracle Whip my whole life. All of the music is good, but after *actively* listening to the entirety of the music catalog on the thumb drive, these are the albums that resonate: the eponymous *The White Stripes* album, Wolfmother's *Cosmic Egg*, Matchbox 20's *More Than You Think You Are*, Destiny Potato's *LUN*, and the most resonatory, by heads and shoulders, The Birthday Massacre's *Hide and Seek*. That one's just cool.

Frank Sinatra's just a little too far removed from my world to fully appreciate. I get the appeal, but it's nothing I can imagine myself ever being in the mood for. I sense that Patch included it more for cultural education than to convert me, so I may end up spending some time with it notwithstanding. I hadn't even heard of Norah Jones before, so I looked her up. I may have spent a worrying amount of time lingering on her face. This may or may not be relevant, but I was quite hungry at the moment and her eyes were like mirror glazed gingerbread cookies. They looked yummy.

CHAPTER 59

> "People are always so anxious to get things out in the open where they can put a name to them, even a meaningless name, so long as it has something of a scientific ring."
> – *The Haunting of Hill House*, Shirley Jackson

It's starting to get cold. The ceald is one of the reasons I've stayed in Utah so long <<too lazy to move being the primary>>. Cold means wearing sweatshirts and wearing sweatshirts de-contours the lingering references to lapses in dietary self-control. And cold means blankets. If happiness took a physical form, it would be a blanket. <<I do use my heating, but when it's winter without and Mountain Dew within, a piker's grudging sixty-eight degrees needs appurtenances. Blankets are free warmth.>>

I was tidying up and noticed my handwritten Rosetta stone for Patch's secret code sitting on my desk. I have a couple of dead hours so maybe I'll translate that leather-bound notebook I found in the first file box.

Everything about Patch was stately—he was wool and leather and brass and shoe polish. I've never seen this notebook before, but if I were to get Patch a notebook, this would be the intuitive choice. Maybe in some other timeline I *did* give him this notebook. <<Thinking through the possibility of that postulation will have to wait for my next long run.>>

The first couple of pages are just non-contextual math and equations. It looks fairly complicated, like he's trying to reconcile opposing physics on multiple axes. Verticals and laterals, vectors intersecting vectors. It would be cooler if I knew to what it was referring. The next few pages sound like fragmented fumes of frustration. He'll start a math problem, scribble it out, and abridge his vexation. A lot of it is fitful, trial-and-error stream of consciousness with comments like, "Frameset must be bounded!" and, "Why can we measure lateral exhaust?" and, "Inscrutables *leave* the frameset!" Some of this sounds familiar. He keeps making a reference to something hypothetical he calls a *bliqueline*. I don't recall encountering that word in the Manuscript. Though, with the volume of fresh, vent-centric vocabulary, I could have encountered it ten times without notice. The bliqueline, at least as it's described, is accessed within the frameset but links to something outside of the frameset. His notes are like the dismembered body parts of a dozen victims of an explosion—legs, eyes, and heads are strewn across the page in their lurid, sanguinary litter. I can't figure out which arms go to which torso. One thing is Emperor's new clothes clear, though: whatever a bliqueline is, whatever a bliqueline does, it is the answer to everything. The symbol for an exclamation point in our code is three lines radiating from a central point on the baseline and they're plentiful. It looks like bliquelines were his cardinal pursuit at the time of his death <<staged death>>.

Maybe it wasn't so much that he could map the vents, or had maps of the vents, or mapped the tracks of the vents, but that he knew something about bliquelines that made him this war's wildcard. Maybe the Mero and the Subverts are after these bliquelines as well and Patch knew something they didn't. Just spitballing here.

DAY 43

Chapter 60

"Men are more easily governed through their vices than through their virtues."
– Napoleon Bonaparte

Assignment #8: TEMPERANCE

Yes and no are the hallmarks of choice, but they are not without their nuanced weights and measures. The college of our cultural philosophy has christened dissipation and intemperance as man's foundational expression of freedom, even in the face of its attendant ruin, and, as such, no has become an affront to the sanctity of that freedom. When a well-defended fortress of no is breached by an occasional yes, then abandoned for a less-conscious, habitual yes, then replaced by a foregone yes, then ruled by a desperate longing, that rendering of freedom becomes slavery.

As conscience impedes desire, the repudiated demands an explanation. Without a why, we struggle with a how. Without a how, we are beasts of the field and fowls of the air governed by cues, suggestions, and stimulation. As the virtues of self-denial are revealed over time in consequences, the establishment of the why requires patience. Our cultural philosophers are brilliant at short-circuiting this revelation, exploiting our impatience, and heralding the ruined as victims of abuse, circumstance, prejudice, anything but their own intemperance. These cultural philosophers provide for the coexistence of indulgence, ruination, victimization, absolution, and self-acceptance, all the while subjecting accountability to witch trials.

I suppose, for our purpi, this is calling the night dark. Vice is slavery and no serious person would argue otherwise. On this topic I could sermonize for a marten's age, but I see little profit in belaboring the obvious. Since we haven't the time to plant every seed and examine every eventual fruit, I will supply the why and frame a how.

Crap on a beanstalk! This is going to be about Mountain Dew, isn't it? I knew it! I knew this was going to be about dropping me off in the middle of a desert of denial and having me walk home! Mountain Dew is the waters of the river of life! It is the all in all! It is the fuel that fueleth the doings of the righteous! <<This is what I get for being so vociferously thankful for hostage-taking poisons.>> Damn it, Patch! Just kill me now!

You have been provided plenty of ore from which you can smelt dazzling vistas and diverting entities, but now we must pause to remove the dross. Transcendence involves both adding the positive and subtracting the negative.

The ecology of the Gontlets permits all residents full view of the activities of the frames. As an umbraled hull, you cannot see, but are seen. You have no privacy, there are no masks, you keep no secrets but what is locked in your mind and not betrayed by behavioral tells. Solitude is a stage production, darkness is a spotlight, and addiction is your head on a charger. Imagine your reaction when a stranger tells you something about yourself they should not know, that no one should know; that start is enough pause for an Exile to sink her hooks into your belligerent curiosity with promise of innocent indulgence. The Lifers will use these character cracks to blindly antagonize. The Blanc-Becs may try to be helpful, oftentimes clumsily and officiously so. Malicious or not, it is the same result: delay. Your disengaged umbra will have a bright recollection of the sensations attending your experience with the physical, especially if those experiences have been repetitively and positively reinforced, inflaming your umbra with refreshed mosquito bites. Offers of indulgence, though mostly impossible in the Gontlets, will tempt to consideration. Liberation is more reliable than resistance.

Liberation is more reliable than resistance. Interesting.

Once a participant in the Gontletian ecology, hauntings of the hull, psychological splinters, physiological echoes, they will all conspire to expose you to destruction. If interactions are unavoidable, they must be unfettered and supersentient.

Why number two: ceded nods to the hull atrophy the umbra and countervail kwazants. Addictions develop stimulus-response loops entirely within the hull itself and their demands bypass integration and confederacy with the umbra. Kwazants, at its essence, is the protraction of the interval between thought and action. The more pronounced that interim, the more involved the umbra will be in that parley as intention, purpose, inclination, deliberation, and volition become counterbalancing factors to an unimpeded stimulus. I have said enough about the advantages of profound kwazants, but be it firmly lodged in your introspections, subordination as a lendemain is imprisonment and swift psychological decomposition.

Yes, I understand why this must be, but this should be the final exam or something! Introducing this evil so early implies that it's going to get worse! It can't get worse!

Last why: if the umbra has left the table during negotiations with the hull regarding its satiations and satisfactions, it will become perforce a coattail-clutching accessory. It will be so loath to depart its master, it will, upon violent separation at the apical frame, claw its way back to the hull while descending the verticality of the vent. In such cases, it creates a depth-reducing stickiness, and you will be unable to descend as deeply as would otherwise be organically determined. This may seem neither heads nor tails at the present, but much study is invested in desired depth, and this stickiness can be a meddlesome variable. If you are trying to descend to the age of sixteen and you only manage twenty-one, the purpose is defeated.

Oh, I don't like that prospect.

Though it can be argued that the umbra and the hull are integral aspects of a single entity, and both are reasonably considered, as far as identity is concerned, two sides of the same coin, these two aspects are, and ever will be, at war. They are like husband and wife—individual wills, unified flesh. Both want singularity, power, accomplishment, autonomy, actualization, and control, but they have to figure out how to tame those aspects in themselves and in each other to maximize their demanding wills with balanced capitulation because, in their reciprocity, they are infinitely more powerful an entity as a salt molecule than as free ions. The umbra cannot achieve kwazants without the hull, but it must keep it on a short leash or they are both dead.

I am sure you already know where this is headed <<yes, yes, yes, just slide the knife in>>, *so I will not insult your intelligence with a prolix proposition. Be honest with yourself and renounce your most salient vice, viz. no more Mountain Dew. I do not want you to just give it up. I do not want you to trick yourself into vitiating cravings. This needs to be a mental exercise that involves reasoning and negotiations and articulating sensation with as much precision as your objectivity and vocabulary allow. This is a weed that needs to be pulled out by the root and not hacked at the base. This will allow for a substantive conquest that hardens and fortifies rather than just leaves a void. You will spend a lot of time thinking about thoughts, but, in the end, this weakness will become your greatest strength.*

Now go! And then stop!

Now all I can think about is how good a Mountain Dew would taste right now. How do you go from strict, daily obedience to the slightest suggestion of Mountain Dew to . . . just nothing. Won't cold turkey give me a heart attack or something? This can't be healthy!

At least this assignment subtracted something from my daily routine instead of adding another task. Extra time is way yummier than a luscious panacea that makes the world right, for sure.

I am so cooked.

CHAPTER 61

"I may not have gone where I intended to go, but I think I have ended up where
I needed to be."
– Douglas Adams

I went skydiving again today, more to cleanse my palate before this next phase
of Manuscript walloping than anything else. I needed to get my mind off of
Mountain Dew. Every time I passed a Maverik or a Holiday or a 7-Eleven, my
body tried to break out of itself. I wasn't entirely sure what Patch was talking
about when he said I'd need to articulate sensation with precision, but now I get
it. *My body trying to break out of itself* isn't very precise, true, but it's day one
and I'll need to be introduced to these feelings before I attempt to characterize
them with any precision. It felt like my being had split in two and one half was
clawing through the other to commandeer the brake pedal and steering wheel.
One half was howling the nastiest of profanities at the other half that was weeping and throwing its hands up while zooming helplessly past pearly gates and
golden streets. Both halves wanted to stop, but . . . maybe I was cracked into
three parts and the other third was being the adult in the room. This story has a
sad ending and I don't want to talk about it anymore.

I still can't believe all I have to do is invoke skydiving and Russians materi-
alize. Do they live at the airfield? Do they *own* the airfield? I'm not complaining,
I just hope they're not sitting around waiting for my call. I'm not important
enough a person to have people waiting on me.

Yuri let me use the suit Patch and I designed. It worked exactly as we theo-
rized. But I had a strange moment up there on one of the jumps today. I know
using the term *strange* is vague, but something vague is perfectly descriptive.
<<High-altitude, steep density differentials probably aren't the safest places for
me when all I do is hallucinate.>> I was experiencing contradictory realizations,
all of which were acutely incontestable. And when you experience these antino-
mies at fourteen thousand feet, you have to settle with *strange*.

I was in freefall, in this suit, manually regulating my net density, slowing to
speeds as low as thirty-five miles per hour, and the earth started moving *away*
from me. My deceleration in freefall translated as the earth retreating. I had this
superhero moment, suspended, hovering, flying as it were, no cables, no supports,
no propulsion, no contingencies <<other than a parachute, I suppose>> in this
world above the world. I was the freest man on earth—unreachable, untouch-
able, invincible, you could say. The mountain-bound patchwork world just
watched me at its distance and I almost forgot my mortality. Which reminded
me . . . I was unsupported, plummeting, wholly exposed to an annulus of threat
and danger with nothing to hide behind, no duck and cover. I was a trackable
target with movement restricted to straight down, more or less. I was the most
vulnerable man on earth—reachable, touchable, vincible, you could say. It even
dawned on me that another airplane could shred me to ribbons with no pros-

pect of scampering, rolling, or diving out of the way. Birds, in fits of territorial nastiness, could abuse me, helter skelter, with beaks and talons, and self-defense in such a fray would be something fit for a meme. If skydiving wasn't the only means available to sling one's umbra out of a hull turned pudding, I would think it was one of Patch's metaphors for life. He was figurative like that. But I was keenly attuned to the dichotomy swimming in my plunging <<ascending?>> breast. In order to become immortal, in order to sidestep the update, I would have to cash in my mortality. All of this training, all of this repetition, it's all designed to fine-tune my death. Is that not insane? Are the paths of the vents that reliable? Are they mapped as accurately as we think they are? And even if they are, what if I just plain miss the vent? All of this will have been for naught. Am I ready to cash in my mortality for the remotest of possibilities? And now I'm back to thinking about Mountain Dew. Crap. All this effort to flee the clutches of its sweet caresses and wicked grin and I'm right back in its scaly, angelic arms.

Day 47

CHAPTER 62

"Habit rules the unreflecting herd."
– William Wordsworth

Patch warned that I'd be thinking a lot about thoughts. Little did he know I'd be overthinking thoughts and categorizing them with a whiteboard full of matrices of mayhem and diagrammatic carnage <<it rivals the canvas of the least medicated of mathematical artists>>. The term *thought*, it turns out, is as specific and useful a descriptor as the term *thingamabob*. Like any organism, it's simple until it's subjected to magnification. Then intricacies overwhelm. It's remarkable how much goes on in my head and how little heed I pay it. I thought I'd at least be my own play's actor, but, after magnification, on the spectrum of theatrical metaphor, I'm much closer to spectator <<groggy after a big meal>> than director.

For some years now I've fancied myself a thinker, but after this little exercise, honesty forces me to downgrade that status to *entertainer of thoughts*. And that's being gracious. This may not be going on in anyone else's head so I won't make generalizations, but most of my thoughts are either reacting to environmental stimuli, vacantly batting around unsolicited injections <<who knows where these are coming from—some of these hailstones far exceed my intelligence and some lie in the absurdly deleterious outer limits of my character>>, or simply responding to direct inquiry or request. I'm like a slightly less attentive Siri or Alexa.

Patch would always say that life begins when you no longer follow a verb or preposition, meaning that you're not really living if you're the direct or indirect object of your life. You're the driver or you're a passenger; there are no intermediates. As I pay more attention to my attention, I realize that these parts of speech are dictated by the degree of control I seize at the flash <<*flash* isn't ideal, but it's the best I can do to convey the very sudden appearance of something>> of the inflection point, the fugitive *now,* the moment I become aware that some content has become available for my consideration. Constructive, destructive, passive, active, reactive, injected, implanted, triggered, un-triggered, relevant, irrelevant, good, bad, neutral, facilitated, un-facilitated, welcomed, unwelcomed, absurd, lucid, deprecating, laudatory, inspiration, temptation, intuition, daydreaming, the more I thought about it <<not a pun>>, the less relevant the nature, the source, or the quality of the thought became. The moment I become cognizant of a cerebral visitor, fixedly and inextricably present, the proof of the pudding, as they say, is in the *thenceforth.* This may all seem very reactive, but, according to my matrix, most thought <<as an umbrella ambiguity>> is not consciously introduced. Certainly, I don't have to self-sabotage by actively shoveling in fresh ordure or hanging out in a dry stack, but once a thought finds itself on stage, I can either give it the hook or give it lines. And since so much of my thought seems to be roused by the scrim, the backcloth, the heckling, I figured, if I want to be my sentence's subject, I either replace the décor or leave the theater. Jousting thoughts at the tiltyard is one approach, but running them through with a sword in their dressing room seems more efficient. I think that's what he was getting at anyway, acting rather than being acted upon, introducing thought rather than entertaining thought, controlling my own narrative. It's all about seizing on that inflection point and, when possible, staging rather than reacting. This was substantiated when I re-routed my travels to avoid convenience stores. And I'm not advocating removal from society to curb vice, but hanging out at the soda fountain during withdrawals is just asking for it.

I should get a girlfriend, not necessarily to replace that wrung out Mountain Dew saturation <<because that would defeat the object>>, but maybe to marginalize the savagery of my first-world problems. I hear love is very transfixing.

How does one go about getting a girlfriend?

DAY 49

Chapter 63

"Life is not a matter of holding good cards, but sometimes, playing a poor hand well."
– Jack London

Blackgoat didn't text yesterday. The hospital called and said they wouldn't need me last night. Mom cancelled on me for lunch today. It's an omen, I know it, though I'm not sure if it's a good omen or a bad omen. Does the word *omen* imply bad?

It could just be that it's Christmas tomorrow. People get busy with family and loved ones and friends and other humans they enjoy being around. Mom didn't mention anything about getting together for the holidays, so that doesn't hurt my feelings or anything. But if it was meant to sting, I probably deserve it—the last ten years aren't studded with Christmas invitations from me. Like Patch would frequently and pitilessly remind me with the curled end of a mustache pointing at his squinty censure, *Your pain is self-inflicted.*

Acknowledged.

Sadly <<for me; happily for others>>, life rises and falls on the degree to which you invest in others.

Mom said something about bridge with friends. Didn't know she played bridge. Didn't know she had friends. How would it be? But if cards are involved, money is involved. Mom doesn't play, Mom gambles. And now she has the means to be a high-stakes roller. I was a first-hand witness to her luck at the Bingo Palace—I give that account six months.

CHAPTER 64

"The trouble is not that I am single and likely to stay single, but that I am lonely
and likely to stay lonely."
– Charlotte Brontë

Alone, like every Christmas Eve for the past ten years. Profoundly alone this
time; I don't even have my carbonated, canary confederate keeping me company. Between the kids at the hospital and my Russian brawtya <<they taught me
the Russian word for *brothers*>> and my friends on the sixth floor of the Moran
Eye Center <<I don't know any of their names and mostly try to steer clear of
them>> and lunches with Mom and scrimmages with the pre-pubescent football
dummies at the park, being alone is kind of a drag. I'm becoming a regular
gadabout. Look at me, Elliot the merrymaker. The strides I've made . . .

This should be a night.

I'm getting better at ferreting out the bushwhackers hiding in the trees at
the inflection point, so I'm not as wrung as I thought I'd be. So ironed out, in
fact, that I grab my dining table's centerpiece to tempt fate. Take 1 to 2 tablets
by mouth every 4 to 6 hours as needed for pain. I must have been in some pain
to think I'd need thirty of these for relief. I roll the thinly titian, barrel-vaulted
battlefield a quarter turn. No hoplites. No battle cries. The dead are buried; the
polluted sky reeks of the bitterness of dried blood. Everything as it should be.

My loneliness hits a pothole and its blackness runs me into misadventure. I'm
more rubbernecking past it than regaining consciousness in it, but it's so sudden
and misplaced I pause to reflect. It's her. It's what's-her-name. The whole of it,
the skyline, the contour, the horizons of my whole existence seem to rise from
a plane to their stature in a topographic timeline. It's all there—history, time,
development, significance. She's in every rise, every fall, every elation, every
depression, every crop, every raincloud. We're each a phosphate backbone,
winding around each other in the structure of everything. I don't know what any
of it means. I can't tell if she's haunting me or part of me is haunting something
else. I've spent lifetime after lifetime pursuing, courting, dying for her, living
for her, and her death is pushing me around in its slosh. This aggravated loneliness is her absence. What is this? How can I be mourning the loss of a complete
stranger, a *fictional* stranger?

Paradoxically, it does mitigate the loneliness.

Inflection point: get the pictures from your whiteboard. My matrix says:
passive, un-triggered, neutral, welcomed, constructive implant. <<I may have
taken this thought sorting exercise a little far.>> I retrieve the pictures.

There's something otherworldly about happiness in its extemporized and
organic element. This is me. I really looked like this. I really laughed like this.
Despite a lot of dark clouds at home, I was happily tethered to a self-fueling sun
that would say things like, *Don't spend your life trying to please people; the
only ones that appreciate those efforts are the ones that are exploiting you!*

Pre-injury Elliot, sixteen <<PIE16>>, that's my last and first page. I'll leave this time travelers' war behind me and ride my update-resistant lendemain as far as it will take me, preferably through fifteen NFL seasons as a linebacker for the Pittsburgh Steelers.

I think I'll watch *The Nativity Story* and go to bed. It's the most Christmasy thing I can think to do.

Merry Christmas, Elliot.

DAY 50

Chapter 65

"There is nothing noble in being superior to your fellow man; true nobility is being superior to your former self."
– Ernest Hemingway

Mountain Dew is what makes Christmas merry. Now it's just Christmas. No offense, Jesus.

I just slept for ten straight hours. Other than post-skydiving wipeouts, I can't remember the last time I slept for seven uninterrupted hours, let alone ten. My break from Mountain Dew has nothing to do with it!

Assignment #9: HUMILITY

Merry Christmas, ya wee spaz! I hope your stocking is brim-bursting with those tongue-cankering wintergreen lozenges! <<How does he remember this stuff?>> *Elliot Christmases were always the best Christmases. Remember that Christmas we gave your mom two hundred lottery tickets and a case of Diet Coke and she sat at the table for five straight hours scratching tickets, muttering to herself, banging her glass on the table when it was refill time? A real gas, that!*

I considered pausing our endeavors for the holidays, but breaks are for moss-gatherers. Besides, Jack Lambert never took breaks. <<Those are dastardly machinations that absolutely work on me!>>

We have learned from fateful experience that expansion of mreg is often coincident with expansion of ego. Kwazants, it appears, is a tide that lifts all boats. Individuals are so pleased with themselves for their progress and its consequent affirmation that the self absorbs more of the attribution than is practical. Profits are not reinvested in the company, as it were, but spent on lavish vanities. This Trojan horse adorns our courtyard as a memento of victory until its slow, pathogenic leak manifests symptoms, fatal symptoms (ingratitude and hubris being primary), in all the colored rooms of Prospero's abbey. Many of the manuscript's ensuing assignments are designed to remind you, convince you, of your helplessness and your nothingness. Excellence is not achieved in a vacuum; the pitons are timeworn and well-established.

For this assignment, I want you to spend the span of next Monday's business hours hopping from one introductory lesson to the next. These have to be group lessons, not private. This is about parading and embracing nescience, so do not choose group lessons that lend themselves to creating private enclaves in public places. I do not want you spending the day hiding behind a canvas, then a sketch pad, then a computer screen, so vary your exposure and level of participation. Alternate between active, musical, artistic, technical, recreational, etc. In such naked circumstances, you have a penchant for insouciance or playing the motley fool to caricaturize your incompetence. I want genuine, maximal effort in every instance and no caveats or face-saving excuses. Accept the fact that you are not a perfectly cut diamond. The more your public understands how misshapen you really are, the more clearly you are seen. <<My public?>> *You will find that living in a glass house saves a lot of time closing doors and drawing curtains.* <<Says the most cryptic man alive.>>

Do not presume that death implies ignorance—I have eyes in the brick and ears in the mortar of all the walls in Salt Lake City. If you do not want to do this every Monday for the next six months, just plow through it like you would a good blocking scheme!

Always using a love of football against me. Never reveal a love of anything to this man!

Now go plan your Monday and get on with it!

This is blender-spun horrcitement. Excitor? I love the idea of learning new things, but hate the idea of learning new things through embarrassing, public displays. I have my dignity to think of, no? I have money, why can't I just hire tutors? I get it, looking stupid in front of one person that knows you're a rookie is way less humiliating than whole rooms of people whispering and shaking their heads.

The only way out is through, I guess.

His list of possible angles gave me ideas. I've always wanted to learn how to play the violin, dance the tango, fight like a cage fighter, draw faces, and patch up somebody that just got stabbed four times. Oh, and I've always wanted to be more flexible, so maybe some yoga.

DAY 51

Chapter 66

"The best way to keep a prisoner from escaping is to make sure he never knows he's in prison."
– Fyodor Dostoyevsky

I'm in Crispin Castlebright's apartment <<my apartment, I guess>>, surrounded by the souvenirs of my youth's innocent happiness—not so much as tangible relics, but as the hazy reconstruction of an anamnesis. I didn't have to answer questions three, I just gave James, the <<my>> security guard, a twenty-ounce bottle of Mountain Dew <<that I, myself, can't enjoy!>> and a Tiger's Milk bar and scooted in. No cleaners this time.

I continue rummaging through the notebooks. I'm better at making sense of documented explanations than deciphering what's going on with this loom of interlacing animal tendons <<that's what it looks like anyway>>. *Alternate Circulating Hemoglobin Vectors and Underwater Breathing; Gene Design and Nucleotide Rephrasing; Bliquelines and the Native Thread.* There it is. I knew I'd seen something about bliquelines in here. That's what I was translating from his leather-bound notebook in the file box. I don't think I knew that bliquelines were part of the whole vent-diving scheme when I was here last. One of the downsides of firehose vocabulary. I should start a glossary.

I photograph all the pages, but its content and diagrams suck me in and here I am trying to squeeze my enormous body into a Louis XV armchair sideways for a more thorough inspection.

This would be way more satisfying with a fresh-out-of-the-freezer Mountain Dew. I should write down the sensations born of my physical and psychological itch at this moment with precision, but this bliqueline business has left me rapt. Besides, my phone is on the table and I'm packed into this chair pretty tightly.

The first several pages discuss the ascending cycle of decompression up the frameset. Inter-frame Gontlets are sealed into the petram at an age of one hundred and twenty years; the pressure accumulated by compressed Gontlets is released into vents that are in contact with the petram; shallower <<younger, I guess you could say>> vents intersect with these deeper, self-contained, pressure-storing vents in their corkscrew descent, accepting the rising exhaust; and again in turn; and again in turn; and again in turn until it intersects with a vent that is in contact with the principal apical frame. Blah, blah, blah, I remember all this.

The nautilus-south archived vents, say, will always form a continuous column from the petram to its most superior end <<between nautilus, anti-nautilus, and the four cardinal directions, I remember there being eight total archived vent options>>, but if the current nascent vent is a nautilus-north, the pressure built up in the nautilus-south archived vent column will have to wait for an intersection with the nautilus north column to release some of its accumulation through the nascent vent. It looks like the compression of an aged-out Gontlet is released into all archived vents making contact with the petram at that moment evenly, so each of the four continuous columns will have to intersect with each other to release the totality of pressure. Once it reaches the nascent vent, the pressure is discharged into the open system at the principal apical frame via that circulating nascent vent. Yes, okay, so . . .

Blank page, blank page . . .

Okay, so, maybe not as simple as *discharged into an open system. Open system* I guess means our atmosphere, the supra-principal apical frame Gontlet. The open system, itself, it seems, requires its own decompression. What? His depiction of the Earth <<principal apical frame>> and all the frames falling below it are similar to his other flattened, global disks <<I know that three-dimensional *global* and two-dimensional *disk* are incongruent; I'm making sure it's understood that the entirety of the world's surface area is included in each flattened facsimile>>, like poking a hole in the South Pole and peeling the world up from the bottom until Antarctica is the rim of a flattened disk whose center is the North Pole. Forming the perimeter, just beyond the Antarctic rim to the south, he has the depiction of a boundary or a wall that provides some fenced, exo-structure to the frameset. It almost looks like Pringles <<frames>> in a Pringles can <<the fenced, exo-structure>>. It's a little strange trying to conceptualize the Earth like this, but it can't be any simpler trying to depict these frames as spherical shells falling downward without also imagining them shrinking in surface area and volume into a central oblivion.

As the open system gradually amasses these additional emissions, a critical mass is reached that triggers a lateral expulsion of the aggregate through breaches in the cylinder of the Pringles can. These breaches, according to his diagrams, look like adjustable slats on vertical blinds. Maybe like one-way valves. It says that this exhaust is a finer, slightly more toxic matter than our atmospheric gases and that feedback loops in the atmosphere trigger the expulsion. The critical mass is reached in a similar fashion to the additive effects of excitatory post-synaptic potentials on a neural membrane—once a volume threshold is reached, it is an irreversible reaction.

So, the pressure ascends vertically through the vents and then horizontally through the Pringles can at the Earth's surface? Why does that concept seem so familiar? Have I already read this stuff? A promnesic weight is keeping my diaphragm depressed and rendering my lungs unfillable. It's not just déjà vu, it feels like I've forgotten something that *just* happened.

And where do bliquelines come in to all this? More pages about this lateral expulsion . . . more pages, more pages. Wow, really? You have a system as complex as vents and frames and Gontlets with all its circus freaks and the petram and decompression, and you have to throw in theoretical stuff as well? Oh, I guess it's not entirely theoretical—apparently, some loose-lipped Dovolniya mentioned bliquelines and the *native thread* to a foolhardy pikirovatel thinking he could window shop in the Gontlets <<the window-shopping part is extrapolation>>. Holy hell for Hannah, just when you thought you'd wrapped your head around something, the intelligence reveals that our frameset isn't the *only* frameset. At least not the only *possible* frameset. Though it doesn't explain how, bliquelines have their origin within this frameset, what is referred to as the native thread, and link to or terminate in or initiate <<or all of these>> alternate framesets.

I pry my half-again Houdini body out of the submerged safe that is that chair and loudly stretch my back. I roll the kink out of my neck and pack myself back in.

It seems like a bliqueline creates a copy of the frame, and that frame then pivots laterally from a point on its rim <<a single point on the Pringles can, I guess>> to form the base of a frameset tangential to the native thread. It is a separate frameset that begins to stack in Pringles-in-Pringles-can fashion from the foundation-forming copy. Patch indicates that nobody knows how many tangential threads there are, if there are any at all, because the population copied with the frame now also exists outside of our system, outside of this native thread, and there is no access to this thread through the Gontlets. That he knows of. The wall of any frameset's Pringles can <<if I could think of an analogy better than Pringles in a Pringles can, I would use it>> seems to be an impassable boundary other than through bliquelines. So, Patch mentioned earlier that the Dovolniya exist outside of our frameset and that the Inscrutables escort some of the entities of the Gontlets to a location outside of the native thread. Is this all part of that tangential thread universe? Do the people living in these tangential threads know they're living outside the native thread? Or even know that they used to live *inside* this native thread?

More questions than answers, as per Patch's ways and means.

So why are bliquelines the grail? Why would he be so interested in getting out of this native thread? Is there some quality of the tangential threads that makes them a more coveted arrangement? Contemplations for a long run, I suppose.

I think the security guard is just messing with me now, but I heed his instructions to wait twenty-nine seconds at the bottom of the stairs before leaving the building all the same.

When I get home, I write, *shrinking significance* and *the thrill of alternate realities* on my gratitude list. As I walk away from the list, I realize that Mountain Dew didn't even come to mind.

DAY 52

CHAPTER 67

"He, who every morning plans the transactions of the day, and follows that plan, carries a thread that will guide him through a labyrinth of the most busy life."
– Victor Hugo

I had to wake up to an alarm today. If I wasn't already daily reminded of the pleasures of waking up, I would think that somebody threw me off a three-story building, kicked the stuffing out of me as I lay maimed and unconscious on the concrete, and then forced a gallon of whiskey down my throat during the night. And to insult my injury, I'm shorting my sleep for reasons optional and odious. But, alas, I'm up, and a dozen scrambled eggs await!

Today's agenda:

8:00 – 9:00 a.m.: Violin

10:00 – 11:00 a.m.: Fencing <<I couldn't find any drawing lessons in Salt Lake for today, so I went with fencing; if I'm going to be the heir, I'll need to learn swashbuckling.>>

12:00 – 1:00 p.m.: Tango <<The fencing lesson is up in Kaysville and I should probably shower before embracing a stranger.>>

1:30 – 2:30 p.m.: First Aid

3:00 – 4:00 p.m.: Mixed Martial Arts

5:00 – 6:00 p.m.: Yoga

It's going to be a long day.

CHAPTER 68

"It doesn't matter what it looks like, it matters what it feels like."
– Bryan Kest

That was extortion! Sixty dollars to rub rosin on bow hair and play a scale? What the dickens is that about? This little brat was walking around, holding on to his elbows behind his back, pointing at people that have clearly never touched a violin in their lives, and barking, "Wrong!" when their bow maladroitly misplaced a note. I think eternal remuneration should be augmented for people my size—eighty-pound great-grandmothers don't have to overcome the very real temptation of dismantling twerpy little snots and stuffing them into violin cases. From a kwazants perspective, it was a useful exercise. In this new Patchiverse, I assume every exchange, social or otherwise, is a tightly controlled, scrupulously monitored experiment. I'm just here to manipulate the results. Being good is easy when you think you're being watched. I should probably stop thinking like that; being good for its own sake is probably preferable to being good because being bad is embarrassing.

The fencing was pretty cool, but I was abysmal. I was looking for a chance to say, "I am not left-handed!" but I wasn't even competent enough with my good hand to think of starting with my bad. And that one was free, so it only cost me a little pride <<maybe more than a little since they paired me up with a nine-year-old girl who worked me pretty good>>.

I don't think I've ever been on a dance floor <<I know I haven't>>, so the tango lesson was noteworthy. I was the only participant that showed up without a partner, so I was confiscated by the instructor to serve as her demonstration dummy. Showering was prescient. I may not be able to prevent a nine-year-old girl from running me through with an épée, but I can dance. My whole body just seemed to apprehend the geometry and cadence of it. It was as intuitive as timing the gaps to the flats, where a running back would be cornered and awaiting destruction. I might make a habit of that tango stuff.

I was at a table with an ex-Special Forces guy who was training to be a civilian paramedic for the first aid class. He'd had some combat medic training so I came away with some competency in treating shrapnel and bullet wounds. If someone plans on being injured around me, I just hope they're shot or blown up. They're dead otherwise.

The mixed martial arts class was bitchin' <<partly because it was free as well>>. They paired me up with one of their regulars. We spent the entire hour in circular parries and punches, starting slow, moving faster, starting simple, adding elements, first with hands, adding legs, initially rote, adding extemporaneity. We didn't stop moving for an hour. I may not be able to feel my shoulders right now, but, holy shit, I know kung fu. <<I don't think any of that was kung fu.>>

I just pulled into the parking lot of the yoga studio. Death by Yoga. How clever is that. It's a funky lotus design with a dark figure sprawled out in the middle, as if dead. For some reason it looks vaguely familiar. I know I'll look like a total idiot, but this should be fun. Hopefully yoga doesn't require the use of shoulders.

Everyone is coming in with a mat. I didn't know I was supposed to bring a mat. Hopefully they have loaners. I know it will have a whole community's funk and disgustingness smeared all over it, but I'd rather not compound my spectacleness. There's always soap.

This place looks more art studio than yoga studio, with its curvilinear white-scheme brick walls and unfinished duct-labyrinthed ceilings. I check in with the girl at the front desk and ask about a mat.

"It wouldn't be much of a yoga studio without 'em. You'll find them in cubbies in the main studio at the back. Just follow this hallway to the end."

I do as directed. The hallway is high and wide and paneled with what looks like acid-washed concrete. On the left and right are massage rooms and saunas and a hot yoga room and a yoga accessories shop. I think to buy a mat, but then it looks like I should know what I'm doing. And it will be a waste of money since it's likely I'll never do yoga again. If I borrow one, I won't betray their low expectations when I sprain a joint doing something simple, like a rear twisting lotus <<I just made that up>>.

It doesn't take long to realize that I'm the only male in the establishment. I thought the girl at the front desk held that congenial smile to be polite; I now realize she was humored by my imminent, multi-tiered spectacleness. I don't know how I didn't foresee this. All of my insecurities are ablaze in white fire and every step is a squirt of lighter fluid. The whole of my surface area is heating up. I must look like a beet, a giant zombie beet, avoiding eye contact, walking stiffly ahead. Pull yourself together, man! This is the last one. Just get through this hour and you're done forever! Nobody knows you here and you will never see any of them again as long as you live! <<There I go jinxing things again. Now I'm going to run into half these people next week.>>

I'm diverted by the optical illusion at the end of the hall where the studio is expanding at a disproportionate rate to my approach. The building is perched on a bench in eastern Bountiful, at the base of the mountains, and a wall of western-facing windows is stretching the room's dimensions to fit the enormity of the valley spilling to the horizon below. It's an incredible view and all I can think of is how much the rent for a place like this would be. I'm a true romantic.

I cut straight through the studio and stand at the window, marveling. The sun looks like the epicenter of a war, lines and fronts of clouds and sky bleeding their beautiful blood. This conversation piece gives me a little comfort. But nobody says anything. Because, as I turn, nobody's in here. I quickly grab a mat and tuck myself into the remotest corner. I don't want to be called on. I just need to think of all these people as seven-year-olds with blood disorders and cancer and I should be fine. No offense, Hudson, I'm in survival mode here.

As I wait for additional arrivals, I wonder how hard I'd need to throw someone to break those windows with their body. This is the kind of stuff that passively fills my mind. It's on the matrix somewhere.

Three enter as a group. They glance at me. I smile. Two more arrive. They glance at me. I smile. Two more. They glance, I smile. Glance, smile, glance, smile. My smile is more an apology for sullying their sanctum than a pleasantry. And I see now that I'm dressed all wrong. Apparently, yoga isn't done in athletic shorts and a sweatshirt. In my defense, I'm between stretchy pants and tight tank tops at present. At least there aren't any mirrors in here, that's a relief.

I mimic the regulars with my mat placement, designer water bottle positioning <<didn't bring a water bottle>>, folded towel arrangement <<didn't bring a towel>>, and the orientation of my foam cube <<not even sure what that's supposed to be for>>. Everyone is doing these technical looking stretches and I feel like an idiot just sitting on my mat like a jock, my forearms resting on my knees. There's a total of fourteen of us, all facing the setting sun, anticipating the *next*. Something feels . . . I don't know, *tangled* about this sunset, like it's going to explode and end all life on Earth. Maybe I'm just remembering how it felt on the first day of a new school, all these strangers sitting around, facing the same direction, waiting for the entrance of a teacher that was sure to ruin their lives. And in she comes, the teacher that is sure to ruin my life. Ruin my next hour, anyway.

She's quite stunning from behind, with an untamed night sea raging and billowing from a succumbing scrunchie, the black . . . wait . . . night sea . . . wait . . . why does this description sound so familiar? So, so familiar . . .

Holy shit. Holy, holy shittiness! What is this about? This can't be! It's her. It's what's-her-name.

She's real.

She's standing right in front of me, naked as a jaybird <<she's fully clothed; my mind is just throwing up right now>>, clear as the moon and fair as the sun. I'm not dreaming. This isn't a dream. She hasn't even turned around yet and I can tell from just a pale tincture of her reflection in the window, it's her. I know it's her because I can feel little bits of me, maybe bits of the umbral me, being yanked toward her. Everything about her is that asymmetrical me that isn't me. What on earth is she doing here? How is she real? I'm sure I'd remember somebody like that if a previous chance encounter had put her in my head to dream about. Distinguishing between dream and reality is difficult in the middle of a dream, but easy in the middle of reality. I know I'm not dreaming. Even with all of your dressed up flimflam, Patch, this isn't possible. Dreams stay in dreams; they aren't exported for amusement.

I should be a jellied heap of syncope and head trauma right now, but for some reason, I'm feeling . . . affirmed. It feels like I've turned up the volume on my life all the way so I could hear something, anything, and then someone starts screaming on the audio. You'd think it would be painful to simultaneously feel everything and sense nothing. Maybe it is; I can't make sense of anything that's going on in or out of my body right now.

"Welcome, everyone, my name is Peyton and I'll be—"

I smash my open hand into my forehead. "Peyton! It was Peyton!" I heard the loud smack sound when I'd slapped my forehead, but from the room's reaction, it's clear that the words came out as well, loudly. And here I was worried about coming across as a little slow in the brain. I start massaging the back of my neck and sheepishly lie, "Sorry, uh . . . that's just how I remember names." I puff my cheeks out and push my eyebrows up into my hairline so I don't burst out laughing at their expressions.

"Thank you, Gigantor, for caring enough to want to remember my name. And a special welcome to *you*; we don't get many men brave enough for yoga around here."

"Oh, no, I'm horrified right now." <<I really need to give my brain a little time to decide what comes out and what doesn't.>>

"But you're here and you're on a mat. That's ninety percent of yoga, right there."

I can't think of anything to say so I just nod. Like a dope.

"Okay, let's get started. Come to the front of your mat and stand in mountain pose. I want you to move your sternum to the sky and try to ground your heels. This is about getting length."

Even her voice is exactly as it is in those dreams. Everything about her is filling the whole room.

"Nose breathing only." Her voice is like high fructose corn syrup.

I'm making too much noise falling out of poses that I can't physically hold. I'm breathing loudly in and out of my mouth. I'm grunting even. I can't figure out how to replicate some of their positions. I'm getting glances, but I don't want to take my eyes off of her. I'm trying to do downward dog with my head up because there's an exquisiteness to the shapeliness of those yoga pants that my nagging agastopia simply can't disregard for an instant, social shame and all. That figure, that flexibility, those lines, modeled from stretched cotton by the decrees of the heavens, anchored by the black swells of a thrashing sea—this is proof that God exists.

The shrinking sun breaks my concentration. It looks like a half-sucked butterscotch, smooth and discolored by the rising smoke of Utah living. How are they not distracted by this sunset? Everything about this scene will spoil any prospective promise of enjoying the beautiful.

"I want you to lay mindfully back into shavasana and let all the tension you're still holding onto sink consciously into the floor."

Now this is a pose I can hold.

"Empty your mind and just focus on your breath. Fully complete your inhalations and exhalations and just sink."

So, is it over? Laying limp on the floor doesn't seem like a mid-workout sort of exercise. That was both the longest and shortest hour of my life.

Anxiety is starting to creep in like breathing in the Arctic. I feel it piggybacking on the oxygen, all the way down to the cells. I'm moving from scripted to unscripted and I'm not so good with unscripted. I have to play this just right, but I know that's not realistic. Entertaining the notion that this whole day could be vapor as of tonight's update seriously pisses me off.

I take my rolled-up mat to the cubbies and she intercepts me.

"You did good, Gigantor."

I can't tell, but I think she's mocking me. "Oh, gosh, I feel like I embarrassed yoga."

"You showed up. You got on the mat. There's no better yoga than that. The yoga gods accept your sacrifice, even if it did make them weep."

I'm laughing on the inside, smiling on the out. I don't encounter funny women that often. <<I don't encounter woman of any variety that often.>> It's just so weird interacting with her when I'm awake—hearing her speak, watching her move, engaging in conversation without reading minds, or sharing a mind. It's like meeting someone you've only ever seen in movies.

"Hey, so, doing yoga for the first time, and I don't *know* that this is your first time doing yoga, though it's obvious that this is your first time doing yoga, usually just angers people and they never get back on a mat. Especially people with tight shoulders the size of baby heads like you. I give two free classes because people don't usually discover this fountain of youth until the second time. Unless that second time is six months away, and then it just angers them again. So, come back soon, free of charge. And there's no actual fountain of youth, so don't be snoopin' around the broom closets or I'll have you thrown out."

Then she smiles. It's a smile with which I am well acquainted. I'm pleasantly melting all the same.

"Don't let your successes carry you away, and don't let your failures sink you. Like anything, progress is made in increments. Keep at it; you'll do great."

Then she slaps me on the butt.

I stand there like I've been rebooted. I don't know if I should be offended or excited or offended that I've been so publicly excited. I'm just there, waiting for my operating system to load.

"Oh, come on, isn't that how you jocks encourage each other?"

"Yeah, on a football field!"

"Okay, then. The only difference between a football field and a yoga studio is . . . hm, there is no difference, so get a grip on yourself and snap out of it. Consider that one a freebie."

I let a breathy laugh out through my nose. I'm roaring on the inside. I wonder if she can tell that my eyes are devouring her; I'll need a belly full to digest her for the next few days.

"Now go sign up for another class! I teach Mondays, Wednesdays, and Fridays. I'll expect to see you three days a week without any of your grousing."

"Yes, ma'am." I hold the mat up and ask with a wrinkle in my nose, "Do you have anything I can use to clean this mat off? I think I made it gross."

She smiles a curious smile. "We have people for that, you big gym rat."

Then she knocks the mat out of my hand and walks away. "Wednesday!" she says without looking back.

I rally all of the platoons of all of the companies of all of the battalions of all the brigades of all of the divisions of all of my faculties to imprint that departure onto every alcove of every subdivision of every lobe. I glance back at the sunless, civil twilight whose battles have moved beyond the horizon and left their beautiful, bloody casualties scattered across a bluing battlefield.

Life rises and falls on . . .

What the hell just happened?

Chapter 69

"Every time when I look at you, Well, I seem to find another thing behind the story. Every time when I look at you, Well, I seem to find another dream behind the glory."
– "Sun Dial," Wolfmother

I have this issue where the more exhausted I get, the farther sleep slips away. And I don't think I've ever been this exhausted. I won't refer to this as a reality because I'm not convinced that what happened today was real, but the mere possibility of such a reality is already becoming a tumor growing inside me, overtaking all of my organs, whispering in the here and there and everywhere of a graveyard like an unfindable ghost. The fantasy was a lullaby, the reality is insomnia. *Reality*, that is. You take the good with the bad, I guess.

How are you real, Peyton? How is it possible? Even in the context of the frames and Gontlets jumble, I can't see how this could be possible. Is she in on it with Patch? But if she was, how did she find her way into my sleep?

She called me a big gym rat. That's a good sign. *Gym rat* implies fit and muscly <<and stupid, usually, but I'm trying to be positive>>. Vast improvement from a few weeks ago where I would have gotten *pear boy* or *pudgy turd*. And why did you have to be a yoga instructor? Yoga is evil! Why couldn't you have been the tango instructor? But that hair . . . how I would love to drown in the heaving vortices of that hair.

I've never been high, but I wonder if this is close.

DAY 54

"He who cannot put his thoughts on ice should not enter into the heat of dispute."
– Friedrich Nietzsche

I think my lungs engage in some level of gas exchange directly with my bones because when I breathe this cold air in, it makes crispy frost of my marrow. In the best possible way. Georgia was a lake of fire; Utah's counterpoint is glorious.

I know I'm doing yoga tonight, but I thought I'd get a workout in since the only exercising I'll be doing in that yoga studio is massaging cramps out of inaccessible joints with hyperventilation and hands on hips. So gaily down the lane I skip <<near sprinting with shouldn't-be-legal Peyton fuel>> to my favorite park. I walk the last fifty yards so I have enough gas for the workout.

I'm prepared to recruit a few money-grubbing pre-pubescents to be part-time trainers <<humiliation dummies>>, but sort of relieved that the park is empty.

Seriously, out of nowhere! Out of bloody nowhere! Not five seconds after I slow to a walk, this dude appears at my side, dressed for, and in the attitude of, taking a morning stroll! I was sprinting! He's not even out of breath! How could he have caught up with me and not be out of breath? Where in hellfire's half-breed did he come from? There's nothing to hide behind—no bushes, trees, structures—nothing! I'm starting to realize that *how* is a pointless question in the Patchiverse.

I jerk away from his sudden proximity like he's a giant insect and bark, "Dude!"

"Bonjour, Monsieur Dillinger."

Oh, great. Another one of these. At least I don't have to wheedle his Frenchness out of him.

"It is avec plaisir to faire your acquaintance."

Even without his hopscotch Frenglish, I can tell he's foreign <<a hoodie with sleeves removed at the seams is a dead giveaway>>. You'd think he'd try to be more American if he wanted to fit in. Maybe he doesn't, or doesn't care. He looks slight enough to fold in half. If I could keep him folded in half, I think I could fit him in that storm drain. Kwazants, Elliot! Crap, yes, right, fine. Okay, what would Patch do here? What would you do here, Patch . . .

"I had great respect for your grand-père. We all did. He was a true gentleman, lordly born and manor bred."

I'm still thinking.

"I do not believe that he is dead. Men like that do not die. I do not believe that you either think he is dead."

Now I've got it.

"We cannot find him without your assistance. I approach you without deception—I am a member of the Merovingian. I do not hide this. Your grand-père was a great ami to the Merovingian and we owe him a grande debt of gratitude."

Just what I'd expect from threat-herding tacticians: derail the heir with vain adventures, then hang him on your trophy wall.

My silence is fermenting the pauses between his thoughts. Why would he need to say that he's not hiding the fact that he's a member of the Merovingian? It implies that others have approached me that *are* concealing that fact. His honesty hardly merits trust if his confederates are cozening. I guess they're coming at me with all the tines on their fork of weirdness: Blackgoat, the man-boys at the clinic parking lot, this Francophonic hallucination, some with official cover, some with full disclosure, all with the same objective—waste Elliot's time.

I have arrived at my destination. I stop walking and take my time facing mon ami. I guess there's no sense in trying to evade the surveillance of all these all-seeing eyes. I might as well have it out. "Do all of you guys know where I live?"

"Bien sur, we do."

"Blackgoat as well?"

No response.

"Why would you need to know where I live?"

"Like it or do not like it, you are one of us now. We like to protect our interests."

He said that with a little too much duplicitous, agent-of-a-power volubility. I know that if my encounter with Peyton, even the dreams themselves, are scrubbed in the update by some depth-generated alteration, I will be none the wiser, but I'd prefer that not be the case. I need to tailor my pursuit of kwazants, not just to fully subordinate a native umbra, but to safeguard this version of the frameset. If that's something I can even purpose.

"I appreciate your concern for my grandad. You're right, he's not dead. But I'm afraid I can't help you locate him since he doesn't want to be located."

"You *know* where he is?"

"Bien sur, I do."

He's studying my pleasant, unblinking face. "Monsieur Dillinger, it is imperative that we meet with your grand-père. He discovered some vital information that he was to discuss with us before his reported demise. I do not mean to be insistent, but this is tres important, Monsieur Dillinger."

"I do comprehend your urgency, and he did mention that you would be keen to discuss this matter with him, but I'm afraid that's impossible."

"Monsieur Dillinger, I—"

"He did want me to pass along a message: he has found the bliquelines, he knows how to access them, and any effort to alter the record will only hasten his . . . enterprising resolve. I think you understand the consequences of any unsolicited interference, as he is the *sole* proprietor of this intelligence for a considerable depth. I assure you, he will contact you when he is ready to contact you."

At the mention of bliquelines, his face was rapid fluctuations between a wrinkle of horror and fury and helplessness and muscles tightening to veil those tells.

It was an ineffectual poker face. I'm not sure if I didn't just make my situation horribly worse with that bluff, but I was apprehending its brilliance as it was spilling out. Some molten power was enlarging my whole being and I felt like a freakin' steely-eyed superspy. Booyah!

I slap him on the shoulder with a big, dismissive grin and it unbalances him a little <<the slap, that is>>.

Chapter 71

"Pain is temporary. Quitting lasts forever."
– Lance Armstrong

"Well look what the cat dragged back in."

I'm so giddy I have absolutely no idea how I responded. I'm as much a spectator in this conversation as the girl at the front desk grinning at our voluptuous badinage. I should probably get a hold of myself, though. I have no authority on this subject, but I feel like the second encounter might be a little early for unchecked histrionics.

She looks at me like I just told everyone the punchline to her joke. "Get in there, you! And no more of your cuttin' up. This is serious business." She shakes her head and tuts like a British grandmother.

I promptly jog down the hall.

I set up in the same place, at the back, so I'm not in the direct line of sight of anyone. I'd like to confine my spectacleness to the very un-yoga-like sounds I make.

"Okay, people, we're going to do something a little different this time. I know most of you are fairly advanced, but we're going back to the basics for the newbie's sake. The poses don't have limits, so if you want to challenge yourself, just probe the limitlessness. Experiment with your depth, symmetry, and positioning. I'll talk you through the modifications of these poses as we go, Gigantor, so don't drift off."

I give her a thumbs up from the back of the room.

Here we go . . .

Downward dog, no problem. It's just a pike press you hold for a minute. Piece of cake. Maybe not. It's like a pike press you hold forever. Up to forward fold, thank the heavens. Plank, upward dog, back to downward dog? Seriously? Align the hands, fingers spread, index fingers pointing forward, push out of your shoulders, sit bones to the sky <<whatever *sit bones* are>>, heels move toward the floor, whether they get there is immaterial; we want sensation, not perfection.

"Get out of your ego. There's no health benefit to going deeper in a pose than the person to your left. You're here, you're feeling something, you're breathing; that's perfect yoga."

She was born to teach, no question. However, I'm starting to focus on the more melodic aspects of her voice and it's twisting me up.

I'm doing something called triangle pose and it feels like my chassis just exploded.

"I want you to find that boundary between sensation and discomfort, between challenging yourself and pain. Consult your breath. If you're sacrificing your breathing for a pose, then back off a little. But remember, your breath is a meter, not a master. Your reactivity to the discomfort is your master and you can defy masters. You can be uncomfortable without being a slave to it. You can respect where you are and still be a little belligerent."

Breath is being sacrificed. I'm backing off a little. Now I'm backing off from where I just backed off.

Child's pose . . . stars and garters, I thought time stood still for a while there. Hopefully that means it's almost over. That hour was longer than Monday's hour.

My forehead is resting on a spongy puddle of my own sweat and I don't care. She's right, this does feel pretty good. The invigoration is counterintuitive; normally after a workout I feel like sitting on a couch for six hours sucking down a gallon of Mountain Dew through a fat, red straw. <<Mountain Dew . . .>> I don't know about fountain of youth, but I do feel like I just drank from a pool that will make me young forever.

I store my mat and walk to the windows. "This is quite possibly the best view in all of Utah. How did you find this place?"

"It's a long story and I don't think you have what it takes to appreciate so great a story, so I'm not going to tell you."

"Really hurtful."

"So, what do you think? Have I convinced you that you need to overpay me for long-term, contracted, public yoga humiliation when all this stuff is free online?"

"That was a pretty good pitch. Tell me more about the *all this stuff is free online* part." <<I don't know who's doing this! I am so not this witty!>>

She has this woebegone look about her face and she gulps, "Okay, look, my mom has cancer and I really need the money to pay for her treatments."

I'm speechless and stunned by her impudence. "You're an excellent yoga instructor and a horrible liar."

A wicked grin rolls across her face from the philtrum out. "Okay, it's not my mom, it's my dad. And it's not cancer, it's syphilis."

"In that case, sign me up. I hate the thought of a man having to live with syphilis."

"Excellent choice, Gigantor. Your charity will be rewarded. By some cosmic force. At some point."

When I get home, I write *Peyton* on my gratitude list. I almost add a little heart after her name, but I remember that I'm a grown man.

DAY 56

Chapter 72

"There is something so amiable in the prejudices of a young mind, that one is sorry to see them give way to the reception of more general opinions."
– *Sense and Sensibility*, Jane Austen

Pre-Christmas season life resumed quickly after Christmas. Thankfully, too—it's exhausting living in the extremes left of madhouse and right of closed for business. I'm not very celebratory, so there's nothing festive or cute about such disruptions.

Blackgoat texted on Thursday. This time he said no problem if I couldn't make practice, but he would like to schedule me for a personal try-out. He's a tenacious vent grate, that one.

Sophie's Place was a packed house last night. I think there were more parents and nurses than kids this time, which kinda bugs. When you speak to kids, you have to be both more and less respectful. Fluency in kid-speak requires dumbing everything down without being patronizing. And kids are less forgiving when they discover you've lied to them. They're a little more black and white.

Adults are stupid but think they're wise, so you have to patronize with tepid respectfulness. When it's an even mix, I feel like I have to hybridize my speak, and it just confuses everyone. So I decided to avoid eye contact with the adults and just focus on the real people <<kids>>. I guess there's too much intrigue in the Gontlets to keep the adults away. Or maybe they're just concerned that I'm going to indoctrinate their kids with otherweirdliness. I try to make it sound more like a Jack and the Beanstalk tale, but these kids are too intelligent to keep it bobbing at the surface. One kid even asked if people try to kill each other in the Gontlets and if they had wars there. I was afraid the parents were going to shut me down after that doozy, but they all just sat there patiently, stroking their chins, awaiting my reply.

I was dying to tell Mom about Peyton at lunch, but I didn't want to get hopes up. Peyton is like six degrees out of my league <<on a seven-degree scale>> and I don't want to be berated for letting a thirty-pound, flailing, slippery, shapeshifting fish slip away. I think a could-have-been would make her more anxious than a never-was. And I wouldn't dare bring those dreams up. She's already getting a little weird about things.

I'm sitting in my truck on the north side of the Death by Yoga parking lot drinking in this impossible view. Elemental light is drawn from the sun's fire, the earth's soil, and the sky's blending wind and water. Everything is perfectly endless.

I arrived too early and my confidence and self-consciousness are having competitive foot races. I regret how loose I was last time and intend to tighten it up. She seemed cool with it, but I feel like social mercies have short leashes. Just be cool, Elliot. There's no rush <<"Lies!" screams my dying heart>>. I'm wondering if last night's update overwrote everything that *actually* happened with Peyton yesterday. Anything's possible, I guess. Which makes me intensely dislike this update rubbish. I need to get me a lendemain so I'm not erased every day. Who can plan in such conditions?

But then I think, if I Pik, I'll be going *back* in time. If I go back in time, I'll have to wait until this present to encounter her for the first <<second-first>> time. Or would I have to wait? Why couldn't I just start going to yoga earlier in the new timeline? For that matter, why couldn't I go back to PIE16 and find her there? <<Though I would probably need more information than just her first name.>>

This is perfect—Peyton is talking to another patron in the lobby. I don't have to try to be slick. She notices me, so I flash my new Death by Yoga emblem stamped symbol-of-commitment yoga mat as I pass.

"Mr. Dillinger." <<Mr. Dillinger? What happened to Gigantor?>>

"Miss" <<I desperately hope she's a *miss*>> "Peyton."

It's going to take a while to get used to the torment of that reality-infiltrating dream face.

Everything's pretty tame today. I'm curbing my desperation and she's focusing on class. I'm able to hold heavily modified versions of the poses <<meaning they only vaguely resemble the Gumby people around me>> for the duration of her torturous eternities and she recognizes my efforts without making a big thing of it. We're acquaintances for the hour. I try to abscond at the hour's expiration, but she accosts me.

"Out of curiosity, why yoga?"

"Why yoga . . . I think because strength and speed aren't the only things I want to be able to do with my body. I could improve my range of motion and flexibility and yoga is good for that sort of thing."

"Oh. I wasn't expecting a real answer. I'm the only girl you've talked to here," <<how does she know that?>> "so I didn't think it was to pick up chicks, but I thought you were going to say you lost a bet or something."

"Some of us are serious people with serious girls. Goals! I meant goals! Not girls. Sheesh."

She huffs out a few tss-ing chuckles. "Okay, Mr. Range of Motion and Flexibility. Whatever."

"What about you? Why yoga?"

"I will answer your question if you understand that I wasn't asking to be asked."

"I wasn't mirroring," <<I was absolutely mirroring>> "I'm legitimately curious."

I can tell she's a person that doesn't trust easily, but she responds, "The most successful people are the ones that don't swap their strengths for their passions. Lucky you if they're one and the same, but it's not as common as people pretend it is."

"You don't like teaching yoga?"

"I think I've convinced myself that I do so I don't chase fancies into poverty."

"Is it too intrusive to ask what your passion is?"

"Yes, now away with you! You look like you're seriously interested and I'm about to blow my rape whistle!"

I stand there for a minute to see if she actually blows a whistle. "As you wish. Your loss though, I was about to tell you how little I cared about your passions, your pursuits."

"*Sense and Sensibility*, right?"

"I have no idea what you mean. But he does have the smartest bitch of a pointer."

She punches me in the chest. "You are something else, Elliot Dillinger. I love that movie."

"Yeah. Me too. My mom forced me to watch it once with her and then I gladly watched it the next fifty times."

She makes a nearly imperceptible, "Hmm," sound and then walks away.

I probably should have made more of that exit in my mind, but it's not often that something that beautiful walks away in yoga pants. Who overthinks an exit when such images are available? I hope that's not a mreg shrinker.

DAY 58

Chapter 73

"It was a night plan and it's morning now. Night plans aren't any good in the
morning."
– *For Whom the Bell Tolls*, Ernest Hemingway

I woke up this morning in a cold sweat. The chilling realization that it was Sunday
meant I forgot to do the assignment yesterday! What the Hubert Humphrey is
that about? I'll tell you what it's about! It's about Peyton! Murderess! She is the
ice-nine around which all of my thought is crystallizing!

The idea wormed its way into my head on Friday night that I was going to
ask her out, like on a traditional date, and I found myself in this tunnel, undeterred, steamrolled by my irrational impatience until, hell to hamburgers, it was
late Saturday night. My daily routine is so soused and structured as it is, it's
hard to distinguish a Wednesday from a Saturday. I'm just glad I didn't write
any of those draft propositions down on paper. There's no cross shredder fine
enough, no forge burning hot enough, no acid caustic enough . . . Patch had me
read *For Whom the Bell Tolls* when I was a teenager and write a whole essay on
this one line, "It was a night plan and it's morning now. Night plans aren't any
good in the morning." These propositions were definitely night plans—mortifying, cringeworthy night plans that make you want to pile mountains on top of
yourself. And I can't throw Mountain Dew in the shards of this broken vase as a
scapegoat—this was all Elliot in his lovedrunkenness.

Peyton was right, I need to get a grip on myself and snap out of it.

I have a feeling that Patch meant for these assignments to be done on
Saturdays, so I'll just resume next Saturday. Hopefully they aren't designed for
specific dates or I've really fuched it up.

Day 59

CHAPTER 74

"Behold, I have played the fool, and have erred exceedingly."
— 1 Samuel 26:21

My skin and muscles are trying to conceal a sprinter's pace heart rate. I'm focusing on Peyton's face, but it's having a perverse effect. Probably because she's the one effecting this choking angina in the first place. Maybe I should go back to the sunrise for now. *The darkness of shadow barricades itself behind the threads of a salten web, bright parapets ensuring the bailey's passab—*

"I'll say, Mr. Dillinger, you astonish me."

"Astonish?"

"You're almost a regular now. I never saw it coming. We have guys in here every now and again and once they discover that girls aren't that impressed by uncoordinated muscle, they scoot."

"Clearly, I'm not here to impress."

She has a reflective kind of smile. "You always have just the right thing to say, don't you."

"Uh . . . no." <<Don't you dare mention all those disgraceful drafts, Elliot!>> "If you ever think I'm saying just the right thing, you should look around for a ventriloquist."

Her thorax lifts her shoulders with one sharp heave of humor.

I'm not really sure what to make of her lingering gazes, but I know throwing a gala for them in my head is not what she intends for them. Elliot, get a grip on yourself and snap out of it!

"I beg leave to depart, ma'am. If I don't limber up a little, I'm bound to break a hip or something. My ligaments have very little elastic apparently."

"Off with ya then! I'll try not to destroy you today."

I'm going to need that mercy.

"Okay, people, since Mr. Dillinger is all caught up with us," <<caught up? What?>> "we're going to embrace the discomfort today. If you have to come out of a pose or modify, that's fine, but know that we often save some for the last lap when we don't need to. Every lap is the last lap today."

I go a little deeper in the poses. I hold them a little longer. I work on focal points and technique. This is by no means easy, but it's getting easier. I'm realizing that concentric contraction and isometric contraction are the most distant of cousins.

The sun is setting on the hour and I'm in child's pose, so nervous my shoulders are goo. I try to flex them to see if they're even functional, but they just start quivering.

I'm slowmo-ing my packing up routine to make sure I'm the last one out.

"You survived."

"Unfortunately. Hey, I have a question."

"Let me stop you right there . . . just kidding, go ahead."

She's so relaxed it's actually relaxing me. "I know we basically just met, but I was wondering if you would be interested in going out with me on a date." I try to enunciate each word so I don't have to repeat it.

My face is bracing for a detonation. Hers is collapsing into the dread of having to put the family dog down. Her answerlessness is distending in all directions. All the negative emotions enshrined in the human experience are the individual components of the grand finale of a fireworks show going off in all my internal and externality.

"Oh, I'm so sorry, Elliot—"

"Of course, you have a boyfriend. It was a long shot, but I thought it better to be a man and ask you out properly rather than be a coward and come up with some slippery way to ask if you had a boyfriend."

"No, it's not that."

"So . . . you don't have a boyfriend?"

"No. That surprises you?"

I cock my head back and say, with a little too much *duh*, "Very much so."

"Why would you ask me out if you thought I might have a boyfriend?"

I hadn't rehearsed this far into the proposition. The truth reaches the finish line before a customized face-saver. "Totally worth the risk of rejection, I guess."

She gives me a very serious, quizzical look that fades back into putting the family dog down. The beginnings of a response become a polite smile. "Sorry, Gigantor," <<oh, no, we're back to Gigantor>> "I just don't date attractive guys. They're too full of themselves and never stop looking for the next conquest."

I'm flush with genuine confusion. "So . . . are you saying yes? I guess I'm not sure what that has to do with me. That should work in my favor, right?" I'm honestly not trying to be coy. Is that a circuitous yes or a flattering no?

I can tell from a look of pitiful ambivalence that shrill yeses and noes are exploding in her head. "It's a no. I'm flattered, believe me, but it has to be a no. I'm so sorry—"

I hold my hands up to stop her apology and I can see that my hands are shaking. "Nope. No need for an apology. Just a shot in the dark. I will cry myself to sleep tonight, but I promise not to make things awkward and I'll never bring it up again. Just business as usual. Promise, never bring it up again."

Dead light from a nautical twilight illuminates a gloss describing the blackest of tide pools. She's not crying, but it looks like she's about to. Her mouth departs from the rest of her face in a sad smile. She punches me in the chest again, but it, too, is sad. Then she turns and walks away.

Crap. I think I just ruined something big.

Chapter 75

"It is far better to endure patiently a smart which nobody feels but yourself,
then to commit a hasty action whose evil consequences will extend to all connected with you; and besides, the Bible bids us return good for evil."
– *Jane Eyre*, Charlotte Brontë

I should be more wretched than I am. This manifest defeat feels more like a
successful trial run, like everything I've been doing with this Manuscript is working. I don't regret asking her. Nor am I ashamed of the feelings I related; they
were natural and just. Oh, gosh, Elliot, now you're quoting *Pride and Prejudice*
to yourself. The day just became sad.

I had never seen Peyton before that initial yoga class. There's no reason
so clear a picture of her should emerge in dream after head-scratching dream.
There's no sufficient explanation for why she should be me and I should be her
in these dreams. It is unmistakably her, no question, so what is the connection?
Why her? Why me? To the naked eye, it's happenstance. All accounting, then,
must reside in outlying domains, realms of practical impossibilities. And this
comforts me. Understood or not, this connection is swirling around me, just
waiting to be apprehended. I've made my interest known, now I can calmly,
affably engage with Peyton on her terms. No rush. The connection isn't going
anywhere.

I feel worse for what I did to Peyton than I do about my rejection. Her life
was probably pretty stress-free before I burdened her with a yoke of funhouse-
style discomfiture.

DAY 61

"It's easy to cry when you realize that everyone you love will reject you or die."
– *Fight Club*, Chuck Palahniuk

You can be excruciatingly, recklessly in love with someone and be totally unaffected by their indifference to you, right? <<Wrong!>> I was fascinated by some girl that stepped out of my dreams and into an incarnation over whom I am now madly, malignantly head . . . heels. So what? This happens every day. It's nothing to tweak about. <<Wrong!>> I am calm as a summer's morning. Everything is as normal as ever my life has been. <<Wrong!>>

I grunted much less this hour. I'm breathing mostly through my nose now. My chassis doesn't feel like a sciatica storm anymore. Peyton sounded like . . . like the only Peyton I've known in the flesh. It's as if I never tried to torpedo our good thing.

As I roll my mat up at the conclusion of the hour, I can feel someone hovering. I entertain the prospect of a flying side piercing kick <<made that up>>, but if it's Peyton, it might make things worse. And I know it's Peyton. My giddy meter is spiking.

"I want to talk to you."

I keep mat-rolling without turning around and reply to the voice still winding around me, "Who is *I* and who are *you* . . ." I'm laughing too hard at myself to finish my flippant mindlessness. As I turn, Peyton is glowering with her tongue in her cheek.

My contrition loudly whispers, "I already apologized. I've been acting normal. I said I wouldn't bring it up again, I didn't bring it—"

"Okay, calm down, speedball! I said talk, not scold!"

I'm that grimacing face emoji. "Sorry."

"I'm changing my mind. I want to go on that date with you."

"What? Really?" I think my excitement sharpened those syllables up and they slashed my poker face.

There's a hint of a smile in her cheeks somewhere. "Really."

"Should I ask if *you* lost a bet or something?"

Glowering, tongue in cheek.

"Kidding. Am I allowed to ask? Did you come to the realization that I'm not attractive after all?"

"No, idiot. I meant what I said about that. It's just that you had this real look of confusion when I implied that you were attractive. That was an impressive display of modesty. I like that. You really don't think you're attractive." She's more musing now.

"Because . . . I'm not."

"Right," she says with an eyeroll. "But then you showed up today, even after I rejected you. You showed up when things could have been really awkward. And you weren't awkward. And you didn't make it awkward for me. And you didn't bring it up again. That was . . . cool. So you get a date with me. This is your one chance, so don't ruin it."

"Oh, I have every intention of ruining it. Ruining it with awesomeness." I laugh at myself again and have to cover my mouth so it doesn't run away. The glee in me is spitting out like boiling oil.

She flicks me in the chest and says, "Here's the catch, Mr. Dillinger." She's jabbing me in the chest with her finger every third word. "You have to come to my class four more times before we go on this date. I want to squeeze every penny out of you in case you try to get frisky and I punch you out."

"Deal. I wouldn't have it any other way. I promise I won't get frisky. Whatever *frisky* means."

"You paid up for the Leah, now I need to make sure you pay honestly for the Rachel."

I think to mirror by jabbing my finger into her chest as I respond, but my finger, thankfully, recoils. "Leah may have had a fruitful womb, but Rachel was way hotter. Well worth the wait. And I think Leah had buckteeth, that's why she had to trick Jacob under the cover of night. I'd rather have the non-buckteeth Peyton."

I don't think she was expecting me to know that story. She has that lingering gaze again. I don't know enough about these boy-girl encounters to know if that's an omen or a nostril-flaring malison, so I take the opportunity to sink all the teeth of my cerebration into her face and chew up and digest her image for the coming interlude.

"That reminds me . . . uh . . . never mind. Maybe for another time."

She steps between me and the exit. "Out with it, Dillinger."

"It's nothing. It would sound like I was trying to weasel my way out of our arrangement."

"Out with it."

"It's seriously nothing. Four more classes, got it."

"You have to go through me to get out of here, you know."

I don't think a dozen of her could prevent me from leaving. "Fine, sheesh. So bossy. I was just going to say that I go to Primary Children's every Thursday evening and read to the kids there. I was just wondering if you were interested in joining me. It's just a service thing, no big deal. Not a date. I think the kids would like you."

"You go to a children's hospital once a week and read to kids?"

She makes it sound grand. "It's just one hour. Nothing extraordinary."

Lingering gaze . . .

"I'm filling in for another class tomorrow night. You said every Thursday, right? Can I come the following Thursday?"

"Really? You would come?"

"I rejected you to your face a couple days ago. Do I seem like the kind of person that does things they don't want to do?"

I smile. "Okay, then. See you Friday?"

"Sure. Assuming one of us doesn't die before then."

Well that was grim.

Chapter 77

"Reality is just a crutch for people who can't handle drugs."
– Robin Williams

The last eight entries of my gratitude list read *Peyton, yoga pants, Peyton, Peyton, the fountain of youth, Peyton, perspective,* and *reckless abandon.*

A noticeable lack of Mountain Dew entries. It's remarkable how fickle human obsession can be. I would claim status as an *ex*-Mountain Dew addict, but then some grammarian will turn up and remind me with a powerful thumb that life needs indirect objects too.

A couple of months ago, sitting quietly on my couch would have been ache and arrhythmias and dark seizures. All gambits, all stratagems would have been deployed to befoul the mere whisper of thought-impregnating quiets. Now it's therapy. I've become a buoyancy in this swaddling fluid of sensory deprivation. I just completed my first of four dowry-accruing yoga classes <<sixth overall>> and I'm in that post-shower, invigorated exhaustion, right between wired and sleep. The noiselessness is drawing the day's sweepings out in its osmotic lure. Images of Peyton are organizing themselves into an art show, lining a meandering maze of white walls.

Something is bothering me though. If things work out with Peyton, what of the Manuscript? What would be the point? What moron would choose youth over happiness? Over love? But, then, I did dream about Peyton before I met her, so maybe Patch's contrivances are more about Peyton than high school football. I know this gentleman's war is a theme in the documentation, and bliquelines are significant, but he's like this, setting an elaborate stage just for you to appreciate a simple monologue. Did he know I'd find the key to the code so I could translate the notebook? Did he know I'd go to his <<my>> apartment and research bliquelines? <<Oh course he did.>> Hell's butt balls, Patch, I'm back to fretting. Pik-ing, kwazants, the Russians, maybe these are all figures on a sand table to wargame my earlier introduction to Peyton. Maybe it's just a slow rolling bait-and-switch, the conclusion of which I was to eventually arrive at and embrace. Like I said, you can't second guess this guy. In the end, whatever I do, he meant for me to do. He's not a loose end leaver.

I know tomorrow is another assignment, and I skipped last week, but I need more sorting time. I don't want to keep burrowing deeper into the Manuscript if I'm contemplating U-turns. Besides, I have a life-pivoting date approaching and I don't want Morocco or swashbuckling or plummeting pikirovateli competing for my attention. The date is all planned, of course, but I don't want to run the risk of a conflict. No offense, Patch, but Peyton wins this time.

DAY 66

Chapter 78

"Beauty is eternity gazing at itself in a mirror."
– "On Beauty," Khalil Gibran

I've been supplementing my yoga with plyometric, isometric, and calisthenics workouts to cheat my way to more impressive stamina and flexibility. Nothing screams *love* louder than destroying yourself to impress someone.

I moved to the front of the room, but don't have the nerve to teacher's pet my way to the center, so Baby's still in a corner. My outline in the sunsetting window is steady, almost sculpturesque. My warrior one isn't being used as whispered examples of what not to do anymore. My hips are squarer, my angles are ninetier, my thighs are scissorier, my lines are straighter, my longevity is winning the tug-of-war with agony. Peyton isn't publicly congratulating me anymore, so I must be improving.

The fountain of youth analogy is apt. I've never felt so good after feeling so awful.

I'm always a little <<horrifyingly>> self-conscious when Peyton approaches me after class; there's no way I'm not ripe after that sudor soak. I haven't seen her nose crinkle yet so maybe she's become numb to stink.

"So, Monster Man, assuming you can hold out for two more classes, what is this date of ours going to look like?"

I'm feigning exasperation. "It looks like what it looks like!"

Her eyes die and she jams her tongue into the inside of her cheek. One day I'm going to photographically capture that expression extempore. Then I can die happy.

"It's a secret. Just know that you're going to *hate* it."

"That's one way to keep me coming back for more."

"Absolutely hate it."

"As long as it's not dinner and a movie, I think I'll be okay."

I breathe in through my teeth and start massaging the back of my neck. "Oh, crap. Looks like I have some reservation canceling to do and some tickets to return."

Her palms meet with a gasp and she rests the ends of her index fingers on her lips. "Please tell me you're kidding. Were you really going to take me to dinner and a movie? Please tell me I didn't just ruin it." She sounds romantic, almost sad that she'd missiled that idea right out of the sky.

I really want to twist this knife, but she's already at a high level of distress. "I would never take a classy girl to a movie theater. Have you seen those seats? Not fit for a peasant, let alone a queen . . . -ly thing. Way too disgusting for a butt as nice as yours." <<Reminder: spend more time with thoughts.>> "Not that I've looked."

"Then you've wasted some good opportunities, you liar."

"I'm not really that conventional anyway, so I'm glad those are your only stipulations. I'm just relieved you didn't shut down robbing senior citizens and water balloon bombing homeless camps."

"Eh. That stuff gets boring when you do it all the time. I just don't want to have to tell our kids that our first date was dinner and a movie."

That comment un-centers me. "We have kids?"

"Well, you know what I mean. Just in case, who wants that to be their story?"

I'm pleasantly melting again. Then I remember the dream. The dream where she's falling and I have to construct her soft landing with balconied high rises. She was pregnant in that dream. Could a woman like this really entertain the notion of having a family with a man like me? Grievous to be borne <<for her, I mean>>!

I'm just glad my mom wasn't here for that conversation. I think all the squeaking and squealing would have given me a migraine.

DAY 67

Chapter 79

"You mean you'll put down your rock and I'll put down my sword and we'll
try to kill each other like civilized people?"
– The Man in Black, *The Princess Bride*

I've spent too much time daydreaming this past week so I resolved to crack
knuckles and put shoulder to wheel today. If practicing card tricks and studying Russian can be considered shoulder-to-wheel. I spent more time memoriz-
ing *The Princess Bride* screenplay than anything else. Cerebrally shoulder-to-
wheel for sure. The difference between the screenplay and the movie is stout
enough to double the workload and quarter the certainty. It's like Russian and
its incognito English letters—their *c* is our *s* sound, their *b* is our *v* sound, their
p is our *r* sound, etc. Just obnoxious.

There's so much lactic acid building up in my brain that I have to rest and
recover with push-ups.

I know these activities—the card tricks, the breath holding, the memorization—all serve their purpose in the Gontlets, but the dual-routed benefit can't be ignored. The long-suffering of rewiring individual muscle fibers to
disobey its design and function, contravening the hysterics of thrashing survival demands, plowing through snowbank after snowbank despite a caterwauling
fatigue—I can feel concentric rings of expansion and power consuming more
of the boundaries beyond my skin. I'm definitely a broader-shouldered vitality
than the worm I was at this moment <<I'm holding the pill bottle>>. It may not
be as apparent when I share the road with Utah drivers, but I feel like that will
eventually be corrected incidentally and organically as kwazants blooms from
inside to out. I've been so reactionary because I perceive everything as a threat
to my life, like everyone's out to kill me. Once I have enough non-lethal experience with humanity, I'll realize just how pathological that mindset really is and
I'll, more or less, shrug it off.

DAY 68

Chapter 80

> "If it's a penny for your thoughts and you put in your two cents worth, then someone, somewhere is making a penny."
> – Steven Wright

"Stop trying to cram yourself into somebody else's aesthetic. You're here to be you as much as possible. Don't betray yourself by betraying your breath. If your breath is telling you to back off, back off, restore the fluidity of your breathing, then come back to the best version of you. Consolidating gains for a few classes is way better than getting an injury trying to jam yourself into someone else's aesthetic. Be you until you can safely be a better version of yourself."

She's roaming around the class correcting alignment and symmetry. I intentionally misalign myself.

I'm craning my neck to see the sunset while doing something called half moon. Nobody else is multi-tasking like this. They're so serious about their yoga they'd let this sunset go unappreciated.

As I roll up my mat, I notice that Peyton is already gone. I start evaluating all of my life's micromovements to determine if I'd done something to scare her off. I'll hang out in here, retying shoelaces and drawstrings, rerolling my mat for perfect flushness at the ends to alibi my loitering. She returns and walks straight to the window, admiring the sun's unfathomable artistry.

She's talking to the windows. "When is this date of ours happening?"

I join her at the windows and also speak to them. "If it's not too short notice, this Saturday is the most ideal day for what we're going to be doing."

"Do you ever notice how the clouds steal all the glory in a sunset?"

That's such a me thing to say. "Yes. I do. They're very selfish."

"Utah has some great sunsets."

"It really does."

The silence we're soaking in gives me great comfort. Conversational lulls make me anxious, but she seems unfazed. It takes some of the pressure off of always trying to fill them with my hasty jabbering. A seesaw waterfall of conversation is ideal, but more so I prefer thoughtful, hand-selected topics to filling the toilet water of those pauses with my madcap verbal diarrhea.

I'm not rashly palliating a blood pressure-spiking pause here. "The more I look at sunsets, the more I'm convinced that we, the humanity *we*, don't know anything about anything."

"That's an interesting observation from something that happens every day, but I get what you mean."

We're quietly absorbed again.

"Saturday is fine. Since you're insistent on secrecy, you should at least tell me time, location, and how to dress."

"I'll pick you up at 10 a.m. right out here in the parking lot. I don't want you to have to divulge your home address to a stranger. And dress warmly, comfortably, and casually. You'll need full use of your limbs. You're not afraid of alligators, are you?"

"Sloths, but not alligators."

I'll have to get used to this quick draw wit. I have limited exposure to clever minds that work on a hair trigger.

Day 69

CHAPTER 81

"I became a good pitcher when I stopped trying to make them miss the ball and started trying to make them hit it."
– Sandy Koufax

A Costco run is in order—I ran out of Nesquik powder. Milk is just milk when it's nothing but milk, but add some Nesquik and it's about forty percent as good as Mountain Dew <<which is as close as any consumable can get>>.

I only plan on getting one item but I get a cart because it's Costco and you never know.

I used to love shopping at Costco because of the wide aisles. I could fly through the store, ticking thirty items off a shopping list in eight minutes. Not so much anymore. It's either a family of five all walking full abreast; retired, window-shopping recreationalists walking at seemingly negative speeds; the wannabe Europeans walking on the wrong side of the aisle; the unbelievably oblivious leaving their cart in the middle of the aisle while they casually check an item forty feet away; or coagulations of several couples in their happy encounters clogging the main arteries. Despite the widest berths in the American shopping experience, it's virtually unnavigable.

I strategize a route through the lowest population density: protein powders, canned fruit, along the side wall to the bottled drinks. When I arrive, there are already two relatively attractive girls blocking my access to the Nesquik display. They're having a hushed conversation about price per serving and where they could find it cheaper in town. Everything about the scene is just . . . wrong. I've never seen a girl in her twenties buy Nesquik before. I've never seen a girl in her twenties publicly fret about price per serving, let alone two girls in their twenties publicly fretting about price per serving. They're not dressed like thrift and economy are life's major concerns. They don't have a cart; they, like me, came to Costco for just Nesquik? Could saving a couple of cents per serving be worth the gas and time to get it elsewhere? It seems very waxy and staged.

I approach circumspectly.

I'm about to violate personal space with my cart when they both turn and look at me. At a distance they were relatively attractive, up close they are *extremely* attractive. Which makes this encounter a bona fide parody.

"Sorry, ladies, I just need to grab one."

They both shuffle back a step without a word. One of the girls is staring at me with a degree of unmasked awe. She glances back at the other, then back to me.

The less impressed says, "Don't, sis."

"What? You're the one telling me I need to be more assertive."

This is either a Mero orchestration or one of Patch's dramas. I might as well just kick up my feet and settle in. "I'm sorry, did I intrude on something?"

"My sister says I should be more assertive with guys, but I guess she meant when *she's* not around."

"Let's just go, Bree."

I'm curious, so I pry. "What is your assertiveness telling you to do?"

She stands up straighter and shows a little conviction as she lays out her plan, "Get your number. You're a fit, attractive guy, and, according to your ring finger, you're single." <<How do girls notice this stuff?>> "I thought, if I'm not unattractive to you, maybe we could go out some time."

"Fit and attractive?"

"Yeah, fit and attractive."

"Well, that's more flattery than I deserve, I'm sure, but I do have a girlfriend. I do commend you for your courage and always welcome the flattery, but I am spoken for."

"Girlfriends come and go, you know. In my experience, if you're not married, you're single."

"If you were my girlfriend, you wouldn't mind if I gave a beautiful girl my number?"

She's paying less attention to my point than to my implication of her beauty.

I lower my volume a little and step a foot closer. "I've been having these dreams over the past couple of months about this girl I've never met or seen before. Weird dreams and weird situations. I'm either saving her from falling or we're creating civilizations together, but in all these dreams I can't really tell where she stops and I start. There's no clear division between us as . . . I don't know, entities. It's like we overlap or move through each other or something. It's strange. But we're always somehow tethered to one another. Sometimes I'll say something but it comes out in her voice. Sometimes she'll think something and I'll know it was my thought. Sometimes I even feel like we're just one being. Everything about her is this magnificent improvement of me and I'm this magnificent improvement of her. We are this endless, boundless force. I hesitate using the pronoun *we*, because I can't tell if that *we* is just an inexplicable *I*."

The sister has this twist about her face, like she's mad that I'm about to make her cry.

"The strangest part is, and it's totally impossible and unbelievable, but I met her the other day. I don't know how things like this work, but she's real. She's a real person and I met her. She's even more magnificent in person than in the dreams." <<I can hear my voice drifting away and nostalgic.>> "She has this black hair that moves like the ocean and these eyes that look like black pearls. And her voice is like that lingering breeze after a thunderstorm. You know how you meet some people and immediately forget every stupid thing you ever cared about? You just want to pour everything you are into this person because their happiness has an easy reciprocity to it."

My arms are getting involved now. "I'm just this lone, fraction of a being muddling through his days that happened to stumble on his reciprocal, his perfect compliment. She's everything I'm not in the best possible way."

The sister is pushing tears back up the sides of her nose.

Ms. Assertive has defeat and a miserable sort of envy in her voice. "Okay, I get it. I get it." She takes her sister by the hand and starts to lead her away.

"Also, ladies, next time somebody puts you up to something like this, you should hold out for more money."

They resume their departure, shoulders not quite as square.

Okay, then, where was I? Nesquik . . .

DAY 70

Chapter 82

"Life is like an onion; you peel it off one layer at a time, and sometimes you weep."
– Carl Sandburg

I have to wait for Mom to chew her bite of pasturage, swallow, and wash the residual down with water so she doesn't choke when I tell her about my date tomorrow. I don't know if it's the poor air quality here, but this is the third woman that has cried or nearly cried in my presence in the past week. I'm very attentive to my oral health, so I don't think it's that.

She puts her silverware down and lowers her head. Oh, no. Her whole upper half is inflating and deflating with some theater. Is she having an episode? "Are you okay?"

She gets out of her chair, walks around the table to me, and puts her twiggy arms around me. "This is all I've ever wanted—grandchildren."

"I'm pretty sure I said *date* and not *grandchildren*."

"Just be quiet and let me enjoy this."

I pat her shoulder and realize there's some chiseled girth in there, not just the skin-insulated bone my pin-pricked organs were bracing for. "What's going on *here*? Doing some water aerobics or something?"

She has that how-dare-you look. "Water aerobics . . . I'm in my fifties, Elliot, not my eighties. I started going to a kickboxing gym."

I assume she's kidding and leave it at that. There's a fair chance she's not kidding.

She thought Peyton sounded delightful and said as much at least thirty times. The thing she was most curious about was why I was doing yoga.

Chapter 83

"You can't wait for inspiration. You have to go after it with a club."
– Jack London

I wrenched my neck in class today. Why did I have to flush *all* the pain killers down the drain? Three certainly can't kill me. I was admiring <<ogling, if I'm being honest>> Peyton while all my limbs were splayed hither and yon. Serves me right for being so interested <<lusty>>.

I can see the road of my life forking again. I really hate forks, but my mind tends to polarize everything into mutual exclusivities, so I can't see anything but rights and lefts. All of my being fibers are shrieking, "Linebacker!" and all the same being fibers are shrieking, "Peyton!" I don't have enough time to pursue both so I just need to pick a side and commit. Although, here's this <<epiphany!>>: I could just use the activities of the Manuscript as date ideas. Maybe Peyton would be willing to do them with me. Then I wouldn't have to lay one on the altar as a sacrifice to the other. It's a bi-bird murder stone! I like this idea. I was wondering how I was going to keep her interested in me.

Though I feel this obligation to Patch, and I'm sure Peyton was somehow factored into his equations, getting on with my life has a higher probability of success than timing the collision of fired bullets to die and resurrect. If it has to be one or the other, it's Peyton. <<Though, hearing myself say that, have I not considered that by abandoning the Manuscript, the thing that brought us together, I may be losing Peyton as well? How terrifyingly annoying this all is.>>

I should get some sleep. Big day tomorrow.

DAY 71

Chapter 84

"Dating is pressure and tension. What is a date, really, but a job interview that lasts all night."
– Jerry Seinfeld

I pull into the Death by Yoga parking lot in my venomous snakeskin, roid-raged, toothless linebacker, testosterone machine, feeling the muscles of my shoulders and biceps and chest thicken, certain I could snap the mountains in half, and I'm immediately reduced to a chunk of banana suspended in a Jell-O mold. This is the first time I've seen her with her hair down. She's in jeans. She's smiling. I'm trying to breathe all the looming heartbreak out of my chest.

I'm the kind of guy that believes that everything he's associated with, and the condition of everything he's associate with, is a reflection of his character, so I spent a couple of hours detailing what amounts to my resume. The new car smell doesn't hurt.

I pull up beside her and make sure the passenger side door is locked. I don't want her subverting my limited opportunities for chivalry. I walk coolly, gut in, chest out, shoulders back, around the front of the truck.

I try to affect my voice so I don't sound as smitten as I am. "You look simply jaunty this morning."

"Is jaunty good?"

"It is when *I* use it."

With a little flair, I open her door, which I forgot to unlock. So I apologize all the way back to the other side of the truck and demand she not let herself in. I offer my arm so she can clamber into the Mount Olympus that is my truck.

"This is definitely a man's vehicle. Other than it being spotless."

"Yeah, I figured since I was a man I might as well drive a man's vehicle." <<I don't mention the effeminate red blob of a cheerleader car this vehicle replaced.>>

"Did you just buy this for our date? It smells brand new."

"Would that be weird if I did?"

She nods. "So where are we off to? What's the big secret?"

"We'll get there when we get there! Wait, what was the question?"

"So help me, Dillinger!"

I can tell she's at ease and a little excited. It's easy to be at ease in your element and in public encounters that can be egressed easily, but she's trapped in this vehicle with me for an indeterminate duration and has no idea where we're going, and she's still at ease. I don't want to read in to things, but that indicates some level of trust or asylum. And I love that she calls me Dillinger. The last time I answered to that name was when my high school football coach would whip me up into an offense-devastating frenzy.

"Before I answer that, I just don't want you to be freaked out about all the weirdness that will be your day today. I don't mean that what we're going to be doing is weird, but I somehow attract weirdness. It seeks me out. And usually finds me. I'm probably making it worse just saying that."

"Don't worry about weirdness. My dad was a professional celebrity impersonator. One of my brothers is a professional ventriloquist. My mom wrote children's books that don't have any words. My little sister is a state-level accordion player. It doesn't get any weirder than that."

Now *I'm* worried.

"Out of curiosity, is there any specific weirdness I'm supposed to look out for?" she asks.

"Nope. Just general weirdness. Except the Russians. But they're more Russian than weird. And Frenchmen feigning interest in me. That gets weird sometimes. Have you ever personally, in person, seen a man with a handlebar mustache curled at the ends?"

"Not in real life, no."

"Then maybe look out for that. They multiply around me."

"Handlebar mustaches, Russians, and French stalkers, good to know. That doesn't sound too bad. I like a little variety."

As we westerly I-80 ourselves out of the city, our conversation settles into a giant beanbag chair and we just enjoy each other without airs or audiences. I keep the topics wrapped tightly around Peyton, mostly because she has an interesting story. I find myself a sinking, jejune topic. In order to understand a client's expectations and requirements, I have become conversational in most disciplines and a maven in the art of intelligent, conversation-extending inquiry. From the outside, one would mistake it for nerves, but I'm excessively interested in figuring out how this girl found her way into my dreams. I should probably pace myself though—I don't want to run out of things to talk about. Me and my hatred of conversational quiets and all.

Civilization has all but vanished away in the mountains-obstructed rearview mirror. Utah is revealing its true desert identity with its earthy drabs and furrowed hills.

"The gods are smiling on us today."

"Oh?"

"It's supposed to be near record highs where we're going, low-sixties it says. Ground temperature, at least."

"Opposed to . . . subterranean temperature?"

I dip my head under my windshield's upper limit and clarify, "Well, it'll be about thirty degrees cooler where we're going, so every little bit helps."

She glances up in case I was looking at something specific. Then the light goes on. "Are you taking me skydiving? Are you freaking taking me skydiving, Dillinger?"

A decompression needle punctures the apprehension I've been amassing from the moment such foolhardiness entered the first date pros-cons deliberation. Skydiving on a first date . . . impolitic! Her excitement is that hissing of decompression.

"Oh, Hannah be hailed, I thought that proposition might blow up in my face."

"Are you kidding? I've always wanted to go skydiving!"

She unbuckles her seat belt, summits the center console, and hugs my right arm with nearly the whole upper half of her body. "Thank you, thank you, thank you! This is going to be so great!"

My past, present, future, my heritage, my destiny, my soul and body all want to do something to reciprocate the affection, but my prevailing cooler heads just freeze me in a Peyton-appreciating paralysis. I already dread having to quit her for the day. How do I go from thunderously, agonizingly alone to this sense of full integration in weeks? Whoever's behind it, it's genius.

Peyton is singular. She is unabashedly faithful to the rudiments and shreds of which she is comprised. All of which are highest grade and finest quality. After her display of gratitude, she settles back into her seat, buckles her seat belt, and, with sugar-spiked animation, tells me about the time her parents bought her a gift certificate to go skydiving but the company went out of business the day before she went to cash it in. I have to keep reminding myself that this is not one of the dreams.

"So you're an adventurous one, are you?" I ask.

"Adventurous is my other middle name."

"What is your other *other* middle name?"

She giggles. "Gail."

"Just . . . Gail?"

"Gail . . . ord Perry?"

"Whoa, how do you know who Gaylord Perry is?"

"How do you, more like! I grew up in San Diego. We're big Padres fans."

"You like baseball?"

"No, I mean the hockey team, the Padres."

Snarky.

"Peyton, you're a girl that likes baseball! I would say you're a unicorn, but I seriously hate the overuse of that analogy. So, you're like . . . an alligator with a tough, twisty horn coming out of its head!"

"An alligator?"

"It's like a unicorn, only scalier and can't run as fast."

"I don't know if I like being a slow, scaly unicorn."

"You'd rather be a horse unicorn with azoturia?" I say. "Horses get that, you know."

"Are those my only two options?"

"Yes."

"Surely there are sloth unicorns."

"I thought you said you were afraid of sloths."

"Well, yeah, but not sloth *unicorns*. They're quite friendly," she says.

Her wit makes this conversation feel like it was scripted, like we're mouthing each other's words when it's not our turn to speak.

The sun has monopolized the sky. It's the middle of January and it's sixty-two degrees in Wendover. I consider the possibility that Patch orchestrated these conditions. There are no irrational considerations anymore.

I can see my comrades loitering at the fence as we pull into the airfield's parking lot. Dimitriy is noticeably more jazzed about our arrival than the others, but they all look somewhat amused.

They all approach howling, "Peyton! Dyevushka!" Despite thick Russian accents, I tell her I have no idea who they are and she should just ignore them. She looks at me like I surprised her with a pony and she wants to run to it.

"If you must. Make sure you give them all high-fives—they like high-fives."

She finds all the handles and running boards and rungs and platforms to descend the truck <<because it is a process>>. I don't think I've ever seen someone beam like she's beaming. The sleeves of her sweatshirt are pulled up over her hands and she has them pressed against her face. I can't see her mouth but her cheeks invading her eyes divulge a smile. She gives them all an energetic high-five. She truly is everything I am not.

"You are the famous Peyton that Naslednik tells to us! We are meeting you in great honor!"

Yuri cleans it up. "It's a pleasure to meet you, Peyton." He points to the others, "Dimitriy, Ivan, Sasha. We should get going. If we leave Dimitriy in one place for too long, his exuberance gets us in trouble."

She glances back at me with a smile as wide and bright as the sky itself.

We follow the Russians down to the Enola Gay Hangar for training.

Rapture is bursting out of Peyton's casual tone. "They seem fun."

"You have no idea."

"How did you find these guys?"

"They trained me."

"You've done this before?"

"Oh, yes. In fact, I'll be training you."

"Really? You are full of surprises, Dillinger."

"It's a recent development."

"Will I also be hooked to you for the jump?"

I'm Dimitriy this time. "No hook to! We don't do hook to! Peyton like free bird first time!" <<Free beard fierce time.>>

"Wait, I'm jumping on my own?"

"Well, we'll all be there with you, but, yeah, you're on your own. Hope that's okay."

"That is awesome beyond awesome! I don't need no stinking tandem!" She rolls her upper body into a coil, squeals, and then unwinds. "Don't they frown on that for first-timers?"

"We're kind of a rogue outfit. Good or bad, we're accountable to no one."

"Yes! You did good, Dillinger. This is going to be so cool."

I love her fearless grace. My mind keeps saying *adorable*, but she's something profoundly more virginal <<not in a sexual way, but more like sheltered, preserved aristocracy>> and with provenance. Again, everything I am not. A perfect stranger infiltrates her yoga world only two weeks ago and now has her in a memorialized hangar <<that even looks like a hideout used to plan a ransom collection>> at a nowhere airfield with a bunch of even stranger Russians about to toss her into the open throat of the troposphere, and she's so exultant she's biting her bottom lip and her legs are bouncing like a Neil Peart solo. I admire this level of trust because I am trustworthy; as a general trait imparted to the rest of humanity, it horrifies me.

I run her through all the same drills on which I was raised in this venture. She's rattling back the instructions vocally and molding her body into perfect anatomies of mid-air renderings. Her flexibility is in no way distracting. I think she might be hustling me though with the whole yoga instructor thing—she's infinitely more intelligent than I am and concretes the abstract before you can say Jack Robinson. Maybe that's just yoga's natural corollary—training your body to be your brain. I do envy that; other than tracking Walter Paytons through the chain-link fence of an offensive line, I lack that faculty. However, if we, together, are to be a totality, I can at least console myself with a thirty percent contribution. You can't be everything, after all.

I watch her as we climb to sixteen thousand feet. She's about to make her maiden plunge into the unsupported and there is no hint of nervousness. Is it obliviousness or fearlessness or implicit trust? Not that any of them would bother me—it beats overthinking, terror, and cynicism. She's having a happy conversation with all four of the Russians and somehow including each of them individually. She seems to have stumbled onto a topic about which they're all passionate <<either soccer or Russian politics>>. Yuri most of all; and Yuri is as Russianly dispassionate as they come. I know I've already been to the heights of the heavens, so I know what that's like, but if there was a cloud higher than nine, that's where I'm at. Over the moon, maybe?

Sasha rolls the door up. Now I'm nervous *for* her. I don't recall Dimitriy telling Peyton that she'd leeyive. Please don't die today, Peyton.

As she jumps, as we join her, as we stabilize her, as we rehearse the chute deployment in freefall, I have that strange sensation of seeing myself. It's like my vision is glitching and I replace her every eighth frame. This time my hallucinations feel like a conspiracy, like a malevolent prefiguring. The whole sky is laughing at what's about to happen. An unwarranted dread presses on my chest like I'm freefalling through the plum viscidity of the bottomless pit. I need to get it together so my date doesn't meet an untimely black lambda.

She's watching me, awaiting my signal. It might have been a bad idea for me to direct—my ability to justify staring at her has me in a precarious trance. I hold up my fist: three . . . two . . . one . . . We retreat, she waves everybody away, then she disappears. As smooth as yoga.

Dimitriy, Yuri, and I deploy so we can stay with Peyton in the air; Ivan and Sasha deploy late so they're available for her on the ground. Within a few seconds we skirt her in the hems and seams of some of the Eastern Hemisphere's greatest skydiving talent, so I feel better about the situation. Even in that open throat of the voracious, sound-gulping sky, I can hear her exploring the walls of our tutelary vesicle with all her hooting and yelping, the volume of which is unreasonable for someone her size. I want to tell her to cool it so the Russians don't fall in love with her too, but I'm too busy indulging in the indulgence.

I can see her pacing in a circle while Ivan and Sasha follow behind and gather up her entrails.

She takes a big breath and shouts, "So great! That was so great!"

I hardly get my feet on the ground and she wraps me in a bear hug—meaning her hands barely make it to the lateral extents of my back. Half of her face is buried in my chest so I only get half comprehension. "Elliot! That was unbelievable!" She grabs my suit at the shoulders and tries to shake me but only shakes herself and yells, "Unbelievable!" like each syllable is its own word. Then she's back to pacing in a circle.

My comrades are respectfully, voicelessly nodding at my triumph. Dimitriy sneaks up to me and gives me a high-five.

"Peyton?"

"Yes, Elliot? Elliot, that was unbelievable!"

I've graduated from Gigantor to Dillinger to Elliot. Hopefully this lasts long enough for me to find out what follows in this evolution.

"It was unbelievable, yes, but you may want to save some energy for round two."

She snaps to attention with her index fingers centered on a face-splitting smile. "For real? We can go again?"

We're all just standing there, grinning at the show that is Peyton.

"Well, what are we waiting for, people? Move it!"

And then we go again.

We only ended up going twice in all; everything was so perfect the second time, I didn't want to jinx it. This time she hugged everyone at touchdown. I thought, from the amount of graphically sexual profanity they use, they would have been a little less mousy about a hug from a cute girl. Except Dimitriy, who picked her up, thrashed her about, and nearly squeezed the juice out of her.

The Russians did well. She gained four big brothers that will go to the ends of the Earth for her. The intensity of loyalty <<worship?>> Patch garnered <<garners, not dead>> puts him in the demigod category.

All the way home, Peyton was cramming me into her brain with breathless paragraphs, regaling me with the nuances of every observation, perception, and consideration from airborne to grounded. I was grateful for her seatbelt or she may have spider monkeyed her way around the cab in heedless revolutions. And I thought border collies had a lot of energy. <<She would have liked Patch. Immensely.>> I'm starting to see our lopsided reciprocity, our 60/40, as it were, in a kind of inverse proportionality—her rapture is paradoxically soothing. All social, conversational, body linguistic, and expressive expectations are muted by her un-paused, fast-forwarded, maniacally gesticulated narrative. Experiencing this level of structural happiness is satisfying. *Balances are always preferable to a party of unbridled, visceral vomit!*

Pulling into the parking lot of Death by Yoga switches her off and she sits there quietly, looking toward the darkened western sky over which she had so recently lorded. It's a natural conversational stop sign, your final destination, but, juxtaposed with two hours of mania, her silence sounds like sadness in the void. Maybe it just seems so because we're about to part ways.

My butterfingered desperation wants to prolong the date somehow, but I know that will just expose my butterfingered desperation. Thankfully she cuts the thought off at the knees.

"Okay, Dillinger," <<crap, we're back to Dillinger>> "you're off the hook. You're all paid up. That was super, super fun, the best way to go skydiving. The best first date ever. But don't feel like you have to—"

I reach over and wrap what looks like an animal paw around her diminutive forearm before she can finish whatever stupid thing she was about to say. All of my features are engaged in lacerating eye contact. "I'll see you on Monday."

She flashes a smile that I think means *I was hoping you'd say that.*

"Stay right there!"

I slide to the ground, jog to her door, and help her find all the grips and grapples to the ground. As soon as she finds her footing, she tries harder to reach my spine and buries her body into the bottom two-thirds of mine. I don't freeze this time, but my body's trying to take me down from its chemical overwhelmedness. She's so small I can overlap my arms and reach opposing shoulders. Then, without analysis or pageantry or expectation, she just bounces away. I'm not a kiss on the first date kind of guy <<I've never actually kissed a girl, so I don't know that for sure>>, so I'm disappointedly grateful for the unruffled obviation.

After a safe distance, she turns, "Oh, also, thanks for being such a patient and polite driver. I like that in a man. Very gentlemanly. Made me feel safe." Then bouncing.

Uh oh.

CHAPTER 85

"You know you're in love when you can't fall asleep because reality is finally
better than your dreams."
– Dr. Seuss

I'm in bed. My eyes are burning even though they're closed. Everything about
me is asleep except my consciousness, which is doing burpees at the moment.
What is it called when you do burpees and cartwheels at the same time? Carpees.
I'm staring at a text I just wrote and trying to convince myself to delete it. I hate
having these contests with my ambivalence; so much time wasted second-guess-
ing, overthinking, doubting. Even that overdose dilemma seemed simpler. The
fiftieth iteration of the text reads:

Ms. Peyton, thanks for the unrivaled fun today. I know this violates all courting etiquette, but if you're not otherwise engaged tomorrow afternoon, would
you be interested in joining me for lunch at my home at 11:00 a.m.? I make some
mean mashed potatoes. No biggie if you have other plans. Or if you just plain
don't want to come. I know it's short notice.

Should I not shove this process along? Is this too much too soon? Did that
last part lack confidence?

Sending it is edging out not sending it only because I'm convinced nothing
is really permanent or immutable in the Patchiverse. And because of the dreams.
My gut tells me that our intersection is packed deep in inaccessible layers of
time. If she says no, I retreat to a position of patience and coast. I have the luxury
of time after all.

I hit send, mute the volume, and place the phone face down on my nightstand.
I don't want to know.

Within ten seconds my nightstand growls. Apparently vibrate isn't considered volume. A response is a promising sign, right? But a quick response? It's
like a jury taking twenty minutes to return a verdict. It's never good. Again, all
appendages of all matters of the heart are a map with only my native city chart-
ed. And I just wandered into the farmland outside of town.

I'm back in the mire of ambivalence. I don't want to look. I have to look.
Come on, Elliot, get a grip on yourself and snap out of it! I'm always ashamed
of myself when I consider how Patch would handle these situations. It wasn't
so much that he was fearless, he had somehow forgotten that fear should be
a consideration. And he loved unraveling things in a manner that enriched all
involved. He was the gentlest of cattle catchers and never had cause to apologize or regret. Why can't I think like that? *Be of good courage, and let us play
the men for our people, and for the cities of our God: and the Lord do that which
seemeth him good.* Yeah, that sounds good.

Peyton: u have a <<house emoji>>?

I'm not sure what the connotation is there. I feel like I'm taking too much time overthinking this. My reflex is sarcasm or a Your Mom joke, but I fear either might be bridge-toppling demolitions with a female acquaintance of a mere two weeks.

Me: I do.

Then: ofc i'll be there idiot. u had me @ <<potato emoji >>.

Oh. Okay. That wasn't so hard. I don't know if the name-calling was altogether necessary.

My response: Great. I've needed an excuse to fire up the grill. I have bottled water, but if you're one of those people that feels like they have to bring something and you're not a water person, bring drinks. Just no Mountain Dew. I'm in a program.

Peyton: program? can't w8 to hear about that. cu @ 11.

Now I'm stressed about whether I should respond to that or not.

DAY 72

CHAPTER 86

"I've been living alone so long, everything about me's private. I'm surprised
anyone's able to understand a word I say."
– *Mother Night*, Kurt Vonnegut

I'm staring at her through the peephole wondering how long I can get away
with this before she gives up and leaves. Seriously, she makes Aphrodite look
like a gorgon hag with bad acne. She's in a dress. Why is she in a dress? Did I
imply formal? Am I now too informal?

"Well, hello, Ms. Peyton. Come in. Sorry I took so long, I was actually just
staring at you through the peephole." <<Marinate, Elliot! You have to let those
thoughts marinate!>> As inappropriate as it might be, these unfiltered moments
are hilarious to me and I have to engage in these weird behavioral ensembles to
choke down the laughter without upping the jig. Some laugh at people that fall
down stairs or on ice and hurt themselves; I laugh when my thoughts assume a
voice.

"Boys are so funny."

"I had to make good and sure it was you and not that Peyton impostor that
roams around my neighborhood, randomly ringing doorbells. She's so annoying. Make yourself at home. Bathroom is right there on the right if that's something you eventually need. Cherry Coke, good pick. I'll fridge that joint."

"Elliot, this place is a palace!"

"Really?"

"I live in a shoebox with a roommate that never leaves the apartment. And I
think she has that fish odor syndrome. Or just never showers. It's so disgusting.
People are so disgusting."

"I'm definitely not trying to one up that, but I'd take living with someone
over living with no one. It gets a little lonely around here sometimes."

"Well, you have me now. I'll take this place over shoebox with stinky girl any
day of the week."

I know she's just making casual conversation but the glibness of those words
is grinding me to a hope-chasing powder. As a pathological people pleaser, if
I have the means to help, I want to help, but I can't think of anything more
excruciating than living with Peyton as a roommate. I have to choose my words
carefully here.

"You're welcome any time."

Her eyes bounce off of me with a sort of desperate hopefulness and she
wanders further into my living room.

"You look very nice all dressed up, if I may say."

"Oh, yeah, this, I came straight here from church. Didn't want to go back to
my apartment. I thought I'd bring the stink with me if I set foot in that place."

"You go to church?"

"Yeah. It's Utah. Most people go to church here."

"Could I go to church with you?" I honestly wouldn't care what we were doing, I just want to be around her.

"Maybe, if you had all your demons exorcised first, like with that forehead-slapping 'Demons Out!' thing."

My face spills into an arrangement of drooping openings. She looks so serious it doesn't occur to me that she might be kidding. Like I said, I'm not used to this quick draw wit.

"You should see your face."

"You are so mean."

She laughs a disbelieving laugh.

"But, for real, can someone do that 'Demons Out!' thing to me?"

"Maybe. But not at my church."

"Not to change the subject, meanie, but everything is ready to eat if you're hungry. I'm not trying to rush, but I do like eating hot food hot."

She's trying to squeeze her eyebrows into her upper lip and she says, "Your house is spotless. You have food ready for your guests when they arrive. You're single, you're not at all attractive and you have a house. You were normal all day yesterday. What's your story, Elliot Dillinger?"

For some reason, when she said the words *Elliot Dillinger*, the mortifying realization that my gratitude list, fraught with Peyton references <<some bordering on lewd>>, was hanging on my fridge blasted through me like a razor-sharp nor'easter.

"Hold that thought!" I dash to the fridge, tear the list down, and run to my bedroom. "Sorry about that, secret time travel documents and stuff," I explain when I get back.

That stunt might have soiled all of her positive observations.

"I noticed yesterday you were pretty good at deflecting attention away from yourself. I don't think you're going to get away with that today."

"Deal. Anything you want to know."

"What was that on the fridge?"

"Anything you want to know but that."

"Dillinger . . . I got all dressed up for you today."

"I thought you went to church?"

"Dillinger . . ."

Patchiverse: nothing permanent or immutable. I trudge the long walk of shame back to my bedroom and retrieve the gratitude list. A little honesty never killed a relationship, right? <<That's probably the number one killer of relationships.>> But can you really call ours a relationship? We've been on one date. Please don't misinterpret this list, Peyton.

"I will absolutely show this to you if you sit through the backstory first. It won't make much sense without the backstory. Even with the backstory you may still have some concerns. But, again, anything you want to know. To my detriment, I'm sure. I'm a pathologically private person, but you don't seem petty or vindictive, so I'm okay sharing. I'm really not okay sharing, but I'll share. Just with you. It's pretty embarrassing. I'm a very private person. Did I say that already? Your church teaches you to be merciful, yes? This would be a good time to show the world what you've learned. Lots and lots of mercy."

Her smile is stretching by magnitudes as I ramble on. "Mercy and understanding. And maybe some brotherly kindness. There's something in the Bible about brotherly kindness. And patience. Just overall non-judgmentality as much as you're able. I have good reasons for everything on that list."

"Okay, shut up now!"

"Okay, I'm done. Remember mercy. Mercy and understanding."

"Let's eat."

She's a healthy eater. That's my polite way of saying she can pack it away. I nailed it with steak and potatoes, I guess. She closes her mouth when she chews unless she's talking, then she urbanely covers her mouth with the thumb side of her knife hand while she speaks. You can tell she comes from a big family because she surrounds her plate with one forearm and keeps the other, the one armed with a fork, elbow-on-table and stab-ready. She's perfect.

I talk while she eats. "This isn't for pity or anything, but my dad died when I was thirteen. He was in the army, died in Afghanistan. He was hit by an IED. My grandad, my dad's dad, kind of took over the father role until I was close to eighteen. He was amazing. He was a lot like you. You would have loved him. He would have loved you. He's like no one you've ever met, by ranks and degrees. Well, he died a few months ago, too. I went to his funeral. He did amazing things."

I can feel my chest and throat trying to squeeze tears out so I have to pause between sentences. <<What ninny cries on a second date?>>

"The Russians, they were very loyal to Grandad. He was Scottish and they use grandad rather than the American versions. They're quite strict about that. I normally called him Patch, but that's a whole story itself. Anyway, when he died he made me executor of his will. One of the things he left me was a manuscript he drafted himself. It's like a self-improvement program. Maybe more like a character building program. Apparently I didn't have much character."

Her silverware is down, her elbows are on the table, her hands are curled backwards at the wrists and tucked into her neck. She's watching me intently. I can only maintain eye contact for brief blinks or Aphrodite 6.0 will derail my train of thought. That kind of beauty is the embodiment of a tension pneumothorax, an alien invasion, and the end of *Terms of Endearment*.

"It was his dying wish that I follow this manuscript, this program, to the letter. He really saved my life when I needed a dad, so I feel like I owe him this. Every Saturday or thereabouts I'm given an assignment that I have to work on. Sometimes it's just a one-time thing, something he wants me to experience. Sometimes it's a skill I have to develop. The first assignment was to start a gratitude list and add to it as often as possible, any time I encountered something I was grateful for. For which I was grateful." <<I gesture to the ceiling; I'll get it one day, Patch.>> "This is my gratitude list."

"Is it personal?"

"Quite."

I can feel my shoulders and elbows shaking a little, like I'm bracing for someone to stick me with a one-gauge needle. I thought, for sure, she would respect my privacy, but, instead, she holds her hand out. I've realized in my limited interaction with people that being an only child has denied me familiarity with most human proclivities. People develop normal behaviors when they're stuck in ecosystems with similarly-aged peers with whom they don't have to pander to too much diplomacy. Dealings with parents and adults is, in most respects, the opposite. I got a lot of practice with deference and politeness and respectfulness, but very little with arguing and brutal honesty and thickening skin. And friends, even good friends, don't come close enough. You're not stuck in a house with them day in and day out, forced to put up with, forced to play nice. She clearly comes from a big family.

I hand the list over. She takes it but doesn't look at it, just stares at me for a few seconds. A long few seconds. I think she's surprised I actually handed it over. Since I don't feel like I have anything else to say, I just stare back and take snapshot after snapshot of that gorgeous, flawless, heart-stopping face with the swells and surf of her hair abiding its boundaries.

"I think I'm on assignment number ten now. From the look of it, I'm about halfway through. I've had to take a break for a couple weeks because of unforeseen . . . uh . . . diversions."

"I'm assuming that's a reference to me," she says while flipping through the pages.

"Yes and no. But mostly yes."

She chuckles at some, some depress her eyebrows a little, she nods at some. "So the truck *is* new. Dig up Patch's body? Pacific Ocean . . ." She's getting to the end and my heart is contracting so hard I can feel a pulse in my knees. Remember, Peyton, mercy!

She mutters, "Yoga pants," and smiles. When she gets to the end, her eyes start jumping back to earlier entries, then she covers her mouth and hides her face behind the list. Her breath starts stuttering, she's sniffing, and she sneaks her napkin behind the paper.

Oh, no. Crying is not good. Crying is bad. All crying is bad, but *really* bad when I can't tell if it's happy or sad crying. Or even *angry* crying. I can't even think of why happy crying would be good right now.

"Oh, Peyton, please tell me you're not crying. I don't know what to do when people cry."

Her words are coming at me from the sides of the list. "Don't worry about it! You're fine. There's nothing to do. Just wait it out. I'm fine."

I obey. I don't really see an alternative. I'm too afraid to ask her what caused the tears. Which shouldn't matter, because I don't want to know anyway.

She's fanning her face with the list and I get brief glimpses of her face at the extent of each swipe. "I just really like your handwriting," she says while she recovers.

I'm audibly chuckling. Again, she's everything I'm not.

"So . . . what does the Mountain Dew have to do with this? According to this list you seem pretty grateful for Mountain Dew."

"One of the later assignments was to give up my most prominent vice."

Her voice is still a little weepy as she says, a little dumbstruck, "Mountain Dew is your most prominent vice?"

"I guess. Other than, like, your typical human frailties—pride and vanity and impatience and stuff."

She comes out from behind the list and hands it to me. The napkin is damp and mascara-scarred.

"Sorry for that peek into an idiot's mind. Like my grandad would always say, *Your pain is self-inflicted.*"

She takes a circular, composure-recovering breath. "You don't need to apologize, believe me."

I restore the list to its home. "I'm telling you all this the long way around, I guess, to say that my Saturdays are pretty full."

"What other kind of assignments have you done? You said you're on ten. What were the other nine?"

"Oh, you want to see?"

"Of course."

I pull a deck of cards from my pocket <<gotta stay frosty for the Gontlets>>. I'm so excited for this. I've done this card trick, the Three Travelers, for the kids at the hospital with adult observers, but this is my first strictly adult audience. You can't be sloppy with adult audiences. They get eagle-eyed. And they spend the whole trick telling you how you're doing it <<and they're always wrong>>. Adults are annoying.

She's following my eyes as much as she's following my hands. When I'm done, I can't tell if she's unimpressed or just trying to work out how it was done. Her eyes just keep bouncing back and forth between my eyes and my hands.

She holds her silence much longer than my other victims.

"Okay, hold on. Here's something else . . ." I lay down on my living room carpet and instruct her to time me. I drag my inhalations all the way to the top and my exhalations to the bottom for a dozen cycles, then give her the signal. It turns out to be an uncomfortably long three minutes and fifteen seconds.

"Did you just hold your breath for over three minutes?"

"Yeah. That was another one of the assignments."

"So, his dying wish was for you to do card tricks and hold your breath for long periods of time?"

Without the context of the Gontlets, it does sound a little useless. "Well . . .yeah. But it's more about the process than the activity itself. You learn a lot about patience and discipline when you take the time to develop these skills."

"Okay, I can see that."

"Also, I was trained how to beat a polygraph test, learning to skydive is part of it, I had to devise and implement the program at Primary Children's to read to the kids every week, stuff like that."

"It actually sounds like a lot of fun, like a scavenger hunt every week. What is the next one?"

"I never know beforehand. I find out on Saturdays when I read the next assignment."

"You never read ahead?"

"Never. I was instructed not to or it would spoil the intent of the program."

"That, in itself, is discipline. I always read the last page of books first. Well, so, are these assignments designed specifically for you or can I do them with you? They sound fun. And who couldn't do with some extra discipline and patience?"

And I thought I was going to have to spend the next few hours herding her to that conclusion. "Really? You would want to do this with me?"

"Unless you want this to be your thing. It won't hurt my feelings. I just thought you might want some company. And it sounds like fun."

"No, absolutely. I think that's a fantastic idea. I would love the company." I'm Agent Smith trying to stop Neo from exploding out of him. "It's just that . . ."

I let my sentence trail off for too long and now she has a brooding look of annoyance. "Out with it, Dillinger!"

"Well, I just don't want you to think you owe me anything for taking you skydiving. I don't want you to think you have to repay me with charity or anything. I'm a literal kind of person." I'm usually entertained when these unrestrained sentiments leak out, but I really wanted to punch whatever moronic third-person kept talking until that thought was finished.

"Skydiving? I *like* being around you, idiot! I like *you*. Now stop with the self-loathing and accept the fact that you're the kind of person that people like to be around. That *I* like to be around. Seriously, charity! I turned that date down, remember? Then I said yes and I didn't even know what we were doing. I know I made it sound like I came here today to escape stinky fish girl, but I was beside myself when you texted last night. Good men are hard to find, Elliot Dillinger. Those girls you do yoga with three times a week, I told them all to stay away from you or I'd cancel their memberships and ban them for life! You should hear them salivating over you behind your back! It's disgusting!"

<<There's that unlikely volume. And now yoga is going to be awkward.>>

"And you asked *me* out. Out of thirty girls, you asked *me*. You haven't said a single word to any girl there except *me*! Do you know how hard it is to find an attractive, fit, intelligent, fun, funny, normal, put-together guy that doesn't have a lot of baggage? And likes baseball? And reads to sick kids? And whose craziest addiction is Mountain Dew?" I want to answer, but my vanity is too busy humoring itself. "They don't exist! They're not sloth unicorns or alligator unicorns, they're actual horse unicorns! And then you just . . . and then you just . . . I think I've said too much already."

"No!" I startle her by how quickly and loudly that came out. "I mean, you can keep going if you want."

She grabs my arm, drags me to the couch, and sits me down. Then she plops herself down right next to me and rests her head on my shoulder. I notice that her head and my shoulder are the same size.

"Elliot."

"Peyton."

"We were destined to do this program together. You know it and I know it. Just say yes."

"I already said yes!"

"Say yes without suspicions or misgivings. Say yes because it's the right thing to do."

"Peyton, darling, I know I'm asking a lot, but would you be willing to participate in my grandad's strange character development program with me?" She doesn't immediately answer so I attach the addendum, "I promise it'll be fun."

"Only if you understand that I'm not doing it out of charity or kindness. I'm doing it because I like being around you. And I like your house. And those mashed potatoes *were* really good. I'm not even really that kind!"

"That's what I'm putting on your headstone, 'Here lies Peyton Gail . . . insert last name . . . the kindest person we know.'"

"I'll haunt you for the rest of your life if you do that. Is this whole thing your shoulder?"

"I think so."

She rests her contralateral hand on the crook of my elbow. My mind is a soup of disbelief. Everything about my life for the past couple of months has felt like a movie set. I badly want this to be an organic chaos that wasn't scripted or staged or rehearsed. Even if it's just this moment, I want something to be unquestionably authentic. The world can have everything else; I just want the extract of this ten seconds of being in love.

"Now that I've been properly set down, can I ask you something?"

"As long as it's a really good question that doesn't make you look stupid."

"So many rules . . ."

She squeezes my forearm.

"You had a lot of brothers, didn't you?"

"That's your question?"

"No. But you talk like a girl that had a lot of brothers, like you had to fight boys all the time to get your fair share."

"Three. All older. What's your real question?"

"When you said you don't date attractive guys, is that really why you initially said no when I asked you out?"

Her pause is so long I think she might have fallen asleep. "After showing me that gratitude list, I think you've earned my honesty, but I don't want to answer that question. Not yet."

"Why not?"

"Because if you don't think I'm weird now, you'll definitely think I'm weird after that answer. And I don't mean quirky weird, I mean entrapment weird, *Fatal Attraction* weird. Maybe another time."

"Okay."

"Maynes."

" . . . what is the hair called on a horse's neck? Are we playing jeopardy?"

She punches my shoulder with the pinkie side of her fist. "It's my last name, idiot. Peyton Gail Maynes."

I think of everything that rhymes with Maynes. Then I move to the initials to see if they're already an acronym for something or spell a word I can use as a future nickname. That's when it feels like all my skin shrinks. Her initials are PGM. PGM! Those were the initials on that stinking handkerchief the Mariner put in my spy suit! Damn it!

There goes a good night's sleep.

Chapter 87

"We must hurry. There is nothing to fear here."
"That's what scares me."
– Satipo and Indy, *Raiders of the Lost Ark*

It's that scene at the beginning of *Raiders of the Lost Ark* where Indiana Jones is squaring up against the golden idol. He pulls a bag of sand from his satchel, weighs it by heft, deems it excessive and empties it by a handful, crouches down, faces off, makes the switch with some delicacy, stands in the relief of victory, re-fits his wide-brimmed, high-crowned sable fedora and . . .

That's the frame I'm stuck in—looking around, unable to move, waiting for the pedestal to collapse, waiting for Peyton to figure out how out of my league she is, waiting for the darts and arrows to fly, waiting for something or someone to obliterate our acquaintance over a Carcassonnian midnight stroke, waiting for the stone chamber to topple down around us, waiting for any number of late arrivals on a train station split-flap display to clack to the surface and erase us.

The dreams, a flesh and blood reality, our chance <<masterminded by a living, conniving scamp!>> encounter, the farcically smooth transition from first sight to one flesh <<reading into things a little here>>, our interlaced, interwoven, interlocked, helicase-resistant pyrimidines and purines—it's all impossible and yet historical. Well, historical for the time being. This is a concept I cannot abide, this impermanence. I know Patch said the frameset wasn't as mercurial as hypothesis would suggest, but with all these unlikely encounters, I feel like I'm a knot to be untied and a shoe to be unlaced. I feel like I'm a target for these nightly revisions. I'm finally fixed in an airy satisfaction and I'm not able to enjoy it; I'm more stressed out than I was pre-Peyton.

I'm starting to see that Peyton isn't a sassy flirt at all, she's the kind of girl that grows into? settles into? a conviction and defends her position with a thousand cavalrymen. <<I was going to say *hoplites*, but that would be a badly mixed metaphor.>>

I just got a text from Mom:

Hello, my handsome son <<string of happy *emoticons*, as she calls them>>. How did your date go? When can I meet her? I don't see any harm in bringing her with you to lunch this Friday if she's available, do you? If it didn't go well, don't bring her. See you soon! <<Party hat, heart, thumbs up and smiley face emoticons.>>

DAY 74

Chapter 88

"Virtue is health, vice is sickness."
– Petrarch

I put all my vice energy eggs into one Mountain Dew basket, so I never really had the time or inclination to pursue any others. It was the center of my daily anticipation, and so satisfying that if I had any vice juice left, it was reserved for anticipating the next day's Mountain Dew.

Patch may have designed that temperance assignment for purpi related to the Gontlets, but I wonder if he foresaw to what extent this detoxification would be a vice unto itself. I know I'm working out daily and being in love is its own power plant, but the vitalization is more addictive than the vice itself. It's almost as though the act of *not* drinking Mountain Dew has become a more potent stimulant than the rush of the initial hit <<if I can call a sip of Mountain Dew a hit>>.

It's a good thing, too, because I've become a locomotive that departs at dawn and arrives at dusk.

DAY 76

CHAPTER 89

"Quarterbacks should wear dresses."
– Jack Lambert

I'm armchair quarterbacking the prudence of inviting Peyton to lunch last Sunday. Even though it was, by all accounts, a smashing success, I don't want to seem clingy. As she reports, she was beside herself when the invitation was extended, but she is a girl, and I'm sure she appreciates a chase rather than a manhunt, one that involves less sprinting. I saw her at yoga <<and I thought all those lusty broads were being nice because I was the new guy>> on Monday and Wednesday and thought that would redeem my weekend suffocation. But then I couldn't bear it another day, so I invited her to dinner before we went to Primary Children's. She said yes, if you can believe that.

Yoga has become the affirmation that things are still progressing. As long as those ten pre-departure minutes are playful and she says all her *Dillinger*s with an exclamation point, the train is still on the tracks.

We're at Fuji Sushi in Centerville. I hate spending money on food <<because Mountain Dew is $1.06 for 566 calories and has always been a superior meal replacement>> unless it's sushi. I don't know if it's justification for eating healthy or if eating sushi makes me feel swanky or because sushi is the supernal morsel of the divinities, but I'm at peace dropping a day's pay on a platter. And Peyton, bless her heart, loves sushi. We are MFEO.

We're waiting for our food and a wave of ice seems to roll up Peyton's lumbar, thoracic, cervical vertebrae. She stiffens, goes quiet, and smiles everything from stupefaction to amusement to skepticism. She snaps a finger and points at herself, evidently to converge all of my attention onto a singularity that happens to be her face.

"I feel like you're staging this to mess with me."

My head is having right-left convulsions as I say, "I'm sorry, I have not the pleasure of understanding you. Of what are you talking?"

"Don't look, but at your six o'clock, maybe your six-thirty, there's a guy" <<she nearly mouths the rest>> "with a handlebar mustache curled at the ends. Just as you predicted."

My sense of humor collapses into a volcanic sill and smoke twines in hypnotic helices out of my ears and nostrils. Every extra in my play, every uninvited cameo, every French accent, every accosting, every handlebar mustache, curled at the ends, is a potentially bad tomorrow. Amnesic, but disastrous.

I want to keep Peyton in the dark about the true nature of the Manuscript until I'm confident she won't turn me in to the FBI or have me committed or, worse, dump me. I can still feel the steam trying to find its way out of the helix/anti-helix maze of my ears and it's imperative that I stay ahead of these infuriations so they don't give my sourness arms and legs. And fists. Patch was fiery. Patch was wild. But he was a poet and a philosopher and a peacemaker, and if he was in this situation, he would . . . crap, what would he do? Anyway, maybe it's time to set a new standard: What would Elliot do? I'll tell you what Elliot would do, he would nip every Peyton-erasing threat in the bud with a smile and a handshake. <<My definition of handshake is very loose.>>

I politely excuse myself and walk directly to my loitering nemesis.

"I beg your pardon, sir . . ."

The mustachioed looks up from his book, *For Whom the Bell Tolls*, as deep-fried luck would have it. "Can I help you?"

"Nope. I just wanted to commend you for how brilliantly you pull that mustache off. Very classy."

"Thank you."

"High Life?"

He smirks. "High Life."

"I mean, you don't pull it off like the Cartographer did, but not bad."

His smirk deepens and thickens into an approving grin.

"Do you have something you want to tell me?"

Against all genteel social convention <<I'm getting used to this>>, he closes his book, gathers his coat, stands, and stares at me for some seconds before responding. "There are no allies and enemies in this game. Individuals have loyalties but they also have agendas, individual agendas. Consider yourself the bank that's lending to all participants in a world war. You're just concerned about the fees, interest, and foreclosures. A resolution to the conflict is not in your best interest. You don't know where you are yet, but you soon will. Then it will be less a matter of who to trust and more a matter of how to get them to trust *you*."

"Why didn't you just come up to me and say that? Why all the cloak and dagger?"

He peers around me at Peyton. "Just respecting your timetable. There's a lot at stake here. But he assured us that you'd . . . how did he put it? You would *Jack Lambert* the entire system. He sees you as some kind of Neo, somebody that doesn't open doors, but removes walls. There are a lot of unnecessary walls."

He tries to leave but I block his departure with my fit <<as everybody is calling it>> body. "Say my name. What's my name?"

He laughs something deep and rolling and plays along. "In Project Mayhem, we have no names, Elliot, you know that."

I walk back to Peyton like a freshly-fed zombie.

"What did you tell him?"

My response is a macerated jumble stuck in my teeth. "I told him he had an awesome mustache."

"And then . . . you just stared at him for like three whole minutes?"

"Well, I was asking him how he got it to look like that and stuff. Seemed affable. My grandad had a mustache like that. He used High Life."

"Are you going to confront everybody with a handlebar mustache, curled at the ends?" she asks.

"Every. Single. One. It's like an Easter egg hunt."

CHAPTER 90

"The soul is healed by being with children."
– Fyodor Dostoyevsky

"Filter in, filter in. Remember what that big octopus lady from *The Little Mermaid* said about lurking in doorways . . ."

I don't know what this is about, but every girl that comes in smiles and waves at Peyton. I've been doing this for weeks, these are my people, and Peyton gets all the waves and smiles on her first day? Though I didn't smile and wave when I first saw Peyton, the entirety of my animas and immaterials was doing airborne snow angels and radiating like an ecstatic idiot, so I get it.

There are fewer adults here today. Maybe they got the hint. There are a couple of dagger-staring, wallflower nurses trying to murder Peyton with the wrinkles on the bridge of their nose.

"Okay, so where did we leave off?"

A redheaded seven- or eight-year-old who has something taped to the outside of his nose points at Peyton and asks, "Who is she?"

"Who is who?"

"The girl sitting next to you. Who is she?"

I look to my right and left and question his vision. "You see someone sitting next to me?"

"She's right there! She has black hair! She's right next to you! Just reach your arm out and you'll feel her!"

I slowly stretch my arm in the wrong direction.

"Other side!"

I glance to my left and jump in my seat with a start. They think this is hilarious.

"Oh, yeah. Pardon my indecorous manners. Esteemed colleagues, this is Peyton. Peyton, this is . . . all the kids. Not in the world, but . . . in this room."

She waves and smiles a smile that eclipses the sun <<at least it would if it wasn't already dark out>> and rests its weight on that looming heartbreak. One of the nurses peels off the wall in the back and leaves the room in high dudgeon.

"Peyton is my bouncer. If she catches any of you poopin' around in here, she's going to sit on you."

"I will do no such thing. In fact," she shields her mouth with the back of her hand and whispers, "I'll probably give you five bucks!"

"Don't believe it! She owes the IRS six years in back taxes!"

For this I get slugged. I think the kids are more entertained by this production than the Dovolniya.

A little girl with braces and a sinister hairline asks, "Are you guys married?"

"Okay, let's not get sidetracked here. Yes, Peyton is the most interesting thing in the room, but we have Gontlets to get through! Gontlets are mysterious!"

She hammers on. "You guys make a cute couple."

"Peyton could be sitting next to a turtle turned inside out and she'd still make it a cute couple."

And on and on. "Why aren't you married? Does one of you have commitment issues?"

Her tone is flat and her head is listing like she's coming out of an anesthesia hangover.

"You are very interested in our situation, I see. Peyton and I just met a couple of weeks ago <<I'm trying to cadence my syllables to a more toddler-appropriate march and fanfare>> and she's coming down from the heights of the heavens to see if us mortals are even likeable. And have tolerable hygiene." Hopefully that's arcane enough to prompt a change of subject.

And I'm wrong.

Sinister hairline girl asks, "Do you wish you could go back in time so you could meet Peyton sooner?"

What is going on? I don't like how she's using Peyton's name with that undead tone.

"Well, if I went back to a time before I met her, prior to a couple of weeks ago, she wouldn't know me anymore. That would be horrible."

She's digging in now. "Well, isn't that what this is all about, with the vents and the frames and the Gontlets, to go back in time? Wouldn't you want to find her wherever you go back to? Wouldn't you want to be able to spend more of your life with her?"

This language . . . it's too careful to be coming from a brat that needs to run a brush through her hair. These aren't innocent musings. And I can feel Peyton looking back and forth at me and little demon girl with some suspicion.

"Let's just say this: if I went back in time, to a time before I met her, I would spend all of my days trying to be the most likeable mortal around for when I did meet her."

My eye corner tells me that Peyton is looking at me lovingly and she runs her hand gently across my upper back a couple of times, which pulls me into a sort of fugue of euphoria. I act unaffected so she doesn't perceive the power she wields.

"But maybe Peyton would be different in a different past," she starts again. "Maybe she wouldn't even exist—"

"Nope! Young lady, you've reached your question quota. Who wants to hear about the Blanc-Becs who don't even know they're in the Gontlets?"

The rest of the evening floats along in its typical Thursday night current, but I feel more winded and my joviality has to fight through this jading hopelessness <<I remember this same sensation of life-sucking despair when my dad would fill the house with the *Blade Runner* soundtrack>>. This girl knows something. She knows something and she knew exactly what to say to unsettle me, to, well, to piss me off. She was a mouthpiece for some calculating coward. I'm sure that's the case, but I don't have a lot of confidence in my surety because I'm letting the listlessness of an uncomfortable, medicated little girl, agent or not, get the best of me. I don't like that about myself, that un-dammed emotional reactivity. It needs to be checked at the threshold with some deliberateness and foresight. The most ravishing of all of God's creations is within arm's reach, in my corner, being affectionate, being supportive; that should be enough to frustrate all the wiles of the wicked. Or leave them unheeded at least. But it's that seed, that possibility that the update could not only erase our acquaintance, but that it could efface her very existence. The dread, the abject loneliness halts my cooling blood at the thought; I just have to make a U-turn and go back to happiness and oblivion or I'll lose my mind. And my mind gets lost easily.

Peyton and I watch everybody leave and find ourselves alone in the stuffiness of walls that hoard sound. We look at each other like we've just been through an ordeal.

"Saturday is the next assignment."

Peyton gets up and stretches like she's about to practice yoga. "Do you get nervous when you have to do one of these assignments?"

"Like the dickens."

"They haven't been too bad so far, have they?"

"On paper some of them have been horrifying. I'm a paranoid hermit, I'm not fearless like you, so the skydiving one was just consciousness-challenging stress until I was on the ground. But no, they haven't been too bad so far. The funeral was the most stressful, and that wasn't even one of the assignments. But I just know one of these days he's going to have me kill a family or release all the animals from a zoo into a major city or something."

"Do you trust him?"

"Trust who?"

"Patch. Do you trust him?"

"Present company excluded, he's really the only person I trust. Not posthumously trust, but currently trust, since I don't believe he's actually dead. But, yeah, I trust him. I have no reason not to; he's never steered me wrong. But having Patch in your life is like being locked out of your house—you have to find alternative comfort zones in the wild. Or just make the wild your comfort zone. So I trust him, I just don't always like how he wants me to get from A to B, because it's always the bumpiest route."

"Well, then, bumpy ride or not, that family needs to die. Those animals need their freedom. Them city folk need to learn themselves some wilderness survival skills."

"I know that too much flattery calls my motives into question, but you are an extraordinary person, Peyton Maynes."

"Me? Hardly. After witnessing that display, that intense, lively kind of conversation with young kids about topics I thought were way complicated and abstract, I'm pretty sure you're the extraordinary one. I've never seen someone interact with kids like you do. It seems so unlikely, this big, quiet muscle man and these chirpy little kids, but they love you."

"They've *grown* to. They were waving and smiling at you before they even knew you were in the room!"

"They accepted me because they already love you. That's the way it is. End of discussion."

I know this sounds weird, but when she's adorable like that, it makes me want to devour her, starting at the hands.

"You're not nervous at all about these assignments, are you?"

"It's been a while since I've had this much fun, so no. Bring it on. But now, Dillinger, we need to go to Nielsen's, order some frozen custard, and sit in the car long enough for you to explain to me what all that time travel talk was about."

Crap. I wish it weren't true, but life rises and falls on hard honesties.

Day 77

CHAPTER 91

"Love is not affectionate feeling, but a steady wish for the loved person's ultimate good as far as it can be obtained."
– C.S. Lewis

I don't feel very good about it, but I told Peyton a series of velvety lies last night. Actually, I'm fine with it; the last thing I want to do is come across as some kooky time travel nerd. Classy girls prefer you keep that stuff to yourself until you can fend off attackers and settle them in a big house. And even then . . . But I don't think it would be useful to worry Peyton with implications of imminent abandonment. Because that's not my plan. I'm not saying Patch is lying to me about vents and the frameset, but he has been known to convincingly construct the fantastic to elicit some desired effect. And Peyton may be the dangling carrot of his desired effect. There's no way to tell what he's really after, but whatever it is, wittingly or un-, she's the magnet on the end of the fishing line in the kiddie carnival game.

Patch used to subject me to these elaborate ethical scenarios when I was a teen. He made it seem like there was so much to being human that you could tie yourself in knots deciding what to eat for breakfast. Or if you should even eat breakfast at all. He offered so many variables and considerations and nuances to every situational chiliahedron, I started to wonder if human interaction was worth the headache. It probably contributed to my reclusivity. But he was expert at disentangling this tangle by decocting the purities out of the muck. *How you make people feel is more important than being blindly bound to binaries! Stop worrying about their motivation and start worrying about your contribution!* He didn't dwell in the gray so much as his blacks and whites erred on the side of a cheerleading tough love. When we'd read the New Testament, Patch would point out how Jesus was aggressive and reverent and meek and insulting and forgiving and scolding and reticent and confrontational and tender and sympathetic and cutting and loving and name-calling, and every reaction was inexplicably customized to the individual, to the occasion. All that to say, there's probably some reasonable utilitarian justification for why I told her all the Gontlet and vent and frame mumbo jumbo was concocted to entertain sick children. I was so conversant with the particulars of the scheme, so fantastical with the flourishes, she was sufficiently convinced. Or she thought it was all factual and I was just screening it with fantasy to give it a blur of absurdity. Her facial expression didn't change much, so it was hard to tell.

Either way, she still wants to see me tomorrow, so my head's still above water. For now.

I'm stuck in a wispy love cloud on the way home and I'm letting people cut in, ignoring the jackasses that disagree with my speed, waiting patiently for the delayed green-light go's, all with no more rage than appreciating the darkness and desolation of this undisturbed hour with a stupid grin on my face. I feel at least one magnitude bigger physically and ten magnitudes bigger umbrally.

It's not just this immediate source of validation that enlarges a confidence that breeds a fearlessness that magnifies meekness and amplifies humility, it's . . . a general sense of being in love, I guess. It's finding the switch to the fluorescent bulb-lined walls of your dimly-lit life so you can finally sort out where everything goes. You understand what really matters in the world and you're able to put everything else in perspective. It's a perspective irrespective of the self's horizon as it eyes the beyond to the requirements <<intimations, even>> of another self. It is concentrated selflessness. Kwazants, it seems, is nourished by this being-in-love overspill. The longer the valve stays open, the more collateral runoff spills off the impermeable fountain of the self. But, if I'm being honest, it's also the unqualified terror of some stupid little thing blasting the whole condition to bits <<like hospitalizing someone for an aggressive lane change>>. It isn't a virtue of entirely pure motive, to be sure, but it's reliable concrete footings until you can fill in the foundation. Good behavior is as much omission as it is commission.

Even before my encounter with Peyton <<real Peyton, not dream Peyton>>, I could feel fruit growing through the weeds. Now sequoias are crashing through rocks. I'm not necessarily saying I'm a *better* person, it's just a lot easier to be a *good* person. And I love that she's so perfect I don't have to make any excuses for my infatuation or question my judgment in any way. Not that I'm in a position to be choosy.

I'm ready for native umbra subjugation! <<Now that I say that, I hope the native umbra isn't cognizant of its subjugated status. How awful would that be.>>

DAY 78

Chapter 92

"Diplomacy frequently consists in soothingly saying 'Nice doggie' until you
have a chance to pick up a rock."
– Walter Trumbull

Since the first nine tenths of each assignment are usually Gontlets and Exiles and
stuff, I think I'll just give Peyton the sanitized summary.

Assignment #10: POWER

Welcome back, laddie! We're back to business, aye?

Okay, smarty-pants.

*I know I have painted the Gontlets as the Devil's mosh pit that will bury you
in its pandemonium, but you wield more power there than I have suggested. You
will discover in the Gontlets that, as an itinerant, you possess faculties superi-
or to that of many of its tenants, the most useful of which is the understanding
that you are a transient and not a permanent resident. You know that you are
a disengaged umbra and that a lifeless hull lies unaccompanied at a shallower
apical frame. You know where you are, why you are there, and that your excursion will be of brief duration. This is leverage, powerful leverage, but it mustn't
be paraded and it mustn't be abused. It should facilitate your sojourn without
impeding others'. As the activities of the Inscrutables suggest, the Gontlets are
a waystation, not a destination.*

*As previously mentioned, some of the entities of the Gontlets do not quite
understand where they are and what they are doing there. As regards this
feature, the Exiles exploit and the Dovolniya explain. The Blanc-Becs, and the
Lifers, to a significant degree, are quite tractable. Doubt and confusion are
their overlords and they pine for information and explanations, even if their gut
belies its veracity. Their officious natures will occupy you, their inquiries will
impede your progress, their concatenations will curb you. Panic has a tendency to resort to ignoble intrigues, and in this iron maiden you will be tempted to
sate their appetite with newspeak and idle reports, even promise of return-trip
intelligence, just for a swifter extraction. This should be avoided as it elates the
Exiles, complicates the work of the Dovolniya, and makes quicksand of any subsequent forays through the Gontlets. The entities have ample time to commit your
pledges and visage to memory. There are things one could say to part them like
the Red Sea, but indulging their curiosity with fictional placeholders and dulcifi-
ers is akin to bowing to the majesty of an individual suffering from delusions of
grandeur. It is mutually assured destruction. Kwazants is not a frames phenomenon; it does not stop at the train platform.*

So I can't tell any of these people they're dead?

You will find that forging the Gontlets is actually quite simple, but that simplicity comes at a kwazants-castrating cost. You do not want to engage with any entity in the Gontlet, but as that is an unlikely scenario, you will need to master the art of statecraft rather than warcraft while holding a bazooka.

The Exiles will be all smiles and sugary rage, but they are accountable to masters as well. I do not mean to say they have a job to do and, right or wrong, just want to make their mothers proud, but making a lot of noise will attract the zombie horde. They do have their kryptonite, but, again, its use constitutes kwazants-castrating mutually assured destruction. They know this. They count on your desperation to employ it. They are infinite and indestructible, so rather than break them, you are more inclined to break yourself against them. But even the Exiles, the obscene wretches that they are, who merit no civility from anyone, should be handled with the same courtesy and decorum as your grandmother. Those that turn civility and kindness on and off like a switch eventually get used to fumbling their way through the dark.

Emotional entanglements of any variety are concrete shoes in the Gontlets. Unfortunately, to gain a full appreciation for this power, the Gontlets themselves will have to be your primary schoolmaster. Thenceforth it can be a matter of quiet contemplation in the safety and security of your living room, so just know that being nasty or heartless to save one's own skin jeopardizes the umbra's ability to find that skin. Emotions are sticky in the Gontlets.

In some form, you will need to experience the thrill and world-crushing domination of this power and its distended rapacity so, in the sobriety of the hangover, you can reverence its potential for devastation and avoid being its addicted bedfellow. Waving hands and commanding unquestioned obedience is an opiate. Once you have tasted its superhero syrup, you will need to learn how to keep it holstered.

So, I wield this power to understand why I must never wield this power? Sounds like a parent letting a kid drop an f-bomb just to get it out of his system.

Barring a genocidally buffered dictatorship, firearms afford the layman powers that most closely resemble that of the gods. They giveth and taketh away. They defend and destroy. They elicit compliance and coercion. They preserve law and order and subjugate societies. They check governments and unbox anarchy. They preserve and pilfer freedom. They are the ultimate instrument for good and the ultimate instrument for evil. Wielding power and witnessing its capacity for devastation is the easy part, it is the fun part. Taming power, harnessing it, focusing it, safeguarding it, ensuring that the circumstances under which it is drawn are dangers clear and present, that is the challenge. Power of any genus should be the subject of sedulous study so its symptoms are readily recognized and swiftly salved.

Westbound 1600 North jumps Legacy Parkway and continues on its west side. At the northeast corner of Bountiful Pond, north side of 1600 North, stands a complex. They are waiting for you there. I hope you got a good night's sleep.

Shooting. This should be cool. I've shot guns before, but I'm definitely not a shooter.

I text Peyton: Are you ready for this?

Her response is a thumbs up. Then she texts a picture of a fish carcass. That must be her roommate.

Me: I'll be there in fifteen minutes. Is that too soon?

She texts the picture of the fish carcass again.

She needs to cool it with the adorableness or she's going to find herself handless. Or worse.

CHAPTER 93

The stench must be dyspneic because she's standing out in the parking lot in twenty-eight degrees. My eyes aren't big enough or my retinae aren't developed enough or my occipital cortex isn't specialized enough for me to process this exploding hypernova beauty properly. I think I'd have to be a fruit fly-hawk hybrid to do it justice. It's like trying to appreciate the score of *The Last of the Mohicans* <<my dad's favorite, played it all the time>> where the notes are represented as aromatic, tactile light. Our brains are only good for single file, not several abreast. Peyton is the embodiment of several abreast. Oh, gosh, why did I say that.

Her teeth are chattering.

I scream from the warmth of the cab, "I know it's cold, but stay there!" I make sure I unlock the passenger side door this time and appear at her side with my arm held aloft like the rung of a ladder. She scales the side of the truck and settles her little body into the seat.

"Why hello, Ms. Peyton. Looking snappy as ever."

"First jaunty, now snappy. You better not be mocking me."

"I promise I'm not. It would be like the bishop stopping one square away from the queen."

"I get that reference. Good analogy. Knowing your place really simplifies your life." She grabs the blanket folded on the center console I brought along for her just in case. "Hey! Is this for me? Please tell me this is for me!"

"I guess it is now."

"If it's really for you, I can wait my turn. But I'm so cold," she says, drawing out the *so* for emphasis.

"I don't get cold. It's why I love Utah. I brought it for you, so it's all yours."

"See, Dillinger, you're a lot smarter than you give yourself credit for."

She quickly becomes the stuffing of a burrito and tries to control the teeth chattering.

"You just need to beef up. I bet those women strongman competitors don't get cold."

The ferocity of her glare is neutered by the tommy gun chompers. I crank the heat to eighty-two <<I didn't even know car heaters could go that high>>.

All her words are spaced out with banging teeth and stuttering inhales. "So, where are we going? Please tell me it's inside!"

"We have to go into the mountains and stand still in our underwear for a whole hour."

She tucks her head into the blanket and screams.

While she's hunched into the blanket, I try to start a fire with the friction of my hand on her back. "Oh, that feels so good," she says, melting into herself. "Don't stop doing that. How are you not cold?"

"I told you, I'm a reptile. Only mammals get cold. You should look into one of those mammal-to-reptile conversion kits. But to your question, I'm not really sure how to answer. He gave me more a destination than an activity. I only know what we're doing in a general sense. Do you want to know?"

"I guess not. I don't mind being surprised."

"It's not far, so the suspense will be short-lived."

Her teeth aren't chattering anymore, but I'm so warm I'm about to throw up. I turn the heat up to eighty-four, direct all the vents toward Peyton, roll my window down, and stick my head out. The heating in these newer cars is very effective. "These assignments can be stressful and exhausting sometimes, you know."

"Maybe for you, sissy boy."

Ouch. "Okay, tough girl. I better not hear any beef out of you before mile twenty-two then."

"You better be kidding. I ain't doin' no winter marathon unless it's watching Harry Potter movies on a couch with a whole lot of popcorn."

Date idea catalogued.

We turn left off Frontage Road onto a dirt road that runs along a culvert. At the end, I pull through a narrow gate and park at what looks like a small military outpost on the outskirts of Fallujah. I roll to a stop as four men and two women approach the truck. From head to toe, they look like the outfitted cast of survivors in a zombie apocalypse movie with things tucked in things tucked in belts and cargo pockets. They look pretty badass.

"Wait here just for a second. I want to make sure we're at the right place."

She's more than happy to oblige as she fine-tunes the flaps of the vents.

Before I can open my mouth, one of the welcoming committee calls out, "Welcome, Elliot! It's really great to have you here. We've been looking forward to this."

"I guess that means I'm at the right place."

"You're at the right place."

I whisper even though I know Peyton can't hear, "I know you were just expecting one, but I brought a friend. Is that against the rules or would she be able to participate as well? I'm not sure how Patch . . . or . . . however you know him sets these things up."

"No, we were expecting two." He points to the Venus in the truck. "Peyton, right?"

Before I answer, I scroll through all the dark corridors and abandoned tunnel-ways that could have led to that information. A non-dead Patch spying on me? The Russians know these guys and tipped them off? Again, a pointless exercise. They know and I'll never know how they know. "Yeah, Peyton."

"Yep, we were counting on both of you to be here. Come on in, let's get started."

I gather a thawed Peyton and we're ushered into a portable-type building. The two women and one of the men tell me they're stealing Peyton and the four of them disappear. So much for that date. At least I'm spared the humiliation of being exposed as a bumbling novice for an hour.

Correction, four hours. Well, the *first* four hours, anyway. Shooting .22 rifles as a teenager, as I'm now to understand, does not in any way qualify as shooting. What I thought was to be a day of shotguns demolishing watermelons and soda bottles turns out to be an eight-hour operator crash course. Safety, mechanics, handling, cautions, considerations, stance, sights, aiming, not aiming, surroundings, movement, magazine change, cover, clearing, slicing the pie, dynamic entry, jams, tap-rack-and-fire, low ready, high port, sector of fire, CQB, center-fed, sight picture, and on and on and on. I have a headache and haven't shot a single bullet yet. Sorry, round. Cartridge? What happened to standing in front of a paper target and emptying a magazine?

I hope Peyton is getting all this instruction as well. She probably lives for these kinds of field days. I'm too stressed out about shooting someone and I haven't even held a gun that fires yet.

These guys are machines. We've been at it for four hours, hundreds of drills, banging away, and they're still dancing around me like a team of scientists working out the kinks of my creation. Consider this prevailing philosophy—now clear the whole structure. This is an alternative philosophy—now clear the whole structure. Watch your profile. Shadow awareness. Now you're the two man. Now you're the three man. Again. Again. Handgun to rifle, rifle to handgun. Watch your profile. Reload. Station to station. Platform to platform. Innocents, walls only work as cover if they don't know you're there, get behind the engine block. I was reverencing the power of firearms during the basic rules of handgun safety; it's progressed to fear-of-God grade veneration.

As far as training goes, Patch sure knows how to pick 'em.

We break for lunch. There's a whole Firehouse Subs spread. I offer to pay and they laugh. I hear *cash cow* among the laughter. Peyton walks in the building with her team. You'd think she spent the last few years in combat with these people—she's excited and comfortable and conversant. Everything I'm not.

As she sits down next to me she grabs the back of my neck and my shoulder and hisses, "Elliot, this is so fun!" Then she looks at me with a contented smile. That's thanks enough.

I think she left gouges in my neck with her fingernails but the dark pools forsaken by the receding surges is like lidocaine. I'm sure my sweat will let me know later just how deep those fingernails went.

I brag, "I already killed two elephants."

"You haven't shot a single round yet, numbnut. You know it makes a noise the whole world can hear when you shoot a gun, right?"

"We used pillows and potato silencers."

"You lie out of your face, Elliot Dillinger. Your grandad's not going to send you to a tactical range to learn how to shoot through pillows. Get a grip."

I can't keep a straight face anymore and I say, "It's a new thing. They call it cloud-fu. It's a lot of pillow fight training."

"Well, while you were having your girly sleepover training, I was learning how to shoot down fighter jets with a glock."

Given the company, this conversation is making me a little self-conscious, so I'm scanning my sectors of fire. From the trainers' reactions, I don't think I've crossed any lines yet. Half are humored, including both women, but three are watching us with drooping looks of ominous gloom, like one of us is about to die, like we wouldn't be having this much fun if we knew what was skulking around the blind. Spooky. I know enough about Patch and his projects to know that, on an errand of the Manuscript, I am immortal. Hopefully Peyton is immortal by extension.

They take the pair of us outside. The sun is finally having an effect on the temperature and mid-forties is almost pleasant. Now we're all together. Pie slicing, room clearing, single man, team, movement drills, weapons transition, drop mag, reload, acquire, switching shoulders. Go again. Go again. Four more hours. No breaks. One thing to the next to the next. It's like on the movies where hired guns have an afternoon to arm and train the townsfolk to defend their village on the morrow.

I'm moving at about half of Peyton's speed. I don't know what slows me down more, being behind her with that fantastic view, being in front of her while she's barking, "Pick it up, Dillinger! Kidnappers need to die!" or the overall entertainment from what a monster this activity has turned her into.

All of this technique, all of these considerations, all of this hyperawareness, all of this control, all of these precautions, carefully defining sectors of fire, muzzle control, positioning to minimize damage beyond the target, the whole industry, the whole endeavor is designed to reverence the power of the life-snuffing tumble of a little metal nugget released by a subtle muscular twitch.

Live rounds, finally! They want me to go first. Objectives. Targets. There's a tone. I dart, cover to cover. Limit exposure. Profile awareness. Don't lose your target on reload. Burnt powder is filling my nostrils like the incense of my worshipping subjects that prostrate themselves before me with a muffled clang. I feel like a god. Or a special agent of the gods. Then I hit a target I wasn't supposed to hit and all of that imperious might nebulizes and gets lost in the dust I'm kicking up. I profane, hope nobody heard it, and finish the course.

Peyton is way better. Quicker and more accurate. She's able to snap this weapon that's as long as her leg right into place and fell targets like she was firing rounds of hopefulness. She never hits the wrong target and I have to hear about it all the way home.

It takes us forever to leave for the day; Peyton won't stop thanking them, praising them, and hugging the female instructors. She's everything I'm not. I shake hands, grunt, and nod my head, man-style.

We sit in the truck for a few quiet minutes, trying to catch our breath. We're both filthy and sweaty and don't care. The rest of our lives will be spent talking about this day.

"Are you telling me we get to do that every week?"

"Well, maybe not shooting, but I would imagine something exciting."

"I'm just glad it wasn't giving up Mountain Dew or something. I'm sure that taught you a lot about yourself" <<she giggles at the prospect of Mountain Dew being an addiction>> "but this is way more fun!"

"Agreed. I do miss my Mountain Dew though."

"Can you imagine how much a day like that would have cost if you paid out of pocket? That's insane! Thousands of dollars for just one of us! And we didn't have to pay a cent!"

It's evident that growing up without a lot of money facilitates gratitude in these instances. Whatever the source, seeing her smile, seeing this genuine excitement, it makes me want to have kids with her.

She says we have to go to Carl's Jr. on the way home, that she'll pay. This time I'm laughing. I'm the cash cow, after all.

DAY 81

CHAPTER 94

"If all else perished, and he remained, I should still continue to be; and if all else remained, and he were annihilated, the universe would turn to a mighty stranger."
– *Wuthering Heights,* Emily Brontë

I don't know what my heart is doing, but it's new. Bad new. Only I could turn being in love into being in pain. My heart feels like it stopped beating but I still have a pulse and I'm still breathing, albeit with some effort. There's this viscous bitumen wedging its way into my pleural space and I wait with restless impotence for the collapse.

I'm trying to clear my head but billions of hatched spiders are skittering across the edges of my mind, making all the walls black. Why can't I just enjoy this moment? Peyton shows up, this blistering brilliance, and the gloom scampers about, readying a reception to its homey darkness. The only way I can prevent the gloom from dimming the brilliance is to keep Peyton within arm's reach. That's not even realistic in a practical sense, let alone as a pawn to forces fickle and unmanageable.

So I sit in the middle somewhere between love and loss.

I don't know how much Patch can protect me from conspirators. I don't even know how intense or involved this war really is. Maybe I'm just overthinking this and my reactions are comically exaggerated. They might not care a wink about me, and this tickle I'm sensing is nothing like a hook in my cheek. But it's this uncertainty, this rug pull, that has me walking down these black-walled halls. I think it would just be selfish to pull Peyton into this world of rockets and bombs with no bunkers.

I know it's not reasonable to be unraveled by unknowables and unstoppables and uncontrollables, but in this case, ignorance is the antithesis of bliss because an ignorant loneliness is way worse than a happiness braided with dread. And I just know, on some level, whether I'm cognizant of it or not, that if the update took Peyton away, it would haunt me to my death. But if I could know what was changed, even if I couldn't immediately change it back, I would at least have our history and some dry powder.

Even though I plan on doing all the Manuscript assignments with Peyton, I don't have any intention of Pik-ing. I just can't foresee how that will impact <<let alone improve>> our relationship. Maybe in theory, but I don't get the impression that theory counts for much based on the ocean of unknowns in the explanations of these assignments.

I don't want to wake up tomorrow with no memory of her and I don't want to jeopardize this fairytale courtship. I don't want Peyton to become my living, breathing, flesh and blood ghost like Dad was to Mom before his death and I don't want to start over. These stupid ambivalences. It's like I've come full circle.

I don't want to seem ungrateful, so I add *having it good for a while* to my gratitude list. I change it to *having it good for as long as I have it good*. I change it to *ten seconds with Peyton (every other second is more than I deserve)*.

CHAPTER 95

"'Tis better to have loved and lost than never to have loved at all."
– "In Memoriam A.H. H.," Alfred Lord Tennyson

God Almighty, I am nobody. I merit no special favor. I have made no particular effort to establish a relationship with thee and thy majesty, and I understand that *we are men of action*, and that *lies do not become us*. I'm not being disrespectful when I say that. If thou truly art omniscient, then thou wilt know that I am being sincere. I have been slow to call on thee in my prosperity and to give thee proper credit for the prosperity that is so commonly my experience, so I understand that thou wilt be slow to hear my entreaties. Thou hast blessed me abundantly with people that have loved me with whole pieces of themselves, with which they have freely parted and left burning as sweet savors on sacrificial altars. Please bless them for these offerings. They were made in love and genuine concern and I have been a truly fortunate beneficiary. It is my desire now to make similar sacrifices of my own. I may not have much to offer, but I beg, I beg with all the influence I can effect in the heavens with whatever measure of goodness and righteousness I have achieved in my short time on this Earth, with whatever favor can be bestowed on my behalf, that thou wilt accept a sincerity without blemish or spot and bless Peyton with the greatest measure of happiness that can be fathomed in this lonely world, and that I can contribute as much to that happiness as is possible for someone so insignificant and powerless. I know that thou knowest my heart and that I would dig through mountains with my bare hands and swallow rivers for this girl, and I beseech thee with all the energy of my soul that we can be connected . . . bound through time and eternity if it be her desire. Because it is mine. Amen.

DAY 82

Chapter 96

"Remember not only to say the right thing in the right place, but far more difficult still, to leave unsaid the wrong thing at the tempting moment."
– Benjamin Franklin

My next text conversation with Peyton goes like this:

I know I alluded to this last week, but are you still interested in going to lunch on Friday with me and my mom?

what do u think

<<She's so great.>>

I will interpret that as a polite and sassless yes.

I get to meet ur mom!

Is that a Your Mom joke?

no, idiot

Yeah, she's something. I'm not trying to jump the gun or anything, but caution with the topic of grandchildren. It's the cheap way to her heart.

good to know. I'm going to have a new bestie on Friday.

I'm not kidding. She'll start calling hotels for us.

would that be such a bad thing? <<pensive emoji>>

PEYTON GAIL MAYNES!

I'm kidding!

*not really kidding

I don't really know what to say here that won't be something I can't unthink for a month

ur so cute, Elliot Dillinger

lunch Friday. txt me time and loc when u have that info.

<<I better just leave it at that. Good hell, woman. Introducing such scenarios in a man's mind is like introducing a knife blade into flesh—it's a hard wound to close.>>

DAY 84

Chapter 97

"You've accidentally given me the food that my food eats."
– Ron Swanson, *Parks and Recreation*

I made this arrangement with Mom: you choose the restaurant, I choose the hour. I needed to make sure it was that post-lunch rush, pre-dinner trough since this encounter was going to be a high-pitched display.

Peyton and I are sitting in the truck outside of a barbecue restaurant at 3:15 p.m. I don't know why I'm so nervous. I'm not looking for my mom's approval; I know Peyton is going to blow her away. I think falling in love with someone splits your character open and lays it bare—it is your truest admission. Being a private person generally means I'm not interested in people's observations of my character. And Mom has been pretty frank about some of my recent bare-laying reports, like her confusion about me doing something like reading to kids. It's this frankness, whether it's in my favor or Peyton's, I hope she keeps to herself.

"I thought you said your mom only ate leaves and seeds and stuff. This is a barbecue restaurant."

"Yeah, that is strange. It's the right address. She's been a little weird lately, maybe this is part of her syndrome."

"This is very exciting."

"It's just barbecue."

"I get to see where Elliot came from!"

"Oh, that. I did *not* come from this woman. Well, maybe technically, but you would have to meet Patch to see where I *really* came from."

"Well, you say he's not dead, so maybe someday."

My nervousness is pooling blood in my chest so I just nod. "Let's get this over with, I guess."

"Elliot . . ."

I turn to look at her. She can tell I'm nervous. She has a big smile on her face and squeezes my forearm. Then she bounds from the seat and disappears to the ground far below. It's not so much that she's everything I'm not, she's everything I could never be.

Peyton enters first with her hands balled up in little fists under her chin. Mom is sitting at a table next to the window. She has clearly seen our approach and is already making sounds that would alert all dogs in a two-block radius.

She takes Peyton's hands and pulls them away from her body, as if to inspect a specimen. "You darling, darling thing! Elliot said you were the cutest thing alive," <<oh, great>> "but 'cute' doesn't even begin to describe how precious you are, Peyton! I have never seen a woman so stunning in my whole life!"

"Mom . . ."

"You hush. I've been looking forward to this moment for a decade."

Peyton is relishing the lavishment. "Yeah, Elliot, let her appreciate the moment."

I shake my head and mourn the loss of part of her to my mother. I know that, regardless of a woman's loyalty to a man, she will situationally shift that loyalty to any other woman in the room, even if that woman is a total stranger.

"I am so glad you approve. I'm sure it hasn't been easy to find someone good enough for such a fine young man as your son. You've done such a fantastic job raising him. He is so good."

Okay, maybe I'm wrong.

Mom wraps her chiseling arms around Peyton and squeezes appreciation into her. "Oh, dear, dear girl, how good of you to say that. I know he's my only child, but he is my favorite. I'll admit, though, I always wanted a daughter, too."

"Well, if you do end up with a daughter, it would be something of a twofer—grandkids probably wouldn't be too far behind."

Mom cinches her arms in a tighter hug.

Peyton is really pleased with herself right now. She winks at me. I mouth, "Digging your own grave."

The hug lasts an uncomfortably long time, but it doesn't seem to bother Peyton.

As we sit, Mom starts in on the warnings. "Just don't let his obsessive cleanliness put you off. He's always been like that."

It's more a scolding tone this time, "Mom . . ."

She waves off my demands and continues, "When he was a teenager, he used to bring baby wipes to restaurants and wipe the table and seat off before he sat down."

Great. Now I can't wipe this nasty table off without looking weird. "Because they were disgusting! Case in point—look at this table! Don't they wipe them off between customers? This is so foul. You know what, hang it . . ." I pull a baby wipe out and start wiping.

Peyton finds this hilarious. Mom is stroking Peyton's back in case that sound isn't laughter.

"Son, I taught you to keep your arms off the table for this very reason!"

"But I can still see it! I can't eat with the last eight customers' spillage staring at me! They're a bunch of savages! I don't know if this fell off their plates or fell out of their mouths while they were chewing. Utahans aren't known for closing their mouths when they chew, you know! And even when they wipe these tables off, they use the same gross rag on every table the whole day! The water they pull that rag out of looks like chunky sewage! They may as well just smear all the leftovers around on the table with their hands and leave!" I'm simulating all this with contrarotating hand circles.

"Lower your voice or they'll hear you! We haven't ordered yet and I don't want them spitting in our food. They do that, you know."

"I hope they do hear me. Maybe they'll start cleaning their tables properly. And if you suspect them of spitting in your food for the mere hint of doing their jobs, why on earth would you ever go out to eat?"

Now Peyton is rubbing Mom's back. But the table now meets my cleanliness standards so I change the subject. "So what's with the meat restaurant, Mom? Did you find a nice coleslaw recipe here or something?"

"Very funny. I don't *just* eat greens, you know, but they're just not enough for all this kickboxing. Can you believe how much energy meat gives you? And it tastes so good!"

"Sounds like something I've been saying for years."

"Yeah, yeah, you're so smart. Ms. Peyton, Elliot tells me you're the best yoga instructor on the continent."

"Continent, huh?"

"Mom . . ."

"Hush now. You've had your time to get to know this wonderful young lady, now it's my turn."

I pull out another baby wipe, remove their elbows from the table, and give myself something to do while Mom embarrasses everything. I don't care how stupid this makes me look, I found more disgustingness that I thought was just wood grain the first wipe down.

"You came home from practice every day, dirt and grass and sometimes blood from head to toe. How in the world did you play that filthy sport for so long when you have such a problem with a few crumbs?"

"When you're on a football field, you expect to get *dirty*. When you're at a restaurant, you don't expect, you *shouldn't* expect, your arms to be the canvas of a Jackson Pollock! It's seriously turning my stomach just talking about it."

"Football?"

"You didn't tell her about your football days?"

"Eh. That was another life."

"Another life? It seemed like it was your *whole* life for a while. Oh, was he a wonder. Every college in the country wanted that boy."

"Really?" Peyton is cutting me obliquely with squinty, objurgatory eyes.

"Heavens to Betsy, what a crazy few months that was. That boy had people from every big college football program calling, sending letters, some even sent recruiters to our house! USC, Alabama, Ohio State . . . can you remember who else?"

"There were a bunch."

"So much interest in that kid's extraordinary talent."

"That picture on your whiteboard, that's you."

"*Was* me, yeah." I sound more forlorn than I am.

I think Mom can see that this topic is affecting me and changes the subject. Sort of. "Then he injured his knee and that was that. And with football out of the way, he found out what he was really meant for and is even more brilliant at that than he ever was at football. And he was *so* good at football."

"Oh? What is that?"

Mom shakes her head again, this time more slowly. "Son, it's okay to be a private person, but you're eventually going to have to open up to *somebody*. Peyton isn't going to try to burn you with a few of your particulars."

Peyton looks heartbroken, like what Mom just said was divined by clairvoyance or something, like how dare those allegations ever enter my mind. She's right about me being a private person, but wrong about my hesitation to open up. "I have no problem telling Peyton anything she wants to know about me. Peyton knows this. It's just that Peyton is so much more interesting a subject. Her stories are so much better. And happier. She has a brother that invented a sport that has state-level tournaments in thirty-one states. How fun is that? Besides, when she's talking, staring at her doesn't seem creepy. Who could ever tire of looking at that face and listening to that voice saying pretty much anything?"

Peyton, in her fearless social validations, gets up from her chair, walks around the table, and wraps her arms around as much of my body as she can and nestles her head into the back of my neck. I can't help but parade my defeat of those allegations with a big smile. Mom smiles back, like we'd pulled something off together.

"Don't sell yourself short, kiddo. You have some pretty great stories as well."

We order. The food arrives. We take our time eating. Mom is discovering how charming and captivating Peyton really is. I more observe than participate in this unveiling. Watching her in her element is my new favorite thing, and my admiration is having this strange camera effect where focusing on Peyton blurs pretty much everything else. Everything about Peyton is unreal and impossible and I can't snap out of this dubious dream state. The more hopeful it appears, the more hopeless I feel. Everything is falling in place and falling apart. Maybe this is why I'm so comfortable around her, plowing through these incongruities—I'm not fully convinced this isn't a dream. The last three months have been improbable enough; the last month has been back-lit fantasy.

"Now, Elliot, this may be very un-motherly of me, but you need to shut up for a minute while I have my say."

I motion with an open hand for her to continue. She's been pretty well behaved so far, so I don't think she can do too much damage at this point.

"I love you. Now keep your mouth shut." She shifts her body to her left and looks more directly at Peyton. "Peyton, you sweet, sweet girl, I know I'm just the mother, and what I say doesn't, nor should it, count for much, but I want you to know something without any favoritism on my part. I have been watching Elliot from the very day he came out of me," she says, snapping a finger and pointing at me in case this is where I intervene. "I have directly observed his every coming and going. I know you don't need a lot of convincing, but he is, despite all of a mother's bias, the greatest man you will ever meet. His grandfather, who I'm sure you've heard endless tales of, was an extraordinary man. His father was the *best* man. Elliot is better than them both. Unless you're one of those weird, new age girls who breaks up with men because they're too nice, don't let this one go. It will be a source of lifelong regret."

Peyton half-hugs Mom. I can feel the formation of tears clinging to my corneas, just waiting for a critical mass, but I convince them that you don't cry in dreams and it dams them up.

"I know a good man when I see one. I'm not going anywhere."

"Elliot's not going anywhere either. Are you, my good son?"

And all the heartfeltedness is gone. Why? Why do you have to dot every compliment and cross every confidence with these crabwise insinuations? We were having a moment!

I feel like I have to reclaim some autonomy and manhood, so I break in, "When I first asked Peyton out, she said no. I was a little disappointed but I wasn't discouraged. I knew something she doesn't know I knew. Without revisiting the proposal, without any mention of it from me, the next day she said yes. She doesn't want to tell me why she changed her mind overnight, but I'm pretty sure I know. She may not think I know because it's so unbelievable, it's so impossible, it's so strange that nobody could guess it. But I'm pretty sure I know. It's the same reason I wasn't discouraged by her initial rejection. It's the same reason why no matter how far we may try to get away from each other, we would snap back like an exacting elastic."

Peyton grabs one of my hands with both of hers and buries her face in my knuckles. I continue, "It's this strange, strange event that makes us both wonder if we knew each other in some other life or some other world. Which we did, I'm sure of it. It's the same reason why after only a month, being apart sort of tears us a little. The reason she said no is the same reason I asked her out in the first place. No matter how far I may go, no matter how far I may *end up*, I will always snap back."

Without revealing her face, Peyton whispers a choked up, "Sorry," and makes a beeline to the ladies' room.

Mom is looking at me with some wonderment. She says, "You sure have a way with words, my son. I'm still trying to figure out if that's good or bad."

My smile is relaxed and sanguine. "It's good."

DAY 85

Chapter 98

"There was only one catch and that was Catch-22, which specified that a concern for one's safety in the face of dangers that were real and immediate was the process of a rational mind. Orr was crazy and could be grounded. All he had to do was ask, and as soon as he did, he would no longer be crazy and would have to fly more missions. Orr would be crazy to fly more missions and sane if he didn't, but if he was sane he had to fly them. If he flew them he was crazy and didn't have to; but if he didn't want to he was sane and had to."
– *Catch-22*, Joseph Heller

I don't set an alarm for Saturday mornings anymore because knowing I'm falling asleep on a Friday night makes my mind an all-night alarm. The night bridging Fridays and Saturdays is like being in a womb with a gun battle raging in the postpartum. I can't rest when all I'm looking forward to is the fray.

I'm up at 7:30 a.m., my mind bounding across the icy boulders of all of today's possible scenarios: tracking the hum of my native umbra's beacon—finding a noisy bobcat in the woods at night; plowing through the Gontlets—running through a high-crime neighborhood naked; getting my bearings after recoupling—waking from a medically induced coma in another country. I shouldn't give him any ideas—I'm sure he's in my head somehow.

The last few days have had me on a rickety sky bridge, but other than a gruesome headache, I feel pretty good. However things turn out, I feel like the bitter end will be a net positive.

Okay, Flipper Crunch, let's see what bull I'm taking by the horns today . . .

Assignment #11: EXPOSURE

Not promising. Especially in the winter. This is karma for teasing Peyton about standing in the mountains for an hour in her underwear. Although, now that I say *standing in her underwear*, a little hypothermia never killed anyone.

One of the fundamental differences between a tourist and a resident of the Gontlets is that tourists are confined to a single Gontlet. The residents are free to traverse the frameset's temporal and spatial three-dimensionality. You are on a chess board, they are on a broomstick at a Quidditch pitch. To the untrained eye, two-dimensionality may seem an advantage of simplicity, but the curious commuters of the X, Y, and Z axes will unequivocally unseat that misapprehension. Imagine a single screen whereon a dozen films are simultaneously projected, and the operator of each projector is independently and arbitrarily speeding up and slowing down the pace of the film. Then give yourself vertigo and indigestion for good measure. Since the Gontlets are more like being in water than on land, you will need to become inured to stereoscopic shark attacks. You need to be at peace with sun and moon, earth and air, cloud and ocean, fore and aft, port and starboard, all trying to murder you with uncoordinated assaults. As multi-dimensional awareness is not a feature to which we plane-bound brutes are acclimatized, you will need some degree of exposure. Though studies in human learning indicate that immediate involvement is the only reliable teacher, and only the Gontlets can adequately elucidate this phenomenon, there are simulations convincing enough to keep these considerations lodged in your peripheral awareness. As your domain, a single Gontlet, will be two-dimensional for you, I will not subject you to peril of such three-dimensionality at this time. You'll have enough to consider with 360-planar-degrees.

Of course, the logical analog is to lock you in a room with a pack of undernourished coyotes, but, in my mercy, I have arranged for something more treacherous but less lethal. It is perfectly suited to your geography—nothing exposes you to more clear, present, and immediate danger than riding a motorcycle on roads populated by Utah drivers.

Yes! I was hoping this would eventually be one of the assignments. I bet you five bucks there are two brand new motorcycles sitting in my garage at this very moment, having found their way in there with stealthy Patch magic. I'm so certain, I throw the garage door open with a loud, "Ha!" like I've cleverly foiled some plot. I am wrong. There is nothing. He probably anticipated my reckoning and withheld them out of spite, that snake. Although, it's been a few years since I've ridden a motorcycle, so I'm not sure I could confidently drive it away if it was in my garage. He probably foresaw that, too.

You just checked your garage, didn't you? Ah, the wee smartarse in his pink wellies!

One of these days I'll outsmart the outsmarter.

File box number two, three, four, and five have all the gear you will need. Go to 765 North 2200 West in Salt Lake. It is a military installation, so you will need an escort to proceed through the gate. A Master Sergeant Satter will be waiting for you. Dress warmly.

File box two, three, four, five . . . I skip my lid-lifting ritual this time. If he wanted to prank me with his *pure deed jolly rogery*, he would have done it already. Why is there two of everything? This is a girl's helmet! These have been sealed in my house this whole time! How would he have known about Peyton before *I* knew about Peyton? Elliot, you have to figure this out if you ever hope to get ahead of this witch! Okay, so . . . Patch could be <<is!>> alive right now, spying on me, watching me do all this stuff with Peyton. He Pik-s back to, say, four months ago, before he packed those file boxes. So, now he knows that Peyton will be with me and packs for both of us. That's possible, right? But what was in the boxes before if it has always been the same number of boxes? Crap. Why do I keep forgetting about that damn update? There's no way I would know if there were the same number of boxes because my reality would have split-flap displayed up the frameset in fast-forward from whatever changed in the past and I'd be none the wiser. There could have been fifty of these boxes yesterday, but now my native umbra knows <<has been made to accept>> that there are however many there are. So there's no way, without a lendemain, that I should be wasting my time on these unsolvable equations. Could you really rapid-fire Pik like that though? Wouldn't you have to space it out a little to give kwazants some time to accrue so you are assured total subordination? <<Even though I know I can't figure it out, I continue trying to figure it out.>>

Texts with Peyton:

Darling, precious Ms. Peyton

<<Sleeping emoji with the zzz's>>

Sorry to wake you. It is time. We have assignments to complete!

<<Nerd emoji with the spectacles.>>

I regret to report, this one will be outside.

<<Red-faced emoji with symbolized expletives taped across the mouth.>>

You must dress warmer than you've ever dressed in your life. If you've ever seen *The Christmas Story*, dress like Randy's mother dressed him for his walk to school.

But make sure you can put your arms down.

<<Weird green robot with electricity arcing over its head>>

I'm coming to get you. Is 15 minutes to soon?

<<Picture of a fish carcass.>>

CHAPTER 99

"When I'm riding my motorcycle, I'm glad to be alive. When I stop riding my
motorcycle, I'm glad to be alive."
– Neil Peart

We pull up to the gate of the United States Air Force Roland R. Wright Air
National Guard Base <<I'm reading that mouthful off of lettering mounted on
a brick wall>> and the pink desert rock, the ornamental grasses, the purple sage,
and the boulders at the entrance, the fact that it has landscaping at all, makes it
nicer than every army base I ever lived on. And I've lived on a few.

Master Sergeant Satter is standing at the gate, coat-less, rubbing his hands
together. He is a lean, wispy, shadowy entity with a military mustache, and when
a breeze kicks up, the front of his uniform collapses onto the back of his uniform
so you can tell there's nothing in there but a rib cage and vertebral column. He
has an agitated, jaw-flexing intensity that makes his face more muscular than
gaunt. It was like Death joined the military and took his duties chew-on-his-
own-teeth kind of seriously. The name *Satter* turns out to be a misnomer—he's
quite cheery.

"Mr. Dillinger, Ms. Maynes, it is my great honor to be your host this fine Air
Force day."

So cheery, in fact, that he's calling this sky of swirling demons and menacing
gray figures with angry beards and dark horns a fine day. And he seems invigorated by the breezy thirty-four degrees.

"How does everyone know our names?"

"The Cartographer was a celebrity. *Is* a celebrity. All his nearest relations are
celebrities by association."

We follow Sergeant Satter to a large parking lot on the east side of the base
next to a fenced compound. <<This is one of the great advantages of living
on military bases—vast, largely unused parking lots. They are the blank slate
playgrounds where every child of every soldier learns how to ride a bike, roll-
erblade, drive a car, and ride a motorcycle.>> Other than two sparkling crotch
rockets <<I can't recall the accepted industry term>>, one red and one black,
and an older roadster, the lot is bare. Nobody works on Saturday, Sergeant Satter
tells us.

"So, how did you get roped into working on Saturday? And for strangers, no less."

"I have two primary loyalties, Mr. Dillinger. One is to the Constitution of
this great United States of America and the other is to the Cartographer. The
Cartographer shares my first loyalty, so I never have to compromise my loyalties
or question the Cartographer's directives."

I think Peyton heard all that. It kills me that I can't mine this conversation
a little, but there are only so many lies I can keep track of. She's already looking
at me like I'll have to explain all that later.

I present Peyton with her Patch-gifted armored jacket, gloves, helmet, and boots that look like we're going to take a fashionable, hopping stroll on the moon. She's quite pleased with the ensemble and I can see that same kill-the-kidnappers ferocity in her jutting chin and sinking eyebrows. The gear does make you feel a little invincible. With flagrant disregard for my own personal well-being <<and with a helmet on my head>>, I point to the front of my helmet and dare Peyton to punch me in the face as hard as she can.

Peyton grew up in the foothills of East San Diego. In all my conversational contribution-deferring attentiveness, I have learned that Peyton already has extensive experience with motorcycles. She would sneak her brother's dirt bike up to the hills outside of El Cajon and ride till it got dark. She never learned how to refill the gas, so, as punishment, her brother would do things like steal her phone and break up with her boyfriends or set off fireworks in her room in the middle of the night or just punch her in the legs so hard she couldn't shift the gears on the bike for a week. Or walk properly. And when the bruises from her last knee-capping would heal, she'd steal it again. She laughs while reporting these accounts, but she can see my masseters wriggling under the skin and tries to calm me by convincing me that that's just part of growing up with brothers. Maybe I *didn't* always want siblings. I don't think those kinds of siblings would have survived me.

I'm sure it will be a fairly level learning curve, but I expect to be outshined today. Again.

There must be layer upon layer of sun-sucking storm systems stacked in the heavens because it's looking a lot like the sky is gathering up the last of the atmosphere-bent light for the day. All we can see is the bottom of a dark continental shadow that I fear will crush us like a hydraulic press. None of this seems to bother Sergeant Satter. He keeps looking at his watch and my pathological peoplepleasing wants to ask if we're keeping him from something, but I don't think any amount of insistence would compel him to abandon his post. His teeth chewing makes him look quite severe.

In typical military fashion, Master Sergeant Satter's first hour is devoted to safety. <<This was my dad's biggest complaint about the army: safety briefings.>> The circumference of the valley rattles like we're in the lumen of thunder's throat. Then the functions of all the bike's buttons, handles, grips, levers, pedals. Down to first gear, up to second, third, fourth. It's all flooding back. We get on the bikes, start them, find first gear, and work out the clutch/acceleration action. We start rolling, feet off the ground. Second gear, back to first, turn, second gear, back to first, turn. Patch likes repetitive learning. We loop the parking lot a few times and then follow Sergeant Satter onto the running track. This allows us space to get up to third gear and back down in time for ninety-degree turns. I look off to the west and realize that we are literally *on* the airport, only a short Jersey barrier separating us from the runways of an international airport. Now I want to race an F-16.

Sergeant Satter is still checking his watch. He can see that we're pros after half an hour and drives us back to the parking lot. Which is a little disappointing; the shape Peyton's body makes while leaning forward on a motorcycle is something I could endure all day.

He stops us and then drives twenty or so yards ahead. Lightning is crawling down the walls of the sky and freezing long enough to look like a being with barbarous intent. Sergeant Satter is now *staring* at his watch. The cracks are so loud, so close, I can see Peyton's whole body wincing. It's like the thunder is coming for us. He removes his helmet, jacket, gloves, boots, socks, and walks twenty feet farther away.

"Mr. Dillinger, Ms. Maynes, it has been a pleasure, but this is where I take my leave."

Peyton and I look at each other as if the other might be able to explain what he's talking about. Or what he's doing for that matter. He says *take my leave*, but it doesn't look like he's *going* anywhere. He's just standing there, his head bobbing up and down between the sky's charcoal underbelly and his watch. At least keep your socks on, man, it's freezing out here!

The wind is sweeping his words away, but I make out, "Remember, Elliot, there's no point in exploring the heights with unexplored depths!" He looks at his watch again. "It's like the Cartographer always said, 'The grass may be greener on that other side, but it doesn't—'"

If I didn't actually see it, I would have thought we were under attack and that a guided missile had found its witting target. But I did see it. I'm sure Peyton saw it too—her scream outlasted the peal of Vulcan's hammer striking the anvil. It was so loud I thought we should have been knocked to the ground, but we were both standing, albeit shrinking and shielding our eyes.

The glorious finger of an old and gnarled god reached down from the billowing coal dust and touched Sergeant Satter who, by all appearances, became a bolt of lightning himself, circumscribed by sparking arcs of gold and white light like a Tesla-coiled chrysalis. Then he fell like a mannequin and jerked there until the electricity was done with him.

My first thought was to Peyton. Screaming indicated that she was at least alive. Traumatized, maybe, but alive. I wanted to get to Sergeant Satter, but, sorry dead stranger, Peyton comes first.

It sounds more like a declaration than inquiry as I cut her screaming off. "Are you okay?"

"Am I okay? What the hell was that? Is this part of the weirdness that follows you?"

She's okay. "Ride your bike to that guard shack as quickly as you can and tell them what happened. I'm going to check on Satter!"

"Just call 9-1-1!"

"The military doesn't work like that. The guards will know what to do."

That girl can move. I think she's always wanted an excuse to speed away on a high-performance motorcycle. For the most part, I didn't want her to see Satter in case it was as gruesome as that failed <<or successful, maybe>> skydive on the Salt Flats.

As I run to Sergeant Satter, I can already smell him. It's not pleasant. My ear is at his mouth and I'm looking at his chest <<meatless rib cage>> while feeling for a pulse. <<That CPR training was timely.>> I can feel residual electricity running through and cramping my knuckles. I notice that his feet are laying in the center of a chalk circle inscribed on the asphalt. Crap. I yell over a loud clap of thunder, "Sergeant Satter, can you hear me?" One eye is looking straight at me, the other is looking at the mountains to the east. That's not good. No pulse. No rising and falling of chest. No breath. His blouse is zip-up <<much more convenient than the sturdy buttons that secured my dad's army blouse>> and I unzip it. The zipper is still warm and my fingers ache a little from its electrical dithering. Is this normal <<a question you never ask on a Patch errand>>? "Sergeant Satter! Hold on! I'll get you going here!"

I separate the halves of the blouse and . . . I don't get it. What is this? Is this a joke? A tangle of bright silver and tarnished-looking copper wires are wound around his entire torso. I'm not touching that. I can't do chest compressions on that. The skin underneath the wires is black and still smoking a little. Using the fabric of his blouse, I turn him over to see where the wires converge and they're helixed around a metal rod running the length of his spine, ending at the base of his neck. Did you turn yourself into a lightning rod, Satter? Patch! What are you about these days? Poor Peyton will never recover from this.

One of the security guards tries to pull me away from the body, but I'm too heavy for him. The other pulls the blouse together. Peyton is standing over us with one hand over her mouth, the other over that hand. Squeals are squeezing through the fissures between her fingers. I snatch her up in the hoop of my arms and chest.

"You guys go!" one of the guard's insists, pointing toward the exit. "We'll take care of this! Leave in your truck and we'll get the bikes to you!"

We both stand there like he'd asked us to set ourselves on fire.

The one with a lot of chevrons on his rank patch stands up, grabs the grip of his holstered firearm and, with surprising military decorum, yells, "Get off my base right now!"

We don't require a second appeal. As we drive away, it starts raining, *really* raining. I've never seen it rain like this in late-January. I don't think I've seen it rain like this in Utah, full stop. I think to go back so they can get in the truck, but I don't want to get shot.

We're driving down 2200 West and Peyton has me pull over.

She's shaking her hands out at the wrists. "Elliot! What the hell was that? Why are you not freaking out right now?"

I unbuckle her seat belt and drag her entire body over the center console and onto my lap. <<That was surprisingly easy.>> She's so small I can overwrap her body even when it's folded up. Her breathing is fast and shallow and I can hear a little huff with each exhalation. She's trying to rest her head on my chest but she's too fidgety. Her hair smells like what hair would smell like if it were a freshly baked dessert. I rest my left cheek against her head and keep my mouth shut as long as possible. She finally relaxes and wraps both her hands around the back of my neck and interlaces them there. Pulling her onto my lap was meant to serve a variety of purpi: I couldn't think of any words that could sandpaper the corners off this atrocity, I don't want to be making eye contact if I have to add additional layers of lies, I want her to feel safe around me, and . . . this is kind of nice.

I finally speak up. "To answer your question, that guy was struck by lightning right before our eyes!" I'm trying to mirror so she doesn't feel like she's the only one freaking out. "He was wired up like a freakin' lightning rod! He stood there until that lightning kicked the crap out of him! Who does that?"

Her breathing has slowed. Her hands slip from their braid behind my neck and fall to her lap. She's very relaxed. She's very, *very* relaxed. "Peyton?" Yeah, she's asleep. She's like one of those fainting goats that go unconscious if you startle them with electric death.

DAY 86

Chapter 100

"Geniuses are like thunderstorms: they go against the wind, terrify people, clear the air."
– Soren Kierkegaard

I sat in the truck for the better part of an hour yesterday holding Peyton while she slept. Strangely, I sat there unable to fathom how life could get any better. I knew, of course, that it could, but the moment was overwhelming my foresight. And I got to breathe her hair for a whole hour. All I want is to be her indestructible carapace, but, until that moment, she seemed so sturdy and self-reliant I didn't think she'd ever need one. She had me carry her all the way into her apartment, past her stinky, sedentary roommate <<I didn't see her face, only the fish carcass picture my mind was superimposing on it>>, into her room, and tuck her into bed. She was asleep before I could get her shoes off. I sat for another fifteen minutes staring at the half moon of her face framed by the rising tide, the clouds of her comforter, and the sandy beach of her pillow.

I had to go on a long run to reset my breathing.

I haven't heard from her since. I hope she's not done with me. Though I wouldn't blame her if she was. I warned her about the weirdness on the first date! It would just mean I'd have to go back to being patient. Not my strongest virtue, but well worth the sacrifice. I wonder if her roommate will tell her that, on my way out, I recommended they get some air fresheners for the apartment because it stunk of rotting fish. You may think that a kwazants-contracting cruelty, but it's the nicest thing anyone could have said to her. Though, from her expression, she may not have thought so.

I'm across the street from Patch's <<my>> apartment. I thought I'd see if I could find any information on that human lightning rod angle. He hasn't mentioned anything about the *heights*, as Satter called it, but I know that stunt was Patch-prompted. He's a fanatical record keeper; he must have written something down.

The storm from yesterday is still battering Salt Lake City. It didn't rain this much the whole of last summer. It's perfect study weather though—the tumult is drumrolling a beautiful white noise on the apartment's many windows.

There were so many notebooks piled on the open table space I didn't think to check all the drawers and letter slots of all the bureaus and hutches and credenzas. Every cubic inch of space is an archive. I can't believe this stuff is just sitting here in an apartment. Governments the world over would assassinate whomever they had to assassinate for this information under the guise of protecting national interests.

There's a very stately looking antique oak bureau against the wall that seems to be glowing <<not really, it just has a key sticking out of one of the drawers' locks>>. The drawer is full of composition notebooks that have clearly seen their day. The top one is labeled *Notes: 1968 – 1972*. I've always loved Patch's handwriting—it's like a draftsman freelancing as an illustrated horror novelist on the side.

Stayed awake for the update tonight. Changes are still fresh when I'm awake for it. Waiting for the morning is gripping buttery dreams. Rossindra drifts farther away. She was already helping a customer when I arrived this time. It's getting harder to retain how it played out in other iterations. I think she said something to me when I entered the office last time around. Buttery dreams. Previous notes confirm, but it's hard to trust those anymore. Can't be sure now if the update isn't incorporating day-old changes of changes. System trying to cleanse itself, I gather. Native umbra, multiple lendemains <<he's had multiple lendemains since the sixties?>>, *it would be madness to keep track of every iteration when modifications are nightly. What did and didn't happen yesterday? I have a memory, a dozen echoes, and some sepia dreams. If nothing changes at the next update, I have a memory, six echoes, and a couple of overexposed black and white photographs.*

That's depressing. And who is Rossindra? I've never heard mention of that name. One of the notebooks is just maps and charts with speeds and depths. This is quite extensive. Some of the pages list times he <<or someone>> Pik-ed, air densities at different elevations, velocity at impact, date of retrogression. I photograph all pages of this notebook for future reference.

One notebook is titled, *Gontlet Death and the Inscrutables.*

Third recycling and he still dies. Same date, same time. Nothing she does can alter it. Giving up hope. If circumstances are somehow altered, different manner of death, but always same date, same time.

Intel from Eric himself as Dovolniya: Umbrae removed from Gontlets and frameset by Inscrutables cannot persist beyond original Gontlet death date and time. No longer part of the system beyond that point. Can only return to frameset as Dovolniya, but cannot be recalled to hull beyond date/time of original Gontlet death due to alterations made by trouplongeurs. Convincing her to withdraw from loop.

Wait a minute . . . Eric? *Eric* as in Dad? Is he saying that Dad is one of the Dovolniya? And when he says *she*, is he talking about Mom? Patch, do you have Mom Pik-ing to try to prevent Dad's death?! This explains everything! Scolding splashy rumrunners, speaking French and Russian, getting freaky cryptic at lunch . . . You've got to be kidding me! So how many times have I lived my childhood with all that jumping? If he says *circumstances are somehow altered,* does that mean his death in the army was, historically, his manner of death the last time she Pik-ed and that's why my native umbra has logged that memory? Is that why she treated Dad like a ghost months before he actually died, because she already knew the date and time of his actual death? This is insane! My own mother, for the love! I photograph everything in this notebook. Posterity may find this interesting. If I can beat the update to a posterity.

I scrounge around in other drawers. A lot of technical stuff. Here's one labeled *Butterfly Effect*.

Even without targeted manipulation, first iteration always most tenable. Butterfly effect creates aberrations that mushroom up the frameset with each subsequent recycling. System reconciling and stabilizing totality of system-wide effects of trouplongeurs' alterations. It appears that the system discourages repeated, focused manipulations. Recycling to period prior to first iteration can reestablish a deeper entry as first iteration and avoid butterfly effect. May improve control of narrative with situational awareness and environmental familiarity.

Intel from Dovolniya: use bliquelines to exit frameset, vent-less system and unalterable for first one hundred and twenty years. <<Ah, vent-less system. Now I think I understand the significance of bliquelines. No vents means no Pik-ing. No Pik-ing means you can't change anything. You'd be at the mercy of fate but enjoy a freedom from the rearrangers.>> *Petram not established and does not begin to fuse for first one hundred and twenty years, no need for decompression. Must be accessed in pairs—one must be a lendemain with experience in Gontlets. No Gontlet with bliquelines, but single mind cannot endure duration of travel. Need to find entrance to bliquelines. Need to find plus one.*

I know I wouldn't be reading all this material if Patch hadn't intended for me to somehow encounter it, but it's hard to tell if he's advocating for Pik-ing or warning against it. If the only way to be with Peyton, reliably be with Peyton, is to peek at the updates or travel through bliquelines, I have to Pik. If Pik-ing will only create a rip current that pulls me farther away from her, there's no way I'd do it. I'd just take my chances. Anytime I'd try to simplify some complex principle with black-and-whiteness, he'd say, *One plus one equals two! The rest is up for interpretation!*

Can't find anything about riding the lightning.

Chapter 101

"Do you smell it? That smell . . . a kind of smelly smell . . . a smelly smell
that smells smelly."
– Mr. Krabs, *Spongebob Square Pants*

It's 6 p.m. I'm all about giving people their space, but after watching someone roast themselves like a kabob, I just want to make sure she didn't fold into a trauma-induced oblivion or something.

Text to Peyton: I'm officially worried.

<<Sleeping emoji with the zzz's>>

You can't possibly still be asleep!

FRT, I slept 26 str8 hrs. Thx for not taking advantage of me. I want to be awake for that.

PEYTON!

<<Toothy smile emjoi.>>

Then: I'm kidding!

*not really kidding

Encouraging that in a guy is like trying to dam a river while floating down it! right, don't touch me.

Well that ruins tomorrow's date.

speaking of that, will u come pick me up for class tmrw? PLZ! I'm so much cooler showing up with a b/f in a big black truck!

<<Boyfriend, huh?>>

You know I will. Just don't make me go into that apartment again.

did u say something to fish-stink? There are plug-in air fresheners in all the outlets.

It sounds like an animal is rummaging around in my garage so I check the garage camera on my phone. Sure enough, someone has counter-burgled two motorcycles from <<into?>> my garage. I'm okay if they just call ahead and let me know, Patch. You just trained me how to handle firearms, remember? And I don't like surprises!

DAY 88

Chapter 102

"This doesn't feel right, feels like everyting's further away, dead as the night-life, hindsight, watching another mistake. You never feel right, long nights following into the day, pale as the street light, pure white, washing the color away."
– "Pale," The Birthday Massacre

This is awesome—I experimented a little with some buttons I found on the helmets and it looks like they're wired to communicate with each other. It won't have to be an alone together trip.

It's 6:15 a.m. and no more than thirty degrees out. Peyton is bundled up like Randy but can put her arms down. She's really the cutest thing.

I-80 is busier than I'm comfortable with as a rookie rider, but it becomes hauntingly post-apocalyptic <<without the abandoned cars and feeding zombies>> the moment we pass Skull Valley. I feel like I just won the Light Cycles round on the grid in that *Tron* video game and I'm just riding a line in empty space until the next phase loads. There's enough moonlight to shade the scattered clouds with cobalts and azures. Listening to her tunneled voice in this openness at this speed with these colors fills me with a nervous guilt. I know I've done nothing to deserve this kind of stillness of mind.

I have her ride in front so I can admire the lines she wears so well and we talk about whatever. I try to make my life sound boring <<which, compared to hers, it really is>> so that voice dominates the airwaves. I'm listening, but it doesn't really matter what she's saying. She could make the particulars of her cycle sound like Karen Carpenter. She's getting shrewder about mining information from my reluctant veins <<Out with it, Dillinger!>>, but her narration of sibling rivalries is too entertaining. And that voice . . .

We park at the Salt Flats Rest Area and walk across the lunar surface with its lunar glow from the light of its lunar sun. We keep our helmets on for warmth. She says we look like space travelers out here. I say her mom looks like a space traveler. She says she's going to write that down and tell her mom later. That'll be a good first impression.

We sit in one of the flattened valleys of this alien planet, surrounded by the towering, two-inch ridge of a wind-scribed scale. The warmth of the solar sun is starting to nudge the ceald of the lunar sun to the edges and we both sigh. The bright eye peeking over the horizon exposes the breadth of the scaly creature.

"I've never done this before."

"It's something, isn't it?"

I take my helmet off, lay down, and rest my head on the helmet. She crawls onto my torso and rolls herself into a ball on her side for warmth at an angle that allows her to keep an eye on the sun. I wrap my arms around her like heat-conducting silver and tarnished-looking copper wires and they cover a surprising amount of her minimal surface area. I've never felt this big and this small before. I can feel her dissolving into me. Her hair smells like the first rains falling in the rarefied air on the tops of the mountains of a new world.

"Why did you change your mind when I first asked you out? Why did you say no and then yes?"

"I still can't tell you."

"What if I guess?"

"I don't want you to guess, because I don't want you to *know*. You're smart enough to know if you've correctly guessed no matter what I say."

"You know you're going to have to tell me eventually."

"I'll tell you when we're married. That way, if it freaks you out, you're still my prisoner."

"Well, Stockholm syndrome kind of prisoner, anyway."

That must have been the right thing to say because she curls into a tighter ball. We're both talking to the sunrise because we're too cold to move our heads.

"I'm really very interested, so we better get married soon."

"Are you proposing to me, Elliot Dillinger?"

"This would be an ideal moment, wouldn't it? I'm afraid if I got down on one knee I would freeze there and you'd have to go for help."

"Down-on-one-knee kind of guy, eh? Very romantic."

"Oh, no, you deserve something way more romantic and elaborate and public than down on one knee."

"Don't you dare. I would say no to your face. Again."

"You would?"

"Probably not. A girl's gotta bluff every once in a while."

It goes quiet. The sun is warming and spellbinding. It looks like there should be celestial theme music playing from the seams of the firmament. It's almost too quiet. I thought it was always windy at the Salt Flats?

"Elliot." She sounds far away and a little sad.

"Peyton."

"What you said at the restaurant, do you really believe that people can know each other before they ever meet? Like remembering some acquaintance from a kind of pre-world world?"

"Yes."

"That makes sense to you?"

"Yes."

"Why?"

"Probably for the same reason you won't tell me why you said no to our date initially."

"I kinda doubt that. You may think you know, but you don't know."

"I think you'll be surprised when it's finally out. If you're concerned about me freaking out about your explanation, you'll have me institutionalized when you hear my reason for asking you out in the first place. Well, the *primary* of the eighty reasons I asked you out in the first place."

"Really?"

"Really."

"We should each write our explanations down, seal them, and read each other's on our wedding night."

"That is not what I want to be doing on our wedding night."

"Next day then."

"The next month, maybe."

She giggles something out of a numb jaw. It goes quiet again.

"Elliot."

"Peyton."

"Does all of this seem unreal to you?"

"Yes. Unreal and unbelievable and impossible." <<I'm back to lazy, mindless verbal diarrhea that I should have enough sense to sit on before something irreparable comes out.>> "So much so it makes me nervous. I saw what happened to my mom when she lost someone who was her everything. It was heartbreaking. It was devastating."

"Do you think it's better to be alone than to be with someone you know would devastate you if you ever lost them?"

"No." I think I answered before I fully processed her question. "I've been alone. Being with someone you're always nervous about losing is way better. At least you have that someone. Being alone would just be throwing the baby out with the bathwater. Nervousness and someone will always beat no nervousness and no one. The nervousness just makes you more vigilant, more . . . protective. It makes you grateful for every moment you're able to have with that person. I misspoke if I made it sound like the nervousness would prevent me from being with that person. I can handle that kind of anxiety when it's paired with something as beautiful as . . . with something truly precious." <<Careful, Elliot.>> "Being alone is for people that know they have nothing to offer."

We're laying on this salty reptile, tucked into the sun's sheets, knowing the other wants to say something personal, something permanent, something risky.

"Not many girls get to say this, let alone actually enjoy the sensation of it, but I feel, in all ways, totally safe with you. I would never say anything to obligate you in any way, but I'm being very careful to safeguard this . . . the very possibility of *us*."

"In all ways, there is nowhere safer in this world, in these cosmos, than in these arms. Just *thinking* about flexing these muscles registers on all seismic and geologic scales. But, slight exaggerations aside, I want you to *know*, I want this to sink deep into every part of who you are, that I would never intentionally hurt you, Peyton. Not in any way. I'm incapable of it. I was raised by people that truly loved each other and showed it every day. That includes Patch. They're the only examples I've ever had of love and devotion. I would go to the ends of all the earths, the heights and the depths," <<probably shouldn't have used that phrasing after the Satter incident>> "every point in all of their timelines, to confront all the forces that threaten or jeopardize the certainty of that *us*."

"I think you've already proven all of that to me. But it is nice to hear it." I can hear her cutting off a thought over and over. "I don't want to generalize this because I don't care about *every other girl*, but you are everything I've ever wanted in this life, Elliot. It makes me nervous, too, like I just found a briefcase with ten million dollars in it and I can't figure out what to do with it to keep it safe. I don't feel like I deserve it this good."

"As long as you draw breath, Ms. Peyton, I'm all yours. You may think you have it good, but the man you truly deserve does not, nor ever will, exist. Men aren't made good enough. But I'd be more than happy to be that placeholder until some god claims you."

I squeeze her a little too hard and she squawks out some of the compression.

DAY 90

CHAPTER 103

"I want to get inside the dark side of you."
– "Take a Picture," Destiny Potato

Since I never had a brother or sister, not in the traditional sense anyway, Peyton thought I needed a crash course in the ways of the sibling. She says growing up an only child is like growing up blind or deaf—you only get half the experience. And it's not just a handicap of privation—when your siblings during your formative years are your parents, you end up knowing much about *their* culture and nothing about your own. I think this lab hour <<no less than twelve hours, she says>> may expose how little I know about my generation. Most of my peers' references go over my head. And the ones I get, at least on an academic level, I don't understand culturally. It's almost a foreign language, a really stupid foreign language that isn't nearly as funny as they think it is. It's like an inside joke where the insiders are eight. Except for Your Mom jokes. Those never get old.

Early February in Utah, she says, is perfect for this kind of training because I need to learn the indoor stuff first. There's a natural sibling evolution that begins primarily indoors, she says. She's very certain of these facts. And it's more organic, this evolution is, when Mom and Dad aren't home. <<Her parents, she reports, were never home, so she claims sibling master status.>> Peyton considers herself the Swiss Army knife of fun—all she needs is a deck of cards, two pennies, some rubber bands, a piece of paper, two pencils, a skateboard, a canister of tennis balls, a few refrigerator boxes, and a couple of comparably-aged siblings, and she can keep you entertained for an entire summer.

Throughout the early afternoon hours we play penny soccer and penny golf on the dining table, paper triangle football, tennis ball wars throughout the house, another funky war game using rubber bands to shoot little paper bullets, and a game <<if you can call it that>> where you see who can break the other's pencil first. Are there no sports fields or movie theaters in California? I know it's chock full of beaches.

"You Californians are weird."

"Well, this is just what we do the six days a year it rains. And when Mom and Dad go out on Friday night. And when we're grounded. San Diego has two seasons, hot summer and cold summer, so we're normally outside from sunup to sundown, all year round. Usually playing Butts Up. All you need is a wall and a tennis ball. That and launching water balloons into neighboring neighborhoods. The cardboard boxes were only entertaining when we were little and could cut holes in them and make cities we could crawl through. We're supposed to skateboard all the way to Taco Bell and back for dinner, but no way I'm doing that in February. We're using the truck for that. Oh, dang! I forgot to bring the

Dreamsicles! Not that that's a sibling thing, but that's what we lived on—frozen burritos and Dreamsicles."

I don't think we grew up in the same America, Peyton and I. I've played that paper triangle football game, but the rest are like precursors to the precursors of becoming a serial murderer. They're either so violent or so delinquent or so mind-numbing that the next logical step is give all the randomness and violence a purpose. And you should hear her grinding her teeth when she's fashioning the paper projectiles for that ballistic rubber band game. She clearly wants blood. I didn't know you could fold paper to the density of osmium. <<Summer diversions are much more sophisticated when your sibling is a wiry old Scot that has a tumor somewhere pressing on some gland that releases some hormone that turns wheat bread into amphetamines.>> Then we start with the card games. War, Speed, Slapjack. That keeps us occupied for the rest of the afternoon. But we have to stop when Peyton goes full-blown sibling on me. We have this big, blow-up fight <<that's what siblings do, she says, and she's really getting into it>> about who got their hand down first on the jack, and when it gets unhinged and savage, she starts wailing on my head with an open hand, tears off down the hallway, and locks herself in the bathroom.

I just sit here, my ears ringing, my scalp burning, my eyelids still fluttering from the repetitive violence of the offensive, wondering if this should reach the threshold of red flag. I must be reacting like an only child; this is her correction: "Hey, dummy! You're supposed to tear after me and try to break the door down!" She waits for a reaction in my lost silence. "I don't hear any doors being torn from their hinges! You just got beat up by a girl, you fat baby!" My equilibrium's still floating up through the daze. "How do you expect to eat dinner at the same table as me when everyone knows you got beat up by a girl and you didn't do anything about it and I don't have bruises somewhere on my face? You can never show your face in public again! You may as well kill yourself or leave the country! *You can't hit girls* applies to everyone but sisters, moron! Where is your self-respect? I'm going to tell everyone at school a girl slapped you and you cried like a sissy with headgear and little golden curls! Are you afraid of the second wave, sissy boy, is that why you're hiding in the corner with your little blankie, suckin' on your binkie?"

She's really good at this sibling stuff. Master status is no exaggeration.

I'm trying to force my buoyant, only-child mind into the yellow depths of her derision but the taunts are like rain to my counter-firebombing. She definitely has the advantage when it comes to vicious provocation. Everything I think to say just confirms her victory. "It's my door! I can't tear my own door down!"

"It's my door! I can't tear my own door down!" she taunts, her voice affected like a six-year-old. And then repeats that statement over and over with a heckling wail. Now she's just non-stop mock-sobbing.

I may have mentioned, I've been to California. I spent some time down there with my cousins when I was ten or something, before my dad died. I wonder how far away from Peyton I was at that time, physically, I mean. Is Oceanside that far from El Cajon? She would have been . . . eight? Anyway <<the geography isn't really relevant here>>, my cousins had a neighbor with a pool in their backyard and we went over a few times to swim. Like, actual *swimming* swimming. Most of the time when you claim you're swimming in a backyard pool, you're really just lounging, but we were playing this game called Marco Polo <<Californians and their made-up games>>, and this required calorie-torching, hardcore swimming. I had never heard of, nor played, Marco Polo up to that point in my life. The Pacific Ocean was the oracle that divined for me my aquiline nature <<again, I know I'm using *aquiline* incorrectly here>>, so doing anything in a swimming pool was like being in my living room. I pick up on sports quickly, and it didn't take me long to discover that swimming is noisy. When I was It, rather than calling out, "Marco," I would just tread water quietly, listen for movement, and then split the depths with my aquilinity <<incorrect usage *and* made-up word, yes, I know!>> until I ran my hand into, invariably, some inappropriate anatomical location or a sandpapered concrete wall that would open my flesh. <<I take all sports at all levels seriously.>> From my brief exposure to siblingitude, it seems synonymous with lawlessness. You want me to be a sibling, Peyton? I will sibling. But I will play this game my way, in the depths, in the silence, like a shark. No Marco, no Polo. Just good old-fashioned Jack Lambert style decimation.

As she harangues my cowering dignity, I slip out the garage door, grab a thirty-two-gallon plastic trash can, and circle to the back of the house. Even outside I can hear her booming trash talk. <<Again, such an improbable volume for someone her size. Those lungs have muscles!>> My bedroom has a door that exits to the backyard and I glide in with my elephantine stealth. I slip down the back hall to the bathroom and pound on the door so hard I can see the top third caving in at the top. Her thunderous tempests stop abruptly and she's quiet. I tiptoe a lap around the house, grabbing a fridge magnet as I pass. Nobody siblings better than immature boys who have face to save.

I hide around the corner from the hallway that leads to the main living area with the trash can upside down, high over my already elevated head, like Fezik waiting with a boulder for the Man in Black's head to come into view. I only ever use this trash can for yard waste and I wash it out after each use, so it's clean. The ruthlessness of my siblingitude has its limits. I can hear these timorous, squeaky, "Elliot?"s from behind the bathroom door. The world is frozen— even the fridge is confederate in this game of stealth. I think she knows she's in trouble. The lock clicks and the door swings open wildly, twanging against the baseboard door stopper, but there's no movement after that. Come out and play, Peyton . . . <<She's right, having siblings is magnificently fun.>> She's in socks, but, dumb girl, you're breathing too loudly! And thank you. She's right around the corner now. I chuck the fridge magnet against the wall opposite the hallway and it explodes in the echoic confinement. Right when I hear her little chirp of alarm, I crash the trash can down on her head and move it back and forth violently until she crumples to the ground and is sealed under the bin. Then I bend over at the waist, leaning the weight of my upper body on its base. I'm seeping these hysterical, muted laughs as she tries to find a seam.

Muffled and miles away, she yells, "That hurt!"

I affect my voice like a six-year-old, "That hurt!" and mock-sob.

"Elliot, so help me! Let me out!"

I mimic, "Elliot, so help me! Let me out!"

I'm laughing so hard I collapse to the ground and wait for the negative pressure in my emptying lungs to equalize its vacuum so I can take a breath. She slowly, pathetically lifts the bin off of her and kneels there, rubbing the top of her head.

This aggravates my fit.

Through a pouty, miserable frown, she says, "You're enjoying this sibling stuff way too much."

My voice is still buried in maniacal cackling, "I want to do my childhood over!"

The corners of her mouth are sinking into her jawline and she's still rubbing her head. "That really hurt my head . . ."

Every time she says that, I laugh harder.

She is no longer amused.

"Who ever knew that being mean was so much fun!"

"Okay, Dillinger, sibling day is over!" she yells over my unextinguishable laughter.

She starts wailing on my chest with an open hand and the laughter takes over the rest of my body. I don't think she anticipated hurting her hand more than it hurt my chest because she's shaking her hand out with a further deflated helplessness.

I roll over, grab her whole body, and roll back, cradling her on my chest. She doesn't even weigh enough to dampen the heaving paroxysms of my laughter so she lays there, pinned, bouncing about on my chest.

When the cachinnations abate, I start rocking, right and left, right and left.

"This is how every day ended growing up—we would get along and play for eight hours, then try to murder each other for thirty minutes. Then we'd get along and play again. It was a healthy balance."

"I don't know if there's anything healthy about that balance. But you're right, it's definitely a different lifestyle. I realize that I didn't really have a childhood. And you were really getting into it. Were you really that mean?"

"Oh, way worse. I was an artist."

"How could little Ms. Peyton be so cute and so mean?"

"Survival, man."

"But, you're so happy and calm all the time. Well, most of the time. Until someone puts a gun in your hand or sits you on a motorcycle."

"That's *why* I'm happy and calm all the time, idiot. I survived my childhood, nothing can kill me."

"So, when you're out in life, interacting with people, are you sibling Peyton, or are you yoga teacher Peyton?"

She looks at me like I'm stupid.

"Oh. I guess I better watch my p's and q's."

"Yeah, you better. I can't believe you put me in a trash can. How did you get so good at being a sibling so fast?"

"Good teacher. And you called me a fat baby!"

Now she's laughing. "I was going easy on you. I didn't want to make you cry for real. If I was being mean, I would have said that you were the reason that Mom and Dad never come home and that if your own parents couldn't love you, nobody would ever love you in your whole life and that you should just die."

"Seriously? You said that to your own siblings?"

"Wow. You really are an only child."

"Thanks for sibling day. It will go down in infamy. I can't believe you fell for that fridge magnet distraction."

She keeps rubbing the top of her head. "Yeah, that was a nice touch."

"Do you need an ice pack or something?"

She scoffs, "Siblings *punch* you where you're hurting, they don't offer you ice packs. Besides, it didn't hurt that bad." She's still rubbing her head.

"You said sibling day was over. I'm back to being the doting boyfriend. Come on, I'm starving." I stand with her in my arms like she was nothing more than the family cat.

After our Taco Bell field trip, we sit on the couch and talk until the planes stop flying out of Salt Lake airport. The adorableness of her expressions and inflections and gestures rattles me with that chest-coring loneliness, like I've already lost her. Those hands that I want to eat, they're starting to vanish finger by expressive finger. She's already becoming that ghost. How long can I hold my breath in this drowning dichotomy, this simultaneity of love and loss? It's getting harder to breathe through it.

The empty pill bottle on the dining table is trying to tell me something. I get the sense it's trying to be helpful. I ignore it in case Peyton thinks having a conversation with a pill bottle is weird.

"I know it's late, but please don't make me go back to that rotting fish freak. The plug-in air fresheners just make it smell like dead fish sitting in a pail of baby powder on a hot afternoon. It's not right."

"You want to crash here?"

She importunes with a little desperation, "Please, please, please, please, please."

"No, that's fine. Well, but one condition. You have to be okay with me giving up my bed. I'll sleep on the couch. The couch is just as comfortable. You're a girl and you need your privacy. And, your lucky day, I washed the sheets this morning, so they haven't been slept in by a gross man."

"Were you always like this?"

"Like what?"

"Gentlemanly."

"I never thought of myself as gentlemanly, but, yeah, I've always been like this."

She's chewing on her upper lip and has a probing look of uncertainty.

I inventory all the necessary accouterments for bedtime business: towels and wash cloths are under the sink; here's a brand new toothbrush, an unopened tube of toothpaste, and some floss <<I'm a planner //read: prepper//>>; baby wipes are here; extra toilet paper is under the sink; I put extra blankets at the foot of the bed because little waif of a Peyton is going to freeze in sixty-six degrees. She's gone very quiet and still, like she's watching a vision pour from her mind into a physical reality before her. She's looking at me with that same sad desperation that Vivian haunted me with behind the glass lid of that coffin on East Broadway. Maybe that's what she does when she's tired.

I do my business in the guest bathroom and use my otherwise harrowing super senses to take stock of her bedtime routine. I'm not pleased about having to clean a bathroom I never use, but having her here is worth indulging a compulsive disorder every now and again.

She calls my name and I count to ten so she doesn't know I'm already standing right outside the door. I knock, yell, "Come in," and enter <<something Patch, a big *Fletch* fan, did regularly>>. She's already in my bed, and, with the comforter tucked up to her chin, all I see of her is the midnight ocean tumbling over the rocks and sand. I know this kind of beauty is enough to elicit bitter arrhythmias, but it's something else, there's this other element of her slipping farther away every time she's this beautiful that makes me ache like my heart muscle is cramping or the valves aren't opening anymore. Maybe I have a legitimate heart defect.

I sit on the side of the bed and see myself looking up at Patch as was so common a scene in my youth. True to Patch form, I run my fingers through her hair, pushing it away from her face, until my fingers get stuck. I want to say, "I wonder if you will ever know how much you are loved," but I consider the setting <<dark room, goddess in my bed, no idea what she might or might not be wearing under there, Peyton's previous texts of not so tacit naughtiness>> and just stare at the moonlight making a *Phantom of the Opera* mask of her face with its smoothing pallor. The light sits atop the bottomless tide pools of her eyes like an oil. There is more yearning in her expression than fatigue, and I know I need to make an escape before my heart stops, full stop.

"You know, it's a king-size bed. You don't have to sleep on the bleeding edge of it."

She admits, with a voice of disconsolate mousiness, "I've only ever had a twin bed."

"Wow. You really are a fifth child."

She almost smiles but the yearning quickly resets itself. I slip to my knees at the side of the bed and push wave after crashing wave, swell after intractable swell from the polished sand of her forehead. My eyes are trying to sate their voracity, but the hull's sensory blanket is just too wet. And I'm trying to stave off a heart attack. You should go right now, Elliot. Just say good night and walk away. And . . . now. Go . . . now.

Every contractile filament of my hull is pushing me closer, most of the philosophers of my umbra want me to exit in a gentlemanlike manner, but the gravitational longing of her eyes is reasoning directly with the hull and I'm pulled right to the point of the slightest sensation, almost imperceptible but for the tangle of bright silver and tarnished-looking copper wires electrifying the entirety of both hull and umbra. The sensation is already evanescing from my lips and I press just further enough to re-galvanize the sensation. But it keeps slipping away, like she's already receding into the whims of an update, vanishing, dissolving into her own sand and black surf. I need to keep her alive. I need to somehow pull her from nativity and put her in some umbral pocket. If I just immortalize this sensation, she can never melt away into other realities, others' realities. I start moving my lips slowly, gently across hers, back and forth, just at the threshold of sensation, just at the sill of my Eternity. But I am in denial; soon I will want more, and I will have to press and press until she's either my prisoner or an apparition. And neither are compatible with the kind of love with which I want to love her.

I recede from the night-washed slopes of the moonlit dunes and scarps but it feels more like she's slipping away from me. Her eyes are still closed and I can see her chest rising and falling through the comforter. *I wonder if you will ever know how much you are loved.* I don't know how long we were at that horizon, but it wasn't long enough. When her eyes open, and she sees me backing up toward the door, it's clear that she doesn't think it was long enough either. I wonder if you will ever know how much you are loved, Peyton. My eyes lower as if to apologize for possibly taking advantage of a situation, but that heart-wrenched longing treading in the light of that oily surface absolves me.

As soon as I hear the click of the closing door, despair hangs weights on all my organs, like I'm back in that lone and dreary world and all the devils are laughing.

One day, you precious woman, you will know how much you are loved. But not yet.

DAY 91

Chapter 104

"I think we dream so we don't have to be apart for so long. If we're in each other's dreams, we can be together all the time."
– *Winnie the Pooh*, A.A. Milne

I'm back in that sumptuous, white depthlessness of my Eternity. There is nothing but its structurally white illusions of dimension, and it is a beauty I more feel than see. I can follow its infiniteness in all directions and perspective is powerless to shrink its milky sky at the horizonless horizons. This time, the mirage of height, width, and depth are only tapering opposite my vantage. No hard lines or intersection-betraying shadows, just the innuendo of a mostly-erased rice paper portico. It is a nexus, the gap junction between myocardial cells that contract the heart of an illimitable. It is the arcade to Peyton's Eternity.

She's there, in her Eternity. I don't see her, but she's communicating with me. I don't really know how to explain it—when she imparts some thought to me, it's as if she's possessing me, like our minds are sharing space in a weird collaborative energy. But when I communicate some thought to her, there is a separateness, like she's back in her Eternity. She's skipping back and forth, like something's wrong with the continuity of the reel.

She wants me to see what she's done with her room <<expanse>>. I'm coming, I say. I squint so I can find the outline of that white on white portico. I see it. But . . . there's something else. At least I thought there was something else. It was there and it's gone. No, there it is. And it's gone. Maybe it's just my bad dream eyes. Should my dream eyes have floaters? There it is again . . . and gone. I can't tell if they're black pathogens quickly absorbed by the white blood cells of the coconut plasma or if they're flashes of pathogens darting sub-Eternity to supra-Eternity. Either way, they feel like disease. They feel intrusive. I know they're not supposed to be here. *Nothing* is supposed to be here but what I will to be here. This is my room, my expanse, my Eternity. There's another one. But this one stays. I move, by the mere will of a location, right beside it, and it's gone. It is an infection and the sumptuousness is becoming cankerous. Every time I move to confront another intruder, I lose sight of our gap junction and have to reorient. Peyton is nervous for me and the concentricity of our minds starts to jar and separate. These black streaks are everywhere, coming and going in flashes, lingering like fleas for a moment before jumping out of sight. I forget the portico; this is my home! I can't ignore this infestation! My delay is being misunderstood. The imbrication of our communications is disjointing and I can no longer hear them, only see them, flashing here and there like the disease itself. The transitioning entities are more sticking around than passing through. They are crowding and accosting and accusing and corralling. We're disconnected, Peyton and I. I can't hear her. She can't hear me. I can't see the portico, I can't see any tapering, the infiniteness of the horizon is painting over our gap junction with its interior eggshell enamel. There is nothing but horizon now, there is nothing but endlessness, there is nothing but spots and smears and streaks and an angry host with blood on its teeth and contagion in its eyes. I can't remember her name anymore. I scream something so viscerally misshapen that the nuclei of the whiteness itself start to crack and my Eternity starts folding and unfolding . . .

I realize I've awakened when I see Peyton sitting on the loveseat, her hands cupped over her ears, her black eyes wide and trembling, tears rolling in straight lines from the center of her eyes to her jawline.

I don't know if it was the dream or knowing that I'd somehow upset Peyton, but I can feel tears spilling from my eyes rather than finding individual routes down my cheeks. I'm a contortion of heartbreak and relief and I can't bring myself to blink. My body isn't crying, just my eyes.

She springs from the love seat and jumps on me, wrapping her whole body around my top half. I can feel her chest sputtering and it's cutting her quiet whimpers into irregularities. I wrap my arms around her and hold onto opposite shoulders. All I want to do is squeeze her so hard that she fuses with me, that we become an indivisible entity.

She pushes herself away from me by my shoulders. I can see that I've frightened her <<terrified her>> and she looks at me like I've never been looked at before, like she's agonized by my agony. "What happened? Was that like a nightmare or something?" Her voice sounds like it's bleeding.

I wipe a fountain of tears from her eyes. "Something like that." My voice sounds worn out.

"That noise you made, I thought someone was trying to kill you from the inside out!"

"I'm sorry. I'm so sorry. It's nothing. Don't worry."

The tide of my tears is no less stemmed, so I know she doesn't believe that.

"Don't worry? Don't worry? How does somebody not worry about something like that? What on earth were you dreaming about?"

I force a smile and look at her for what seems like a horizonless Eternity. "All of my dreams are about you, Peyton. Awake, asleep, they're all about you."

Chapter 105

"All of life and human relations have become so incomprehensibly complex, that when you think about it, it becomes terrifying and your heart stands still."
– Anton Chekhov

Texts with Yuri:

Юрий, мне нужно, чтобы ты оказал мне большую услугу. Короткое время выполнения. Много усмотрение.

мы готовы.

Translation:

Yuri, I need you to do me a big favor. Short turnaround time. A lot of discretion.

We're ready.

DAY 92

Chapter 106

"I'm not running away from my responsibilities. I'm running to them. There's nothing negative about running away to save my life."
– *Catch-22*, Joseph Heller

Yakima is laid out like a giant lobster with its gray body of rooftops and industry, its green-checked pincers of agriculture to the northwest, its trailing tail to the southeast. I wish I could build a house up here; everything is beautiful and peaceful at this height.

All the readings on the suit look good. My relative density is down, my speed is steady, I just need to hold still and let the geoguidance do its job. I can feel the middle and ring fingers tensing and the dactylopatagium stiffening and relaxing. The suit knows where I need to be and how soon I need to be there.

Dimitriy simulates a high-five in the air. I don't want to disrupt the suit's guidance so I just nod. The rest give me a thumbs-up, recede, and deploy. I'm going to miss these guys, these blood brothers from another mother's blood brother's mother-brother. At least for a couple of months. Dimitriy most of all. Most people are living, but Dimitriy is one of the few that are *alive*.

I'm at five thousand feet. Just stay still and trust the suit, Elliot. My heart feels like somebody just turned the gravity dial way up. I was doing some work for a medical university's pathology department a few years back and I had to watch a few autopsies for research. On one occasion, this little pregnant lady was teaching the new pathology residents how to do autopsies. From other autopsies I'd viewed, it didn't look like all autopsies were done this way, but at the base of the neck she cut through the trachea, esophagus, and some vasculature and simply yanked the entirety of the thoracic and abdominal viscera out, helping the diaphragm and kidneys and some colon off the body wall with violently digging fingers, like a tree plucked up from the roots. After a few supplementary cuts, she laid the whole tree of life on a steel table with a sickening plop. It seemed so barbaric and unholy, even to one already dead. But that's how I feel right now— eviscerated and hollowed out, my heart plucked up by the roots, my life on a cold, steel table.

I wish there was a way to explain this, Peyton. I wish there was a way to just love you in the present. But now there is no present, only multiple *presents*, each conspiring to sever us in asymmetrical ways. You are the all, you are the everything, and, in a circuitous way, I'm going to make us unseverable. My first suicide was all about me. This suicide is all about you. Please understand. Pin your wings so, when I re-emerge, I don't arrive in a whirlwind. I would say you saved my life, but that's nothing. You burned me to ashes and created a new creature, one that has only existed in the upper echelons of heaven.

I'm at three thousand feet. All the readings still look good. Steady at seventy-one miles per hour. The last time I was at Patch's <<my>> apartment, I studied the maps and tracks and calculated the circulating nascent vent to be outside

Yakima, Washington, rolling over the uneven landscape, at this very moment. Thanks to the quadskelion nature, the ninety degree shift, of the launch of each successive nascent vent, it puts me in a slightly warmer climate this fine February morning. Ground temperature outside of Wendover is supposed to be thirty-four degrees today, about four degrees at fifteen thousand feet. That would have compounded the unpleasantness of this outing.

Until I see you at Death by Yoga for the first of two free classes, I have my dreams of you, Peyton. I have some housecleaning to do in the meantime.

One thousand feet. As the air thickens at this lower elevation, the suit adjustments feel like they're trying to steady an unsteady top. The black lambda is like a kraken, lurching from the surface of its shrinking sea to swallow me.

When I read *For Whom the Bell Tolls* as a teenager, there was a quote from one of the guerilla leaders, El Sordo, that I committed to memory for some reason. I think it was his honesty that struck me, the honesty of a man whose fate was all but decided by virtue of his occupation. It's exactly how I feel at this moment, at two hundred feet, the kraken's jaws unhinging, the sensation of caressing Peyton's lips with my own still buzzing all over my skin. "If one must die . . . and clearly one must, I can die. But I hate it."

Life rises and falls on . . . Maybe it's that simple: Life rises and falls.

Acknowledgments

A lot of voices have gone into the drafting of this novel. I started taking my medication again, so, happily, we're down to just three or four now. I won't say I couldn't have finished this project without this person or that, because I totally could have. It would have been unintelligible madness and eternal paragraphs and an unrecognizable universe, but I could have done it.

Thank you, Kate, for having the courage to call crap, "crap." Thank you, Erica, for calling nothing crap and allowing me to be an unemployed hobo so I could realize a lifelong dream of disgracing myself in print. Thank you, Courtney Larkin, for limiting the number of times I repeat myself, for accentuating the relevant, and striking through my unmedicated moments. And a genuflected and heartfelt thanks to the great God of the heavens and the earth for not destroying me before I could get this story out of my head and onto paper before it became a trampling reality.

About the Author

Jack Passey lives in Salt Lake City, Utah, with his wife of thirty years and his wife's dog that refuses to die. He has been to colleges and has earned degrees.

Jack has never been to a workshop, has never taught anyone how to write, was never a finalist or on a shortlist (and is not likely to be with this book, either), and has never won any awards. Nothing Jack has written has ever been anthologized.

Jack was a government spy for twenty years and some of the source material for this book may or may not be government secrets. *Ankou's Unsharpened Scythe* is Jack's debut novel.